The Author

FREDERICK PHILIP GROVE was born Felix Paul Greve at Radomno in West Prussia (now a part of Poland) in 1879. Raised in Hamburg and educated at the University of Bonn and later at the University of Munich, he began his career as a poet and translator into German of many English and French writers, including Balzac, Flaubert, Gide, Swift, and Wilde. His first novel, *Fanny Essler*, appeared in 1905; his second, *Maurermeister Ihles Haus* (Mastermason Ihle's House), in the following year. He left Germany in 1909 for the United States.

In 1912, under the new name of Frederick Philip Grove, he began teaching school in Manitoba, and continued in that profession until 1924.

Grove's first book in English, *Over Prairie Trails*, is a sequence of seven sketches of his weekly trips through the Manitoba countryside. His first novel in English, *Settlers of the Marsh*, establishes the essentially tragic pattern of his fiction, the heroic pioneers who seek domestic and material happiness but seldom realize their goals.

Grove's autobiography, *In Search of Myself*, begins with a fictitious account of his early life in Europe and moves on to a largely accurate presentation of his life in Canada.

In 1929 Grove left Manitoba to accept a job with a publishing firm in Ottawa. In 1931 he settled on a farm near Simcoe, Ontario, where he spent the final years of his life.

Frederick Philip Grove died in Simcoe, Ontario, in 1948.

Frederick Philip Grove

A SEARCH FOR AMERICA

With an Afterword by W.H. New

"America is a continent, not a country."

M&S

Canadian Cataloguing in Publication Data

Grove, Frederick Philip, 1879-1948
A search for America

(New Canadian library)
Includes bibliographical references.
ISBN 0-7710-9957-6

I. Title. II. Series.

PS8513.R68S42 1991   C813'.52   C90-095213-X
PR9199.2.G766S42 1991

Printed and bound in Canada

McClelland & Stewart Inc.
The Canadian Publishers
481 University Avenue
Toronto, Ontario
M5G 2E9

*I reverently dedicate this book
to the memory of*

*George Meredith
and
Algernon Swinburne*

*and to one of that illustrious triad
who is still living, namely*

Thomas Hardy

for

*"Canadian literature is a mere bud
on the tree of the great Anglo-Saxon
tradition."*

Author's Note

This book, during the last thirty-two years, has been written and rewritten eight times, becoming a little shorter every time. That, at last, *I* picked up courage to release it for publication as it stands, with all the anachronisms which are an unavoidable consequence of such a method of composition, is due entirely to the encouragement of two of my friends who have known the manuscript for a number of years, namely A.L.P. and W.K., both of Wesley College, Winnipeg.

Rapid City, Man.,
December, 1926.   F.P.G.

Contents

BOOK ONE

The Descent

"As long as you keep in the upper regions, with all the world bowing to you as you go, social arrangements have a very handsome air; but once get under the wheels, and you wish society were at the devil. I will give most respectable men a fortnight of such a life, and then I will offer them twopence for what remains of their morality."

– Robert Louis Stevenson

I Emigrate

I WAS TWENTY-FOUR years old when one day in the month of July I took passage from Liverpool to Montreal. I was not British-born; but my mother had been a Scotswoman, and from my earliest childhood I had been trained to speak the English of fashionable governesses. I had acquired – by dint of much study of English literature – a rather extensive reading and arguing vocabulary which however showed – and, by the way, to this day shows – its parentage by a peculiar stiff-necked lack of condescension to everyday slang. My father, Charles Edward Branden by name, had been of Swedish extraction, himself rather an Anglophile. For many years previous to my emigration, I, too, had affected English ways in dress and manners; occasionally, when travelling in Sweden or in the countries bordering on the Mediterranean, I had connived at being taken for an Englishman. I am afraid, if I could meet myself as I then was, I should consider my former self as an insufferable snob and coxcomb.

I must explain at some length what induced me to go to America.

When I was a boy, my parents lived "in style"; that is to say, they had a place in the country, a rather "palatial" home, and a house in the fashionable residential district of a populous city on the continent of Europe. The exact localities are irrelevant. Every summer, as soon as at home the heat became oppressive, my mother, whom I adored

and whom I remember as a Junoesque lady of very pronounced likes and dislikes, used to pack up and to go to
the French coast – to Boulogne, Harfleur, St. Malo, Paris-
plage – or to Switzerland – the Zurich Lake, Landshut,
Lucerne. She preferred the less frequented places, such as
were prepared to meet her demands for comfort without
being infested by tourist-crowds. And invariably she took
one of her ten children along, mostly myself, probably
because I was the youngest one and her only boy. She died
when I was an adolescent.

About a year after my mother's death I went on a "tour
of the continent", planned to take me several years. The
ostensible reason was that I intended to pursue and to
complete my studies at various famous universities –
Paris, Bonn, Oxford, Rome. In reality I went because I had
the wandering instinct. I by no means adhered to the prearranged plan, but allowed myself to be pushed along.

I will give one example. At Naples I made the acquaintance of a delightful young man – I forget whether he was
Dutch or Danish – who knew the artistic circles of Paris –
Gide, Regnier, and others. He somehow declared that I
was the invariably best-dressed man whom he had ever
met, a highly desirable acquaintance, and just the young
Croesus who should interest himself in modern literary
aspirations. He wished me to meet his Parisian friends and
offered me cards of introduction; and although I had not
been thinking of France just then – rather of Egypt and
Asia Minor – I promptly took the next train to Nice and
from there the Riviera Express to Paris. Soon I was all
taken up with that particular brand of literature which
was then becoming fashionable, filled with contempt for
the practical man, and deeply ensconced in artificial
poses.

My reputed wealth opened every door. I sometimes
think that some of the men with whom I linked up – or
upon whom I thrust myself – men, some of whom have in
the meantime acquired European or even world-wide reputation, must have smiled at the presumptuous pup who

thought he was somebody because he threw his father's money about with noble indifference. It is a strange fact that they received me on a footing of equality and led me on; they had time to spare for exquisite little dinners no less than for the nonsensical prattle of one who gave himself airs. Of course, there was an occasional man who kept himself at a distance; but on the whole I cannot avoid the conclusion that these idols had feet of clay.

Whenever my father enquired about the progress of my studies, I put him off by affected contempt. Anybody could pass examinations and take degrees; I was going to be one of the few Europeans who counted. Of course, nobody but myself ever valued me at exactly that figure. I had not done anything to make others aware of my worth. It would, however, have been a tremendous shock to my self-estimation, had I been able to foresee that one day I should value myself at exactly what the world valued me at while I remained utterly and absolutely unknown. I simply was not in a hurry. My aims were lofty enough. To master nothing less than all human knowledge was for my ambition – or, had I better say, for my conceit? – no more than the preliminary to swinging the earth out of its orbit and readjusting, while improving upon, the creator's work. What puzzles me to this day, is that my father seemed to accept these ravings at their face-value – though maybe the revelations which followed a few years later made it appear somewhat less astonishing. I was, after all, a true scion of his stock.

But you must not imagine that I went idle, for I did not. My work lacked simply that measure of coordination which might have made it useful for the purpose of earning a living when the necessity arose. I mastered, for instance, five modern languages, wrote an occasional tract in tolerable Latin, and read Homer and Plato with great fluency before I was twenty-two. I dabbled in Mathematics and in Science, and even attended courses in Medicine. Theology and Jurisprudence were about the only two fields of human endeavour which I shunned altogether.

Meanwhile, having seen in an incidental way a good deal of Europe, I longed for more extensive travel. In my reading I had, so I thought, pretty well exhausted the literatures of the world – difficile est satiram non scribere – and so there remained the world itself to see.

An opportunity offered when an uncle of mine took a transcontinental trip to Vladivostock – it was before the days of the completion of the Trans-Siberian railroad. I accompanied him and returned to Europe by way of Japan and Singapore. Hardly home again, I struck at my father's pocketbook by asking him for ten thousand dollars to finance a year's tour around Africa. I got the money and made the trip. America beckoned – not so much Canada, or the "commercialised" United States – both of which I despised – as Mexico and Peru with their great traditions.

Then the entirely unexpected happened.

I asked my father for an interview and submitted to him my intention of spending a year or two on the continent of America. Without a word of argument or explanation, he drew his cheque-book, made out a cheque, and pushed it across the table at which we were sitting.

We were in the library of his town-house, a high and imposing room done in dark oak, with its walls nearly hidden by the vast array of books which he had assembled during a half century of what I imagined to have been a most successful career in the business of raising trees for the reforesting activities of various governments around the Baltic Sea. He was the tallest and most distinguished looking septuagenarian I have ever beheld. To the very day of this interview he had lived like a "grand seigneur" of the old school – with three ideals: social prestige, liberal culture of the mind, physical prowess. He was six feet five inches tall, with a long, narrow, still fair-haired head sitting on wide, straight shoulders, and a slender body still under perfect control, encased in an immaculate "morning-coat". To imagine a man like him without money would have been an absurdity.

I had asked him for ten thousand dollars. When I glanced at the cheque, as a preliminary to slipping it into my pocket, I saw that it read for seven hundred and fifty. The world seemed to reel – I did not understand. My father was looking at me with great and expectant seriousness; but not without kindness. It even seemed as if behind his earnest and nearly anxious look there lingered in his grey, white-lashed eyes a twinkle of humour.

Then he spoke substantially as follows.

"When fifty years ago, your mother married me, my boy, she brought me about half a million in addition to the landed estate which I owned. My father had been a peasant, but a money-maker. We have been calling him a landed proprietor, probably to cover the ignominy of our origins; but when he started out, he owned only a very small farm. He amassed property – under my hand it has melted away. To-day, after allowing for a fair valuation of all these things that still go as mine" – he looked about as if he could cover it all with a glance – "there are no more than ten thousand dollars left. I am glad that your sisters are married and provided for. As for you, I might hand you what is left and blow my brains out. You surmise that that is not my way.

"I have often longed to drop all pretence, to quit this 'mansion'," – he smiled at the word – "and to retire into the country in order to live as I should like to live; that is, to buy myself a small cottage, with one or two rooms, to appoint it in the simplest manner, and to prepare myself for the life to come by reading about the life that is past. These books which were the pride of your mother were to be the consolation of my old age. To put it briefly, I am on the point of becoming a hermit.

"I might say in self-defence that during the half century of my wedded life I have always lived in clothes which did not fit me. I married your mother because I loved her. She married me because she liked me. I was young, brilliant, rich, a skilful spender. She expected me to keep it up; I did not disappoint her. She died when it was time for her to go.

Since her death all my worries have ceased because I am free to do as I please. Ever since she closed her eyes, I have been engaged upon the task of winding up my affairs. You have been away a good deal, or you would have been aware of the fact that unusual things were going on. I have finished my task. So much for myself.

"Now as to you. For several days I have been worried about the best way to broach the subject. I am glad you introduced it yourself.

"You will acknowledge that I have been a good father. I have given you the most liberal opportunities to finish your education; I have invariably and unstintingly supplied you with money or paid your debts; I have sent you around the world and even kept up appearances as far as I myself was concerned, in order to assist you in those social aspirations which you have no doubt inherited from your mother. You are well liked everywhere; everywhere great things are expected of you. Among your closest friends are men of letters, artists, scholars, men of the world, and diplomats. All you need to do in order to find promotion waiting for you is to make a choice of whatever calling you prefer, and then disclose your present position to the leading men in your chosen field; they will place you where an honourable and successful career cannot fail you. I know you are a genius," – he said it without the ghost of a smile – "now is the time to show the world what you are. That little cheque will help you to get established."

I had listened under a spell; no thought of mine had been for the cheque any longer. I was so bewildered that I did not know what to do or say. At this mention of the cheque I looked at it and impulsively pushed it across the table, back to him.

He laughed. "No, no," he said; "I do not intend to leave you stranded. It would not be fair, I should feel worried. You will oblige me by keeping the trifle."

I crushed it into my pocket and ran over to him. He gripped my outstretched hand, but by that very move held me at a distance. Then he said in an entirely unemotional but not unfriendly way, "Don't let it for a moment enter your head that you should feel sorry for me. As I said, I am shaking off ill-fitting clothes in order to be better fitted. I see Paradise ahead."

With these words he ended the interview. I left him alone.

There followed a series of other interviews. The phrase, "Awfully sorry, old man, but I don't see what I could do for you," recurred more than a few times; in fact, till it became an obsession. I drank from Timon's cup.

Especially hard was I hit by the refusal of one of my former friends, a young millionaire-writer whom I had, before he came into his money, repeatedly treated to rather expensive hospitality; he had made two trips with me, one to Paris, one to Venice; both had been made at my invitation and at my expense – or rather, my father's. Now he refused me the loan of one thousand dollars which I wanted in order to return to my studies and to pass such examinations as would enable me to take advantage of the only opening that any one could find for me. This opening consisted in a position as lecturer on archeological subjects offered by a few university men who had been my disappointed teachers – disappointed, because they, like others, had accepted me as a genius till I dashed their expectations of what I might be and do to pieces by my lack of perseverance along a definite and limited line of endeavour. This young millionaire – son of a manufacturer of European fame – had the nerve, as I called it then, to point out to me that he considered it a bad investment to loan money to a man who intended to do nothing more lucrative than to embark upon a university career. I judge him somewhat more charitably to-day.

Meanwhile I had promptly though regretfully given up my habit of travelling about in reserved sections of "trains-de-luxe" which carried only first-class compartments. Like other poor people I bought third-class tickets for single seats; I frequented medium-priced hotels, and generally adapted myself to my reduced circumstances. I sold a diamond-brooch left me by my mother and a small steel sailing-craft which I had been keeping on the Baltic. For nearly a year the proceeds of these and similar sales kept me in funds. The reader will wonder why I did not use this money to put myself through my Ph.D. Well, I can only say I wonder myself, for I know as little about it as he does; but maybe it will appear less incomprehensible later on, when we meet with more such decisions and indecisions. For one thing, though, the money came in instalments; I did not, at first, think of parting with a legacy of my mother's; she had, that I knew, intended it as a wedding-gift to the woman that would be my wife; I held it in trust. But the reader might just as well understand from the outset that this story of a few years of my life is not meant as an apotheosis. I do not intend in these pages to gloss over any actions of mine. More than once, as my patient reader will find, I did not grasp opportunity by the forelock when it passed my way. If that is sin or crime, I have paid the penalty and finally still worked out my own salvation; that is all. I even have to confess that the moment I had the money which paid for my sailing-craft, about six hundred dollars, I took one hundred dollars out of it, went to Paris, had just one dinner at Paillard's, took the night-flyer back to Brussels, and was by that one hundred dollars poorer. It was not so easy as it sounds to change from the habits of a young "man about town" to those of a thrifty young scholar.

My father, meanwhile, had also gone to Paris and had, for the remainder of his fortunes, bought a "rente viagère" – an annuity – and a little cottage between Boulogne and Etaples – a coast which he loved as I have always loved it. He was fortunate; for at last he realized his dream, even though only for a short time; and I can imagine how he felt about it, taking it as a final reward for duty well done during a lifetime of disguise.

There was consolation, and a good deal of poetry, too, in the fact that he should have gone there to die; for that is exactly what he did. The letter-carrier found him dead on the concrete steps to his hermitage, one morning late in spring, stricken down, so it seemed, by a stroke of apoplexy. It is a significant fact that I received half a dozen letters from citizens of the nearby town – Etaples – plain tradesmen, who spoke with a glowing enthusiasm of this "gentilhomme" who had passed away. In a shed belonging to his cottage there were found sixty-three living rabbits, the pets of his solitude.

When I received the news, I quietly and quickly wound up my little affairs and took stock. The only man whom I should have hated to disappoint by failing to become a great man was dead. Why struggle? My father's desire for a quiet life in obscurity had become my own desire. I was bleeding from bitter disappointments – my state of mind was Byronic.

As it happened, being at the time at Stockholm, I met one evening, in a certain famous cafe, a young Swedish nobleman with whom I had been intimate, although originally he had been merely an acquaintance from the tennis courts. I was sitting at a small table and brooding. He entered, ushering in his two sisters, brilliant young ladies with whom I had had many a dance. I rose to pay my compliments; but the trio passed me as if I had been air.

I paid my bill, went home to my hotel, counted my money, called up the railway station, found that I could just catch a through-train via Malmoe, Copenhagen, Hamburg, to Ostend, and thence a boat to England, engaged a sleeper, and packed up.

I had, in a flash, made up my mind to leave Europe and all my old associations behind. Not that I felt really hurt or still cared to rub elbows with nobility; but I did not want to be "cut" or snubbed because I was no longer the son of a reputed millionaire.

While dozing in my berth, I determined upon a gamble. Not for a moment did it occur to me to go anywhere except into an Anglo-Saxon country. I might, of course, have appealed to one of my sisters; I was too proud to do

so. Canada, the United States, South Africa, or Australia –
on one of these four my choice had to fall. What I resolved
to do, was this. I intended to step in at Cook's tourist-
office in London – on the Strand, if I remember right – and
to ask for the next boat which I stood any chance of
catching, either at Liverpool or at Southampton, no matter
where she might be bound. As it happened, when, a day or
two later, I carried this idea out, a White-Star liner was to
weigh anchor next day, going from Liverpool to Montreal.
The boat train was to leave Euston Station the same night
at ten o'clock. I bought my passage – second cabin –
received a third-class railway ticket free of charge and –
had burnt my bridges. Thus I became an immigrant into
the western hemisphere.

As I have said, I was twenty-four years old at the time; it
was late in July.

While we were sailing up the mouth of the St. Lawrence
River, I naturally pondered a good deal on my venture. I
was starting a new life at a time when I should have been
well on in my old one. Gradually some conceptions
worked themselves out in my mind. I thought I had a very
definite aim; and I imagined that I also had some very
definite assets to work with. I did not realize at the time
how much I was also burdened down with very serious
disabilities which were to handicap me sorely in the
American game as I understood it. My aim I conceived to
be modest enough. I wanted to found a home and an
atmosphere for myself. Woman might or might not enter
into my scheme of thins. There was the picture of a girl
somewhere in the background of my mind, it is true; but I
thought of her with resignation only. To do what might
win her seemed quite impossible. I had met her in the
heyday of my fortunes at Palermo and attached myself to
her orbit for a week or so, following her to Rome, Venice,
Vienna, Berlin. Now she was one of those infinitely distant
stars which you still see because a few centuries ago they
sent out their light on its path, and it keeps on travelling

and reaching our globe, although the star that sent it has perhaps long since been extinguished.

What I desired as an atmosphere was what I considered the necessities for a life devoted to quiet studies, to the search for contact with Nature, to service, unpretentious and unselfish service of mankind. Cicero's "otium cum dignitate" was what I desired. To this day I believe that to be a worthy aim. To this day I believe that we should be a better people, that our country would be a better place to live in, good as it is even for him who is without worldly ambition, if more people set themselves that aim, no matter whether they are philosophically inclined or not.

Just what that meant in the way of a fortune, is hard to say. But I believe that even in our days of higher and higher costs the interest on about forty thousand dollars would have covered all my wants as I saw them then. This I vaguely hoped to achieve in from ten to twenty years. You see that, as American expectations go, mine were modest enough.

I had no definite plans. It did not matter how I did it or what I might do to reach my goal. The aim was all-important, nothing else of any consequence. I have since lived to see the error in this. To-day my maxim is, What is the goal to us who love the road?

I did not mind, then, what I might be doing, so long as for the time being it yielded me a decent living and enabled me besides year after year to lay by a certain sum, sufficient to insure my independence within a reasonable time.

I thought a good deal of a man whom I had known as a dignified member of the small but select English colony at Dresden. His calling-card showed a "The Hon." in front of his name; and while I knew him, he had lived the quiet and independent life of a scholar of wide views and large experience; not a brilliant, but a carefree life. I had admired him for his perfect form and breeding; and I had always assumed that he probably had never done anything

useful in his life, beyond setting an example of noble leisure to the younger men of whom he ever had a circle
surrounding him. But one day I had received a revelation.
It so happened that I became very intimate with one of
these younger men, a physician who had known him for a
number of years and who possessed his confidence to an
unusual degree. Now this young doctor one day told me
confidentially that the honourable gentleman had been
exceedingly poor when young. So he had gone to South
Africa and learned the business of an hotel-keeper. He
had successively been the porter, the clerk, the manager,
and the owner of a small-town hotel, had lived there for
twelve years under an assumed name, had "made his
pile", and returned to Europe to step back into his proper
place in society.

In my meditations about this man I found only one thing
which I could not approve of. I could not bring myself to
the point of thinking it right of him to return to the haunts
of his youth. He should have stayed in the country of his
adoption, I thought, paying with his culture-influence for
the money he had taken out. Viewing as I did the colonials
as probably sorely in need of such influence, I vowed to
myself that, if ever I should succeed in my endeavours, I
should settle down wherever I had "made my pile" and
spend it, thus paying back my debt and throwing in my
influence for good, such as it might be, by way of interest.
Ecce homo! Crucified to ease and honour.

Another resolve I made was this that, no matter what
line of work I might follow, as a cog in a machine to start
with, of course – I meant to be quite modest – I should
always do a little better than my mere duty, and, if such
were possible, not only a little, but a good deal better. In
this I was honest enough, for there was really no need of
taking such a resolution; I am temperamentally unable to
do anything by halves while I am at it; though, also
temperamentally, I am next to unable to stay with it for
very long if it completely absorbs my energies. I have to
this very day not yet made up my mind as to whether this

is a weak point or a strong one. It has, on the one hand, prevented me from achieving any very conspicuous success along a single, definite line; on the other, it has given me a range of experience in various fields, a knowledge of men, things, processes, languages, and even nations, which I should never have achieved without this defect.

Some of the pages which follow may read like a huge indictment of the Americas. I can assure the patient reader that they were never meant as such. Whoever follows me to the end, will see the unmistakable intention of this book. I have, of course, had bitter hours since I first landed on the banks of the St. Lawrence River. I have sometimes felt inclined, in a spirit of accusation, to put down my education among the liabilities rather than among the assets. I have long since learned to smile at my discomfitures and to think with pleasure even of things that were horrors in the living.

I want to state with all due emphasis that this is the story of an individual, and that I do not mean to put it down as typical except in certain attitudes towards phenomena of American life – attitudes which later study and work among hundreds of immigrants have shown me to be typical. If then, with this distinct understanding, there is no lesson left for the American to learn, that is to say, if parts at least of this story do not uncover weak spots in a great organization, then let these pages go into oblivion as they will deserve.

TWO

I Land on American Soil

A T MONTREAL, when at last I stood in the huge hall of the pier at which the steamer had docked, I felt incongruous and out of place. I felt forlorn, helpless, depressed when I stood there, in front of my fourteen pieces of luggage, with half a dozen overcoats on my arm and a camera in my hand. In thinking of him now, I cannot but smile, I cannot but pity the slim youth in his immaculate clothes, the mere boy I was.

I shall try to describe how I must have looked.

I was six feet three inches tall, with a waist-measure of twenty-six inches. Hands and feet were narrow and long; my shoulders had begun to stoop. My hair was exceedingly fair – of that ancestral Scandinavian fairness that makes me to this day appear like a much younger man than I am. My eyes were blue, arched over by bushy, yellow brows, and set rather deeply in a long, narrow face with a somewhat receding chin.

Add to that a certain diffidence in demeanour – the diffidence of him who is on unfamiliar ground – and the considerate politeness of the man who is used to look upon most of the people he deals with as socially his inferiors – as to be treated with kindliness because they must suffer from the mere fact that they are what they happen to be – none of their fault, of course; they did not mean to be born as such; I was quite tolerant about it: add that, and you will be able to judge what was in store for him in the matter of wounded susceptibilities and mental jolts. Fortunately for the young man, he had also been trained from his earliest days never to betray an emotion, to keep his mask intact.

He was young; and though of a serious cast of mind, he nevertheless looked upon his undertaking – for the moment at least – as something of an adventure, as something that could not help but satisfy, in part at least, his great curiosity as to life, and, after all, as something, too, that might not be so utterly irretrievable as it would seem.

At last the customs-official reached my pile. I remember distinctly the difficulties I had in convincing this man that I was not bringing all these clothes into the country in order to open a haberdasher's shop, but for personal wear. I had to show him the sleeve-holes of every suit as a proof that it had been worn. I also remember that what convinced him at last was my hat-box which contained a silk hat, two derbies, a sailor, and three or four caps. He seemed to accept the silk-hat as conclusive evidence of my good faith.

"Going to tour the country, sir?" he enquired; and I thought it best to let it go at that. "Thank you, sir." And, his manner changed, he touched his cap and walked away.

Two porters stood waiting with a truck. "Cab, sir?"

"No. Toronto Express. Grand Trunk, if you please."

I must, at the risk of seeming tedious, point out the significance of this answer. I have since gone back to Montreal and studied the city. At that time it did not occur to me that there might be something to interest me in Canada's metropolis. As far as cities were concerned, I knew only three in the world that had ever appeared to me worthy of a visit for their own sakes: London, Paris, and Rome. What I saw in them was the setting they gave to their treasures of Art and their jewels of Architecture. It is true, the boulevards of Paris had a further significance for me as the drawing-room, if I may say so, which a great nation had set up for itself to receive its guests in, or as the screen which it had raised before peering eyes to disguise its real mentality, made up of thrift and common sense. I considered Naples, Stockholm, Constantinople as beautiful spots in nature, not as beautiful cities; for me they had been placed where they stood like stagepieces to add a touch of colour which was missing in the landscape. To look upon them, to be interested in them primarily as the abodes of human beings, had never entered my mind.

Nature, Science, and Art – these three were the great realities; what here, in the western hemisphere, forms the first and most essential problem of every citizen – his own success in life, his place in the community – that was for me at the time a mere detail, a trifle to be attended to in due time, but which did not need to engross my thoughts too much. Art and Science I did not expect to find in this new world. Remained nature. Nature, I am sorry to say, meant to me then what it emphatically does not mean to me now; in America I might have summarized it under the headings Niagara, Yellowstone, the Grand Canyon, and maybe the Yosemite and the Big Trees. Everything else was negligible in my estimation.

Now the reader may seem to see in this a certain contradiction to what would seem the natural attitude of the immigrant towards the country of his adoption. He must not forget that reasoning in an abstract way is one thing, and overcoming instincts and leanings that are born and bred into one's innermost being, quite another. I might even go a step further in order unmistakably to define where I stood at the time. As for America, without ever reasoning about it, it would have occurred to me as soon to look for Apollos of Belvedere in Toronto, as to read an American book for anything beyond a certain amount of information. Nor had I learnt as yet to stand transfixed when looking at the Titan frescoes of light effects on clouds of smoke from iron-furnace or railroad-yard. I had not even begun to look for, much less to find, in such things, beauty.

And as for the problems which absorb the best thinking of the western world – the great questions of the social adjustments, the ethnological difficulties as between Frenchman and Anglo-Saxon, Indian and Whiteface, Negro and Caucasian – I should have dismissed them with a shrug of my shoulders as trifles not worthy to occupy such an exalted intelligence as my own. And yet I had come to this country in order to win my daily bread! Whatever there was in me of humility was a reasoned acquisition of my intellect; it had not penetrated within my skin. In spite of my very distinct determination not to form a little island of Europe in the American environment I needed only to let myself go, and I was a hot-house plant, used to artificial atmospheres. Rude draughts of the fresh air of a newer world were required to awaken me fully.

I missed, then, in this opportunity to see, and to get the flair of, a city which to-day holds for me the strongest and strangest fascination. Why I had chosen Toronto as the place to make my first stand in, I do not remember; no doubt I had some reason which seemed compelling at the time.

One of the first impressions I had, coming as I did from crowded Europe, was that of spaciousness. The big station, the roominess of the waiting-hall, the height of the train-shed, and – as I walked along the platform to my car – the length and apparent solidity of the railway-carriages themselves did not fail to awe me a little though I did not show it in the impenetrable mask of my face. I forbore Parlor-car and Sleeper – my train left about midnight – which may and may not have argued for a certain sense of proportion.

When I first entered the smoker of the train, I experienced my first distinct shock. I had, while crossing the Atlantic, studied a guide-book for tourists on the American continent. I knew that most trains carried only first-class coaches. Still, I had – unreasonably enough, of course – expected something of the genteel exclusiveness of an English or Continental first-class coach. I was shocked when instead I saw shirt-sleeved elbows, overalled knees, tramping boots, and collarless necks as the only things which protruded above the rattan-covered backs of the seats. The evidences of proficiency gained in the art of squeezing your body, no matter in what seemingly impossible position, into a reclining posture on a seat which was evidently meant as a mute reproof for all those who ventured to travel at night in a "day-coach" were no less amazing to me. I believe that, with a sinking feeling in my heart, I feared that, after all, I might not fit in with a civilization which apparently lavished its wealth on the "navvy". But, of course, since I was accompanied by what I had already learned to call a red-cap, no feature of my face betrayed the least unfamiliarity with what to me was truly a revelation.

The red-cap reversed the back of a seat in the centre of the car, dropped my suit-case into the space, thus created between two backs, held out his hand, and departed upon receiving a half-dollar which I had in readiness.

I sat down and tried desperately to seem at ease. The large expanses of costly woods, which were left without the elaborate carvings of European de-luxe trains – meant to disguise the inferior materials used – delighted my eye, which at the same time was scandalized by the cowardly indulgence in puny decorativeness displayed in the brasswork of the lamps. Since I could not reconcile the two things – which is always the case where bad taste is obtruded – the former ended by impressing me with a sense of braggadocio. The whole aspect of the car jarred upon me; for a few moments I felt very uncomfortable. I felt that what I saw was typical for my new environment; it made me afraid. During these first minutes in the train I resolved, no matter what might happen, to hold on to enough of my money to pay my fare back to Europe. The reader will see by and by whether this resolution was kept.

Another surprise, this time an agreeable one, was in store when the train started on its gliding motion out of the shed; it went off without the shouting and excitement which I was accustomed to from overland trains in

Europe. "Here is sound sense," I said to myself; "this vehicle starts as if that was its business in the world, not as if it were doing something against the laws of Nature." In Europe it had always seemed to me as if people were highly indignant and full of anxious protests when we dared to depart.

To others also I must have looked incongruous in that scantily occupied smoker. A glance convinced me that, although I had four seats to myself, without careful preliminary schooling any attempt to stretch out and to sleep would have proved disastrous to my dignity. And so far I was not prepared to let go of that precious possession of the new arrival. If any one remotely or closely resembling myself should ever read this record before he starts out on a similar enterprise, I have an advice for him: Let him travel steerage – he will learn a great many useful things and at the same time get rid of the cumbersome impediment of his dignity before he reaches the blessed shores; but, of course, if he really resembles me, he will certainly not be thus advised.

I sat, then, stiffly on my sat, next the window, looking out into the dark and feeling suddenly embarked upon things desperate and suicidal. The empty space at my side was taken up by the stack of my overcoats; the opposite seat was vacant.

By and by I ventured again to look about in the car. On the other side of the aisle there sat in a seat, whose back was also reversed, a smallish, middle-aged man with a clean-shaven, puckered face and in the apparel of a poorly-paid clerk, as I judged at the time; I should know better to-day. He had propped his shoulder-blades against the window-frame, rested his right foot on the arm-rail of the seat, and had flung his right hand over its back. His left hand – the elbow digging into the very edge of the seat – held a pipe at which he sucked in a reflective and disengaged way while staring at me. The very relaxation of his attitude somehow prejudiced me against this man, whom nevertheless I envied for being at ease. I tried to look out of the window again; but soon my eye returned to the stranger. Apparently he had not moved; he was still engaged in what impressed me as staring. Without looking directly at him, I began to study his appearance. In spite of my irritation at being so openly appraised and weighed, I was fair enough to admit to myself that very likely he was quite a good-natured fellow who did not mean any harm. In fact, at last I arrived at the conclusion that he was not really staring at all, that he did not even see me; that his gaze had absent-mindedly taken the direction it held by mere blind chance.

I was on the point of dismissing all thought of him when he suddenly started an amazing series of motions – screwing himself up, as it were, till he stood on his feet; and then he lounged in a dangling, disjointed way across the aisle.

He dropped into the vacant seat opposite myself and remarked, "Fine night."

"Beautiful," I assented with a reserve that hardly fitted the occasion.

Five minutes passed in silence, with myself staring out of the window. I felt expectant, no longer hostile.

"Green here?" he asked in a casual way.

I had been ready to confide in him, to get as much information out of him as I could; but the word "green" shot me back into my shell.

"Beg your pardon?" I countered stiffly.

"Been in this country long?" And this time there was so much understanding sympathy in his voice that I looked straight into his eye.

"Well . . . no," I faltered; "not exactly, sir. . . . Fact is. . . . Well, I arrived to-night."

He blew a thread of smoke through his teeth. "Thought as much," he said.

I believe my pulse went at one hundred and twenty beats to the minute. I was afraid he might hear the sledge-hammer knock in my heart.

Now I want to say a word in praise of the young man that I was. Three weeks before, I should not have spoken to this stranger at all. If, by any chance, he had done something to oblige me – if he had, let me say, helped me with my baggage in a crowded station building where it was impossible to secure a porter – I should have slipped him a handsome tip and dismissed him with "Obliged, my man!" Had he, on the other hand, by mere reprehensible ostentation, spent the savings of his labour on a first-class railway-ticket, in order to pry upon his "betters", and had he, in addition, by mere giddiness or unaccountable failure to realize his "place in life", ventured to address me in a public conveyance – I should have frozen him, annihilated him with one of those glassy stares for which I had been famous among my former friends, one of whom used to say, "Phil can put more opprobrium into one of his fish-eyes than you can cull out of an unemasculated Shakespeare in a day." And here, after only an hour or so on Canadian soil, I was actually answering this man's questions – yes, I had already irrevocably committed myself to his tender mercies by confessing to that most heinous of all crimes – a crime which also involves the most humiliating admission of abject inferiority: "greenness"! . . . I believe that was the first step in my Americanization.

Very likely the look of the criminal betrayed me; and that in spite of the fact that I did my utmost to preserve my mask in impeccable perfection. But it cost me an effort, and the effort involved self-consciousness. Nobody who is self-conscious can get away with the pretence that he is at ease when he confronts a man who by gift or training is used to read human nature at a glance.

That this man read me, appeared from his next remark. "Hm," he drawled reflectively, "I shouldn't feel badly about it, me boy."

Imagine him calling me "boy" – me who had been rubbing elbows with dukes and lords. But more than in anything else, the rapid progress of my Americanization showed in the fact that I yielded myself to the simple good-will with which this stranger stooped from his superior status to one apparently so raw in the ways of the country as I was.

"Good many of us have been there," he went on. "I've been just there meself." He sucked at his pipe.

"Have you?" I asked politely.

He nodded in a pensive sort of way, still absent-mindedly sucking his cold pipe. "Yea," he said, "sure. Twenty-seven years ago."

That remark startled me into sudden admiration. The casual way in which he made it placed him high, very high indeed, in my esteem. I had been in this country an hour and a half maybe; he, twenty-seven years! I was nearly tempted, I think, to figure out what multiple twenty-seven years might be of an hour and a half. It was overwhelming. I had been under the impression that this was a young country. Young indeed! The man had been here before I was born!

"Great country," he continued after a while, "great country! Want to go on the land?"

I had not thought of that as a possibility; but I said, "I might."

"Want to look around first, eh? . . . Good thing to do." And again he sucked his pipe for some time. "Hardly seem the type," he drawled, "hardly the build. . . . Better try the city, I'd say. Know a trade?"

"No," I confessed. Somehow I did not like to tell him that I was a linguist, that I had been deep in studies of classical archeology. I was afraid I might sink too low in his estimation by admitting scholarly propensities.

"Have a stake, I suppose?"

I did not know what a stake was; but the tone of his words seemed to imply that not to have what he meant might be a serious handicap or even a disgrace. So I answered precipitously, "Oh yes, of course."

"That's good," he said in the most indifferent manner possible; "will enable you to look around."

And from that I guessed at the meaning of the word.

He seemed lost in thought. He had resumed his former attitude on the seat, only, of course, with the sides reversed. Now he lifted his right foot high up and put it negligently but accurately on top of the stack of my overcoats. I suffered pangs, for I was exceedingly particular about my clothes; but not by the slightest flicker of an eyelash did I betray my agony. I was too much afraid of losing this only link which so far connected me with that human world in which I meant to strike root.

The train went rickety, rackety, rumble, rumble, wheel on rail. Like ghosts huge trees shot by in the dark. Hills loomed, lakes gleamed, towns slipped silently back into the behind; distance was devoured. Half an hour passed in silence.

"Great country," my fellow-traveller drawled again. "Crossed over from Liverpool?"

"Yes," I replied, glad to hear his voice once more.

And after a while he went on. "My home-town, that. Foul with poverty. Won't see much poverty here."

I felt glad of it. I was fleeing from the very threat of poverty.

"Most anybody makes a living here. . . . Me boy there – only fifteen – that's him, over there – he's sleeping – learns jeweller's trade – gets ten a week . . . "

Ten a week? Surely he did not mean dollars! *Ten dollars a week! A boy of fifteen!* When I should have gladly used the whole of my education and worked every hour of my waking day for one hundred and fifty pounds a year? He could not mean shillings either, could he? I tried to find out without betraying my ignorance.

"How much do you have to pay for board?" I asked.

"Well-l," he drawled, rolling the l like a quid in his mouth. "I'm boarding meself, me and the boy. We pay five dollars a week. Can get it for four, mebbe. But when a man works, he needs the grub."

I wondered. Had he no home? But my question was answered. The boy did get ten dollars a week. *A week!*

My fellow-traveller relapsed into silence. Then he proceeded; and it took me quite a while to make out what the connection was; so much was I startled by the visions of possible wealth that arose.

"Can pay six. More, I've heard."

I mustered all my courage. I felt that, even though I might be encroaching on dangerous ground, even though I might be "prying", much was to be forgiven to a raw arrival like myself.

"Pretty good for the boy," I said, "saving five a week."

"Oh, he ain't saving," he replied; and his tone held a note of contempt. "Doesn't even buy his own clothes. Money's got a knack of dribbling away in this country. A dime here, a nickel there. Soda-fountain, show, Sundaes, – they're the curse of the nation – leastways, unless ye're a drinking man. Then, it's treating."

What could he mean? Sundays? I did not enquire, however, for fear of betraying too great an ignorance for his patience.

"Save!" he went on contemptuously. "Of course, I don't say no. Been a saving man meself all me life. But then it had taken me and me wife five years to lay by sufficient to pay my passage across. The old lady stayed behind till I should have got a foothold."

Who might the old lady be? His wife?

"That's how ye learn to be careful. And when the old lady died – I brought her over, y'know. Took me three months here to save *Her* passage – longest three months in me life – was young then, y'know. . . . Well-l as I was saying, when she died, I kept right on, don't just rightly know why. Sold the house, of course. And the only thing I ever treated myself to, was a trip back home, all over the old country, in state – cost me five hundred, mind ye – But then, I didn't need to earn it – was just a year's rent on some property I own. Didn't like it, though – back over yonder. I mean . . . " And he relapsed into silence again.

Five hundred dollars the rent on some property? Twenty-seven years in this country? The man must be wealthy! And surely, he did not have much of an education.

"What . . . " I began diffidently and stopped. "May I . . . I do not want to be inquisitive, you know. – Might I ask you what your profession is?" I blurted out at last.

"Me? I?" he asked. "Perfession? That's a good one, me boy. Used to heave coal in the docks over yonder. I? I'm foreman in the packing-room at Simpson's, T'ronto. . . . I'm making thirty-five a week, and extra for overtime, because that's what ye really want to know."

"I'm sorry," I started apologetically, for I felt that I must have offended him.

But he interrupted me in his drawling, indifferent way. "Not at all," he said; "if ye have any more questions, shoot. Glad to be of help – if it helps . . . "

I was impressed. My clothing, I counted, would last me for years without renewing. This man, to all intents and purposes a labourer, was making thirty-five dollars a week. His board cost him five dollars. Thirty dollars a week would amount to fifteen hundred dollars a year in savings. If I laid by, let me say, a thousand a year, my goal would seem within reach. I felt quite elated. I, with my education, my knowledge of the world, of languages, countries – with my appearance! A subtle change, I suppose, crept over me. I believe my fellow-traveller noticed something of the sort.

He sat up. Not suddenly, nor in one continuous motion. I could see by the slow, successive stages in which he lifted himself to his feet that age had him in its grip. Not that he was really old – past fifty, maybe; nor did he suffer from any very pronounced infirmity. But somehow I could not imagine myself ever getting up that way – unless life in this country used human bodies up to a greater extent, at a faster rate than it did in Europe.

"You look around for a while," he said when at last he was standing. "Steer clear of bars and soda-fountains and shows. It doesn't much matter what ye do. Read the ads in the papers. . . . Clerking seems to be y'r line. Not much in that, though. But mind, whatever ye do, *stick!* Nothing in drifting. One thing's about as bad as the next one.. Might just as well stick – Well-l, I guess I want to doze a little. Look me up if ye want to. Simpson's. Ask for Bennett."

With a nod of his head and a push of his arms he propelled his body so that it landed in his former seat across the aisle.

I had risen to my feet; but he did not offer his hand; nor did he give me a chance to thank him for so much kindness shown to a young man as green as I must have appeared to him. I sat down again.

"One thing is about as bad as the next one," he had said. "As good," he had meant. I read him in a kindly spirit.

Rickety, rackety, went the train; rumble, rumble, wheel on rail. I looked out through the window again, into the dark. The vastness of it all! It was disquieting! Sleep was impossible, I had food for thought.

THREE

I Secure Work

I HAD RENTED a room, without board, for two dollars a week. I do not remember the street nor the exact location. It was somewhere east of Yonge Street, in a quiet, residential place. Restful it might have been; but for me, of course, there was no rest.

Beginning with the second day of my stay at Toronto, I began to look for work. The stranger in the train had advised me to study the advertisements in the daily papers; that is what I did. Since I meant to save in the most desperate way, I did not even buy the papers. Every morning and every night I went to the various newspaper offices, waiting till the sheets were put on file for inspection. Armed with a note book and a pencil, I made a list of all the positions that were offered and which I thought I could fill. Luck was against me. I remember as typical one incident in this first heart-breaking initiation into the chase. A steam-laundry had advertised for a clerk, "apply there and there at 4 p.m." I went at three, an hour ahead of time, and found a queue of fifty or more applicants waiting. I did not get the impression that "help" was scarce in the city; it seemed to me rather that work was scarce. To this very day I have not yet succeeded in reconciling the contradictory statements which you hear according as you are interviewing those who are looking for help or those who are looking for work. The position was filled, of course, before it came to be my turn.

Far and away the majority of the advertisements began with the words, "Wanted, an experienced . . . " whatever it was. Experience was what I lacked no matter what the line of business might be. I did not dare to apply.

There were also many advertisements grouped together under the heading "Agents wanted." Some of them stated expressly, "Experience unnecessary" or "We teach you". A number of these I answered. Most of the men who received me did not give me a chance to say much. "I am afraid we cannot do business with you." "Sorry; get rid of your brogue, and we might see." Such were two of the answers I received most frequently. Ever recurring there came the question, "How long have you been in this country?" Gradually, during a week of heart-breaking and desperate endeavour, the conviction was borne in upon me that my appearance – among other things the plainly old-country cut of my suits – stood in the way of my success. The man I met sized me up, with a brief, searching look, saw how "green" I was, and dismissed me curtly, sometimes not even troubling to be civil about it.

Three or four of these advertisements led me to men, however, who spoke differently. They were polite and exceedingly sympathetic, even to subserviency. Invariably I found after much preliminary conversation that what they were after was not my services but my money. To hear them, it was astonishing what a small amount invested would do for me. It was astonishing, too, that the sum needed for a start in their particular line of business was always within a few dollars of what I actually had. Not that a larger sum would not have been highly desirable. Since I was to double or treble my money within a week or a fortnight, the larger the amount with which I started, the larger, too, of course, the profits to be garnered. According to them most Canadian millionaires had begun with pretty accurately two hundred and fifty dollars. Unfortunately for them and, as far as I know, for myself as well, I was altogether too regretfully reluctant to part with my money even for so short a space of time as a single week. I came to the point where I felt discouraged the moment a man treated me with common courtesy.

Meanwhile I learned to know the city fairly well. I began to get used to the fact that the amazingly numerous churches advertised their services in various ways – a fact that had greatly shocked me at first. I assimilated the ways of dairy-lunch rooms and high-stool counters. And I became convinced that women who walked or rode about unattended, flaunting their clothes in fashions more "outré" than I had ever seen them at Paris or Nice, could not necessarily be put down as belonging to the "half-world." It is not meant as a criticism if I state that before I was inured to the finer wrinkles of American fashions, it seemed to me as if shop-girl and well-to-do "bourgeoise" alike tried their utmost to look identically like a "cocotte".

Sunday came. All morning I rode around the city on a belt-line car, looking down from the heights over the spacious or huddled streets and feeling baffled, defeated, miserable. I reproached myself for not having called at Simpson's the day before. I needed a cheering-up about as badly as anybody can need it at any time. Pride had stood in my way. Surely, I must be good for something? Surely, I could somewhere find a breach to take this fortress? For by this time I looked upon my fellow-applicants for positions as defenders against me, the intruder. I did not like to look Bennett in the eye once more as somebody prowling about "on the outside". I was willing to do no matter what. His boy was making ten dollars a week; and I was to fall down? That was what I had said to myself that Saturday night.

By noon I felt the need of company so strongly that, after taking a frugal lunch, I went to the beach. Merely to see humanity, I thought, would help me. But I was by this time so thoroughly discouraged that I saw whatever presented itself to my eyes through the darkened glasses of doom. The beach houses struck me as flimsy, the picnic grounds of the island as litters of paper and left-overs of lunches, the crowds as a rabble. Not even the trees or the lake made any appeal. Nothing seemed to be able to pull me out of my wretched self-consciousness and alarm.

Then I sat down on a bench. I did some searching and thinking. I thought of the associations of my past, and I began to see even them in a new light.

My criticism probed into the lives and careers of all the young men I had known over yonder. Those who apparently had been the most independent, had been so because they had inherited money. In other words, they had been parasites! I was horror-struck at the word. Looking back at it now, I am chiefly struck by the ease with which this young man slipped into socialist views and phraseologies as soon as he was stripped of his social pretensions. That could not have happened in Europe – not, at least, at the time; and since the conditions of that time are rapidly passing away, I might add another word. No matter how miserable I might – in Europe – have felt in my innermost heart, the mere deference shown by "subordinates" to my appearance, my bearing, and my clothes would have kept up the pretence of a certain superiority. In Europe I should have lapsed into the most comfortable of all deceptions, self-commiseration: "a smile on the lips, and death in my heart". Here I was simply roused to revolt. Nobody paid the slightest attention to me. If in all this gaiety a girl or a boy had a look for me at all, the girl betrayed no admiration in her eye, the boy felt not subdued by my mere presence. This was truth!

Parasites, yes! And those who had not inherited any money, or not enough to make them entirely "independent", had dropped into careers which were carefully prepared and prearranged for them. These careers were like the track of a railway roadbed. The young men were like the trains. They did not go where they listed; they went where the rails might lead. Tradition governed them all. Of course, I was thinking of the young men of my own class only; the lower strata of society I did not know. I thought of Niels, André, van Els, and Sidney; I tried to

figure them – who had been successful as young professional men – in my situation. Why, they would have been
as helpless – more helpless than I was. How easy it seemed
to follow the beaten road – how different to go out as a
pioneer!

But, had not that beaten road stretched before myself as
well? If only I had known from the beginning that I must
go it? But should I have done so? Was I to go back? It
would still have been easy. I should have been away for a
month or so – on a trip across the Atlantic. Nobody
needed to know what desperate thoughts had held me in
their grip. Deep in my innermost heart I should be possessed of a wisdom beyond all their wisdom – of that
knowledge which comes from having looked down into
that deadly maelstrom which is real life reduced to its
lowest terms. There were still possibilities. I could still
drop into this or that; could surely make some kind of a
living by stepping down somewhat lower than I had so far
contemplated while I was thinking of Europe.

But I knew. As soon as I began to face the thought of
turning back, I knew that all that was impossible now. I
was like one who has received a revelation. Here I was in
a different world. Here I stood entirely on my own feet.
Whatever I might have to go through, if finally I arrived
somewhere, if I achieved something, no matter how little,
it would be my own achievement; I must be I.

Could a man starve in this great country? If so, starve I
would. Could a man go under, plunge below the surface
into that underworld which we call crime? Well and
good; rather become a criminal than turn back on the
road! Here I was, and here I should stay! Somewhere,
somehow I should find a place, a niche into which I fitted
or could fit myself; and when I had found it, then it would
be time for the final search after equilibrium and happiness, not before!

Monday morning's search through the back-pages of
the early papers raised a hope. There were two advertisements calling for waiters in restaurants. I was willing to

do no matter what. I neglected everything else and took note of the two addresses. One of them was on King Street, the other on Yonge Street.

I found both places at once and discovered that neither would be open before eight o'clock. The one on King Street was a large affair occupying the ground-floor of a business block. It looked cosy and exclusive; the huge windows being hung with wide lace-curtains flanked by heavy draperies. Nothing but a monogram woven into the lace of the curtains indicated the name of the place. Through the film of their patterns I caught sight of many small tables deeply hung with immaculate linen.

The one on Yonge Street consisted of a low, narrow building squeezed in between two tall and massive structures. It displayed fruit and fowl in two uncurtained windows which flanked a double-plate-glass door. Through the glass of this door I caught sight of a booth built into the right-hand side of the entrance, and, in the booth, of a cash-register. To the left of the long, narrow dining-room there stretched a long, narrow counter with glass-cases on top in which a white-smocked attendant was arranging pies and pastry. As far as I could see, the place was quite as clean as you could wish. I crossed over to the other side of the street; from there I saw that a large, black-glass sign with gilt letters five feet high ran across the entire front of the building. "Johnson's Café" the inscription read. A similar, but smaller sign, fastened over the door, bore the words, "The Business Man's Lunch."

In my former, old-world days I should not have been doubtful as to which of the two places I was to enter as a customer. I was still too close to that past not to make up my mind instantly to try the place on King Street first.

The very moment its door was unlocked I entered the restaurant. A smooth-shaved young man in a smoking-jacket tried with a bow and a smile to take charge of me and to conduct me to a seat in the rear of the room, where a huge balcony overroofed half its area. I noticed a semi-circular space jutting out from the centre of that balcony, which seemed to indicate that music would be provided for the dinner-hour.

The young man nearly succeeded by his winning manner in changing me, to the profit of his employers, from an applicant for a position into a customer, such was his hypnotic masterfulness in sweeping me forward. In fact, I am afraid, nothing but the lamentable circumstance that all my currency was hidden away in my hat-box and that, unfortunately, I did not carry the hat-box with me, prevented his complete success.

When I realized this phase of the situation, I stopped him short. "Pardon me," I said; "I do not intend to take anything just now. I should like to see the manager."

He turned. "I am sorry," he regretted. "Mr. Wainwright is not in yet. Maybe you could find it convenient to drop in again about noon, sir? Or might I deliver a message?" He still spoke with that compelling, frank, hypnotic smile on his face and with undoubted, nearly ingratiating deference in his tone.

"I read an ad in the paper this morning . . . " I began tentatively.

Instantly his features changed. His lips straightened, the smile dropped out of his eyes. Instead, a grey, steely scrutiny sprang into them. He stood rigidly erect, a medium-sized, alert business man. When I was a boy, I had a "caleidoscope" given to me, a brass-tube resembling a telescope, with a great number of tiny, coloured glass-plates cut in various geometric shapes and set into the wider objective end. When you aimed this instrument at the light, you looked through an eye-piece at a many-coloured mosaic; and when you rotated the tube slowly in front of your eye, suddenly, as a certain point in the rotation was reached, all these little coloured glass-plates would fall into a different arrangement, tumbling about for a fraction of a second in apparent confusion; then, with a slight, clicking sound, a new mosaic presented itself, differing from the first in its general effect and in its figure, but not in its component parts. The change in the face of the young man was like that, as sudden and as surprising. The component parts of the face were still the same; but the expression was altogether new. The salesman had changed into a buyer.

"Looking for work?" he asked curtly. "I am the captain. I hire the help. Vous parlez Français?"

"Parfaitement," I replied. This question restored my confidence; after all, my knowledge was going to count in this business! I spoke with my best Parisian accent. I exulted, for I could see that he accepted a single word as sufficient evidence of my linguistic proficiency. But then came the word which instantly dashed all my hopes to the ground.

"Experienced, of course?"

"No-o," I replied hesitatingly.

"How long have you been here?"

"A week or so."

"Just came over?"

"Yes."

Observe the climax in his questions.

He looked at me with a firm, quiet, thoughtful glance. Like another kaleidoscopic view kindliness replaced in his face the eager scrutiny. I remember that I liked him immensely because he did not at once lower his eye to look at my clothes. He sized me up from my face alone. I fairly longed for him to say, "I shall give you a chance."

Then he spoke; and a feeling of hopelessly sliding down into the bottomless void took hold of me.

"Sorry," he said. "I can see you have been used to look at this business from the other fellow's side. All the more sorry. For that's the type we should like to have. But there are details. Suppose you have never handled a tray full of dishes? I thought so. Has to be learned, you know. Sorry. Why this? Have you tried any other line?"

"Everything," I said in a tone which betrayed my disappointment.

"Sorry. Awfully sorry. But wait. I'll tell you. You try Johnson's. They are shorthanded too. Ask for Mr. Carlton, the manager. If he turns you down, come back and let me know. I might be able to do something for you, there. Beastly place, you know. But you will have to learn somewhere. If you make good there, you can get in here. But I cannot take on a raw recruit. We don't even as a rule advertise. Get our help through agencies. But we were caught, this time. Still . . . No, I can't do it."

And his face broke out into a smile quite different from that hypnotic, masterful smile which he reserved for the guest whom he guided where he wanted to place him.

"Leave your name with me, will you? Try Johnson's, and good luck to you."

He shook hands, and I was in the street.

I came dangerously near crying with rage. This failure to secure what I had been after affected me more cruelly than any previous rebuff had done. Here I could not attribute it to any preconceived notion, any silly prejudice, nor to the antagonized unmannerliness of the employer who did not wish to engage a constant rebuke to his own lack of breeding. This young chap, though likely he had never partaken of my own social pretensions, had my own mentality; I should have liked to be initiated under his direction into the mysteries of this business. And he referred me to a "beastly place" to learn!

I walked the streets till after ten o'clock before I had quieted down sufficiently to see that I must go to the other restaurant and try again. I nearly wished that I might be "turned down", there, too.

I entered the glass-doors at half past ten. I came into an extraordinarily long and narrow, corridor-like room the walls of which consisted of huge mirrors. The front half was level with the street outside. Behind, four steps led up to a higher part, at the far end of which two swinging doors led into what for me was still the unknown. A long line of narrow-winged electric fans were hanging from the ceiling. In the front-room the right hand wall, in the rear-room both walls were lined with tables placed between stall-like, high-backed, leather-cushioned benches

which gave privacy. Between counter and stalls large, cir-
cular tables, seating, and laid for, eight persons, formed a
long, long line. At or near every one of these tables I saw a
waiter in white jacket and black tie, his legs hidden by a
large, white apron.It struck me only now, in retrospection,
that in the dining-room of the King Street restaurant no
waiters had been visible. The same arrangement seemed
to be repeated in the higher room behind.

I turned to the young lady in the booth.

"Just a moment," she said when I expressed the desire
to see Mr. Carlton, the manager; and she tapped the button
of a bell which stood at her elbow.

A uniformed boy arose from nowhere in particular. She
bent her face down to the window in the glass-front of her
booth.

"Caller for Mr. Carlton," she said to him: and to me,
"Please to follow the boy."

The boy led me through the front-room and up the steps
at the end of it. On each side of these steps there was a
sort of niche or recess, hidden from the public eye by two
or three large cretonne screens stretched in bamboo
frames. The one to the left was apparently meant as a stall
for a small orchestra, for I caught a glimpse of a piano and
of two or three music-stands. The other one was the manager's office.

"Gentleman to see you, sir," said the boy into the crack
between two screens; and he retreated.

I entered through the same opening, and, once inside, I
noticed that, though from the outside you could see neither the man nor the desk at which he was sitting, yet the
cretonne was light enough to permit him to watch whatever was going on in either of the dining-rooms. It took
me a few seconds to get used to the dim light prevailing
here before I was able to judge of the features of the man.

Fortunately he was busy with some papers when I entered; and just as I was collecting myself, the bell of the
telephone at his elbow rang.

"Just a moment," he said, taking down the receiver. "Have a seat."

He waved his free hand towards a chair beside the desk.

I looked at the man before me. He was tall, slim, with stooping shoulders. Above all he was grey. The suit he wore was grey; so was the thin hair on the polished skull; so were his eyes; even his skin seemed grey in that light, though later I came to know it as merely pallid, with the pallor of the man who hardly ever goes out to face sun or wind. He was about fifty. The shape of his head was peculiar. The skull sat on a long neck; the nose was curved, fleshy, and mobile; the chin short and receding. The whole head strangely resembled that of a bird. His grey eyes looked out from behind gold-rimmed glasses. Altogether he looked grey, middle-aged, mild, and, at first sight, insignificant.

Like an inspiration it came over me that I had to dominate this man into giving me what I came for. A native American would have said that I had to sell myself to this man. I was glad of the delay. It gave me time to arrange my selling-points. A certain confident elation took hold of me.

"What can I do for you?" he said at last. When he spoke, his long, thin upper lip which was curved and, like his nose, strangely mobile, revealed gold-filled incisors flashing from behind it.

"Mr. Carlton," I began rapidly and with the air of a man conferring a favour upon his interlocutor, "my name is Branden, Phil Branden; I landed in this country not quite two weeks ago. I have never in my life done anything useful; I was raised in the belief that I did not have to. Recently my father died,and I was left without resources. I came to America to make my living. I know you are going to talk of experience. Let me forestall you. I know the restaurant-business thoroughly – from the customer's point of view. Your regular run of waiters do not, although they may be better able to carry a tray full of dishes. Let me make my point clear. It is your business to feed your customer and to serve his food in such a way that he will come back for more. Your ordinary waiter will serve him his steak and wait for him to order Lea and Perrin's or H.P. Sauce to season it. I know just what I should want to have him serve me with my order. So I am going to anticipate his wishes. If I have my weak points, you see, I also have my strong points, just as your so-called experienced waiters. In addition to that, let a Swede, a Frenchman, an Italian, a German enter your place; I shall address him in his own language. That, too, will tend to bring him back. But the best that I can say for myself it that I want to make good. Your place has been named to me by a friend as a good one to learn the restaurant business in. I am for the moment not after wages; in fact, I do not particularly need them; but I want a chance to learn. I look to you to give me that chance."

Mr. Carlton had been looking at me with a quizzical expression on his face while I made this long-winded speech. When I finished, he took up a paper-knife which was lying in front of him, and he smiled more brightly than I should have thought him capable of smiling. I knew, no matter what he might say, that I had gained my point; that certainly put me at my ease.

"You have stated your case pretty well, Mr. . . . "

"Branden," I prompted.

"Mr. Branden," he said. "You have interested me, and that is more than I can say of any applicant who has ever come to me for a job. In order to settle the main point first, I will say right now that I am going to give you your chance. But I shall regard you as an experiment. I cannot quite agree with everything you said, but I am willing to try you out. I will state our own case as frankly as you have stated yours. We – I happen to be a partner of Mr. Johnson's – are in this business not so much in order to please our customers as in order to get their money out of their pockets into ours. Unfortunately some of our customers will, like ourselves, insist on having luxuries like Lea and Perrins' Sauce with their steak. But to that extent the one who asks for it is undesirable. The one who does not ask for it we do not intend to supply with it, because that means money in our pocket. We are delighted whenever a customer orders something which he intends to pay for. But when he orders what he expects us to give away, we comply within reason, but we do so with reluctance. We do not show it, of course. We serve a certain class of customers who as a rule are not too particular. We serve them at a certain price to yield us a profit. Our profit on a single order is not large; so we consider that we are giving value for the public's money. We charge five cents for a cup of coffee. If the customer asked for cream with his coffee we should have to take a loss if we complied without an extra charge. It is up to the waiter to call his attention to the fact that he will have to pay an additional five cents for a small jug of cream. Of course, we also handle the higher-priced orders of more exclusive eating-houses; with those we can afford to serve whatever the customer cares to have, provided he comes for it at the right time. But our rush-hour business is conducted on a narrow margin. At that time we should prefer the man who demands your kind of service to go elsewhere. We want our waiters then to serve our customer as quickly as possible; and we want our customer to eat as fast as he can in order to make room for the next one. We supply a demand. Your idea of service is right to a certain extent, of course. We do not look for ideas in our waiters, though. If you were to serve tomato-catsup with every order of whitefish, let me say, you would do so to the detriment of your employers' profits. And that in a two-fold way. The lunch-hour and supper-hour client of this dining-room is apt to get spoiled. He is apt, if he is given the chance, to take ten cents' worth of catsup with an order that yields only ten cents profit. We prefer not to give him that chance. And besides, to put it cynically, he will linger too long over his plate, if he enjoys his food beyond its mere filling powers. So he will keep the next one from giving us what we are after, our legitimate profit."

Mr. Carlton laughed. "I do not know," he went on, "that I have ever explained these things to a waiter before. You seem to be rather out of the ordinary. But I have a few more things to say with regard to yourself. Do not for a moment think that this is a nice business for you to enter. I have worked my way up in it; believe me, I know it. I have been in it ever since I was a little boy. We operate a chain of eating-places in this city; that is to say, Mr. Johnson does; I am concerned only in this particular dining-room; the others are lunch-counters. Now I have told you already that I am willing to give you the chance you ask for – provided you care to take it on my conditions. I cannot put you on as a waiter at once. But I will take you on as a omnibus. You will have to help the regular waiters out, carry trays full of soiled dishes to the kitchen, help to clean the silver and make yourself generally useful. As you suggested yourself, you will have to learn to handle dishes in the mass. Besides, have you thought of the fact that an American bill-of-fare probably is something entirely different from that of Europe? I advise you to study the menu every day and to familiarize yourself with the kind of orders we serve. As soon as I think you are ready to start waiting on tables, I shall give you a chance to do so, possibly in a couple of weeks. You will have to trust yourself to me in that respect. As for the wages, we pay an experienced omnibus as much as a waiter, six dollars a week. I shall start you on four and a half. The waiter, of course, regards the wages as a comparatively unimportant item. He figures on tips. I believe that the best of our waiters clear up to twenty dollars a week in tips, maybe more; I do not know; they are secretive about it. But they do get tips, in spite of the fact that two things operate against them in this cafe; firstly, the class of customers – clerks, small storekeepers, steamship and railroad employees, etc., men, in short, who are not overly liberal; and secondly, the fact that it is strictly against the rules for a waiter to collect the amount of the check; he must refer the customer to the desk."

Silence fell. I felt sobered. Since I had settled the main point, that of securing "some kind of work", I relapsed into a critical state of mind. A boy of fifteen and ten dollars a week – I and four and a half! But I was determined to accept, of course.

"And the hours?"

"From ten a.m. to two a.m.," said Mr. Carlton. "We expect you to be here at ten o'clock in the morning if you want to get your breakfast. If not, at half past ten. Your work starts at eleven sharp. You get your board, of course. We close the doors at two o'clock in the morning. A customer who enters the place at a minute to two must be taken care of. But nobody is admitted after that hour. Then you will have to clear the floor for sweeping, and mostly you will be ready to leave at a quarter past."

"Very well," I said and rose. "When do I start in?"

"You may report to-morrow morning. Black trousers and black shoes and tie; white shirt, white jacket and apron."

"Where do I get those?"

"At Simpson's. You mention Johnson's cafe, and they will fix you up. You should buy two jackets and three aprons for a start. They will be laundered daily at a charge of fifty cents a week."

"Well, till to-morrow morning," I said and turned to go.

"I shall keep an eye on you. So long."

It is a fact that I felt elated and depressed at the same time. My case may be hard to understand. As a rule the immigrant who goes from one country to another still preserves some connecting-link with his past. He continues in the same work which he has been doing; and, while he learns new ways of doing his work, he moves among the same class of people to which he belongs himself. He may even keep up pretty close relations with his old environment. Letters at least will arrive. I do not mean to use the word "class" here in a sense indicative of air-tight partitions between social strata; in that sense class does not exist in America. There still remains the use of the word as a convenient synonym for "social environment."

I had stepped from what I could not help regarding as a well-ordered, comfortable environment into what had upon me the effect of an utter chaos. For the moment all human contact was non-existent. I felt that not only had I to learn a great many things, the social connections of a world entirely different from the world I knew, for instance; but I also had laboriously to tear down or at least to submerge what I had built up before – my tastes, inclinations, interests. My every-day conversation had so far been about books, pictures, scientific research. Not a word had I heard or spoken about these things since I had set foot on the liner which took me across the Atlantic. In Europe, no matter with whom or about what I might have been speaking, my intercourse with other people had been characterized by that exceeding considerateness which we call culture. Here everybody, even the few that were friendly, seemed bent upon doing what in my former world had seemed to be the unpardonable social sin, and which is described by the slang phrase "rubbing it in". Had I been born as the son of a waiter, I should have taken a thousand things for granted which now caused in me a very acute revolt. Had I at least been born in America, the atmosphere, which I frankly acknowledged to be a more healthy one that that of Europe, would not have appeared so strange, so hostile when it was merely indifferent. Had I lastly not been so carefully trained in the gentle art of doing nothing, I should not, in spite of better judgment, instinctively have shrunk from soiling my fingers.

As it was, I realized with a gulp that I had become an "omnibus" in a cheap eating-house. In order to earn the distinction of waiting at the table on clerks and small trades-people, I was expected to prove my ability!

But I also felt elated. The curious thing is that I actually took pride in the fact that I had been able to "stoop so low". A few years ago I had felt proud because I possessed fourteenth-century manuscripts of ancient authors. Why? I had paid a high price for them. Now I had achieved economic independence and prided myself upon it. Why? The price was high.

It is indicative of the state of my feelings that in the afternoon I walked several times all around Simpson's emporium before I could bring myself to enter and to ask for a waiter's outfit. Unreasonably, I expected the salesman to treat me with utter contempt on hearing what it was I wanted to purchase. It upset all my ideas, or rather my instinctive expectations when I found that not only did he treat me with perfect politeness, but that he even went to quite a little trouble in order to sell me a greater number of jackets and aprons than I had intended to buy. I believe I felt distinctly flattered when he delicately suggested that for a waiter of my fastidious tastes it would be revolting to don a jacket that was just being returned from the laundry, stiff, clammy, unproperly aired. He sold me three; a more daring psychologist might have sold me a dozen just as easily.

FOUR

I Submerge

WHEN, CARRYING my aprons and jackets in a small suitcase, I entered Johnson's Café at ten o'clock sharp on Tuesday morning, the first person whom I caught sight of was Mr. Carlton. Not a flicker in his bespectacled grey eyes betrayed that he had any knowledge of myself beyond having hired me as that impersonal neuter thing called help. A curt, almost severe nod in answer to my "Good morning, sir," and a sign with his finger to follow him; that was all.

He led me through the front-room, along the pastry counter, and to the left of the steps, where, under the orchestra platform, he opened an exceedingly low door, pointed down to a pitchdark staircase, and said, "You will find the lavatory and the locker-room down there. Your number is sixty-four. Hang your things in the locker, get ready, and report."

With these words which were spoken in a cool, matter-of-fact tone, he left me.

I had to bend very low in order to climb down the stairs and to reach an excessively dirty subterranean room. It was lighted by a number of electric lights which seemed dim because their bulbs were covered with thick dust and bespattered with mud whose origin seemed inexplicable. An inexpressibly fetid small pervaded the atmosphere. To the concrete wall at the right four expensive white-tile washbasins were fastened, all of them having hot-and-cold-water taps, and all of them in a state of utter neglect and dirt. Through the far wall led two swinging doors, one of them marked "Women", the other, left one, "Men". I picked my way across the litter of paper and matted, carpet-like dust. On entering the room behind, I caught sight of a long row of tall, narrow lockers to the left; to the right, of a partition which reached neither ceiling nor floor. From beyond this partition a confused noise of voices, laughter, squeaking or slamming locker-doors, and running feet, lifted itself, as it were, above a background of the general swish of female clothes. Through the opening between floor and partition I could see a great number of various-sized shoes moving and shuffling about. Several small boxes were lying on the floor. I noticed that, by pushing one of these to the parti-tion and stepping on it, any one might peer into the girls' dressing-room. The litter on the floor and the dirt on the electric bulbs matched those in the front-room of this underground cave. There was not a window in the whole place. The air consequently was stifling, saturated with the odour of human sweat, foul with the exhalations of slow, dry decay.

With a movement of disgust I turned to the lockers, found number sixty-four with the key in the lock, hung my aprons and jackets inside, pitched the suitcases on top, and got ready. Then I hurried upstairs.

I saw Mr. Carlton standing by the booth and talking to the cashier. I went to the front and silently awaited his leisure. I felt immensely depressed.

When he saw me, he raised his finger and without a word led me back to the higher room in the rear.

A medium-sized young man in low-cut vest and dinner-coat, with a non-committal, clean-shaven, singu-larly empty face came to meet us. Mr. Carlton stopped.

"This is Branden," he said, "the new omnibus I told you about. You show him, Cox." He turned back to the front.

"Had your breakfast?" asked Cox, the head-waiter.

"No, sir."

He led me to the upper end of the room, where that space of the wall not taken up by the two swinging-doors was filled by eight tall, boiler-like nickel vessels with gas-flames underneath. Between them huge piles of heavy white earthenware cups and saucers rested on low tables.

Mr. Cox pointed to the four vessels at the left and said "Coffee"; to those at the right, and said, "Tea".

He turned to the table in the last right-hand stall and threw down a small pad of paper-slips which bore my number "64" printed on them.

"Your check-book," he said. "Whatever you order, you write out on one of the checks; then take it behind to the kitchen, get what you want, and hand the slip to the checker when you pass back into this room. Always enter the kitchen through this door and leave it through that one" – pointing to the right and to the left. "When your order is for yourself, you will write your number once more at the bottom of the check. You'll find butter in the ice-bowl." A nod of his head indicated where to look for it, on the lower shelf of one of the numerous dumbwaiters flanking the stalls. "When you have finished your breakfast, report. Better hurry up."

And he went.

I looked about. There was, in this upper room, a single, solitary customer still lingering over his breakfast. An enormously tall and big waitress with a good-natured, fresh fat face stood by his table – it was in one of the stalls on the right-hand side – and chatted with him in a friendly way.

I turned, took a cup and saucer, and helped myself to coffee from one of the faucets. It contained milk already mixed in. I should have enjoyed some oatmeal, but I did not like to enter the kitchen unattended. So I got some butter and sat down at the last table to the right to make a breakfast of coffee, butter and bread. The bread was good, the butter not bad; the coffee, thin and by no means of the best quality.

For a few minutes there did not seem to be a sound. As far as my eye could reach, the place was utterly deserted. Once more I looked back, around the corner of the stall-partition of green-stained oak, and I saw that the enormous girl was still standing by the table of the belated breakfast guest. She was giggling. I could not help smiling at this very picture of health, girlish silliness, and innocence. Considering what I had seen downstairs, I should not have expected anything as fresh and refreshing as that girl's face.

Suddenly there was a burst of laughter and noise from the lower room in front. I looked around the corner again and saw five or six young men passing up the lower aisle, along the counter. Somehow I was amazed when I realized that they made for the door to that evil-smelling hole below. If they were employees of the place, they certainly moved, to my European notion, in a remarkably free and easy way. They reached the door. There was something like an explosion of mirth among them. They had collided with a small young man who was just emerging from below. Their laughter and exclamations filled the place. Mr. Cox rose out of one of the stalls on my side and, apparently in silent protest, went towards the steps that led down into the front-room. The small young man was taking them at a bound. While doing so, he kept buttoning up his jacket; his apron-strings were still dangling loose.

"Hello, Cox," he sang out, in a cheerful and mocking voice. "Beautiful morning, isn't it?"

I could not hear whether or what Mr. Cox replied; but with the impulse to hurry up, I turned to my breakfast.

"Hello," the same pleasant voice sang out at my side. "New face?"

I looked up and smiled. He was tying his apron and seemed to be dancing about on his feet. He was indeed small though he might just pass as average, with a round, laughing face, neatly parted short, brown hair, and dancing eyes.

"Beats me where they get them," he went on. "Hello, Ella," for the girl was coming towards the table. "Hungry, Ella?" he asked in a bantering tone. "Sit down, girlie; entertain the guest. I'll get you some steak and French-fried potatoes."

"Shut up, Frank," Ella replied in a singularly high-pitched, childish voice and with a plaintive accent. "You make me tired. You know I never take any breakfast. A new one, you say?" And she turned to me with a look of scrutiny in her blue eyes. "Hello," she said and sank into the seat opposite my own.

"How do you do?" I answered, and added, "My name is Phil. I am the new omnibus."

For no reason that I could see she giggled. "Poor lamb," she said. "Where did Carlton pick you up, I wonder."

Frank was meanwhile dancing about, gathering up a small tray, fork, knife, spoon, and so on, and disappeared through the swinging door into the kitchen.

I smiled at the girl. She had won my entire confidence. "Green," I said. "Fresh from the other side."

She whistled. "Well, it beats everything, the way people leave a good thing when they've got it and flock into this land of milk and honey. What did you do? Kill somebody? Hold up a train? Dip into the cash-register?

I laughed. "No," I said. "I wish I had; it would explain things. As it is, I have committed no crime beyond coming to the end of my resources."

She giggled again. "Lucky boy," she said.

"Lucky?" I asked, infected by her mirth.

"Sure," she replied; "I never had any resources to come to the end of. You look like a swell, too. I'm going to call you Slim, if you don't mind."

"Mind?" I said with a slight exaggeration of gallantry. "You may call your obedient servant whatever you please."

"Don't get fresh," she reproved with a touch of peevishness in her tone, while she was slowly getting up.

"Is he making love already, Ella?" asked Frank who at this moment burst out from the kitchen, with a violent kick against the swinging door from which a whiff of steam-laden air and the smell of cooking food reached me. "Always gaining admirers, are you?" And he vaulted into the seat behind her, instantly busying himself with the food on his tray.

"Silly," she said indifferently and stepped into the aisle, stretching herself. "Well, I guess I better polish my silver."

"Pewter," said Frank between mouthfuls. "Pewter you mean, or tin."

Cox, the head-waiter, appeared at our table. He looked at me. "Finished?" he asked as if he summoned me to follow him.

I rose in answer.

He pointed to the low dumbwaiters flanking the stalls on both sides of the room. "Watch those," he said. "Whenever there is a tray with soiled dishes, take it out to the kitchen. No tray must be left on the dumbwaiters. At noon, when the rush is on, you may put some over there." And he pointed to tall shelf-racks which stood, flanked by two hat-trees and umbrella-stands, in the space that separated the centre tables. There were eight of these in the upper room. "But always get them into the kitchen as fast as you can. I'll show you."

And he led the way to the right swinging door.

We entered a low-ceilinged room which was partitioned off to the left by a gigantic, many-shelved wire dish-rack which reached up to the dripping ceiling. The atmosphere was that of an overheated washroom. Steam seemed to ooze out from everywhere. Along the wall to the right there was, first, a large, low, table-top-like wire net, stretched so that it hardly sagged in the centre.

"Here you empty your tray," said Mr. Cox. "Never put it down. Never leave a tray in this room."

When we went on, a gaping chute for the left-overs came into view through the steam; beyond, two enormous, tin-lined vats were being filled with boiling water from two taps.

Two fat, Slavic-looking women were busy there. Both looked up as we passed, one with a brazen, one with a hunted look on her face. Their clothes were damp from the atmosphere. Unaccountably they fancied heavy, dark, woollen garments.

Beyond, we turned to the left, into a corridor along the gigantic dish-rack. We came to the kitchen. At the corner there was a tray-rack, now piled to the ceiling.

"Here you leave your trays," said Cox. "Pass out through that door as fast as you can. Never linger here."

This part of the room was also low-ceilinged; and the heavy odours of frying fat, boiling gravy, and cooking roasts filled the atmosphere in veritable layers. There was a long counter which separated what evidently was the waiters' corridor from the realm of the cooks. At the end of this counter, close to the door into the dining-room, was a boxlike seat for the checker. It was still empty.

Behind the counter there were four ranges, one beyond the other, each about twenty feet long. Maybe a dozen attendants were busy there. All of them were either naked down to their hips, or else wore nothing but a thin undershirt. Their lower bodies were hidden by greasy aprons.

One of the cooks, a tall, angular, gaunt, grey-haired, and grey-moustached man with an ugly gleam in his one eye – where the other eye should have been, was nothing but a raw-looking scar – came across and threw a sheet of soiled paper on the counter for Cox. He did not say a word but turned back to his range where he was basting a huge roast. Cox took the paper, and we passed on.

"Whenever you see that one of the waiters has two trays filled with orders, pick one of them up and follow him out. But never wait here during rush-hours. Your business is to keep the dumbwaiters clear. Never go down into the front-room. You want to know the waiters stationed there. They have their own helpers, plenty of them. There are only five waiters on the upper floor where you are to help. You want to find out who they are before the rush begins."

We stepped back into the dining-room.

A crowd had gathered at the table where I had taken my breakfast. They were engaged in a lively conversation, which stopped when Cox and I emerged. Curious looks appraised me. Several of the waiters passed without a word into the kitchen; two, a man and a girl, went across to the left-hand aisle and started to rattle about in the piles of knives and forks and spoons which filled the last two tables in the stalls. They filled their trays and went to the front.

Cox had been standing irresolutely for a moment. He did not seem to be the acme of efficiency. "Better help to lay the tables," he said and pointed after them. Then he went across to where Frank was still sitting and eating his breakfast.

I followed the man and the girl down the aisle. Each centre table took up as much floor-space as two stalls.

I passed Ella; then the girl in front of me stopped, and I passed her, following the man. He stopped at the third centre table, counting from the steps, put his tray down, and started to change the linen in the stalls to the left. The girl, whom I had passed, began to busy herself in a similar way.

I scanned the man rather carefully while I approached to offer my help. He was small, much smaller than Frank, and held himself very erect, with the rigidity of those who have been cruelly curtailed by Nature in the matter of size. He was at least fifty years old, grey-haired and grey-moustached, with an expression on his face as if he suffered from chronic indigestion and indignation.

"Anything I can help with?" I enquired with a smile and a nod.

He stopped in his work, straightened his back, stared at me, and snapped out, "You can take yourself off. When I need you, I'll call for you. Do you understand?"

"I understand that you are a cad, sir," I replied, turning.

Ella saw me. He had spoken without subduing his voice. Everybody, in fact, had turned and was grinning. Ella smiled and winked at me.

"Come here, Slim," she called. "Roddy doesn't like anybody to help him. It would reflect on his efficiency. Besides I've twice as many tables as he has."

I did as she wished me to. But in passing the intervening table, I caught a sharp look from the eye of the waitress there and heard a muttered, "Well, I declare."

"Roddy is mad," said Ella in a whisper when I reached her table. "He wants to be called Mr. Fields. Besides he can't stand tall people anyway. We call him Roddy; not because his name is Roderick, but because he is supposed to have swallowed a rod when he was a baby. If he hadn't, he could not hold himself so stiff." She giggled. "My," she sighed, "isn't it hot? Just watch. That's the way we lay out the plate. Now you start on that side over there."

I did so, moving noiselessly and quickly.

"Ain't it fierce?" she whispered after a minute or so, with a toss of her head in the direction of the kitchen.

"Frightful," I assented; then, "Mind giving me the names of the folks around here?"

"Not at all," she said. "You know Roddy and Frank and myself. The woman in front is Meg. Her name is Margaret Cox, you know. She is the wife of the head-waiter and thinks herself better than the rest of us. The girl behind is Iva. You're lucky if you ever get to see the natural skin of her face."

I shot a glance at her. "I have no ambition," I said. "Powder and paint are a blessing for some. Does she need them?"

Ella giggled again. "I dunno. I've never seen her without it. She's a good enough kid. But you want to act as if you were in love with her. Unless you would rather have her for an enemy."

Cox passed along through the aisle, throwing two bills-of-fare on each of the tables. They consisted of large, printed cards with a typewritten sheet attached on which the "Specials" were announced. One item caught my eye. I pointed it out and asked, "What is that?"

Ella bent over and read with an unmistakable effort.

"Oh," she said, "Chilly concarn. Can't be described; can only be tasted." Again she giggled.

Frank hurried by from the upper end of the room carrying a heavily loaded tray. "Of course," he found time to mock, "Ella's got him on her strings for keeps! How do you do it, girlie?" And he was gone.

Ella giggled. "Never mind him," she said. "Frank's a good kid. He's the best waiter in the place. We're awfully shorthanded. Harvest has begun in the West. That's why they've put us girls on for the day shift. When they can get all the help they want, nobody has more than one centre and two stalls. But Frank has always had two centres and two stalls. He'd quit if they gave him less. He makes an awful lot of money; they are very anxious to hold him. Well, now you know all you need to. The rest of the crowd, there's sixteen of them down there, you'll come to know by and by – Oh, Lordie!" she wailed suddenly, "can't those people wait till we're ready for them?"

She started to hurry in the most astonishing way for one as heavy as she was.

I looked around. Two customers were coming up the steps, and I caught a muffled hum from the lower front-room. People were beginning to fill the seats there. Waiters rushed past us in the direction of the kitchen. The change was so sudden that it was startling.

"Well, I declare! as our neighbour would say," I exclaimed.

"Oh, that's nothing yet," said Ella while she was rushing about. "You wait till an hour from now. Then it's hell, I can tell you. Hell!" She nearly screamed the last word out.

She ran away, with me staring after her, this time really startled by her expression.

I turned again and watched the glass-doors which did not come to rest any longer. People were pressing in, singly, in pairs, in groups – mostly men, a few girls, rarely a family, men and women, coming together. Soon the seats in the lower room were taken, and the overflow into the upper room began to gather volume. Humanity appeared in waves.

From the rear of the upper room another be-aproned and be-jacketed figure turned up, a man whom I had not seen so far. He as an old man who walked with a shuffling gait, as if his foot-joints were unable to move, a common ailment among old waiters, so common that it is called "waiter's foot". His face struck me as the coarsest thing I had ever seen in human expression. It was bony, with the eyes set deep in hollow sockets overarched by bushy, dirty-white eye-brows. His cheekbones were red and warty; the whole face framed by a straggling, grey beard. His lips were thin and dry, his nostrils dilated with exertion. His jacket and apron were not as spotlessly clean as those of the other attendants or mine. He carried on right hand and shoulder one of those large trays, loaded to capacity with four tiers of tumblers full of iced water, one on top of the other. Slowly, with the skill of a lifetime of practice, he deposited his tray on one side of the racks in the centre and started to distribute the tumblers in front of the ever farther advancing guests. I watched this old man with fascination.

But suddenly I was startled back into life by a snapping voice. Mr. Carlton was standing by my side.

"What are you waiting for?" he said. "Get busy! Get a tray with butter-chips."

His tone was such that I flashed around and should have flung him a sharp rejoinder, not being used to be ordered about. But I caught a humorous flicker in his steel-grey eyes; with a "Certainly, sir," and a grin I was off.

While I was putting squares of iced butter on chips and piling them on to the tray, the flood of customers overflowed to the kitchen-doors. These doors kept swinging now in a steady pulsation. The smell of food began to pervade the atmosphere. When I grasped my tray and started to wind my way through the human current, the electric fans overhead flashed into activity, emitting their purring sound; at the same moment the piano on the orchestra-platform started a maddening waltz.

Out of the crowd ahead Mr. Carlton emerged once more. I was holding the tray in front, my left hand supporting it from underneath, the right hand grasping one of the handles.

"Get that tray on the flat of your hand," the manager snapped in no amiable tone, the flicker behind his glasses again belying his gruffness. "Out of the way of the customers' heads." He gave it an upward swing which, I feared, would throw its load to the floor. "Put it down in front, on the first rack," he said. "Then get busy on the dumbwaiters. Hurry up!"

I rushed to the front.

"Bringing the butter?" the old man greeted me when I arrived at his side. "Just put it down. I'll attend to it."

He was wearing white canvas gloves on both his hands.

When I reached the first of the dumbwaiters, it was already piled high with soiled dishes. I was at a loss what to do. Frank was totalling up a check at the first side-table.

"Quick, Phil," he said. "Never mind about straightening them. Get them out of the way. I'll help you. There!"

It seemed to me that he was lifting half a universe on to my shoulders.

"I'm afraid," I gasped, intending to say that I did not think I could manage the load.

"Yes, you can," he said very quietly. "Off with you! Nothing to it!"

I was on my way. I went carefully, slowly; but at last I reached the kitchen. Fortunately Cox went through just ahead of me, kicking the door open with his foot, for he carried a similar load. If I had not been lucky in this, I should not have known how to get rid of the dishes. He never stopped but merely slanted the tray over the wire net, dropping its whole contents, or rather, letting it slide down while he went. Then he passed out beyond. My momentary hesitation had already caused a congestion behind; I was being hustled forward by shouts and curses from those who followed me. I did as he had done and went on, but not without looking back. There, from the door, a whole line of men with loaded trays passed in, apparently the helpers from the lower room. To the left, unencumbered waiters, checks in hand, slipped by and disappeared around the corner.

I hurried on myself, dropped the empty tray into its place, and was on the point of rushing out to the front when Ella, now flushed and perspiring, stopped me with a touch of her hand.

"Take this," she said, swinging a tray loaded with orders aloft, on to my left hand which I raised above my shoulder, and pressing a bundle of checks into my right.

I pushed on.

"Checks," the checker yelled; but, when I threw them down, he merely speared them on a spindle and waved me on without verifying what I carried.

The next moment Mr. Carlton had me in tow again.

"Whose order?"

"Ella's," I said.

"Here!" and with amazing agility he wound his way through the ever-thickening mass of humans which filled the aisle, waiting for seats to be vacated.

Ella's dumbwaiters were piled high. Mr. Carlton took one of the trays and pushed it on to a shelf in the rack in the centre. I deposited mine and was on the point of stepping over to the rack when Mr. Carlton's voice rang out again.

"Branden, here!"

He lifted another heavily loaded tray to my shoulder, thus clearing a second dumbwaiter for Ella who was just appearing through the crowd. When I passed her, I was struck by the expression of desperate, dumb determination about her set lips. There was little colour in her cheeks, and they were beady with perspiration.

When I reached the dish-rack in the wash-room, Mr. Carlton was following me, doing what I did, helping to get the dumbwaiters cleared. It put a certain exhilaration into my own endeavours to see that nobody considered anything below his dignity.

A small, very dapper and neat-looking man whom I had not seen before, wearing expensive but overdone clothes, flashed past me just as I was about to turn the corner into the kitchen. His command whipped out like a pistol-shot above the pandemonium of shouting voices and rattling dishes.

"No platters! Plates only!"

"Plates only," sang out the shrill, senile voice of the head-cook in verification of the order.

I learned later that this flashy little man of perhaps thirty years was Mr. Johnson, the owner of a chain of eating-places in the city.

Nobody stopped me this time in the narrow corridor between dish-rack and counter.

Behind the counter a casual observer would have seen half-naked maniacs dancing and jumping about in crazy lunacy. In the corridor, waiters were bustling each other, reaching up into the dish-rack, flinging plates on the counter and bellowing orders at the top of their voices. From out of the reeking pit behind me came yelling shouts, repeating every order that was given. Plates full of food were thrown back, on trays held by the waiters. The swinging doors in front kept opening and slamming shut in ever-accelerated pulsation. Whoever passed through gave them a vigorous kick. The checker stood on a chair behind his desk, roaring for checks, swinging his arms, jumping like one possessed; but in reality he did nothing but spear the checks on spindles, although he sometimes tried to keep up the pretence of verifying an order which passed out on a tray.

While I rushed to the front, I saw that Iva, the painted girl, was as badly off as the rest. Only Meg had her dumb-waiters always cleared whenever she needed them, and it struck me that neither I nor the old man had ever relieved her of a tray. "Oh," a thought flashed up, "she is Mrs. Cox!"

Mr. Carlton was everywhere. Here I saw him chatting with a customer as if he had all the time in the world; there he was taking an order for a waiter; and again he was carrying a heavily loaded tray to the rear.

Most of the waiters were themselves carrying trays now whenever they went to the kitchen. Everything was done in a rush; all movements had to be made through a crowd of people waiting for seats; nor were these people at all concerned about the convenience of the slaves that had to serve them.

For an hour and a half I kept it up at the same rate, now helping Frank, now Ella, now Roddy, to keep their dumb-waiters cleared. I stayed in the front of the room; there the crowd was thickest; partly in fulfilment of an unspoken agreement between myself and the old man who shared my task; he kept to the rear where he did not have to take quite so many steps in order to reach the kitchen. Occasionally, not being used to this pace, I felt like a drowning man, swamped under a crushing flood of humanity, more especially when the customers began to clamour for quicker service. Most of the diners, when giving their order, would add, "Rush that, please," as if the whole organization had not already been keyed up to the utmost in the line of rushing. Ella had been right. I could not have imagined anything more closely approaching to my conception of Hell on Earth than these noon-hours were for the waiters and their helpers. I wondered how the people could sit there, looking as if they were comfortable instead of jumping up and springing to our assistance. As for myself, even if I had been sitting there and giving orders instead of helping to fill them, the noise, and above all that demoniacal music would have inflicted exquisite torture on my nerves.

But when things seemed to come to a climax, when trays piled up in the racks, when nothing that I, the old man with the shuffling gait, and the waiters themselves could do in order to breast the avalanche of dishes that streamed from the kitchen, seemed to avail, when things seemed ready for a collapse or an explosion – then suddenly Mr. Carlton and even Mr. Johnson himself appeared, silently and quickly, or giving short, snapping orders; grabbing trays and carrying them to the kitchen, they would give a momentary relief and breathing space.

In the wash-room one of the foreign-looking women piled the soiled dishes into wire baskets suspended from a little wheel which ran on an overhead rail; when the baskets were filled, they swept through the first vat of boiling water, on, into the second vat, and over, in a dangerous-looking curve, to the dish-rack, where the other woman emptied them, leaving the dishes to be dried by a current of hot air and returning the baskets over the remainder of the overhead track to their starting-point.

By one o'clock the worst of the rush was over. By half past one the place began to look deserted. The waiters at the last tables, nearest the kitchen, were beginning to rest.

In surveying the room, I was struck as by the sight of a disaster. Every table-cloth was soiled; every shelf of the central racks and the dumbwaiters was piled with a jumble of dirty dishes. The atmosphere reeked with the smells of the kitchen. The battle was fought; we were left on the field.

I scanned the waiters' faces. Iva was grimy with a paste of sweat, paint, and dirt. Ella was pale, exhausted, transformed. Meg and Roddy looked grimly resigned. Frank was the only one who still smiled and danced about as if he had enjoyed himself hugely. He had been the only one, too, who, during that frightful hour of the midday-climax, had had time and energy left to exchange bantering talk with his customers. The others, when taking down orders, had looked as if they were peering down on the enemy in the trenches.

There is little else to be said about the first day. Towards evening there was another flood-tide of humanity. But with the specials – which were exhausted – the great attraction of the place was gone. The second tide was a neap-tide only. The customers had more time; the waiters did not rush about. Once more the place filled up when the theatres closed. Then gradually the work dwindled down to the waiting on an occasional customer only.

The night-clients came to spend money, not to save it. These belated diners, I found, were the ones on whom the waiters counted for their tips. The girls had gone off duty at eight o'clock; or the men might have fared badly; for, from the type that prevailed among these late-comers, I judged that they would have preferred to be looked after by members of the other sex.

FIVE

I Earn a Promotion

THE VERY FIRST day taught me that knowledge of men is no more an attribute of the underling in America than it is in Europe. All of the waiters and helpers, except Frank and Ella, accepted me as what I was for the time being. I stood on the bottom-rung of the ladder, on a level with those Slavic-looking women who washed the dishes in the room behind. The fact that I bore myself differently; that my clothes, if nothing else, bespoke at least different tastes and a different origin, did not seem to penetrate their consciousness. I myself was beginning to see by the second day of this life that what we call culture, education, breeding is largely a matter of environment, something that it takes very long to acquire but which may, after all, be acquired and, therefore, lost. It overlies the human nature which is common to us all and which is not an overly lovely or adorable thing like a thin veneer which may easily be dented or even pierced. If anybody belonging to the social, intellectual, and emotional stratum from which the greater number of these men and women were recruited had, for instance, insulted me in my old surroundings, his insult would never have reached me. I might have resented it with a cold stare or an ugly laugh; but I should not have felt a wound. Now I did feel that wound though I did not resent it by stare or laugh.

The strange thing was that waiters and waitresses alike regarded themselves as being on a plane above myself, not intellectually or emotionally – they did not even know that such was possible – but socially. That was what I should have least expected. The tables were truly turned. It took Ella's supreme indifference to such demarcations, or Frank's shrewd divination – for he simply expected me to rise – to accept me on a level of equality. In other words, there seemed to be two gates through which you could enter into the democratic spirit: natural good-will and shrewd intelligence. Both, of course, may be inborn or acquired by education. Of the two, the natural good-will stands, morally speaking, on a higher level, for it simply accepts what is best in human nature and rejects what is low or accidental. Frank accepted in me, not what I was, but what I might be one day. All of which went to show that there were social strata in America as well as in Europe.

It might be well, though, to point out a difference. Taking it for granted – though the truth may hurt – that manners, knowledge, culture of mind and heart stand in the last resort for money – money which is being or has been held by individuals or families – the eyes of the European who appraises a stranger is turned back; that of the American, forward. In Europe the poor man is tolerated if he can look upon a great past; in America, if he looks to a future. This, of course, is meant as a summary only of the instinctive point of view of that part of the population which forms the apparent or patent – and therefore superficial – ground-mass of the people. We also find, both here and there, even on the surface, excluding all the latent strata, certain areas in which, by an interpenetration of ideas fostered through blood-relationship, these characteristics are exactly reversed. I once had a conversation with a lady who had been a teacher all her life and who, in a Canadian school, very strongly underlined veneration for the aristocracy as culminating in the king; to me the flag seemed the higher emblem. "Your king is a person," I said, "a human being like yourself. 'Now in the name of all the gods at once, upon what meat does this our Cæsar feed?' " She laughed.

"The king," she said, "is not a person. He stands for our past; he stands for glorious battles fought, for hours of triumph, hours of terrible need. He stands for tattered banners and smoky battlefields. He stands for all that we hold sacred if we are British. What is your flag? A coloured rag!" "Yes," I replied; "the king stands for the past. The flag stands for an idea, an ideal, for the future. And little it matters whether it be the Union Jack or the Stars and Stripes. The king stands for what most certainly has been – can we always defend it? The flag stands for what may be if we are great enough to weave reality out of dreams. The king stands for our fathers; the flag, for our children. That is why I like to see it in the school. I can always defend the flag." – I still think, though that lady was born in America and prided herself on coming from a slave-holding family in the south which emigrated in 1786, I was the better American.

Things being as they were, I was – in those hours of the afternoon and the night when the work was light – very naturally thrown a good deal with that old man who shared my status on the upper floor.

He had no name in this place where he worked; nobody, not even the manager or proprietor, called him anything but "Whiskers". Nor did anybody, except Frank, Ella and myself, ever speak a word to him unless when ordering him about.

He had been born in Ontario and had come as a young lad from a farm. I was curious about him. Here was a man, considerably more than sixty years old, grown grey in this work, a veteran, as it were, of waiterdom. Here was a test of that famous American slogan, "Equal opportunities for all". He had not risen. Why not? Had he not been able to take advantage of the opportunities that had come his way? Or had no opportunity ever been offered to him?

I think it was on the afternoon of my second day at the place that I sat down at the same table with him, at the left-hand side, where so far he had been left alone, an outcast.

"Hello," I said in the friendliest tone.

He looked up at me with a searching look, out of the cavernous depths of his eyes. Then he nodded without a word.

I waited for him to begin the conversation; somehow a trivial remark about the weather seemed out of place in the face of his hoary dignity. But he proceeded with his repast, now and then scrutinizing me with a look in which shyness and criticism seemed strangely mingled. Since I was not eating, he seemed to suspect that I was making fun of him. I felt as if I were intruding, as if I had to find an excuse for being there at all. Yet, that excuse would not be found.

I scanned his features; they presented, as I have said, the coarsest face I had ever seen in my life. The cheekbones stood out in high relief, reddened to a carmine tinge by an exceedingly fine network of enlarged surface-veins. Above, they sloped away to temples so hollow that they seemed to form an acute angle with a perfectly flat forehead jutting out over the caves of his eyes like a penthouse. The cheeks, too, were hollow, as if all the molars in his mouth were gone. Cheeks, temples, forehead were a ghastly white, in strong contrast to the red circles on his cheekbones. Jaws and chin seemed to form a semicircular ridge under the short, straggling white beard. It was a face which seemed to lack the finishing touches of Nature. It was as if roughly hewn out of coarse stone. The more I looked, the more it seemed as if I were gazing at a death's-head, a mere skull on which there was no flesh.

A stray glance of mine sank to his hands. There they were, a living explanation why he wore those white canvas gloves which I had seen the first day. These hands were knobby, gnarled like a stunted oak-limb; their knuckles, like knots in a wiry rope. The metacarpal bones, too, stood like rocky anticlines between eroded valley-folds. To describe the man one must needs resort to geological expression.

While I sat there, facing him, my curiosity suddenly seemed sacrilegious. I did not see in him a person longer; he became a symbol. He was the walking Death-in-Life; he stood for the end of all things mortal, for ambitions foiled or misguided; for that disappointment which is all the more heartbreaking when it is unconscious. He stood for Old Age looking back on Youth; for failure incarnate, such as in the essentials awaits us all, no matter what our apparent success may be. I was confronting things eternal, tragedies beyond the utterance of man.

Curiously enough, the fact that this tragedy might be unconscious touched me with fear. Speech might turn it into comedy, such comedy as is beyond even Shakespeare's cruel jest. I refrained. I felt shaken, moved. But I smiled at him – it must have looked a ghastly smile – nodded, and got up.

He looked at me with a strange, hungry expression on his face.

As it happened, had I deliberately planned to gain the old man's confidence – with a calculation of human nature quite beyond my years – I could not have devised a surer plan.

In the evening, during the slack hours after the supper-wave, it was he who sought me out.

I was sitting down for a moment, secure from interruption by guests. He passed my stall and stopped.

"We must divide the work," he said in a hoarse, expressionless voice. "You take the front, and I the rear."

"All right," I assented.

"And I'll bring the water," he went on, "and you, the butter."

"We'll just reverse that," I said. "Sit down; you're tired."

He looked both ways before he shuffled into the opposite seat.

"My feet!" he said. "They get so tired I hardly feel them." And then he leaned over and whispered confidentially, "Carlton, he must not see me, you know, sitting down. . . . That man is a devil; you don't know him; but that's what he is; you mark my words!" And lowering his voice still more, to a scarcely audible sibilance, but speaking very fast now, "I'll quit him, though; next week I'll quit him if he doesn't do as he promised. Exhibition's coming. . . . They need all hands . . . Then I'll quit unless he does as he promised to do."

"Have you been with him long?"

"Yes, sir," he said, nodding his head. "Yes, sir. Long enough to know him and the likes of him. Ever since he was a waiter in this place. Long before Johnson's time. . . . What are they paying you, young man?"

"Four fifty a week."

"Four fifty," he repeated. "Good wages, that. Good wages when a man is young. I get six. But look at them waiters! They are making the money. That's what a person wants! Waiting on tables, that's where the big and easy money is! Some of them is making ten dollars extry ever week! Tips, you know. . . . You are young, want to learn. Take my advice, young fellow, stay for a while. Till you have caught on to the ways of this country. Funny ways they are. Then quit here. I'm going to quit, you know; next week I'm going to quit. Unless Carlton does as he's promised to do. He is always promising, talking and talking; but he never keeps faith. Has he promised you anything?" His voice had sunk down to a rapid whisper again which towards the last took on a strange note of wistful and cunning expectancy.

"Nothing in particular," I replied; "though, come to think of it, he did promise that he would keep an eye on me and let me wait on tables as soon as he thinks I am able to do so."

This casual revelation had an altogether unexpected effect. The old man hung upon my words while I was speaking; and when I mentioned the two promises, he nodded his head with more vigour and agility than I should have thought possible in one as osseous as he was. But when I finished, he broke into the most abandoned giggle that I had ever heard from anybody but a silly girl, and the giggle changed into a spasmodic cackle, running into higher and higher pitches of dissonance – an exhibition of mirth which had something alarming, terrifying in so old a man, the more so the longer it lasted; and it lasted longer than anything of the kind I had ever witnessed, till it broke off just as abruptly as it had begun.

"Didn't I know it," he whispered, raising his gnarled and shaking forefinger. "Didn't I know it? Didn't I tell you he is a devil? Now, young man, just tell me, didn't I tell you?"

"Yes," I nodded, "you told me; no doubt about that; but still, I don't quite see . . . "

These words brought a repetition of the former outbreak. I looked at him in serious concern, for I feared an accident. It seemed impossible for so much hilarity to come from one like him without provoking wrath divine. It seemed to be against the laws of nature. Probably it was the expression in my face which cut it short this time.

Then he whispered again. "He doesn't quite see it! He doesn't quite see it!" And, as if to reveal to me the very arcana of his innermost knowledge of the depravity of mankind, "Now listen, young man, and remember! I have never told this to any one before. But you have been good to me. You haven't called me Whiskers. Carlton has promised me that, week for week, for the last twenty-five or thirty years! Just think about it and see whether you can make anything of it!" And with great exertion he lifted himself to his feet, shuffled out into the aisle, looked back at me once more, and whispered again, "Think . . . Think . . . "

Next day I tried out how many tumblers filled with water I might be able to handle safely on a tray. I had made up my mind to start work ten to fifteen minutes earlier in the morning, so as to get a sufficient amount of iced water to the front before the rush set in. I was determined to do that part of the work myself.

While thus engaged, I caught sight of Ella who was passing along the aisle. When she saw me, she stopped.

"What are you doing, Slim?"

"Trying to find out how I can make things somewhat easier for our friend, the old man," I replied.

"Whiskers? Poor fellow!"

"Do you think he is being treated fairly?" I asked.

"Well," she said hesitatingly, "what else can they do? It seems charity to keep him in this job. He is too old; he can't do anything else; he looks a disgrace to the place, but they let him make his dollar a day.

"Is he any more a disgrace to the place than the dressing-rooms downstairs, or the kitchen?"

"Perhaps not," she said; "but those the customers do not see."

"That's it. Do you know how long he has been in this place?"

"Since it was built, I believe."

"Yes," I said, "ever since that dressing-room was swept and aired for the first and last time. At six dollars a week! Why don't they retire him?"

"Retire him? What do you mean?"

"Pay him a small sum a week for life and let him go."

"That isn't done, you know," she smiled. "How could they when he does not work?"

I challenged her. "I hear, Mr. Carlton gets three thousand dollars a year and a share of the profits besides. Mr. Johnson, they tell me, clears somewhere around twenty thousand dollars a year from this place alone."

"Oh yes, they are hogs," declared Ella, and I understood that word though I had never heard it thus used before.

"The old man has reached the stage where he wants to quit unless they give him a table."

Ella giggled. The last trace of thoughtfulness had disappeared from her face. "Ain't he too funny for anything?" she said with a laugh. "That's his ambition, you know, waiting on tables. And, of course, he's sprung that bluff on you, too."

"Bluff?" I asked though I understood only too well.

"That he'll quit next week unless Carlton does as he promised to do. I've been here three years now, and he's told that yarn to every newcomer who would listen. He never quits. He's married. He can't afford to. He's got to live like the rest of us."

I dropped the topic; Ella clearly was not ripe for such ideas. Though she might be perfectly awake to the niceties of personal right and wrong, she had in her mental equipment no organ to grasp the idea of a social wrong.

I had food for thought. I did not know at the time just what socialism was or meant. So far I had had a vague idea that it meant the "subversion of the state"; I considered it one of the many paradoxes in which Bernard Shaw indulged that he tried to persuade the world that he was a Socialist, when the whole world knew all the time that he was perfectly respectable and nice. I had never seriously thought of such topics as Old-Age-Insurance. If anybody had told me that I had been talking Socialism to Ella, I should have been shocked and should have answered, "I was talking sense, and nothing else." In this practical case, of which there must be many duplicates in a great industrial organization like that of America, I felt at once, as I feel to-day, that society is at fault if it leaves the provision for old age to the individual's thrift, or, worse still, puts it beyond his powers to look out for himself. "What a country," I thought, "that turns all my sympathies into new channels within two weeks!" But, of course, I forgot that it might have been the same had I "submerged" in that Europe which I had left behind.

Meanwhile I made rapid progress in various ways. Above all, I learned to regard the noon-hour rush with perfect indifference. I did what I could with speed and alacrity; but what I could not do had by Wednesday ceased to worry me. I also acquired the skill that is needed to swing a heavily loaded tray aloft and to carry it out while I was bustled and pushed on every hand. I knew the names and the faces of all the employees of the restaurant; nor did the bill-of-fare hold further mysteries for me.

I received most of the assistance I was in need of from Frank who was always cheerful, always willing to help.

Another trouble arose in which Frank aided. The first day I had, as much as possible, avoided loitering in the kitchen. But in my endeavour to learn all about the various dishes offered I had to face this kitchen as a serious problem. What I saw there was not of a nature to increase my liking for the place. The very atmosphere was disgusting. The wood-work seemed to be soaked, impregnated, dripping with grease. Apart from sweeping up the litter from the floor nobody ever thought of doing any cleaning there. Soap seemed to be unknown in this establishment. The washing of the dishes even was the most perfunctory process imaginable. The chute through which the left-overs were disposed of was the most nauseating sight I had ever beheld.

This dislike was mutual. There was no Frank, no Ella in the kitchen-personnel to befriend me. Whenever I showed my face – except during the rush-hours – I was received with an uproar of the coarsest and filthiest gibes and jokes. They called me "the baron" there, addressed me as "Sir Phil", and in high-sounding phrases spoke to me mostly of things and parts of the body that will not bear print. The reader will understand that it took courage to enter the place.

"Yes," said Frank with his fatalistic acceptance of all things that be, "you want to get used to that. They are a vile bunch. And all of them – as, by the way, take warning, Phil, most of the girls, too – are rotten with sexual disease. You can't help seeing some of it in the long run."

The first day or so I had forced myself to eat the food prepared in this kitchen, with eyes closed, as it were. Then I went hungry most of the time, for I ate only bread and butter. But late one afternoon Frank and I had slipped out through the kitchen to a little platform behind, where the trucks of the supply-houses unloaded their wares; there we were having a quiet smoke.

Suddenly I heard, close to the door, a remark made by the head-cook. "Well, boys, I must get my hands clean. Guess I'll make a batch of biscuits. Get the flour."

Frank smiled up at me.

But the expression on my face was of such utter disgust that his smile faded.

"How do you make out on food?" he asked.

This ready comprehension made friends of us.

"I am afraid, after this, I shall not be making out at all."

"It is not bad in the morning," Frank tried a defence. "I eat their oatmeal."

"Has the kettle ever been scoured in the last ten years?" I enquired mercilessly.

He laughed. "No. That is, I don't think so. I haven't been here more than six months, you know. During that time it has not that I know of. They merely stir the new meal into the left-over porridge. But porridge does not get rancid."

"I have heard it gets sour," I replied to that challenge.

"Not if it is sterilized by repeated boiling," he said with a very serious face.

We both burst out laughing, so that we could not recover till our sides ached.

"At noon I can't eat their concoctions either," Frank confided after a while; "not after having looked on when that one-eyed devil works."

Again we laughed; we were young and easily infected.

"Well, what do you do?"

"Pastry," Frank replied. "The pies are good. They are handled at the counter, in plain view. They can't spoil them."

"Yes, but I have been told we are now allowed to get our own orders from the counter unless we pay for them."

"There are lots of things which we are not allowed to do," said Frank. "You come to me when you get hungry till you learn to pull the strings yourself."

We slipped back through the kitchen. When we were on the point of pushing through the swinging door, Frank stopped me by a motion of his hand. He raised a finger to his lips.

I heard Mr. Carlton's voice. "Not just now, Whiskers," he said in a tone that was not unkindly. "We'll see; maybe later."

"At his old game again," Frank whispered.

We waited a moment, till the steps on the other side of the door sounded fainter; then we returned into the dining-room.

The words had been insignificant. But the tone in which they were spoken was a revelation to me. There was indulgence in that tone, even pity. The manager simply did not wish to tell the old man that what he asked for was impossible. He seemed to know that it would break his heart if he told him. Sympathy and consideration – attributes which I had not been looking for in Mr. Carlton – made him appear less culpable than before. I came near sharing Ella's view; it was, perhaps, mere charity to keep the old man "in his job."

The week drew to an end. I was inured to the practices of the place. The problem of food was solved by the pies and pastry which Frank sequestered on the lower shelf of one of his dumbwaiters.

On Saturday morning we were all surprised by the appearance of a third helper on the upper floor. He was a raw-looking, awkward boy from the country, red-faced, shy, excitable, but willing to work and very silent.

Just before the noon-rush, Mr. Carlton stopped at the tray-rack where I was arranging the tumblers with iced water.

"How do you like it by this time?" he asked.

"Not much to like about it, sir," I replied. "But I am making my living and catching on to the work, I believe."

"Yes," he said; "you are doing well. We have agreed to let you have full pay for the week. At noon you will help Ella and Iva wait on their tables. After the rush you will take the last centres and the stalls alongside for yourself."

I was so surprised that I could hardly say anything.

"Of course," Mr. Carlton added, "there is not much of a chance for you to have many customers at those tables today; it's Saturday."

With a nod he went off.

Here was success! Mr. Carlton was keeping faith beyond his promises! Within a couple of weeks or so, he had said. I was promoted within five days! I knew, of course, that I owed this in large part to the circumstances. In spite of the fact that there seemed to be an abundant supply of help where clerical positions were concerned, these people were exceedingly short-handed. From which I could draw only one conclusion, namely, that the desirability of certain classes of work attracted or deterred the crowds of applicants here as well as elsewhere. Had the management not by chance been able to secure an additional helper for the upper floor, I should probably have had to stay longer where I was. And yet, I had been making good! My very first attempt in the new world was not a failure! There was promise in this fact. I had shown to myself, to my own satisfaction that I had the necessary adaptability. I knew that I should never accept defeat; that, no matter how long it might take, no matter how much it might cost, in the end I should somehow win through to the very goal of my desires.

And while I was going about my work, taking orders, clearing tables, bellowing in the kitchen with the best of them – sometimes nearly overcome with the rush and the repulsiveness of it all – I grew beyond my present status. I was going to quit this work; I was going to fight for something better. But before I did that, I was going to double my present holdings in money. With twice what I had I was going to make another stand in the very front trenches, as it were. Should success fail me, should I find it impossible to break through into something more congenial, then there would be this to fall back on, this one thing in which I then should be able to say that I was not without experience.

These were, of course, not continuous or even connected thoughts of mine. During the noon-rush the customers saw to it that there was no time left for dreaming or planning. Ideas would arise in disconnected flashes, such as will lift you above your present surroundings, such as will carry you even through times of danger; there was triumph in them, such as will take you forward even into the jaws of death. You forget what you are about; you are able to do things which otherwise you might not even have attempted. In spite of the fact that you are really absent-minded, you go about the work in hand with a curious, nearly automatic precision, as if a second vision guided you, as if you were following inspiration.

Incongruous words to use of the work of a waiter, you say! But my life on this continent has taught me that it really does not matter what you do. I can assure you that the psychology of a general who leads his troops to victory is not essentially different from that of a helper in a cheap restaurant. If vision guides, the problems of immediate details solve themselves. I have found Goethe's word, "What you long for in youth, you have a-plenty in your old age," quite eminently true in life.

If the desire to get somewhere is strong enough in a person, his whole being, conscious and unconscious, is always at work, looking for, and devising, means to get to the goal. It is not so much a question of opportunities offered, as it is a problem of searching for, and seeing, things which you would overlook if your soul and mind were not at all times keyed up to, or attuned for, the very things you see. I might put it this way. On some distant mountain you know a treasure. That treasure you are bent upon lifting. You approach the place; you circle the summit; but the very peak you find impossible of access. You are led to by-paths, devious ways; environment takes hold of you; your immediate attention is deflected; you start, let me say, herding cattle in the valleys around the resplendent peak. But unconsciously your mind is still set on your goal; it looks down upon the small things of daily life; and as you will see the connections of gully and rill, brook-chasm and river-valley more clearly from above, so you will also see more clearly the things in hand, the connections between the hour and the exigencies of the next if your mind is lifted to great heights by overpowering desires. While you are living your years with that glacier-clad height in closest vicinity, without consciously thinking of it, you will at all times be looking about for the approaches, for clefts in the cliffs, for slanting ledges which lead around and above the ice-fields. And one day all things that you have seen and noted – for whatever had no bearing upon your ruling desire you did not note – will, as it were, connect up with a sudden jerk that sends you to your feet; the whole landscape will clear like a milky film, and you will see the road that leads to the goal, as if it were unobstructed.

That is the reason why, in spite of all that has been said to the contrary, the great man, the genius, still counts for more than the multitude. That is why in times of stress or danger we cry for the leader to come; we turn to the man with vision, the dreamer rather than the practical man of affairs. Very great achievements are brought about by passion and emotion rather than by practice, training, knowledge. Questions of routine will solve themselves when the ideas and ideals are clearly conceived. Vision is needed; the dreamer is needed. A people of men who place practical things above all others may become wealthy; but a people of dreamers must become great. Great men were those who had vision, and for their vision passionate love.

And here the case of the old man explains itself readily enough. He was overwhelmed with routine. His vision was weak in as much as he threw the burden of finding the path to the peak on others. I was to make this mistake a good many times myself, in that future which now has receded into the dim past. The old man had a desire, but it did not dominate his life; he had never coordinated present and future; the future had never determined and dominated his present day.

But I do not say this in order to exculpate society from its sins. Legislation is never needed to guide the man with vision. But it should protect that vast majority which is without it.

In the afternoon, when I had taken charge of my new stand, and when everybody was resting, so as to be ready for the supper-rush, an elderly, bearded man, an invalid, guided by a young lady in inconspicuous but expensive clothes, came drifting along the aisle, looking right and left. I guessed at what they were looking for: privacy. Not one of the other waiters was in sight; I happened to stand near one of my stalls. So I ventured a slight, inviting motion with my hand, the young lady smiled; the pair came up.

I was quite excited about it. They were the first customers on whom I was going to wait on my own responsibility. Ella looked at me from where she was sitting and winked.

I took charge of the old man and helped him to his seat, disposed of his hat, and returned for a light coat which the young lady carried over her arm.

"We should like some tea," she said when she was seated. "Father likes his strong, with cream. I like mine weak, but without cream. A little toast and some pastry, please."

That was not a large order, to be sure. I arranged what dishes I should need, having carefully wiped them, secured a platter with assorted pieces of pastry and cuts of cake, made the toast myself, and steeped the tea freshly when I was ready. Then I served the whole order as quickly as I could, leaving it to the young lady to pour the tea, and retired from view. Still I watched my customers, took note of what cake was consumed, and completed the check when I saw that they had taken what they cared to have. Then I went over, enquired whether they had any further wishes, and laid the check, face down, on the edge of the table before I withdrew. At the first motion they made to rise I was back, assisted the father into the aisle, reached for his hat, and handed the young lady her coat. They left with a smile and a nod.

I had not done anything except what I should have expected from any waiter in a reputable place. Yet, what I had done, must have appeared like exceptional service, for when I cleared the table, I found a fifty-cent piece under the rim of the young lady's plate. I could not refrain from showing the coin to Frank and Ella. Neither one believed that that was the actual tip received.

I will mention that this pair of afternoon customers returned to my tables every day while I remained in the establishment; and though the tip was not always so generous, it was never less than a quarter, the amount depending, probably, on the chance of the purse.

Late in the evening, during the weary, slack hours of waiting, of sitting, or standing around, my personal satisfaction with the success achieved was to suffer a heavy check. The old helper had all afternoon been going about his duties with a set expression on his hollow face. While I waited on my first customers, he had followed my movements with a dumb, nearly hostile eye. When the supper-hour was over – which practically finished his work – he sat down in the farthest corner, all by himself, resting his hands on his knees and hiding them under the table, in a peculiar attitude of his which had something strangely pathetic. I did not pay much attention to him, I am afraid, but I shall never forget the shock I received when, on passing his table, I suddenly noticed that he held himself very erect, looking neither to right nor to left, and staring into vacancy, with the tears slowly rolling down into his beard.

My success was his deadliest hurt. I did not feel so elated any longer.

SIX

I Meet the Explanation for
One Kind of Success

I T WOULD be pretty hard to analyze the elements which entered into my friendship for Frank. He was not highly cultured, in the sense in which the word culture comprises manners, knowledge, and, above all, tastes and inclinations. He patronized, for instance, all manner of cheap shows. Yet, on my side at least, the friendship amounted to a passion while it lasted. "While it lasted" – for through none of my fault, as you will see, Frank vanished from my life when I left Toronto; the mere memory of this friendship turned into bitterness.

When I first met him, he attracted me by the force of the contrast in which he stood to our common environment. Like myself he could not possibly submerge in the atmosphere of that eating-place. I endowed him in my thought and unconscious appraisal with virtues and sensibilities which were quite foreign to his real nature; and that even after he had revealed part of this real nature to me.

At the time, I had intentionally dropped all consciousness of what had – in Europe – made up my inner life, as contradistinguished from the mere accidentals of the day. I saw the futility of much of its pretensions. I saw that what I had called my "view of life" utterly lacked a foundation on which to rest. This "view of life", which had been a composite of the experiences and conclusions arrived at by a multitude of great minds of the past, was utterly unoriginal and untenable – a mixture of practical optimism and transcendental pessimism, with now the one, now the other predominating. As a matter of fact, it was contingent upon a life of ease, upon mental or spiritual parasitism, or at least upon a sheltered condition. Such views are needed; they fulfil the mission of helping the masses interpret their lives. But from the moment when I resolved upon my great adventure I saw that they would not do for myself. So, when I threw them out of my mental equipment, with them there went into the discard everything else, above all that vast store of memories which was acquired, not by living, but by reading, and which we ordinarily call by the name of education. Thus I arrived at an undervaluation of myself; I looked upon the world, upon other people, and upon myself "de profundis" – from the depths. It took me years of a new and strange life to get back to a proper appreciation of these memories, and though they do no longer predominate, they form a large and important part of what I may call my present intellectual environment. As for original "Views of Life", the last thirty years have taught me one thing about them, namely, that they are possible of attainment only for those who walk on the very heights, or for those who walk in the very depths of life; because only such will dare to place themselves beyond tradition, beyond what I may, for the moment, call morality.

At the time I was abasing myself. As for Frank, a certain clearness of perception, a shrewdness of judgment, a nicety of feeling, an instinctive respect for the other man's point of view, a mental cleanliness which despised pretences and shams – all these lifted him above the rest of the "crowd". I looked up to him. I lived, as it were, on the sea-level; I had the perspective of the frog: above him all things loom.

But there were other things. The "crowd" – with the exception of Ella who was morally clean – had positive characteristics which we two lacked. I will not speak at length of the depravity in "rebus sexualibus" which seemed to impregnate the dressing-rooms. There are episodes in my memory which I do not like to touch on even in thought, much less in speech. But, repulsive as the scene must be, I will try to sketch an interlude which was played upstairs, in the kitchen. I shall do this merely because after much reflection I have arrived at the conclusion that there is only one excuse for a narrative of this kind: truth. Truth is not necessarily so much a matter of often disgusting detail as it is a matter of atmosphere. But, though accordingly I have endeavoured to indicate this atmosphere of the restaurant – the "milieu" – by mere slight touches of the brush, omitting much and leaving other things in semi-darkness, I still believe that, to give it relief, I must set down one glaring colour-patch; without it nobody would quite understand why I reacted in the way I did.

In the front-room worked a little man of of thirty-five or so whom all called Jim. He was of slight build, no taller than Roddy, with a head that seemed to have been compressed from both sides; with sloping shoulders and small feet which had already acquired the shuffling gait resulting from the waiter's flatfootedness. He was everlastingly joking in coarse, mostly sexual allusions, especially in conversation with the girls, all of whom, except Ella, liked him for this "naughtiness". He was married, by the way, and had a family; and he was reputed to be a good father, though a bad husband – bad at any rate in the matter of connubial fidelity.

One evening, when the supper-wave had come and gone, Frank, myself, and a few other waiters were standing in the corridor of the kitchen where some discussion with the cooks had arisen, when suddenly Jim burst in among us, swearing in the most frightful way, red in the face with unreasoning, scornful anger. He was carrying a tray with a plate of soup, which he fairly knocked down on the counter, yelling at the top of his voice, and cursing everybody.

"Blankety-blank," he shouted. ". . . this fool of a fellow! That's the third time the son of a . . . sends me back with that plate of soup! He's merely trying to pick on me, . . . him!" He was hopping about on his feet and waving his arms. ". . . him!" he shouted again; and then, clearing his throat with a mighty effort, he spat into the plate of soup with great exertion.

Everybody except Frank and myself was enjoying this thing; most of the onlookers were laughing.

"Take it back to him, Jim," shouted a voice, "make him eat it, the son-of-a-gun!"

Instantly Jim was quiet. He looked around, perfectly self-controlled, and winked at the crowd. "Sure," he said; "what did you think I did it for? Here, Dan," this to the cook, "pour some boiling water in. This time it wasn't hot enough for the son-of-a-. . . !"

Under general shouting and laughter he shouldered the tray and walked out with the greatest bravado.

Part of the "crowd" followed him at no very great distance, to press into the little orchestra-platform, where he informed them shortly, so I heard, that the son of a . . . was eating it, "spitting and all."

The fact that Frank saw in this scene as little fun as I did – gathered from it, indeed, nothing but disgust – marked him off from the rest more effectively even than more positive virtues might have done.

I should add, too, I suppose, that both of us instinctively felt and soon verified that neither one was "naturally" a member of this trade or limited to it in his ambitions. Frank confided to me early in our acquaintance that he was an engineer by trade – I did not know at the time how wonderfully ductile this term is on the American continent, covering as it does the wide range from the street-car driver to Thomas A. Edison; I understood that he was taking a correspondence-school course in order to prepare himself for advancement; he was planning an elaborate campaign in order to secure the position which he wished to hold. If anything, he was rather older than my-self; which made me sometimes wonder why he was not further advanced in his real career; I was to find out by and by.

Lastly, there entered into our short but ardent friendship one more element: a rather unreasonable admiration for him on my part, on account of his very superior, though very natural familiarity with American conditions. It seems to be a matter of course that a hundred thousand trifles which astonished me should have seemed quite commonplace and nearly immutable to him; he had never known any alternatives to them. To him it appeared to be only one of the manifestations of democracy that people should crowd the street-cars to overflowing, hanging on to straps and stepping on each other's toes; that men and women should rub elbows in the aisles of a sleeper, fumbling behind impeding curtains while dressing. He did not recoil from the common drinking-cup or the general washing-room in public places. Since the customs of the country demanded such indifference, I looked up to him on the score of a callousness from which my sensibilities shrank. The reader who shares my own point of view must not forget that my most immediate ambition, like that of every immigrant, was to differ from the average American as little as possible.

It was during the second week of my waiterdom that we drifted together. On Monday morning I was given the last two centre tables with the adjoining eight stalls. That means, I was, when every seat was occupied, supposed to take care of forty-eight customers at a time. This arrangement relieved Iva and Ella to the extent of one-half of their former work, much to their satisfaction. Even twenty-four seems a heavy allotment for a rush-hour: but the pressure on the back-room was never even nearly as heavy as that on the front-room. I cannot but say that during the noon-wave both Mr. Johnson and Mr. Carlton henceforth concentrated their activities on my stand, so that it was a rare occurrence when I had to take an order myself; they simply handed me the checks to get whatever was wanted. They also did everything in their power to keep my dumbwaiters cleared. On the other hand, during the rest of the day, the work of these tables was very light; and, since the noon-hour was unproductive of tips, I was by no means satisfied with the way things were going.

"You work too hard when the rush is on," Frank said to me when I complained. "Keep cool; take your time. It's the running that tells on you. Pile your trays higher; take heavier loads. Above all, don't worry. Your evening trade will pick up. Next week you can ask for a different stand."

"Why!" I exclaimed. "I'll be glad if they don't fire me."

Frank laughed. "Fire you! They don't fire a waiter in this place when he brings in the second-highest total of checks."

"The second-highest total?" I asked. "What do you mean?"

"Yes," he answered; "you want to ask for the check-list at the desk. You'll find it ready every morning at ten. Your checks totalled fifty-three dollars yesterday. Mine were fifty-nine. The lowest was twenty-nine. So you see!"

"Well," I gasped, "you are the most encouraging person I ever met."

"If you keep anywhere near that mark," Frank continued, "you can have the pick of the place by Saturday. As it is, you have too many tables. You want only one centre table, but farther to the front. Look out for regular customers. They are the ones that tip. Ask for Roddy's tables; then we'll be neighbours; you'll soon catch on to the ropes."

This information put so much spring into my muscles that I by no means heeded Frank's advice. I wanted to be sure that I could ask for whatever stand I pleased and get it. And I might say right here that I did "keep it up" for the rest of the week and finished on the six days' total of sales in the second place.

When, on the other hand, the third day went by and I had again taken in less than a dollar in tips, I became discouraged once more.

"You come to the front to-night," said Frank; "stick around my stand. I'll show you how to get tips."

That is what I did; and what I saw that night, opened my eyes indeed, though I knew at once that Frank's methods could never be mine. I told him so; and thereby, I believe, hangs the tale of the ultimate break in our friendship.

First of all I was struck by the fact that most of the customers who sat at Frank's tables were by no means the higher-class clients of the place. All of them seemed to know just where they were going. That was one of Frank's tricks: he never changed his stand. He might have had his choice of the tables in the front-room; he did not want them. His regular customers knew him, knew where to find him, and did not care to be attended to by any other waiter.

I shall sketch the way in which he waited on two of his typical patrons.

The first one was a young man who might have been a truck-driver or a baggage-handler at one of the railroad stations. Even in this by no means exclusive restaurant he looked slightly out of place. He nodded to Frank when he sat down, exchanged a few remarks, and asked, "Well, what've you got to-night?"

Frank named two or three inexpensive "short orders."

"All right," said the young man, "make it chops. And coffee with apple-pie."

Frank went to the kitchen and in due time filled the order. So far there was nothing extraordinary about the affair. The astonishing part began when the young man had consumed what he had ordered.

He turned to Frank, winked, and said, "Got any more of this?" touching his pie-plate with his finger.

"Sure," said Frank, "lots of it." He stepped up to his dumbwaiter, whisked two pieces of apple-pie on a plate, and pushed it in front of his guest. The same manœuvre was performed once more, with an extra cup of coffee thrown in; none of these items was marked down on the check.

Before this young man who apparently was inordinately fond of pie had finished his meal, another customer, a heavy-set, prosperous-looking man who might have been a butcher or a small contractor came in and dropped into a seat on the opposite side of the room.

When Frank went over to take his order, he merely said, "Hello, Frank! The usual thing."

I was interested in this usual thing and followed Frank into the kitchen.

Frank laughed. "Beginning to dawn on you?" he asked. Then he shouted his order, "One Porterhouse, rare." Meanwhile he was making out the check. When he had finished, he shoved it to me, and I read, "One Sirloin, single."

Porterhouse steak figured on the menu at one dollar, sirloin at forty cents.

Frank winked at the one-eyed cook and pushed a ten-cent piece across the counter; the cook slipped it negligently into his trousers-pocket. It was he who, after the supper-rush, attended to the checking of our orders.

"I see," I said, rather taken aback. There must have been some distance in my tone, for Frank laughed; and his laugh sounded a trifle too boisterous.

"Oh Phil!" he exclaimed; and I could not help hearing a certain weariness in his mocking hilarity. "What's the use? Everybody does it. Tip the cook and serve the customer. You see they are still making piles of money. They charge it up to overhead. That way I get a chance to make a penny, too."

"Where do you get the pie?" I enquired. "Is Walter in with you, too?" Walter was the German-American "boss" at the counter.

"No," answered Frank, "I've never been able to do anything with him. When I have an order for the counter, I just invite a couple of pieces of pie to come along."

"I see," I said again.

And again Frank tried to laugh it off. "The great American game," he said.

When we returned to the dining-room, I was rather silent. But at last I asked, "How much do these fellows tip you?"

"A quarter each," he replied.

"How much are you making that way?" I went on.

"Well, I don't usually talk about it. Nobody tells the truth about his tips. But you keep quiet, and I'll tell you."

"Of course, I'll keep quiet."

He held up the five fingers of his hand. "About that," he said, "a day."

That was my first encounter with American "graft". I felt rather hurt at the discovery that Frank, whom I was inclined to idolize, should have lax principles with regard to common honesty. I also realized at once the bearing this had on my own outlook. If this was the way to earn tips, was I going to get them? These methods, I knew, were impossible for me. I might, under stress of circumstances, have become a thief, a burglar, almost anything. I was no longer so sure of myself as I had been before I emigrated from Europe. Hunger, despair, and helpless loneliness are strange prompters. I had begun to think less harshly of him who sins against society. This fact may be a revelation to some who are dealing with alien criminals in this country. The path of the immigrant is sown with temptation: a temptation of a spiritual kind; he is tempted to charge all his troubles to some incomprehensible vice in the very constitution of the new country or the new society into which he came. His need and distress may become extreme. If he sins, the society against which he sins is foreign to him, just as truly, as he is foreign to it. What he sees of American morals is often, too often, not what shows them at their best. Having set myself the arduous task of telling the truth, I will, in my own case, even go further and confess that, what disgusted me here, was the pettiness of the thing rather; there was nothing in it to appeal to my æsthetic appreciation. Large, bold crime I could have admired where I recoiled from pilfering.

Frank and I had already formed the habit of walking along together when we went home in the small hours of the day. The road which we followed in common was somewhat out of the way for him as well as myself. But for the sake of our company we were both willing to make a slight detour. Sometimes we had, when reaching the point where we must separate, delayed at the street-corner, talking and laughing for an additional quarter of an hour or so.

This night we reached it in silence. But instead of bidding Frank good-night, I said briefly, "Come, I shall see you home."

We proceeded in silence for a little while longer.

Frank felt the tension as much as I did. That reconciled me partly. I could see it by the way in which he looked ahead, staring into vacancy. My unspoken condemnation hurt him: I was glad of it. He understood me; that did him honour. But apparently, too, he had not expected anything of the kind; and that I resented. He had taken me into his confidence with bravado; a master had shown a supposedly apt pupil one of his tricks of the trade; and the apprentice had suddenly turned into a judge. Every motion of his betrayed that he was chafing under the eye of the law.

"Look here, Phil," he said at length; "let's have this out."

I breathed more freely. I was glad that he felt it incumbent upon himself to broach the matter instead of leaving the task to me.

"You don't know," he went on. "You are new in this country. Everybody else in the crowd would think this a clever trick. In fact, as I've said, quite a few of them practise it themselves. I need the money. I've got to have it. You can't know, of course. But I've *got* to have it, fair means or foul. I could not be satisfied with the six or eight dollars those fellows pay. I'm getting eight; don't tell anybody. They might give me ten if I threatened to quit. If I

did not do as I'm doing, I'd make ten dollars in tips besides. That isn't enough."

"The question seems to be, can you make more at anything else?"

"I could, and I can't," he answered impatiently.

"If you could, why not try?"

"No use," he replied. "Not yet. Nothing to it just now.
Got to stick it out for the moment."

My silence seemed to irritate him.

"Look here, Phil," he began once more. "You are new
in this country. Let me tell you a few things. There's Johnson. He owns property in this city. His property is assessed
by its earning power. Do you think, when the assessor
comes around, he gives him the correct figures? Graft! He
names a figure and slips the man a bill – a big bill, I
suppose. Graft, I tell you, graft! There's Carlton. He buys
the supplies for the beastly place. Take the butchers. One
has a better meat at the lower price. The other slips Carlton a hundred-dollar bill and gets the trade. . . . "

"How can you know?"

"Never mind," he exclaimed; "I do know. Graft, I tell
you! Graft again. There's Cox. He's supposed to place the
customers and, of course, not to know who tips and who
doesn't. But you can tell by the mere looks of the fellow, by
the way he steps about and noses around. Who gets the
big tippers? Meg! And you can have some of them, too, if
you slip him a five every week. What is it but graft? Take
a railroad conductor. You board a train without a ticket.
You wink at him and hold out a dollar-bill. Where to? he
asks. You name your destination and get your counter
check just as if you had paid your fare. Graft! It's the same
thing everywhere. You don't know this country yet. Who's
the successful man? The successful grafter, that's all."

I was struck speechless for a moment. Then I saw the
flaw in his eloquence. "Just a moment, Frank. Has it ever
occurred to you that, if what you say were true, there
would be no business possible in this country? The rail-

roads, the big companies and corporations would simply have to quit."

"Oh," Frank laughed, "there are always the suckers."

"You call the honest man a sucker – whatever that may mean."

"A sucker's the man who takes what's handed to him, the gaff as well as the gold-brick, and doesn't squeal," Frank volunteered as a definition.

"Then I'd rather be a sucker than a . . . "

I suppressed the word, and Frank had the grace not to supply it. Again we went in silence for a while.

"Look here, Phil," Frank began for the third time. "I want you to understand this. I might just as well tell you. Carrol's as little my real name as yours is Branden."

"Just a moment," I interrupted him. "Is there no law in this country against assuming a false name?"

"No," he said. "There isn't. Not so long as you do it without dishonest purpose. Of course, if you do it for fraud . . . "

"Good," I interrupted him once more. "That settles that point. I don't see anything wrong in a man's changing his name if he cares to do so, law or no law. But since you've done it, I'm glad it isn't illegal. As for myself, I can assure you I have documentary evidence for the effect that Branden happens to be my real name, though that's neither here nor there."

"Then why . . . No, listen. I want you to get this. I'm hiding. Buffalo's my home town. I'm hiding from my wife."

"Your what?" I asked sharply.

"Yes," he replied and chuckled, though awkwardly. "Didn't know I was married, did you? Well, I am. I'll tell you a few things about that marriage. I was nineteen, my wife was seventeen when we took the plunge. My father turned me out; said I was crazy; he was right; but I didn't know it; so I went on my own. I defied the world. Poor but happy, you know. Paradise in a hut; just read it up in any fool novel. Heaven turned into the usual hell. No children, thank the Lord! Meanwhile I was making good on the job. I was with the Big Four. Took correspondence lessons, etc. Never had had beyond two years of high school. At last I was assistant engineer on the Delaware-Lackawanna; at one hundred and twenty per. By that time the wife was an hysterical wreck. Home was hell, I can tell you. Nagging and scolding and quarrelling, day and night. The worst about those hysterical women is, no matter how wildly they exaggerate in the reproaches they gush at you, there's always a wee, tiny kernel of truth in what they fling at your head; that disarms you. Whenever I wasn't out on a night-run, we sat up quarrelling or arguing – she doing nine-tenths of the talking. She didn't need any microscope either to see my faults! By and by I lost all my self-respect. Drinks never bothered me much; but then I hit the booze. One day I came home – discharged. Well, I tried to face the music. She went off into a fit and threw herself on the floor, screaming and kicking with arms and legs. I packed up. I told her I was going to leave, for good. She scratched my face all up, screamed some more, and then I banged the door shut on that part of my life. Now get this. Before I left town, I saw my father. He's a Pullman conductor, quite well off – graft, I suppose. . . . "

"Frank!" I exclaimed sharply.

"Oh, hell!" Frank shouted, "don't be so squeamish! Take the world as it is; this country, anyway. Well, he agreed to my going into hiding. I'm paying alimony; thirty dollars a week. Those were *his* terms. I was to go under an assumed name: none of my friends to know where I was – only he. And he would shield me so long as I paid the thirty a week, promptly, to him. If I missed one single payment, he said, he'd hand me over to that fury. If I hadn't promised, he'd have had me arrested right off, I assure you. I went into this waiter business because it was the only thing I knew at which I could make enough money without losing time. I've changed my name; I can't use any of my old testimonials and references. I've got to get a diploma from some reputable school in my new name before I can go back to my old work. I've got to start in from the bottom. And while I'm doing that, I can't even make enough money to live up to what I've promised. I've got to get far enough ahead first. I can't even tell them that I've had experience. They'd ask me where. And if I tell them, I give myself away."

"Well," I sighed, "you're in a mess all right."

"You've said it. And now, I suppose, you are ready to pass me up."

"No," I said hesitatingly. "Still . . ."

"Oh, cut it, Phil," he exclaimed. "You know I can help you a lot. You don't want to stick in that hole, do you? I can help you along. New York, that's the place for you. I've been a waiter at Sherry's, a bell-hop at the Belmont. Just for the fun of it, when I was a mere kid. I know a few people there, and they know me. I can give you a start . . ."

"I suppose so," I said. "But that isn't the point. I did not try to make friends with you for what there might be in it for me. I don't think I want to stay in this business anyway. But what is there in our relation for you?"

"I don't know," he replied. "I don't care. I've taken to you, that's all. I want you to think well of me. I'm quite a decent chap after all, no matter what I may be doing in the line of graft. I've known worse than I am, at any rate."

We drifted into silence again.

"No," I said at last. "I don't think I want to pass you up as you call it. But you know, you've given me some jolts tonight. I wish I could help you, but I can't. You must give me time to get used to the new ideas. Guess I'll turn back now."

"All right, I'll turn back with you." And he took me home.

Matrimonial entanglements were nothing new to me. In those strata of society in which I had been moving in Europe, marital escapades were viewed with leniency. The universal tendency to make marriage easy, so as to prevent extra-nuptial immorality, had, in my old environment, reached a point where five-year trial marriages seemed within reach. Everybody discussed such things; not to talk glibly about them, branded you as being behind the times. From there it is no great step to taking the solemn obligations of old-fashioned wedlock as a mere joke. From a strictly opportunistic view-point it seems indeed as if there were no way out of this dilemma. If you want to suppress vice by making it legitimate, you must throw the portals of wedlock wide open. If you still want marriage to mean anything at all, you must open the door of divorce equally wide; otherwise you encourage the weak in breaking the law; and you force misery on those who are morally strong. All which very likely amounts to, "Le roi est mort – vive le roi!" Unfortunately for the opportunists, a mistake has been made in this modern tendency, namely, to open the door into wedlock a little faster than the door out of it; so that a good many – like my then friend Frank – got caught between door and jamb.

I do not mean to defend him – nor to indict. But I do wish to say that familiarity will inure you to almost anything. I had become inured to lax views regarding the sanctity of marriage. Even to my mother an elopement or a case of adultery had not meant much beyond a theme for amused gossip. Frank probably had become inured to "graft" because he had heard of it and seen it practised ever since he was a child. Still, the mere fact that he felt the need of an explanation showed me that he was aware of the moral taint attached to it.

I have, as you will hear if you care to follow me to the end, devoted the major part of my life to the task of "Americanizing" others.* I have, from choice, since I found my "level" in the New World, spent most of my years among that part of the population of this continent

---

* I use the word in the wider sense in which it includes what is commonly called Canadianization. America is a continent, not a country.

which is of foreign origin. Only too often have I, in the midst of these people, met with the profound conviction that in America "graft" is king, sharp practice goes rampant, that "to put one over on the other fellow" is the chief aim in life of every one the immigrant has to deal with. If he is unable to speak the language, he feels helpless, not without bitterness. Nothing was harder to fight than the pessimism created by such impressions.

I do not mean to indict; nor do I mean to suggest a remedy. I have just recounted my first encounter with graft. I have given, as nearly as I can remember, the first explanation with which I met of this disease on the body democratic. I wish to add that much of the suffering I was destined to go through, for a long, long while, was caused by its rankling in my heart which was only too eager to worship the New World. In looking back over the first few years of my life on this continent – while I was still in the plastic stage, – I cannot but be struck by the amazingly large number of people with whom I fell in who lived more or less exclusively on this or that form of graft. There were so many that in another person I should find it pardonable if he had arrived at the conclusion that graft was the predominating trait in the make-up of the average American. Is it that the "grafter" consciously or unconsciously drifts towards the immigrant? Does he there scent his prey? Or is it that the immigrant, coming as he does into a world which he does not understand, here finds the one feature which he by force must learn to understand if he wants to survive?

SEVEN

I Move On

A S I H A V E S A I D, I kept my record up. On Saturday
night Mr. Carlton came over to my stand and asked,
"Would you like a stand in the front-room, Branden?"

"No," I replied. "If I had my choice, I should take Roddy's stand. I believe that would give me a chance to make
some money."

"As you please," said Mr. Carlton. "I can take Roddy to
the front. You are making good; I want to help you. Your
wages will be eight dollars, beginning with Monday.
That's settled, then."

And he took his grey presence away.

I pondered a good deal about Mr. Carlton. How could he
let things go as they were in kitchen and dressing-rooms?
He was quick enough to notice a spot on a tablecloth. I
came to the conclusion that, shrewd as he was in his business, he too was hidebound in those things which he had
always taken for granted. Dressing-rooms had in his experience always been a litter of filth; kitchens had always
been places to be left to the negligence of subordinates;
flies had always been fought by poisonous fly-pads. Nor did
he balk at what was prepared behind the swinging doors.

Of his ability in handling men I had no doubt. He spoke
in one tone to me, in a different one to Jim – though during
the rush-hour this difference disappeared; at that time he
spoke to Mr. Cox, the captain, just as he would have done
to a mere helper.

Beginning with my third week, I made money. I can no longer give accurate figures except for my last or seventh week in the place. That week the total of my tips amounted to between sixty-nine and seventy dollars, an average of over ten dollars a day. The daily average for the last four weeks probably ran as high as eight dollars. The owners had nothing to object to my making that much money, for during the whole of that period I also ranked first among all the waiters in the amount of checks turned in. Probably Frank would have outranked me had he charged everything he served. As it was, my daily business averaged about eighty dollars, and Frank ran a bad second with sixty or thereabouts.

The major part of my income was made at night; which means that I secured as steady customers men who did not consider the cost and went where they found the service they wanted.

In order to make clear how things worked out, I will quote a few examples which have lingered in my memory, possibly by virtue of their oddity.

One night, at a quarter past eleven, a large party, heavily loaded down with suitcases and satchels, entered the place, apparently fresh from a train or boat. The party was made up of a powerfully built, typically Yankee, clean-shaven man of about fifty, a dignified matron, two grown-up girls, a high school boy, and three younger children, eight in all. They somehow drifted through the front-room and reached the steps, for except during the rush-hours Mr. Cox used to take it easy. Frank was busy; I was not. I went to meet them, relieved the matron of her suit-case, and pulled out the chairs of my "centre." They sat down. One look convinced me that this was a family in which the father did the ordering. So it was to him that I handed the bill-of-fare.

"Well, young man," he said, hardly looking at it, "we want some sirloin steak. We want it tender. One rare, the rest well-done. Let's see. Coffee for eight; some sliced tomatoes, French-fried potatoes; and apple-pie for dessert."

"Pardon me, sir," I said; "we have some excellent Porterhouse. Three would do for the party. No more expensive than eight sirloins . . . "

"All right, sir," he interrupted, "use your judgment."

I went to the kitchen and down into the meat-storage room, where I selected three Porterhouse cuts, choosing one which was much thicker at one end than at the other. When I returned upstairs, I tossed the cook a fifty-cent piece and said, "Dress her up a bit, will you? All well-done except the thick end of this one."

The cook never garnished a dish unless tipped to do so.

When I had everything ready, I pressed Frank into service in order to get the whole of my order to the front at one trip. I served one of the steaks to the older one of the young ladies, one to the high school boy who felt quite elated at such honour and tried to avoid his father's grinning face; and the last one to the man.

"This end is rare," I prompted.

"You managed that?" he said. "I was wondering."

They sat for an hour. Then the father called for the check. It amounted to less than six dollars.

"You take the money?" he asked.

"At the desk, please," I replied.

"Well," he said, "that was a good supper, well served. I hope, you don't decline tips, waiter?"

I smiled non-committally, and he held out a five-dollar bill. This party returned every night during their stay in Toronto.

Another five-dollar bill I came by in a different way.

One day, just after the noon-rush, Mr. Carlton brought a man up to one of my stalls. He winked at me, as if to say, "Special attention, please." This man was middle-aged, slender, fashionably dressed, and had the air of being tremendously busy.

As soon as he was seated, he began, "Now listen, young man. I want a clean table-cloth, a meat-special, a piece of pie, a cup of tea. Everything piping hot and . . . quick! I'll be here every day at twenty to two sharp. At two I want to be back in my office. If you show me that you can do it, I'll make it worth your while."

"Certainly, sir," I answered as casually as I could. "I shall have this seat ready for you after this."

To my surprise he took a bill from his fold, tore it into two pieces, handed me one, and said, "You'll get the other half on Saturday if I'm satisfied. If not, you won't."

I held out a menu. He waved it aside. "I never order," he laughed. "Use your judgment." And already he was deep in his paper.

The bill he had torn was a five-dollar bill.

One more case to illustrate.

One day a young man found his way to one of my stalls, a student of some kind, obviously, for he was carrying unwrapped books. I made it a point, of course, to serve every customer with the same precision, whether his looks proclaimed him to be of the tipping kind or not. My colleagues made a joke of that fact.

This young man was apparently so well pleased with the service received that he felt the desire to tip. Poverty was written all over him; if I had not feared to offend him, I should have forestalled any such attempt on his part. When he had finished his thirty-cent meal, he caught my eye, smiled, and raised his finger.

I went to his table.

He held a street-car ticket between two fingers stretched out. I believe it was worth three cents at the time. With an apologetic smile he asked, "Got any use for that?"

"Certainly," I replied.

He, too, came daily after that, and invariably I found a street-car ticket under the rim of his plate.

The attitude of most of the other waiters was one of outright derision at my courteous service for every customer – till I demonstrated them to be wrong even from their own point of view.

One day a party of five whom I had often seen at other tables appeared at my stand. I motioned them to the centre table. There were three ladies and two young men. One of the young men seemed to be in charge.

"Waiter," he whispered to me, "couldn't you fix us up in a stall? My mother objects to the centre tables."

"Of course," I said. And I moved an additional chair across the aisle.

When I had taken the order and appeared in the kitchen, a shout of laughter greeted me.

"Got the tight-wad at last, Slim," somebody said, "eh? Did he spin his yarn about mother?"

"Son-of-a-gun!" shouted somebody else. "Wants a stall for five and kicks about everything; but nobody has ever seen the colour of his coin."

"Get a tip from him, Slim," I heard a third voice say, "and I'll say you're a waiter."

"Sure," I grinned. "I'll get a tip from him."

Everybody howled with amusement.

I gave the people just that amount of service which every customer received from me; when they left, I found a fifty-cent piece under the rim of the young man's plate.

That convinced even Frank of the superiority of my methods over his.

"You're a wizard, Phil," he exclaimed.

"No magic about it," I replied. "Just treat them as you would want to be treated, and they'll treat you as you wish them to."

Frank laughed. "You forget," he said, "we're not six feet three; nor do we have the manners of dukes and lords waiting on kings."

"Well," I replied, "if I awed them into tipping me, as you seem to think, they would not come back, would they? All they want is the service they pay for. If they get it, they are willing to pay for it over again."

"I've tried it," Frank denied my plea. "I've tried it. Can't do it, Phil. Can't do it."

And there the case rested. I had to accept him as he was or to avoid him altogether; and for that I was not prepared.

The whole episode of my waiterdom would be of little importance – for as far as my economic situation went, it was a mere interlude – if it had not been for the fact that it demonstrated to myself my own adaptability. It gave me a fund of confidence which tided me over, during the moments of clearer vision, even through the years in the depths that were to follow. If I had not had this initial success, I might never have become a Canadian. I might have returned to Europe, gone into something "genteel" – or I might have gone down into the underworld with which I was to come into contact anyway – maybe becoming insane or indifferent in the end.

I have already given some reasons why I was disgusted with this particular scene of my activities. It remains for me to outline why I began to find it impossible to face the prospect of years to come in the same occupation. A certain Sunday morning became the turning point in the trend of my thoughts.

It was early in September, and Nature had begun to don those "golden hues that herald and beautify decay". It had been raining overnight, quietly, softly, abundantly, I am tempted to say persuasively.

When I stepped out of the door in the morning, there was relaxation in the air; the strong and vile odour of the humus of the soil pervaded even the city streets. The sky was hazy. Royal purple lay all over the east. The earth seemed like a brood chamber, like a forcing house for exotic plants.

Instead of going into the city to get my breakfast, I turned into one of the parks and sat down on a bench.

For the first time in my life the commonplace in nature – the "Near-at-hand" – took hold of me and gripped my soul; so that I nearly burst into tears. A squirrel chattered at me; I longed to be able to love it. The dahlias stood with glistening drops still on their petals; the elms were strangely silent, as if they were hanging their boughs down, listening to the flow of their sap.

I felt immensely unhappy. I was young. The joy of mere living – to feel the universe in myself when merely stretching my arms – lassitude and contentment – those things were a memory to me, a memory still near, still recent; but not reality. Somewhere in this great country there must be a place, so I felt, which I could fill better than anyone else. To work at what I could do the very best it could be done, that would be joy, that would be living. I felt as if I were chained underground, deep down, deep down, with an uncontrollable yearning to get to the light, to the life of the sun, to the real world.

New York was the place for me to go to, of course. Frank, so he said, knew the head-waiter at Sherry's who, according to him, was a wealthy veteran of the "profession". Yes, he could and would give me a card of introduction. He also was known to the employment agent at the Plaza. He had lived, he told me, in New York for more than a year. He knew a good house where I could secure a nice room for three dollars a week; it was kept, he said, by an exceptionally fine old lady who was sure to remember him and to do almost anything for a friend of his. He would give me a letter to her.

"And, Phil," he added; "you stop over at Buffalo, that goes without saying, and run up to Niagara. While you are there, you might do me the favour and drop in on my folks. I want my father to see that I am not herding it with the bums."

I smiled. "Of course, I'll see your folks if you wish me to," I assented.

"If you care," he went on tentatively. "I'm sure my father would gladly put you on the train for your trip; and you could keep your roll intact."

"I'm not exactly a pauper for the time being," I replied evasively.

The topic was not touched again.

My mind was made up. The strange thing about it was

that there entered little of volition into my resolve. The thing did itself; I did not do it. Sometimes I realize to my amazement that the life I am dealing with has been my own. I honestly try to understand why I did this or that; and I do not succeed. I can only say, I did it. Something seemed to push and move me on.

May I suggest once more a connection that links these observations to some important problems of American sociology? I have often asked immigrants on this continent, Why did you do this? Why, for instance, did you settle just here? You would think that a man who pulls up his stakes in one part of the world will look around, weighing carefully all pros and cons, and will finally decide with shrewd vision that this or that spot is exactly where he wants to go. In the majority of cases, nothing could be further from the truth. Far and away the greater number go blindfolded into the unknown, just as I did. It is true that a few will plan and forecast; but even among these few I have found fewer still whose plans and forecasts have been realized. I asked John why he lived in Ruthensko, Manitoba; and he replied, because George had gone there; I asked George why he had picked this spot to settle down in, and he replied, because Mike had picked it before him. I came to Mike; and perhaps his story was the same, perhaps it was different. He had, so perhaps he said, tramped the country, working at odd jobs, at the chance of the job that offered. Meanwhile, in some innermost, hidden pocket, he had put away bill after bill of hard-earned and harder-saved money. And finally, when a railroad was being built into a certain section, he had found work on the construction gang and gone out into parts unknown. He had had a certain amount of money – not half what he thought he should have had, considering the wages he had been getting and the frugality with which he had lived; for he had been mulcted and bled on various occasions because of his ignorance of conditions and values; nobody had ever helped him to avoid such pitfalls; complaints had merely elicited scorn and laughter at the "greenhorn". A great yearning had taken hold of him; a yearning to settle on his own soil, to be his own "boss"; he had settled down and gone through things that made even my hair stand on end; but at last he had won out in the face of adversity; and now it had seemed the greatest adversity to be alone in foreign parts. So he had written, or caused to be written, letters to friends and relatives; and they had come; a settlement had grown up. He had been drifting and drifting, ordered about and pushed, till he was weary and felt that to be despised by those who were "on" to the ways and the language of the country was no longer to be borne. Like a refractory sheep, he had lain down in his tracks and refused to move. That is the typical story of our rural, alien population, alien in thought, alien in language, through none of their fault. If the rural immigrant finds stumps on his land after he has bought or otherwise acquired it, well, it is stumps for him; if he finds stones, it is stones, worse luck! And if he finds loam, it is great good fortune and none of the fault of the land-shark. But it is hit-or-miss; hit-or-miss everywhere. He has no choice except in theory. Yet, in the long, weary run of it, even he builds Empire.

My mind was made up. Did I make it up? I can hardly say. But I know that henceforth I thrust aside all objections which might turn up. I followed my star.

Then something happened which gave me a motive. I am emphatic about the order of things at this point. We hear a bell in our sleep; and with lightning quickness "it" – whatever it may be that works in our nerve-cells – constructs a whole story leading up that peal of the bell, motivating, explaining it "ex-post-facto", as if we had been dreaming that story for a long while already, and as if the bell had rung at exactly the right moment; so that we marvel at the wonderful connection between the dream and reality and build up a causal nexus, starting at the wrong end. There was not even coincidence. Much of our explanation of psychological phenomena, much of our motivation in ordinary life is of just that order. We do a thing; then we hit on a reason that may explain why we might have done it; at last we believe quite honestly that we had very good reasons indeed for doing what we have done. Thus we build up the myth of our own free will.

In my own case, however, there never was any illusion about the sequence of resolution and motive. It struck me at the time that in retrospection the order of things might become reversed; the very thought of this possibility prevented it from becoming a fact. But it suited my purposes well to give the ex-post-facto motivation as a very plausible explanation of my actions to others.

What happened was this. A day or two after my conversation with Frank – the conversation about New York which decided the issue – Mr. Cox, the head-waiter, got into a dispute with a patron of the restaurant. Meg, his wife, was the waitress. The customer had told her that he had to catch a train and asked her to hurry his order along. Two or three times he had reminded her of his hurry; without eliciting any response from her. Then, Mr. Cox passing his table, he stopped him, not knowing, of course, about his connection with the waitress. He simply directed him to cancel his order and got up. Now it was considered a very bad break on the part of a waiter to let a customer get away without having been served. Mr. Cox himself had been rather free with rebukes when such a thing had happened once or twice at other stands. He did an exceedingly injudicious thing for which there was only this excuse that just then Meg appeared through the swinging door, with the tray on her shoulder.

"We cannot cancel," Mr. Cox replied. "Your order is coming, sir."

"I don't want the order any longer. I have to catch my train," the customer flared back and reached for his hat.

Mr. Cox went white. With lightning quickness he snatched Meg's checkbook up, totaled the amount, and held out the customer's check. "Whether you want the order or not," he said, "you will pay your check."

"I shall do nothing of the kind," replied the customer and made as if to leave.

Mr. Cox, losing his self-control, tried to bar his way and threatened, "You will not leave the place till you have paid your check; I shall call the police."

This moment Mr. Carlton, who was never far away when there was the slightest commotion, came quickly and quietly along the aisle.

"What's wrong?" he asked curtly.

Cox shrugged his shoulders. "Man refuses to pay."

"Any complaint, sir?" Mr. Carlton turned to the customer.

The stranger explained. "I've been waiting for twenty-five minutes. I have to catch a train and told the waitress so. It is my impression that she delayed intentionally."

"When does your train leave?" Mr. Carlton looked at his watch.

The customer gave the time.

"John," Mr. Carlton flashed around, addressing the new helper on the upper floor, "get a taxicab; quick." And turning to the customer, he went on. "We have to apologize, sir. The house will see to it that you catch your train. I'm sorry you missed your dinner."

"Well, now . . . " the customer began deprecatingly.

"Not at all," Mr. Carlton interrupted. "We cannot let you suffer through the fault of one of our employees."

And together they passed along the aisle.

Mr. Cox was raving. "Look here," he fumed when Mr. Carlton returned, "you have no business to butt in like that . . . "

"Cox," said Mr. Carlton very quietly, but with finality in his tone, "don't you know that the customer is always right?"

"Hell," Cox broke out, "you're just picking on me."

"Listen, Cox," Mr. Carlton cut in like steel. "Now I've got to discharge you, of course. Take it as a lesson and learn from it, anyway."

With that he wheeled about and went into his office.

Mr. Cox was scarlet. Meg stood white. For a moment he looked as if he were going to throw himself after the manager. Then he laughed contemptuously, went, without a glance at his wife, down the steps and into the dressing-room, and emerged shortly afterwards in business suit and hat, satchel in hand, to leave the restaurant for ever.

It was Frank who intimated the sequel to me. He chuckled when, half an hour later, I went over to where he was standing.

"Good for you, Phil," he greeted me.

"For me?" I asked.

"Sure," he laughed. "You're picked as the new captain.

"Nonsense," I said. "How could you know?"

"Heard Carlton talk over the phone to Johnson."

I stood for a moment, looking ahead into vacancy. My New York plans seemed to sink, to sink.

But nobody spoke to me about it that day; nor the next; and on the third morning a sleek-looking, powerfully-built, fat young Jew appeared as head-waiter on the scene.

"You see, I said to Frank as soon as I had a chance to speak to him without a witness.

"Too bad," he said; "underhanded game."

"What do you mean?"

"Well," he explained, "the thing got out, you know; and the skunks went to Carlton and said they'd quit in a body if a greenhorn like you was promoted over their heads. They wanted an outsider."

I pondered that.

"It's hard, you know," Frank went on, "to get waiters; it's easy enough to get a captain. Lots of waiters to pick from. This man they got from the Prince Edward. Easy job – nothing needed but appearance."

The new head-waiter who gave his name as George was instantly disliked by everybody except Frank, who somehow laughed and joked him into friendship. The cause of this general dislike was that he assumed his duty of directing customers to their seats with autocratic indifference to preexisting associations. And since I depended more than anybody else on my regular customers, I was the first to come to an open clash.

It was in the afternoon, when that invalid and his daughter appeared who had been my first customers. George took the lead and tried to steer them to the back of the room. But I relieved him of his charge by simply reaching for the old gentleman's hat and smiling at the young lady.

George waited for me at the kitchen-door.

"Look here, young fella," he said sharply, "none of that while I am around."

I shrugged my shoulders. "They are my regular customers."

"Never mind about regular customers," he flared back. "I'm going to attend to that. You take what I give you, or I'll fire you."

"You might fire yourself," I replied. "But as it happens, it suits me. I give notice. I shall leave a week from Saturday."

With that I went through the door to fetch my tray.

Mr. Carlton called me into his office that night.

"I hear you've given notice, Branden," he said. "What's wrong?"

"Incompatibility of character. I suppose," I said. "But that isn't all. I do not like to stay where the rumour of my being promoted precipitates a revolution."

Mr. Carlton laughed. "Oh, as far as that goes . . . But I suppose your mind is made up."

"I'm afraid it is, sir," I replied.

That answer settled the matter.

Most people are familiar with the feeling that dominates a person who is about to take a holiday. You see your immediate and maybe disagreeable duties as if they stood at a distance; you are wrapped in your expectations and visions and smile at the difficulties of the hour. You look after the business in hand with a certain impatience and even absent-mindedness, forgetting that you will have to come back to it after a while. The holiday stretches ahead – interminably, it seems.

That was my state of mind, except for the fact that I did not expect to come back.

And here is a curious thing.

I had not, so far, suffered from the consciousness of doing menial work. On that score, Frank had been more sensitive than I. I was disgusted with the atmosphere of this particular place, with the dressing-rooms, the kitchen, the small-talk current among the waiters. All these things Frank had accepted philosophically; but he chafed at menial service. The work itself had to be done to keep the wheels of the world turning, and I had not at all objected to doing my share of it. Frank, who had really not changed from one environment to another – I mean, as far as the customers were concerned – objected to being forced to fill orders – obey the orders, as he put it – of men whom he otherwise would have freely associated with on a footing of equality. I, who had never before considered myself as on a level – intellectually and socially – with these people, had not considered myself debased by listening or ministering to their wants, although I should not have picked the companions of my leisure from their ranks. All which suggests strange reflections on the workings of democracy.

This attitude – which is essentially my attitude to-day – now underwent a subtle change. Looking back over a gulf of three decades at myself as I was at the time, I see the difference very clearly, but find it hard to define it in so many words.

It was as if I had begun to look at my relations to the customer with a fine and very superior sense of humour. Not for a moment did I abate in the service I rendered. That is proved by the fact that this last week yielded me the abnormally high total of nearly seventy dollars in tips. But I felt like somebody who has made a specialty of the study of certain processes – in this case, how, gracefully and with the most bountiful yield in pleasure, to satisfy your bodily needs – and who condescends to give a demonstration of his art. This deceived me about a deeper feeling; it was an attitude assumed in self-defence. For, from the moment when I had put a definite end to my stay at this particular place, I looked at the whole business with distaste. It remained bearable only when viewed as a lark, as something which you might do in disguise or for a very short time; but to persist in which would be folly or worse.

During the afternoon before my last day Mr. Johnson, the proprietor, sat down at one of my tables.

"Have a seat," he said to me. "Sorry you are going to leave us," he went on, in a business-like way, when I had complied. "What are your plans?"

"I am going to New York," I answered. "I have no definite plans."

"You do not wish to continue in your present line?"

"For a while, maybe," I answered, "hardly for long."

"Well, I suppose you know your mind,' he suggested, and I tried to look as if I did. "I understand you have been in this country only a few weeks. You have no doubt learned something useful. I can only repeat we are sorry to lose you. It is your type which we want. Should you ever return to this city and need it, we shall be glad to take you on again."

"Thanks," I said, not very heartily.

"I hope you won't need it. Wish you the best of success." With that he rose and offered his hand.

I felt convinced that he had been prepared to give me a glimpse at possibilities, at probable promotions; but I had, by the aloofness of my manner, prevented him from doing so. That he had come with some definite purpose, nobody in the whole dining-room doubted. It was too great a condescension on his part to sit down with one of his waiters.

I felt it a duty to call on Ella before she left on Saturday night.

She giggled with embarrassment when I invited her to sit down with me. "So you're leaving, Slim?" she said with a wistful smile that has not faded from my memory.

"Day after to-morrow morning," I said.

A silence fell.

Her face was flushed, her voice playing up a child-like petulancy. "Too bad; none of the nice people stay."

"You are staying" I fenced.

"That's just it," she complained.

"And Frank," I added.

"Oh yes," she smiled reluctantly. "Frank's all right. I thought so, anyway, till you came. Oh, Slim, just think, I've been here now for nearly three years, and I'm over twenty . . ."

I did not like that tack. I came back to my previous point. "What's Frank done to you?"

"Nothing," she pouted. "Only you can't everlastingly go on fooling. No matter what I say or do, Frank will turn it into a joke and get away from under. I want to be able, once in a while, to talk seriously."

"Ella," I said, "why don't you look out for a husband?"

"Look out for one?" she asked; and there was in her voice a strange mixture of impatience and dreaminess. "As if I hadn't been looking out all along! Who'd want me? Bust-measure forty-four, height six feet two – there's too much of me. Men are cowards. They're afraid I'll crush them." And, in spite of the jeering tone, tears were near the surface.

I laughed. "Don't take it that way," I said. "Somebody will come along. Somebody will see that he can't get too much of a good thing. Some man at the other extreme."

"Some Roddy?" she giggled.

"There are small men who are nice and good and who like to be mothered. Don't look for the big and strong, Ella. They want something they can gather up in their arms."

"Who tells you I don't want to be gathered up in some-body's arms?" she pouted.

"It isn't in nature, Ella," I said with a smile. "You take my advice. Look for the other extreme."

Soon after we shook hands and took leave.

Somehow this conversation, more than anything else, seemed to put a period behind the epoch in my life which this parting from Toronto marked. Here was a girl, meant to be wife and mother, a good girl, a clean girl, suffering from the handicap of too much weight and missing her destiny through no fault of hers. I had taken more of an interest in her than I betrayed; and just because it was the onlooker's interest only and I was going to leave her behind so that she would pass out of my life completely and for ever, there was a certain melancholy about our good-by which I felt keenly.

It was quite different with Frank; I did not expect him to disappear from my horizons. We had agreed to write to each other, to keep in touch, and, if possible, to maintain a mutual helpfulness. On Sunday morning he brought me a number of letters; one of which I was to deliver to his father or his mother at Buffalo; the rest, half a dozen of them, containing cards of introduction to various people in New York. In the afternoon we went to some park outside the city, roaming about and planning for the future. Our parting seemed to lack that air of finality which had characterized my last conversation with Ella. I felt it more as the beginning of my holiday.

I had five hundred dollars in my hat-box when I boarded the train for Buffalo on Monday morning. All customs and immigration formalities had been attended to at Toronto.

I could not help comparing myself with the young man who, two months ago, had arrived at the pier of Montreal. "All things flow." I was the same and not the same. I had gone through what, for me, was a tremendous experience; it had changed my attitude towards life. Outwardly I felt very safe, very sure of myself. If any one had accosted me and asked whether I was a newcomer to the country, I should not have answered so openly – maybe not so truthfully as I had answered Mr. Bennett. Without telling a lie, I might have prevaricated, avoiding the stranger's eye. To a certain extent the quiet, self-possessed bearing of this young man was not altogether histrionic. I was an experienced traveller: for the first time in my life I had money in my pocket which was really mine.

As I see it now, I was, of course, not essentially changed; but I had learned something.

I believe I am right in assuming that behind and beyond American commercialism and industrialism there lies a vast world untouched by either. Even part of commercial America is pervaded with the spirit of that other half which, inspite of its greater extent, is less obvious. By slow degrees I have come to accept two character-traits as distinctively American, marking the collective character of the New World off from the collective character of Europe or any other civilization-unit. One of them is a lack of selfishness which rests really on the consciousness of size; it is a willingness to sacrifice, to help along, to let live, to give out of a superabundance available, and to do a thing because it should be done, not because it furthers the doer's interests, but because it is, after all, only fair and right to do it. The other is a tendency of non-interference, an inclination to take things and men as they are – the ability to get around things, to make shift, to accept things as realities, to make the best of them without grumbling – in other words, the power to assimilate no matter what, even graft. Either of these two traits may become eclipsed now and then; for it is not always a nation's highest which becomes audible; but never yet have I for long listened in vain when I was anxiously waiting for one or the other of these two traits – helpfulness and toleration – to assert itself and to clear up what for the moment seemed hopelessly muddled.

At that time, I still saw the surface only, and the surface indications point rather in the opposite direction. To the casual observer America must indeed seem a jumble of unassimilated units; it seems so to many Americans. As for the nation's collective life, it may well appear as a wild scramble of selfishness to him who cannot see the waters below for the ruffled waters above; he judges the quiet deep by the fleeting breakers which loom so high.

If I had known more about the real America, I should never have gone to New York. Bennett would have advised against it. That, I am afraid, is exactly why I did not look him up before leaving Toronto. I preferred to listen to Frank, to his stories of frantic effort and dazzling success. It had never occurred to me to ask him why he did not go to New York himself.

Looked at from the outside, America's population, whether in Canada or in the United States, seemed much less stable than that of Europe. My first impression, gained under the circumstances which I have outlined, was that of a floating tide, changing quickly, unthinkingly, continually – like the winds which blow over the continent. But it is the surface only to which I belonged and to which I still was to belong for years to come. Underneath this frantic motion, this ever-changing surface-agitation, I have, in the course of years, learned to discern an ever-growing, solid foundation which is firm as the rocks, moving only in a quiet, steady, unvarying motion – a motion headed towards clearer insight and firmer resolve to assert itself – a motion as irresistible as that of the Earth herself, and as continuous and unobtrusive. The trouble is that in our cities we stand in the turmoil of the day; nearly all that finds utterance through the voice belongs to this turmoil. In order to catch the real trend of American thought you have to get your ear down to the soil to listen. Then you will hear the sanity, the good sense, and the good-will which are truly American. While you stand upright in the clash of the surface, your ear is filled with the clamour and clangour, the brassy din of fleeting noises which drown the quiet whisper of destiny. The future must redeem the day. And lucky we, since it is coming, coming.

My short stay at Buffalo was the most fleeting episode. I called at the house of Frank's parents and realized with a shock how little the fact that I introduced myself as Frank's friend prepared a welcome for me.

The mother, a stout, middle-aged lady, received me in the parlour, read the letter which I brought, asked a few questions, distantly almost, as if she took no interest in her son, sighed a good deal, looked a good deal at me, over the rim of her glasses, not without suspicion, hoped Frank would come to his senses, and suggested to my perceptions that the interview was a painful one and had better come to an end.

I extricated myself and, after roaming the city for a while and having looked down from the "Front" on lake and river, took a car to the "Falls."

There I saw what a year or two ago I might have gone across the face of the earth to see. And I have to confess that it made no impression on me at all. I am afraid that in much of our admiration for the great sights there is a good deal of sham. To catch the real significance of any aspect of Nature one thing above all is needed – the receptive mood in ourselves. To create it, I found, so many things are necessary, so many coincidences of preparation, such delicate attunements of eye and ear to the accidents of light and sound, that hardly ever does the real experience of the beauty of any one thing come to us more than once in a lifetime. A good many times have I been out on sight-seeing trips; sometimes I did not bring home a single thing of value; sometimes, what made such a trip an abiding possession, was some little trifle which had nothing to do with the seven wonders that I went out to see – some light-reflexes on the mobile ripples of a brook, maybe; or the play of the shadows of some leaves on the ground. But once in a great while, very rarely, in one of those supreme and never-to-be-forgotten moments which are worth patiently waiting for, worth wooing, one of the really great things of our Earth will speak to us because our own condition is just right for just what we see or hear – and then it stands revealed; when we go home, we are different men and women; our life, our very being is changed because we have stood face to face with the Divine.

The falls might have revealed themselves to me, had I been able to linger with a free and unencumbered mind.

As it was, they were just so much water falling over rocks. The trip, foolishly undertaken, put me at outs with myself and the world. In reality it probably was the impression made upon me by my reception at the house of Frank's parents which so strangely unsettled me. I was preoccupied, angry, full of half-realized doubts; and the sight which I beheld was very nearly an intrusion upon my privacy.

My holiday started thus in the most inauspicious manner. I felt lonesome, deserted. I felt inclined to find fault with Frank for having sent me on such an errand. My whole surroundings, the sight-seers, who were indifferent only, seemed hostile. I thought of that last but one Sunday at Toronto. I had felt as if I were chained underground, full of an overpowering yearning to get back to the surface, the life of real men, the light. Now I was very near to a desire to bury myself, to hide away from the view of all those who had their definite place in the work of the world.

For the first time the real problem which confronted me loomed high. It had flashed up once or twice before, but dimly only, not as the all-important thing as which I saw it now. It is a curious fact that its recognition did not deflect the course of my life as yet. If I had seen things then as I was to see them two years later, I should have spared myself untold days and nights of misery. But to open my eyes, that nightmare was needed which for me is named by the name New York. At that time I saw the problem only, not as yet a way to solve it. Its solution looked like a goal that stood at the end of a road which I had to go in order to get there. No road which I could see was labelled Salvation.

The problem which loomed up was this: to find – not my "level" any longer in this civilization of an order foreign to me – but to find, in this labyrinth of roads, and fields, rocks and soils, that spot of humus where I could take root *in order that I might grow*. I had so far accepted myself, my innermost I, as something given, something stable, enduring, as something *that was*. This afternoon at Niagara Falls which has so strongly persisted in my memory – probably, because it comprised some of the most unhappy hours in my life – I suddenly saw myself as a mere germ, as a seed that wanted to be planted. I realized that I was nothing finished; that there were still possibilities of growth in me. But, unless I found the soil in which I could grow, I was bound to perish – *no matter what my outward success might be*. Like a great anguish a fear crept over me. I might achieve what I had set out to achieve – economic success. But that success seemed strangely inadequate now, might it be ever so great. What good could it do me if I won all the riches on earth but lost my – growth?

I thought of my father and of his life, and I shuddered. Was I to follow his path, but with the direction reversed? Had I started life where he left it, and was I now going for ever after to live in "ill-fitting clothes"? I had gone too far to turn back. Besides, turn back to what? To a life of mediocrity under the eye of social contempt? If mediocrity it was to be, why not spare myself the contempt? I was surrounded by bitter waters, and I had to swim. I was at the mercy of winds and waves.

Bitterly I felt the blindness of him who gropes his way in a foreign world. Bitterly I felt the cruelty of those who live their easy lives in well-marked tracks, unconscious of the suffering that is his who is cast away among them.

Still, when I saw the real problem at last, it never occurred to me – as it hardly ever occurs to the immigrant – that the search for that bit of soil which might fill my needs might not be a geographical search at all. The thought never came to me that somewhere in this great city, in any city, any town, any village, there might be a man to whom I could talk, with whom I could discuss the problem just as it loomed before me, and who might point out its quite obvious and unmistakable solution. Economic success seemed a very small thing to me that afternoon and, in sane moments, ever after. Economic success is a very relative thing in any case; it hardly matters. What would have meant economic success to me might have seemed abject poverty to some, wealth incarnate to others. But one thing we all desire and long for; unless we find it, we perish spiritually and mentally – unless we find a way of doing it, for it is a doing rather than a having. And to express that one thing, I might borrow a word from among the words of Jesus: "to live in abundance."

Still, of course, the economic problem persisted. Even after I did what I could to shake it off entirely, this question of the immediate sustenance still was to arise, every now and then, and to obscure the real problem as it had dawned upon me when I was at outs with myself because a middle-aged lady did not receive me as I thought I should have been received.

BOOK TWO

The Relapse

"The cost of a thing is the amount of what I will call life which is required to be exchanged for it, immediately or in the long run."

– Henry David Thoreau

ONE

The Issue is Obscured

WHEN I EMERGED from the train into the huge hall of the Pennsylvania Station at Jersey City, the clouds that shadowed mind and consciousness had vanished. I still remember the bright sunshine of the early morning, the glaring contrasts in the light, as I stepped out of the train shed to find my way to the ferry. It was one of the mercilessly clear, cloudless fall days that soften nothing and which for that very reason are so exhilarating to the young.

The unfinished skyline of the city, as I saw it in crossing the Hudson over to 23rd Street, seemed full of hope. I left my baggage in the ferry-hall and started out a-foot to get my breakfast. While waiting for my coffee and rolls, I studied a map in order to find my way through the network of streets to the address of the rooming-house which Frank had given me.

On my way I saw the Flatiron Building and the Metropolitan Tower; and the sight of both filled me again with that exhilaration which I had experienced during my first few minutes on American soil. But there was a difference. I felt very American on this morning in the metropolis of the western world. I walked all the way, for I was jealous of any obstruction to the free range of my eye. I felt outside of things, but I enjoyed this onlooker's attitude; I was still on my holiday – I was glad I was not yet a cog in the gigantic machine. I should be one soon enough.

At last I reached 14th Street, and I took out Frank's letter to his former landlady, in order to make sure of the address. I soon understood the system of numbering; so I walked on, past Union Square, to Third Avenue; beyond which I began to look for the house that I was trying to find. Several times I went up and down the block, relying upon myself. I could not find it. I began to enquire from residents of the street. No such number had ever existed.

I felt baffled and annoyed at Frank for having committed an inaccuracy. Beyond that no suspicion entered my mind. I still had the name of the lady; but the directory at the corner-drugstore gave no clue; I returned to Fifth Avenue and walked back up-town.

It seems a trifle; but something had gone wrong, had not worked out; I had lost a thread leading out of the past into the present, a guiding clue; I felt disquieted. When I caught sight again of the Flatiron Building and the Metropolitan Tower, they no longer exhilarated me; there was something like a threat in their very boldness and enormity. The glare of the unmitigated sun began to weary my eye. I sat down on one of the benches in Madison Square, opposite the Tower, and began to study my guide-book. I tried to find the name of some medium-priced, quiet hotel where I might stay for a day or two till I got used to the pace of the city. It seemed that I could not find what I wanted. The maze of names and addresses was bewildering. Invariably my eye seemed to revert automatically to such as the "Astor", the "Waldorf", the "Knickerbocker", the "Plaza".

I reasoned myself into indifference. What did it matter, after all? I should stay at the hotel only for a night or so; then I should secure accommodation at some private house. What was the difference whether I spent a dollar or two more than I felt justified in spending?

I picked at random and hit upon Prince George Hotel on 27th Street, between Fifth Avenue and Madison. I went there at once, secured a room – with bath – made the necessary arrangements with regard to my baggage, washed, and left for a trip over the Elevated Railway to Bronx Park. I felt the need of relaxation and meant to have it.

In the evening I returned to my hotel; but when I went to my room, restlessness drove me out again.

I went down to the spacious lobby of the hotel, bought a magazine, and thought to employ the remedy of reading. I wished Frank were there. I longed for company.

In this mood I dropped into one of the deep, leather-covered chairs in the smoking room. I do not remember whether I had started to read or not. I dreamed. At any rate I became conscious, after a while, of the fact that somebody else had occupied the chair next to mine. I did not see my neighbour; not did I hear him. I did not look around. But I felt a pair of eyes which brushed over my body and seemed to touch it, now here, now there. We are occasionally in such a state of sensitive nervousness which seems to call into play perceptive powers beyond those that are normally ours.

I was on the point of rising and leaving the place, when the stranger addressed me. He sat, half hidden between the huge arm-rests of his chair which was turned so as to shade his face and his half-averted figure. The voice seemed pleasant; it had a strange effect. It seemed to hold me, to take the initiative out of my make-up. It rang with a delicate timbre of sadness and sympathy. It seemed to force me into a conversation, whether I wanted it or not; and I yielded to its invitation, at first reluctantly, then not without pleasurable readiness. Was not here, after all, the company I had been longing for?

Our first remarks were trivial enough.

"A beautiful night," the stranger said; and by a turn of his voice he managed to convey in these three words the effect of great and elaborate eloquence.

"Yes, very," I replied; the sheer inability to respond adequately made me laconic.

There followed a good many remarks of a similar nature too insignificant to be remembered or recorded.

"Nobody should remain in the city this time of the year," he continued after a while, speaking quite slowly and looking down at his hands; "much less seek it. The country, the woods, the hills – purple distances, hazy foregrounds. But you cannot always do as you would like."

A silence fell. I should by this time have regretted to see him rise. When you are in an uncertain, undecided, doubtful mood yourself, nothing is quite as comforting as to play the helpful spirit to some one else who is in the same predicament. The very tone of his voice spoke of a sadness kin to my own.

"Are you a stranger here?" I enquired.

"Oh," he replied, "I've been in New York before. Business takes me here quite frequently. But I hate the city, except in the dead of wintertime. To be here in the summer or spring always gives me a feeling as if in the whole world I did not know a single soul. I arrived today. Whenever I get here, I seem to be simply starving for company."

"Yes," I said, "I know that feeling myself. A person is nowhere more alone than in a crowd which he does not know."

"You've said it," he exclaimed; and for a second the slang expression and the alacrity with which it was uttered jarred upon me.

"I suppose," he went on after a while; and his voice resumed that soft and melancholy note which had won my sympathy, "you're quite an experienced traveller. You look that way. I've stayed at home most of my life – at work which I hate. And there is every now and then this trip to New York. St. Louis is my home-town. Life's a funny thing anyway." He laughed a low, melodious laugh at his own triviality.

Often already in my young life had I made the experience that a stranger, if hour and place prove auspicious, will confide to a fellow-stranger things which the other might never have found out had he lived side by side with him for decades. I felt a strange sensation of expectant tension that such a moment of revelation had come. Here was a kindred soul, apparently in troubles not unlike my own. To listen to him restored my self-control. It was soothing. I meant to lead him softly on.

"St. Louis?" I asked with a show of interest.

"Yes," he said with a note of indescribable contempt, "the city of beer, tobacco, and boots. Boots are my line. Had to make it my line, you know. No choice in the matter. What else was there for a Hannan to do?"

He looked up at me with confiding, child-like eyes. "Of Hannan and Morse, you know. The 'National Work-Boot'. I'm not the Hannan of the firm, of course. That's my father. But if you are born into a great business, you might just as well desire the stars as think of anything else."

"Well," I said philosophically, but not without sympathy – the way you might speak to a child when you try to comfort him, and quoting Mr. Bennett of two months ago, "One thing is about as bad as the next one."

"Perhaps," he sighed; "yet I cannot quite admit it. Take my own case. I have a gift for drawing. That is what made me speak to you. When you were sitting there, looking out into the dark, I saw a picture. I saw it all finished, painted, framed, and hung in some famous gallery even. I saw it all, down to the title on the little brass-plate underneath. 'Lord Willowscoop', it read, 'in meditation.'" And again he laughed his soft ironical laugh, as if in self-derision.

I smiled. "Branden's my name," I said indulgently, "plain Branden."

"Not the Brandons of Brandon Beeches?" he asked with a sudden show of interest.

"Not that I know of," I answered simply. "I am a stranger in this country." I had not read Shaw's Unsocial Socialist at the time; the ironical trick went unchallenged.

"Just touring?"

"Oh, I don't know," I evaded. "I may stay after all."

"Beastly country to live in," he said with more passion than I should have expected. "As I said before, take my own case. I wanted to be a painter. Did I get a chance?

Art is nothing. It does not exist. Nobody has ever heard of such a thing. There is money enough in the family. The old man has seen to that. But what is his idea? Since he made a pot of money in his time, I must make another in mine. Sometimes I feel sorely tempted, when he sends me out on one of these trips, to decamp and try poverty and contentment. Life is a rotten thing, alright."

"Things may change," I said. "Besides, if that is the way you feel about it, why not try as you suggest?"

"Oh," he exclaimed, "I suppose I am a coward. A mollycoddle, if you want. Don't seem to be able to muster courage enough to break loose." He jumped to his feet. "Say, old man, do me a favour. I shouldn't be alone when I'm like that. Let's go somewhere. Let's have a glass of beer. Anything rather than sit around and brood."

"Sure," I said good-naturedly and rose. "Whatever you say. Where shall we go?"

"Might drop over to the Holland House," he said dejectedly. "We can talk there. It's quiet this time of the night."

I reached for my hat; we went out, down towards Fifth Avenue, and then turned north.

We walked in silence, and I reflected. I could, of course, not help seeing the contrast between the situation of this young stranger and my own. A millionaire's son, rich, apparently well-bred – I had forgotten that one or two remarks had jarred upon my sensibilities – unhappy through being forced into a station in life which clashed with his inclinations. I, free to do as I pleased, but forcing myself in order not to remain for life what I was, a poor man. And yet there was similarity, too, in the way life played with him and myself. But the strangest thing was that we should have met. I thought of Frank and myself; and now this stranger! The country seemed to be full of problematical persons.

We reached the corner of 30th Street and turned in at the Holland House. There was, in the large, brilliantly lighted room which we entered, only one single guest. He sat near the wall to the right, at a small table, a bottle of champagne in a cooler by his side. A waiter was filling his glass.

My companion started when he saw this guest. We went to the middle of the room, young Hannan nudging me and whispering, "Let's get away from that fellow. I know him. He's a bore."

We sat down, separated from the other guest by some five or six intervening tables. Since Hannan deliberately chose his seat so as to turn his back to the stranger, I had to face him.

While Hannan attended to our order, I appraised this man. He was heavy, massive, forty years old, I judged. Apparently he had been imbibing for some time. His big, prominent, goggly eyes showed that lack-lustre stare of the drinker who is almost stupefied with liquor. He was probably tall when standing; his great bulk expanded below to obesity, and tapered towards the head. The head, too, tapered towards the skull. His cheeks seemed to overflow; so did his chin which reposed in two or three heavy rolls on a low, fold-back collar. His nose was fleshy, his upper lip was hanging like a thick, quivering curtain over his teeth. His hair was scant and grey. His clothes, too, were grey; there was something slovenly about them; the coat seemed to hang in cast-iron folds.

From the stranger my eye slipped back to my companion. It was the first time that I could scan his face in bright light. He was prepossessing enough; and he gained still more by contrast. He was neat, clean, young, pleasant; his clothes were sober, of irreproachable cut and taste. A small, unobtrusive pearl reposed in his expensive, navy-blue moire necktie. He seemed the type of the best class of young Americans.

The waiter withdrew; young Hannan leaned across the table.

"Let's hurry," he said, "and get away. That fellow is sure to bother us. He's an awful bore."

"He does not look any too pleasant," I admitted.

"Tobacco-planter," Hannan whispered. "Money to burn; but no manners. I'm afraid he's seen me already. If he has, he is sure to come over and spoil our evening. A regular boob. He's from Missouri, all right. My father's got a place in the country, next to his. Too bad."

Our beer appeared. The big stranger had all the time been looking at us. His heavy upper lip swayed in front of his teeth as if he were muttering things. When he saw the nature of the order, he sneered openly. "Pikers!" I heard him say, as if to himself. Then he shouted across the room, "Broke, Hannan?"

Hannan did not reply, The stranger laughed.

"Let's hurry," Hannan whispered once more, "we'll go somewhere else." He gave the waiter a sign to indicate his desire to pay for our order.

But the stranger had risen and was already coming towards our table. The next moment he was heavily swaying above our heads. He spoke ludicrously as if to a child, "Is the poor boy from Missouri broke? Poor child! Bad daddy! Come, let uncle Howard pay for a little candy!"

Hannan pushed his chair back, with a fine show of resentment. "Hang it, Howard," he said; "leave me alone, will you?"

"Sure, sure," soothed Howard. "Poor little boy! Out of sorts to-night, is he? Waiter, here! Bring us another Mumm, extra dry. Sit down, boy! Let uncle Howard cheer you up. Sit down; keep your coat on. Come, come!"

I had been looking on in half amused, half annoyed silence, ready to reach for my hat.

To my amazement, Hannan allowed himself to be pushed back into his seat, whereupon Howard dropped tipsily into a chair between the two of us.

Meanwhile a waiter brought the wine from Howard's table; from the rear a second one approached with a tray of high-stemmed glasses and an unopened bottle. Howard was treated here with the deference which is accorded only to well-known liberal patrons of a place.

Hannan still scowled heavily. Then he suddenly smoothed out his brow and with a motion of his hand introduced me to Howard. "Shake hands with my friend, Mr. Branden," he said, winking at me.

Howard pulled himself together with a visible effort and did so, nearly upsetting the glasses in the act. This reminder of a third presence apparently put him on his guard; he tried to hold himself straight and steady.

A waiter poured the wine. We reached for our glasses and raised them. Hannan and Howard emptied theirs at a gulp. I, being bent on observing the two, barely touched the wine with my lips. The waiter instantly refilled the glasses.

Howard turned to me. "A stranger in this land of libertee?" he asked in a drunken drawl.

"Yes," I said, "I'm coming over from the Canadian side."

Howard chuckled. He caught sight of our beer glasses which were still standing on the table, nearly untouched. "You pore fish," He said contemptuously, "drinking beer at a time like this! Hannan, you're a piker! Pa doesn't like to see his money wasted, eh? Got any stuff in you, boy? Don't you even wake up when you get to little old New York? Come on, you piker; let's see who's going to pay for this."

And he extracted from his pocket a handful of silver from which he laboriously picked a silver dollar.

"Oh, cut it," snapped Hannan in undisguised ill-humour. "You're showing off, as usual, Howard. Probably sold a crop or so, and when you've got a few pennies in your pocket. . . . "

Howard laughed uproariously, emptied his glass again, and once more dug into his pocket from which this time he was at great pains to pull a huge roll of bills, fully three inches in diameter. They seemed to be mostly in denominations of one hundred dollars, though the wrapper consisted of a thousand-dollar bill.

"Sold my crop, eh?" he sneered. "Sure I did. Look what kind of crop uncle Howard had. Can afford a little spree, can't he, you little envious crab? You digger and son of a bobtailed cat!"

"Look here," Hannan said, getting hot under the collar, "if you want to insult me, I might just as well go. As for that filthy trash which you choose to exhibit, if you want to know, I think I could match every blessed bill you've got there without as much as writing a cheque. And so, for that matter, could my friend Mr. Branden, I suppose, if he wished to. You don't seem to know that your bragging is in abominably bad taste, especially in the presence of strangers . . ."

Howard had, for a moment, dumbly gasped at this effusion. Then he burst into a guffaw of laughter which shook his huge bulk like the waves of a prolonged earthquake.

"Bad taste?" he roared. "Bad taste, is it? That's what every mother's son says who hasn't got it. Bet you, my boy, that I could sit in a little game with you and put up a hundred to one and still clean you out in less'n half an hour. You pore reptile!" With that he got up; and, turning to me, he said, " 'Scuse me a minute, Mister Branden," and went out.

He had hardly left the room when Hannan bent over and started to speak in a rapid whisper.

"I have to apologize, Mr. Branden," he said "for getting you into this. If I had thought we might meet this fellow, and he being drunk, I should not have taken you here, that goes without saying. But the thing is done; and I hate to retreat. He needs a lesson. I'm going to take that wad from him, till morning. When he's sober, he's right enough – he should not drink. As it is, he's going to fall into the hands of some con-man; then pity his poor wife and children. He's a friend and neighbour of my father's, too. It's only charity to protect him. Let's have the game he proposes. You do as I tell you, and in half an hour we'll clean him out. Then he'll sleep off his drink; to-morrow morning, when he's sober, we'll put him on board his train, with his money safe till he leaves the city. What say?"

"He might win instead of losing," I objected.

"I'll see to that," whispered Hannan. "He's coming back. You do as I'll tell you. We two'll stack against him. He can't win that way; but he'll never notice the trick. We often do it for fun, at home. I'll be the banker for the two of us. Whatever you put in, I'll hand back to you when the game is over. I'd do it by myself; only I might not have enough cash in my pocket. I was bluffing before, you know. We'll save that sot in spite of himself."

He leaned back, still speaking in a sibilant whisper, without moving his lips.

Since I saw Howard approaching, I acquiesced by an imperceptible nod.

Two points I can aver in my defence. Firstly, I had no doubt of young Hannan's entirely honest, yes, benevolent intentions. Howard's condition was such that indeed I considerd his money as being in grave jeopardy from professional crooks. It was doing him a kindness to take care of it for him. I could well imagine what a salutary jolt it would be for him to wake up next morning and to find himself penniless. He would probably live through an hour or two which would not be so easy to forget. The hint about his wife and children had sunk in. The thing took hold of me. Secondly, I had sat in a game before. I had never yet given thought to questions of public morals. Gambling seemed perfectly legitimate to me; why, it pervaded even the public life of Europe with its state-sanctioned lotteries. If anybody had suggested to me at the time that to live on a million won in the lottery-game was immoral, I should have gasped as at an absurdity. From what little I had seen of American life – which was, of course, superficial enough – it seemed altogether built up on, and in itself a sanction of, the gambling chance.

Howard seemed slightly sobered when he sat down. But the idea of a game seemed to fill him with pleasurable excitement. He had by no means forgotten about it.

"Well, boys," he said, "how about it?"

"How about what?" snapped Hannan, once more with his show of angry impatience.

"The game," said Howard. "I offered to play you a hundred to one. I need some excitement in this dull town. The offer is open."

"Sure," said Hannan indifferently, "we'll take you up any moment you say so. But we can't start a game here."

Howard became astonishingly active for one who was so far gone in drink. He called the waiter, suppressed Hannan's attempt at paying his share, threw down a hundred-dollar bill, gave, when he received his change, a five-dollar tip, and asked tersely, when we were getting up, "Where'll it be?"

"Stanley's," answered Hannan, as tersely, "on twenty-seventh."

And, taking my arm, as we walked out, he whispered, "That's only a couple of doors from our hotel."

We left the Holland House, Howard leading by a few steps. Hannan and I followed, arm in arm, like a pair of old and trusted friends.

On the way Hannan whispered again: "Going to play flip. Let him lead. Throw your coin quickly. The game'll take care of itself."

I cannot say but that out here, in the open air, some qualms of conscience assailed me. I should have preferred to take Howard's money outright and to put it in the safe of the Prince George. But, since we were not going to any private club, there were difficulties in the way of such a plan. And what was Howard to me that I should bother about him? Hannan seemed to feel sure that he would lose. Here goes, I thought. Since I had gone so far I would see the matter through. I was entirely altruistic.

We entered Stanley's by a long, semi-dark corridor from 27th Street. The barroom, which must have been closer to 26th Street, to judge from the length of the corridor, was garishly lighted and filled with a noisy, gesticulating crowd over which lay thick, bluish layers of cigar-smoke. A white-frocked coloured waiter flitted across our path as we entered. I still see him with my mind's eye, how he bent over in hurrying forward, and how he suddenly stopped, as it were, in mid-flight when he caught sight of Howard. Without waiting for sign or word, he turned at a sharp angle to his former direction and led the way to a small private room at the left. He opened the door, switched on the lights, allowed us to enter, closed the door, and was gone.

We sat down. In every motion of Howard's enormous bulk was quiet purpose. He seemed hardly tipsy any longer. But Hannan winked at me and with a quiet smile allayed the misgivings which were taking hold of me in spite of all.

"He's an habitué here," he whispered.

The waiter returned with three glasses of beer which no one had ordered.

"Anything else, gentlemen?" he asked.

"Two scotch," said Hannan.

"Yassir," and the attendant ducked out. He had not so much as smiled at any one.

Again he entered, bringing a bottle and three glasses, and vanished.

Howard knocked his roll of bills on the table and showed by every impatient motion that he "meant business."

"What's it to be?" he asked curtly.

"Flip," said Hannan and threw three coppers on the table.

"Just a moment," I spoke up; "how do you play that?"

"A flicker of a smile flashed over Howard's face and vanished. Hannan explained briefly. Whoever led, was to make a bet and throw his coin. The other two had to match the bet and to decide the game by throwing their coins in turn. If all three coins fell alike, either obverse or reverse, the pot remained; if not, the one whose coin differed from the other two took it. Each of us in turn started the betting and threw first.

"Your turn," said Hannan to Howard.

Howard threw a hundred-dollar bill into the centre of the table and flipped his coin.

Hannan threw down a silver dollar, and so did I.

Howard snarled with a contemptuous grimace. "Remember the terms, do you?" he said.

The pot was Howard's.

Hannan who was sitting to the left of Howard, betted next. He threw down a ten-dollar bill; I matched it; and Howard, with a coarse and derisive laugh, whipped out a thousand. The coins fell, and again Howard with a remarkably steady hand raked in the money.

I made it a one; the pot fell to Hannan. He raked it in and left it on the table between the two of us.

There was a momentary pause while Hannan filled two of the small glasses from the bottle. He pushed one over to me, one to Howard. Howard emptied his at a gulp, I touched mine with my lips. Hannan did not partake.

The taste of the liquor seemed to make Howard all the more eager. He counted out five hundred-dollar bills and threw them down. Hannan and I matched with two fives, and the coins span. Again it was Howard's turn to rake in the stakes. His upper lip seemed to wave from one side of his mouth to the other; it reminded me oddly of a heavy curtain blowing in a breeze. His eyes bulged more than ever.

Hannan made his bet five dollars again. The pot fell to myself. When I raked it in and joined it to the pile already lying between us, it suddenly struck me that indeed, even if the stakes had been even, we could not have helped cleaning Howard out since we were playing together. Only the most extraordinary run of luck could have given Howard any winnings at all. As it was, he was bound to be bankrupt within half an hour. I could not understand that Howard did not see through the trick, especially since we left the money lying open on the table and did not disguise the fact that we threw our winnings together. Mostly, it is true, for the next ten or fifteen minutes, Howard was the winner. But his winnings in each pot amounted to two, ten, or at most twenty dollars; whereas what he lost, was never less than a hundred, and often it was a thousand dollars a throw.

The alertness and alacrity with which he had begun the game had left him now. Repeatedly he had his glass refilled. Repeatedly he sank into something like a stupor. At last Hannan had to touch him on the shoulder when it came his turn to bet. He started up as from a dream.

"Sure," he said, "sure"; and he reached for his roll on the table. It had by this time dwindled down to a few meagre bills. He grumbled. Then, as if awaking, he opened and closed his eyes rapidly two or three times, and a heavy scowl settled between his brows. He shot a glance at our joint pile. I expected some kind of trouble. But he merely hissed a scarcely audible remark, reached into his hip-pocket, apparently with great exertion, pulled another roll out, counted off ten bills, slowly and carefully, and threw them down. To my bewilderment they were ten thousand-dollar bills. I took the remainder of my money out of my pocket. It amounted to just sixty dollars. Hannan saw my predicament and, with the slightest motion of his hand, pushed the pile of money which lay between us towards me. I took four tens and matched the bet. I thought I saw Howard shoot a glance at the hand which picked out the four bills from our common winnings. I was not quite sure of it, but the mere suspicion sent misgivings of some impending disaster through my spine.

When the coins fell, Howard bent forward and watched his chance more eagerly than he had done so far.

The pot went to Hannan.

Howard laughed. "Gol-darn it," he said; and suddenly he did not seem the least bit drunk, "You've done it, boys. You've cleaned me out. All but the fare back home. Well, 'scuse me a moment." With a heavy motion he got up and left the room.

As soon as he was gone, Hannan turned to me. "Well," he said quickly, "we'll put that wad in the safe of the Prince George; all but what is your own, of course. There must be twenty thousand here. Some crop! How much is yours?"

All misgivings were dispelled by these words.

"Two hundred and fifty-five," I said, and Hannan began to count,

That very moment I pricked my ears, for I heard distinctly that out in the bar-room a monotonous voice had begun to call my name. The voice came nearer. I could now hear and understand it beyond the possibility of a doubt. "Phone-call-for-Mr.-Branden! . . . Phone-call-for-Mr.-Branden-from-the-Prince-George!"

I jumped up; yet I hesitated. Who should call me? Who knew me? How could the people at the hotel have guessed where I might be?

"Phone for you?" asked Hannan.

"Seems so," I said, "but I cannot imagine . . . "

"Better answer it," said Hannan; "but take your money."

He held out a number of notes among which I recognized two hundred-dollar bills. I grabbed them, crammed them into my pocket, and rushed out. A uniformed boy was just beginning to sing out again. At sight of myself he broke off.

"You Mr. Branden?" he asked.

"Yes."

"This way, sir." And he led the way through the crowd to one of the telephone-booths.

He held the door open and closed it when I had entered; I picked the dangling receiver up.

"Hello," I said.

Pause. Then, "Hello."

"This is Mr. Branden; who is speaking?"

"Central."

"Hello," I said. "The Prince George was calling me, I hear. You've cut us off, it seems."

"Prince George? You want the Prince George?"

"If you please."

A moment later the connection was made. No call had come from the hotel.

A vague uneasiness took hold of me. But it did not matter. Once more I felt for my money. The money was there. I left the booth and tried to find the room in which we had been sitting. All the rooms seemed empty. I did not know exactly where to look for ours. Then I suddenly caught sight of my hat on the hat-tree of the very room into which I was looking. There was the table, too, with the glasses and the half-empty bottle. But neither Hannan nor Howard were there. I felt uneasy again but could see no cause for alarm. Probably they had simply left the room for a moment and would presently return. I had my money. I entered and sat down.

The waiter opened the door. When he saw me, he stepped back with a muttered apology. But before he could close the door, I sang out, "If you please, waiter."

"Yassir," he said and reentered.

"These gentlemen gone?" I enquired with a motion of my hand towards the empty chairs.

"Yassir," he repeatd obsequiously; not a motion in his coffee-coloured face betrayed the slightest interest.

"Oh," I said, surprised and exceedingly puzzled. Then I rallied. I pulled out my money.

"Young gentleman paid the check," said the waiter. "Him as you called Mr. Hannan, sir."

I was still more puzzled. What was the game? Something was wrong; but what?

"Any message?"

"Nossir."

"Look here, waiter," I said in a confidential tone, handing him a dollar-bill which he took with a "Thank you, sir," but without a smile, his face the picture of unfathomable sorrow.

"Look here," I repeated, "do you know either of the men?"

"Nossir," he said very promptly and, so it seemed to me, a little too promptly, "never saw either one before."

This I knew to be a lie; the way in which he had led us to the private room had too clearly betrayed that he knew

Howard at least. I thought of the fact that Hannan, like myself, was stopping at the Prince George. I shrugged my shoulders.

"Very well," I said.

"Anything else, sir?" he asked.

"No, thanks." And I rose to go.

At the office of the hotel I asked for the number of Mr. Hannan's room. No Mr. Hannan was registered there.

I went upstairs, profoundly puzzled. I believe I walked the floor for the greater part of the night; and when at last I went to bed, I could not sleep.

There must have been some trick; but I simply could not find in what it consisted. All those points on which suspicion was based came back to me: the unmistakable fact that Howard was known to the coloured waiter at Stanley's, who yet denied all knowledge of him; the incomprehensible stupidity of Howard's in submitting to a silly mulcting trick like ours; his undoubted soberness at the beginning of the game; the sharp look from the corner of his eye when I began to draw my betting money from the common fund; the fact that the game had automatically stopped exactly when my money was gone; the fabricated telephone-call at exactly the right moment; the disappearance of the two accomplices (for, that they were accomplices in some scheme, I had now no doubt); the deceit practiced by Hannan with regard to his stopping-place – all these things convinced me that I had been the victim of an elaborately laid plan. There were too many suspicious things, there was too astonishing a concurrence of trifles to admit of their being taken for mere coincidence.

What was the scheme? What was its purpose? I had my money. I took it out and counted it over, only to find the amount correct. Even the drinks had been paid for. Where did I come in? If I had somehow been cheated, well and good; I could have taken my loss and gone to bed and to sleep and accepted the thing as a lesson. As it was, the very mystery of it was tantalizing.

Suddenly a thought struck me, and the whole matter presented itself in a new aspect. *I had been sitting in a crooked game!* My intentions has been honest. But does the end justify the means? The fact remained that I had taken part in a conspiracy to take a man's money from him. I felt defiled. The rest of the night I spent in violent self-reproaches. I vowed never to make up with a stranger again. I wished to bury myself, to find a private room and to accept any kind of work – that of a waiter, if necessary – immediately. I began to wish that I had been cheated, that I had lost my money. I preferred being the victim to having placed myself in a position where I might possibly have been the victimizer. And suddenly a still more disquieting thought arose, still more disquieting, because it seemed to carry conviction. It seemed to explain to my heated imagination all the puzzling features of the evening; and those that it did not explain I had no longer any eye for.

What if Howard had really been bled? What, if Hannan alone was the crook? The fact that the telephone-call had come when Howard had left the room, seemed to speak against it. But, might not Hannan have "planted" that boy who had been paging me? Might not Hannan have grabbed the money and made off before Howard returned? Might not Howard, thinking that I had fled with him, have started in hot pursuit of the robbers, sobered as he no doubt had been by that time? If that was the right explanation, no matter how guileless my intention had been, I was Hannan's accomplice or at least an accessory to the fact. Who would believe me innocent?

From that moment on I expected the police. It would have been a relief to see them enter and to be arrested. But no one came. I believe that was the most terrible night I have lived through in all my years.

Dawn broke. I got ready to leave the hotel, locked my baggage, and went to roam the streets in search of a room.

It was much too early, of course. The houses were still closed. But I walked about, went down to the ferries on the North River, back to the East-River, down to Battery Park, and back again to Madison Square.

Then I started to scan the houses for "rooms-to-let" signs. I inspected only two rooms; one was eight, the other five dollars a week. Both seemed too high in price, but in order to get settled I engaged the latter, paid a week's rent in advance, and returned to the hotel to have my breakfast.

When I had made arrangements about my baggage, I crossed over to the cashier's desk, threw down a hundred-dollar bill, and asked for my account. There was some delay. It seemed to take an unconscionable time to settle my bill. The cashier, with my money in his hand, stepped back and used the telephone before attending to my change. Two other men sauntered over and stood beside me, apparently also waiting for the clerk's leisure.

"Just a moment," said the cashier to me; and he looked at the other two men with what seemed to be a questioning glance.

One of them nodded.

The cashier left his cage through a door in the rear.

I became impatient. Ten minutes went by.

Then the cashier stepped briskly back into his cage.

A fourth man had joined the group in front of the wicket.

The cashier, whose serious, yes, severe manner struck me, handed my bill, which he still held between his fingers, through the wicket to this fourth man who was pushing forward and looked at me without a word.

The same moment I felt a hand closing over my wrist, and a quiet voice spoke into my ear. "You are arrested. Don't try any monkey business. Just walk alongside of me, and nobody will be the wiser. If you resist, I'll have to put the billies on you. These two are the house-detectives."

I smiled. "I'll follow you, sir," I said quietly, although my knees shook and my heart pounded as if it were going to burst. "I expected you. I am glad you came."

"All right, come along."

We went through the lobby of the hotel as if we were two guests lounging about. At the curb stood a waiting cab.

"Mulberry," said my captor to the driver.

We got in, and the cab rolled off.

For a while the detective sat in silence. I looked at him. His face was intelligent, frank, kindly. He was thirty-five years old; his hair, brown; his eyes, gray.

I smiled. "I'm glad this came at last," I repeated.

He looked at me with a frown. "Better not say too much," he warned without a responsive smile. "Whatever you say, may be used against you. Your words imply a confession. Wait till you've got a lawyer."

I laughed. "I don't want a lawyer," I replied. "The case is clear enough. All I want to do is tell the truth and take what is coming to me for my foolishness."

I could see that his sternness relaxed. "Well," he said, "you may not feel like that after a while. Ever been up before?"

"What do you mean?" I asked, somewhat alarmed.

"Ever been in jail before?"

"No."

"Ever done anything like this before?"

"No."

"Did you know?" he asked with sudden sharpness.

"Know what?"

"That this is phony?" He raised the hundred-dollar bill.

The scales fell from my eyes. So that had been the game! I felt immensely relieved. It was not half so bad as I had feared. I laughed with relief till tears choked my laughter.

"No," I said at last, "but thank the Lord if it is. I thought it was much worse. I've got more of that stuff here," and I took the remaining bills and handed them to the detective.

"The worst of it is that I have already paid out one bill which probably also is counterfeit, to pay a week's rent for a room."

"Well," the detective said, "if you didn't know and can prove it, they can't do anything to you. But your story has got to be straight."

"My story," I replied, "is straight enough. I want to make a confession. It's lucky that I was the victim and not the crook. I was afraid that I was the crook, or at least one of them. That's why I was glad when you came."

"We'll be at the station in a minute or two," he said. "All this sounds queer. But tell a straight story, and you'll be all right."

We reached the Central Police Station; I was searched, my papers were taken from me; and I was locked up in a cell behind iron-bars.

There was an occupant in the cell already; and as soon as the keeper disappeared, this man, a rather flamboyant youth with a red necktie and shifty eyes, began a nervous conversation questioning me as to the charge on which I had been arrested, and telling me that he was wanted for forgery and embezzlement; he was "in for it"; they "had the goods on him."

About half an hour later I become aware of a stir and commotion running through the huge establishment.

"The cap's arrived," my companion volunteered. "Now we'll be up one after another. But they won't fetch you before the afternoon."

I did not reply and resigned myself to waiting.

But it was not more than ten minutes later before the keeper appeared again. He unlocked the barred doors, nodded to me, and said "Chief wants you."

My companion emitted a whistle of surprise; I stepped out.

A detective in uniform took charge of me; I followed him through a long corridor of cells from behind the barred doors of which many human eyes looked after us like those of so many caged animals. We went down a flight of stone-steps and through a second corridor similar to the one upstairs.

We stopped at a door where another policeman stood on guard. Words were whispered; the guard disappeared through the door. A minute or so later the door opened again, and I felt myself pushed forward into the room beyond.

This room resembled any ordinary office in a large and prosperous business house. Over against the window to the left stood a large, flat-topped desk at which a portly, middle-aged, clean-shaven, and distinguished-looking man was apparently reading a paper. But he shot a sharp, enquiring look at me from behind his gold-rimmed spectacles. At the window stood, looking out, the detective who had arrested me. In front of the right-hand window sat a young lady, pencil in hand, holding a pad of paper on a small table. At her elbow stood a typewriter. Between desk and door I noticed an unoccupied chair.

The captain raised his head and looked at me. After the slightest hesitation he nodded dismissal to my escort and waved his hand towards the unoccupied chair.

"Sit down." he said. "Mr. Mulligan here tells me you have a story to tell. What is your name? . . . Age? . . . Date of birth? . . . Place of birth? . . . Ah, you are a recent immigrant? . . . Well, let us have your story, please."

I told the story as clearly and as truthfully as I could. Repeatedly the captain nodded and smiled in the course of my recital. Mr. Mulligan, though ostensibly looking out of the window, lent a sharp ear. The young lady wrote rapidly in shorthand.

When I had finished telling about my worries during the night and about the relief I had felt on finding that, as far as I could see, I was the only one victimized, the captain swung around in his chair and said with a smile to Mr. Mulligan, "Han the Hook, of course, and Big Heinie."

"Of course," Mr. Mulligan agreed.

"Better give the word," the captain went on, "at the roll-call, that they are in town again."

"I'm sorry," I said, "and to tell the truth, I'm mad that my foolishness had got me into this trouble."

"Oh," the captain laughed, "they've got those who should know better than you can be expected to. As for trouble, you are in America. A little inconvenience, of course; we must ask you to give us the chance to verify some of your statements. When you are dismissed, we must require you to keep us posted as to your address. We might need you to identify the pair, that is all. Too bad you lost your money."

"Oh," I replied, infinitely relieved, "that part of it is nothing. So long as I don't need to reproach myself . . ."

The captain exchanged a look with Mr. Mulligan. "Well, no, Mr. Branden," he said with a smile, rising, "you don't need to do that. It may even turn out that you have been of service to us. I don't think we'll detain you at all. As I said, keep us posted with regard to your address. Mr. Mulligan will attend to you. You are discharged."

He shook hands with me before I left the office in charge of the plain-clothes man who had apprehended me.

TWO

I Scour the City for Work

IT TOOK ME some time to get over the excitement incident upon the happenings of my first day at New York. The great problem in hand, however, was that of securing work and recouping myself. First of all I was going to follow up the cards of introduction which Frank had given to me; I started out to call upon the various addressees. I will not weary the reader's mind by a detailed account of the peregrinations through the city which certainly wearied my body. I did not find a single one of the people to whom the introductions purported to be. I may as well anticipate right here and say that during the months which followed I made in various quarters and at repeated intervals the most careful enquiries; from what I learned, I could not help coming to the conclusion that the addressees of the various letters were altogether fictitious personalities. The very first day I wrote to Frank, but I never received an answer; and when, after a couple of weeks or so, I wrote to Frank's father to enquire about him, this letter also remained without an acknowledgment. Since there was in this an additional thing which puzzled me profoundly and even wounded me, I wrote, after several months had gone, once more to Frank's parents and had the letter registered, explaining fully what my experience with Frank's introductions had been, and asking whether there was any key to the mystery. In reply

I received a brief note from the mother in which she said that to the best of her knowledge her son had never been in New York; that they, the parents, preferred not to hear of him, neither directly nor indirectly, that they considered Frank, much to their sorrow, to be a "bad egg"; and that further enquiries would remain unanswered. That settled Frank. If I were called upon to write his epitaph, I should word it about as follows: "Here lies Frank, the most cheerful jester and liar I ever met, and the most disappointing friend at a distance." Whenever my thoughts reverted to Toronto, gloom would settle over my mind like a fog on the marshes.

I had wasted the day. In the evening I laid out a plan of campaign. Being now, as I imagined, a fully experienced waiter, I resolved not to rely on the advertisements in the papers alone, but to find the addresses of the employment agencies and to apply to them. Nevertheless, as a last thing before going to bed in order to make up for the sleep lost the previous night, I went out into the street to buy the evening papers and to look over their "help-wanted" columns.

When I got back to my room and unfolded the sheets I had purchased, I was dumbfounded to see my portrait adorning the front-pages of the various editions. Glaring headlines proclaimed: "Police makes big haul." – "Clever crook who flooded the city with counterfeit bills at last apprehended." – "Tries to deny but breaks down under cross-examination." I was intensely worried. It took me a long while before I was able to sleep; and the purpose for which the papers were bought was entirely forgotten.

Next morning I was inclined to view things more quietly and to let the whole matter rest. And rest it did; but I anxiously scanned the morning papers for a denial of last night's story; but none appeared. I might add that the story was never set right, in spite of the fact that surely the police must have issued a denial. My revenge has been that ever since, I have considered newspapers as remarkable only for their "square-miles of printed lies."

I was astonished to find that nobody seemed to recognize me. I had imagined that everybody would be talking about the case; and I was nearly disappointed to find that even such a "haul" on the part of the police should pass unnoticed beyond eliciting a momentary interest on the part of the commuter ensconced in his car-seat behind the rampart of his daily paper which defends him against all intrusion on the part of literature. I did not know yet that most people read with their eyes only, not with their minds, the same as they twiddle their thumbs for physical exercise.

Though, with all my recent savings gone, I was in a hurry to find work, I was not at all nervous; but I felt that I had lost two months of my life, a rather serious setback for one in my situation.

First of all I called at two employment agencies – one a commercial agency in the down-town district, the other a "waiter's exchange" somewhere in the central portion of Manhattan Island. At both these the first question asked was that after my "experience". At both I was requested to fill out a lengthy questionnaire which seemed to search into my most private doings during the past five or ten years. When I had filled it out, I stood stripped of all pretence at being a veteran in any trade whatever. The clerks who waited on me took my money – two and a half dollars each; but when they looked at my record, their faces lengthened.

"You haven't been in this country very long?" asked the elderly man at the Fulton Street office.

"Not very," I answered deprecatingly.

"Have you any relatives or friends to take care of you?"

"No."

He pushed my registration fee back to me across the counter and made an ominous-sounding remark. "You better hold on to your money," he said, "You'll need it before long."

"But surely," I said, still with a brave and confident smile, "a man with my education . . . "

"No," he interrupted me fiercely, "your education does not count for that much here. Let me tell you," this in a more friendly and sympathetic tone, "you speak French and German, Italian and Swedish. Well, there are thousands like you here. If you knew how to pound a typewriter faster than anybody else, we could place you at once. Or if, instead of those languages, you knew Rumanian, Slovakian, or some such lingo, we might try. But for French and German nobody has any use except a bartender or a waiter."

I thanked him, of course, and left. So it was a position as a waiter for me, after all!

At the waiter's exchange I was told to return the next morning at ten o'clock.

I was there on time.

The anteroom was filled with a noisy, laughing, polyglot crowd. One after another these people stepped up to a wicket, where a clerk, after enquiring for name and number of registration-card, gave each of them a slip containing the addresses of one or more establishments in need of help.

When it came my turn, I stepped up.

"Oh, yes," said the clerk, looking me over and reaching for the card which I had filled out the day before; "you are Branden, are you? Phil Branden? Speak French and German, I see. Fluently?"

"Yes," I replied.

"Experience? Some, I see. None in Europe?"

"No."

"Well, wait a minute. I'll see what I can do for you."

He stepped back, took a receiver off a telephone-stand, and called a number. A few of his words, during the conversation which followed, caught my ear. "Yes," he said. "French and German. Spanish, too, by the way. . . . What's that? Smart-looking? Yes, I should say. Yes, straight as a pine-tree. No, not very much experience. But I'd give him a chance if I were you. All right, send him over right off."

He replaced the receiver and returned to the wicket.

I looked at him, all expectant.

"Well," he said, "I've fixed you up, I think. Good place, too; at the Belmont." He wrote a few words on my card. "On forty-second," he added. "I suppose you know. Good luck to you."

With that he turned to the next one waiting.

I found the gigantic pile of the famous hotel. Being still unused to my newly humble station in life, I proudly entered through the main portal into the hall. When, at the office, I stated upon what errand I came, I was rather unceremoniously waved away and directed to enter through the employees' entrance on Fourth Avenue. I left the lobby and did so.

On looking about in the subterranean corridor to which this entrance admitted me, I discovered a sign on the frosted glass panel of a door. "A.J. Harris," it read, "Employment Agent."

I approached and was on the point of knocking when the door opened; a small man with a white goatee came rushing out and collided with me.

"What're you doing here?" he asked in unmistakably bad humour.

Again I stated my errand.

"See the captain," he said and pointed along the corridor, hurrying away meanwhile.

I continued my search till I found a door similar to the first but marked "Captain". I knocked.

The same moment a voice from behind enquired, "Want to see me?"

I started and turned. In the half-light which prevailed I saw a tall, massive, clean-shaven, typically American man in a black dinner-jacket standing behind me.

I stated my errand for the third time.

A few, rapid-fire questions followed, in English, French, German, all of which I answered satisfactorily.

Then came the dreaded question about my experience.

I stuck to the truth.

A frown settled on the man's face. "Give you a chance as an omnibus," he said; he seemed to drop the words slowly, like so many pebbles; "the best I can do for you."

"I am willing to learn," I said.

"All right; report to-night at five. You have a black swallow-tail?"

"Yes."

"You'll find me here." And he was on the point of going.

Then I made a mistake.

"May I ask," I said, detaining him, "what the wages are?"

"Four dollars a week," he said; and he fixed a pair of stern, penetrating eyes on my face.

My disappointment must have shown in my features. I know I thought of the fact that my room-rent amounted to five dollars a week.

Unaccountably, utterly unprovoked, in a wilfully insulting tone, he snapped out a few vicious words which left me with a feeling of dumbfounded surprise and indignation; they seemed so utterly uncalled-for.

"I don't want you," he said. "I don't want you at all. Do you think I can change the rules of a large establishment like this, just because you come here, begging for a job?"

His voice had risen towards the last; the next moment I looked after his retreating figure, too much taken aback to speak. I felt inclined to rush after him and to put him, by a few cutting remarks, "where he belonged". Fortunately the futility of bearding the lion in his den came home to me in time, and I was struck with a sense of the ludicrous. I laughed and retraced my steps.

When I emerged into the avenue, a miracle had happened. I was in Europe again; I was a European. My whole present situation was forgotten, submerged in social and intellectual pride. Who was I to walk these paths? I did not care to admit that I had been defeated. Had I retreated? No, I had given up certain positions, given them up "for strategic reasons", as I might have said. Had

I been more of an analyst of mental states, I should have seen that my very revolt and indignation proved me to be defeated. It was no genuine outburst, but resentment. To entrench oneself behind the feeling of superiority is invariably a sign that one has become the underdog. But for the moment this revulsion of my feelings gave relief. I was no longer daunted by the terrors and dangers of a foreign world. I had bravely gone through the worst; I had done the utmost anybody could ask me to do – as if anybody had asked me to do anything at all! In Toronto, rebuffs, courteous or discourteous, sympathetic or unsympathetic, had filled me with vague fears, with a dread of the future, with dark misgivings as to the very possibilities of life itself. To-day's experience, which was really quite similar, wiped away even that feeling of uncertainty, of unfamiliarity with life and its various, unknown aspects with which I had been infiltrated by my encounter with Messrs. Hannan and Howard. I looked down upon such a world. I was glad I had met with the adventures of the last two days. Instead of charging them up to my own lack of knowledge in the ways of the world, I charged them up to America. Howard and Hannan, Frank and this captain of waiterdom, they were all of a type – they were what I had very nearly come to accept on a level of equality! I had simply not been keeping myself at the proper distance; in my present mood I should have snubbed even Mr. Bennett! Compared with such as made up that quartette, I felt very righteous indeed. "I thank thee, O Lord, that I am not as these men are!"

I seemed to see with a very sudden realization that I had been all wrong in my methods; the advice I had been listening to was the advice of ignorance. This last rebuff, I thought, was needed to throw me back on the right track. Here I was, in a new world whose sham civilization was crude, raw, unfinished in the extreme. Yes, America was crude. That was the word. I can hardly convey how much there was of comfort, of soul-quieting, soothing, flattering support in this wonderful word which summarized my condemnation of the country to which I had come. "Crude!" And I? Forgotten was all that humility which I had so carefully nursed. Forgotten was what had driven me out of Europe – the merciless adherence to pre-ordained lines of caste – the spirit of sham and hypocrisy – the lying falseness of it all. I was, suddenly, the representative in a foreign country of an older, of a superior civilization. I forgot that I had come among these "colonials" and "Yankees" to ask them for a living. I felt as if I were conferring a favour upon them by condescending to accept an adequate remuneration for my mere presence upon their shores.

This reaction which was brought about by a mere trifle has often puzzled me since. Many a time I have tried to fathom its significance; but I failed to understand it – except as a mere perversity – till I became aware of the fact that it is typical; that nearly every immigrant into the New World goes through this stage; that some of them, especially English immigrants, seem never to get over it. It is probably something like a last fight put up by the old associations, the old order that had pressed its seal upon mind and soul, the old points of view and ways of looking at things. Everything that was European in the immigrant rallies once more and tries to reconvert him – till at last it collapses and leaves him helpless, exhausted; unless indeed it wins out.

The spirit of this reaction determined my next move. No longer was I going to apply for positions which might be offered in the daily papers. Instead, I was going to announce to the Americas that I was here and willing to listen to applications for my services. In other words, I was going to advertise for a position.

That very day I arranged to run an advertisement for a week in three of the leading newspapers of New York. It was a long advertisement, carefully composed, setting forth all my manifold accomplishments, but omitting those considerations which might argue to my disadvantage; the question of immediate remuneration was treated as negligible. When I read the final copy, behold, it was very good; at least, it seemed so to me. It was, of course, quite an expense to print this essay in display type for six insertions running; to be exact, it cost me in the neighbourhood of ninety dollars. But I felt confident that it would bring results; no doubt the big corporations could use me, or maybe the diplomatic service. Above all, the fact that I had this announcement running seemed somehow to release me from all my responsibilities with regard to myself; I felt that I could sit back and await developments.

I made up my mind not to enquire for answers before the week was over. I thought it best not to read a single one before the very last reply that I could possibly expect had arrived. If I read them as they came in, so I reasoned, I might merely be sowing regret for the future; the better offers might come later, following the less desirable ones. Anxiety to get settled might induce me to accept the first thing that came along. I was no longer willing to work at no matter what.

I spent a delightful week.

It was still early in the fall, the month being September. The valley of the Hudson River and the hills of Westchester County were arraying themselves for the grand carnival of the year. Hazy atmospheres and crisp breezes, alternating, moved the distances backward and forward, as if you were looking at them through telescopes of varying power. There was about my rambles something of the adventure of the first explorers. They had before them the Indians and an unknown continent. I had the unknown continent and the Americans.

Somehow I began, during this first week of carefree roaming which I enjoyed in the New World, to sense something exotic, something of the undiscovered world, something of the smell and scent of wild things in this small fringe of the continent, through which I walked, not observing, not exploring, but in a divine forgetfulness of all my worries and of the large city close by, with all its bustle and hurry and its relentless challenge. There was a beyond to these hills, something which called. There were days when the call became so intense, so concrete as to grow very nearly into a sound. I climbed across fences and walked across lawns, straight up to the crest of these hills, in a bee-line, merely to look down into the valley beyond and then to turn back, unsatisfied, strangely at a loss. I hardly knew what to do with myself, feeling full of a boundless melancholy which yet was infinitely sweet, for it remained entirely veiled and never became so pronounced as to force an interpretation in articulate thought.

Yet there were other moods, too; moods of a sterner, less comfortable cast.

My relation to Nature had been largely a literary one. When I had gone to Italy, I had read and studied what others had thought and felt there: Goethe, Browning, Byron, Shelley; and unconsciously I had tried to feel and to think like them. I remember with special distinctness having stood, as a very young man, on some promontory, somewhere in the Mediterranean, where large rocks had continued the grey ridge on which I stood way out into the blue deep, like "staccato accents in some great symphony". Beethoven, Wagner, Tchaikowsky had written my landscapes for me.

All that seemed very far and distant now. I could not make out at the time where I was heading; but I knew even then that, unknown in their nature to myself, processes were at work which were to remould me, which were to make me into something new, something different from what I had been, something less artificial. I felt as if I were in the hands of powers beyond my own or any human control; as if the gods were grinding me into their grist and grinding me exceedingly small.

I fought these powers, fought them with all my might. Growing-pains are the most healthful sign in a boy; but the boy does not like them; he would cast them off if he could; they make him feel tired when he wants to be active; they make him feel dependent when he dreams of being master.

I should have preferred to condemn; but I could not do

that now, not at least without reservations. I should have preferred to pass sentence on everything, on the country as well as on its population. It would have re-established my inner equilibrium which was shaken and thrown out of balance. I still felt that America – using the word as a collective name for that part of the population of two cities with which I had come into contact – was "crude". But here, in the hills and the woods, there was something strangely at variance with that population. Here there was, not a church, not a society, not a man-made institution; here there was God; but God, too, sometimes seemed cruel.

One day I went to the sea-shore; I do not remember just where, maybe at Rockaway, or on Long Island. It was early in the afternoon; the sea looked intensely, cruelly, unfeelingly blue. I walked along a beach of a blinding white, a chalky white. By and by I sat down; and as I sat there, I felt intensely aimless, useless in the world – homeless, too: the Son of Man has no place where to rest his head. And suddenly I realized that the beach on which I was sitting consisted of myriads and millions of shells, thrown up by the waves from the deep, from their home, here to die, to be ground to pieces by the wash of the surf. It was a great shock. Religion had in my former life never meant anything to me. I had grown up and lived in entire indifference. Here I revolted. At this moment and in the light of what I saw life meant for me largely the ability to feel pain. Why did all these myriads and millions of living beings have to live, if they lived only to die, and to die in such a way, such a cruel, casual way, devoid of meaning? God all-good? I asked. He could be all-good only if he was also all-ignorant, not all-knowing. My whole inner consciousness was like the raw flesh of a frightful wound: yes, I was such a shell thrown on these shores, in the process of being ground to pieces and fragments, in order to furnish the soil for others to stand on and maybe to thrive on.

When I returned to the city, my mood was nearly suicidal.

The week went by; and so there came the time when I had to face the things in hand again. One evening, when I had allowed ample time for all replies to come in, I made the round of the three newspaper offices to collect my letters. There were fifteen in all. I put them in my pocket and went home.

I was full of expectant excitement when I began to open one after the other. Their contents struck me like the news of a great disaster. Not one of them was a bona-fide offer. Not one of them took cognizance of the things which in my advertisement I had stated I knew or could do. Most of them were written on ordinary letter-paper, without a business heading. All of them were proposals to invest my money for me. A few stated definite sums, five hundred or a thousand dollars; most of them left the sums that were needed to make me independently rich in intentional darkness.

In an impulse of despair I gathered them all and burnt them. What was the use? I did not fit in.

This disappointment, coming as it did at a moment when my whole outlook on this new life was despondent, merely confirmed me in my despondency, my attitude of hostility towards God and the world; I closed up in my shell and coiled inside, to lie down and feel righteously unhappy. Unhappiness I felt vaguely to be a sufficient indictment of the system, a confirmation of the justice of my resentment, a justification of my late inactivity. I doubt whether that night I should have changed things had I by some effort of the will been able to do so.

What was I to do? I did not know. I counted the money that was left and found it to be somewhat less than a hundred and fifty dollars.

And now began another desperate search for work. It was not as frantic as it had been during the first week in Toronto; my anxiety was blunted by despondency. The daily round, which always fell far short of the list made up in the morning, became a matter of routine. In the beginning I used subways, elevated railways, surface cars whenever I had more than two or three blocks to go. I took hurried meals at whatever restaurants were handy when my general exhaustion sounded the alarm; I drowned every wish and every longing for relaxation because I saw my last funds steadily dwindle to the vanishing point. After weeks of this, when my capital had frittered away to less than a hundred dollars, I gave up riding and walked. That limited my daily range still more. The number of my calls fell to ten or twelve a day. I did not mind. My attitude had become such that I expected relief only from some lucky chance. I shaved my expenses down to a minimum, just enough to support a bare existence. My daily food bill averaged for weeks on end no higher than forty-five cents a day for week-days, and thirty cents for Sundays when I limited myself to two meals.

Curiously enough, it was at this stage that I began to read again. When the offices closed in the evening, I went home and took out my books.

A few details may be of interest. Let not the reader suppose that I limited my search to the "genteel" occupations. I did not even have any preference for them any longer. I was beginning to look under the surface. I realized that it was not only easier to secure work which would have classified me as belonging to the army of "unskilled labour", but also more profitable. You could hold down and control your outgo so much more readily; your appearance, for instance, had to satisfy only your own standards, not those of others; and by this time I should have been willing to limit my aspirations to neatness and cleanliness.

Sometimes I stood for hours in a queue of applicants waiting for jobs at the office of some contractor, or of the employment agent of a transfer company. One thing I felt sure I could not do, kill living things. Yet for days in succession I went every morning to the yards of the city abattoir and stood in line till the foreman came out and picked the men he needed. I was fortunate in that he always passed me by; at last I gave the abattoir up as hopeless.

Once only was I chosen by an employer, by a contractor who hired me as a hod-carrier for a building in the course of construction in Brooklyn. I started out one morning at seven o'clock carrying bricks up a ladder to the third story of the shell of what was to be a factory. At ten I played out and had to go home and to lie down. It took me the rest of the day to recover. My greatest handicap was a body which would not stand up under heavy work.

For those early morning trips in the search of a livelihood I dressed the part, of course. I had bought a suit of black overalls, so as to cover my expensive-looking wardrobe. When the time of the day came at which I could expect to find office-people in I went home, slipped off my "disguise", changed my shirt, put on collar and tie, and went out again.

Another plan was this. I knew something about books, in fact, had a personal and rather intimate relationship to the best editions of the best books in half a dozen literatures. I made a list of all the New York booksellers and called on at least one of them from day to day, offering my services for a minimum of wages to start with. I came down to offering my work at the discretion of whoever would employ me. If what I might do seemed worth anything to him, he was to give me whatever he thought fair; if not, I should be satisfied to have worked for nothing. Some of the men whom I thus interviewed were friendly; some were not. Those that were not usually asked me some such question as, "What's your game anyway?" Those that were never seemed to be in need of help; business seemed to be bad with them, invariably and without exception. Some however took my name and address, so that they might notify me should in the future a vacancy arise; I never heard any more of them.

I also called on every banker whose offices I passed in my peregrinations, especially in the smaller banks of the downtown districts, where foreigners did their banking.

These offices I learned to enter with a show of great confidence, so as to penetrate without difficulty to the managers and presidents. I found it easier to speak to the responsible executives than to underlings who were hedged about with caution. Sometimes I was gruffly shown the door; sometimes I had a friendly chat. Once a manager regretted very much; he had indeed been in need of just such a man for the information bureau – a clerk who could speak Italian above all; but he had, a day or so before my call, found what he wanted; the man was giving satisfaction; I was too late; but, of course, if I cared to leave name and address . . .

Two further incidents stand out, trifling things; but everything in this desperate search seems trifling; it is only in their accumulation that matters worked up to a pitch where they became tragedy.

One day I found an advertisement in the papers which ran as follows: "Wanted, young man of good appearance and skilful address to interview ladies. Only such as have a more than average education need apply. Experience in any commercial branch unnecessary. Tact and an unusual degree of culture indispensable. Do not answer unless you have at least a college education. Apply personally. . . . "

Just my case, I thought with characteristic promptness and felt at once in high spirits. I cannot help laughing at myself when, in looking back, I see myself answering that advertisement. I dressed with great care for the interview.

A dandified, effeminately adorned young man received me. For ten minutes or so he made a general conversation, handing out small-talk as if I were on a social call. Then he excused himself and left through a door, leaving me alone in a sumptuous office which resembled more the reception room in a well-appointed private house than that of a business firm. Nothing whatever gave me a clue to the line of activity these people might be pursuing.

A few minutes later the young man returned with his partner, a stockily built, burly, middle-aged man with long hair and flowing necktie. He looked like a bohemian of the parlor variety; he might have posed as a sculptor or a painter of peasant stock; his bohemianism was too exaggerated to be genuine.

The young man introduced me with elaborate politeness; and again there began an exchange of mystifying small-talk.

Suddenly they turned towards each other; a mask seemed to drop from their faces; they spoke in rapid French.

I smiled and broke in, speaking French myself, calling their attention to the fact that, if they wished not to be understood, they had chosen the wrong means.

Both gave a brilliant, apologetic smile.

The bohemian turned to me with an expression of candour. "Well," he said, "Mr. Branden, we are very sorry. It is your brogue that stands in the way. Your language is too unmistakably English. We need Yankees. You have everything else. But we want a man who can interview young ladies, college students, in fact . . . "

"You will understand, Mr. Branden," the young Beau Brummel broke in, "they are so flippant; they pick on everything to get the lead in a conversation. Whoever interviews them must not only be able to dominate them completely; he must not give them the slightest thing to take hold of, either. If they find anything at all to make fun of in the man who interviews them, our representative cannot do business with them. As Mr. Lowell said, you have everything else, but you have the slightest touch of a brogue. I am so sorry, Mr. Branden; I am sure you will understand . . . "

Both he and Mr. Lowell offered their hands; we parted as if I were a duke and they mere knights of the lesser gentry.

Of course, I did not understand one iota of it all, but – well, what was the use?

The other incident reminds me of an anecdote in a magazine story. Only its outcome was, of course, radically different; life usually differs from fiction.

It occurred when I had reached my last ten-dollar bill. Many a time had I passed the large window of the branch of one of the international Telegraph and Cable Companies in which a card was displayed, bearing the legend, "Messenger boys wanted". I had seen this card so often that it became a fixture in my memory picture of that street-corner. It hardly conveyed any meaning to me any longer. But one evening, when I saw the moment coming at which I should be entirely destitute, its sight suddenly flashed upon my mind, and it seemed to have a sudden import for me.

"What a boy can do, I can do," thus ran my thought; and in my distress, this inspiration shone like a beacon-light in the dark. I was ready to catch at any straw in order to save myself from drowning.

Next morning I went straight to this office, without even having any breakfast, and asked, upon entering, for the manager.

A tall, lean, humourous-looking man in slovenly attire, a tooth-pick in his mouth, sidled up to the counter and looked at me with a questioning inclination of his head.

"You are the manager, sir?" I enquired.

"Yes, sir," he said in a voice which seemed impatient right then, though probably it was only indifferent.

"I see by the sign in your window that you need messenger-boys," I began hopefully.

"Always room for some more," he replied casually, looking at me with his questioning glance.

"What a boy can do, I can do," I went on and smiled at him.

He tilted his tooth-pick up, puckered his forehead, and stared. "I don't get you," he said with mild reproach in his tone.

"I will make myself clear," I smiled, "I wish to make application for one of the jobs."

His eyes narrowed to mere slits. He gave a short laugh. "Gwan!" he said.

Several clerks who had overheard our conversation, drew nearer, expectant, grinning.

"I mean it, sir," I went on. "I am out of work; I am stranded. I assure you I shall try my best to give satisfaction."

"Quit your kidding," he cut in, this time sharply.

"But my dear sir," I argued with the courage of desperation, "if you would only take me seriously. I mean every word I say. I am at the end of my string. I am an immigrant and find it impossible to secure work. I am willing to do anything at all, down to sweeping your offices, provided it will pay for a meal-ticket."

"Cut it," he interrupted me. "Get a move on you, before I put you out of here. There's the door."

Under a general snicker I made my exit.

That week I began to sell my wardrobe. Suit after suit, overcoat after overcoat, went to the "Jew", as I expressed it to myself. Pitiful prices they brought. For the star-piece which I sold, an evening-dress suit made by one of the most exclusive tailors in London, a tailor to whom you have to come well recommended if you want him to work for you – I had paid him twenty-five pounds for it – I received ten dollars. I hated to do this – not that I minded parting with my things; but I knew that this policy merely meant putting off a little longer what had to come, what was approaching, inevitably, inexorably. I had exhausted my funds; now I was exhausting those of my possessions on which I could realize. Besides, there was for me something repulsive in the thought that others were going to wear what I had come to regard as nearly part of myself.

Why did I not return to Toronto? Well, I wrote to Mr. Carlton, asking him whether I could drop back into my old "job", and adding some lame explanation for my failure at New York. I never heard of the man. That worried me. If I had received an encouraging reply, I should most certainly have started back at once, and probably this book would never have been written. As it was, I thought up a great many reasons which might account for his silence. What kept me from going on the blind chance was the thought that possibly the restaurant had gone out of existence. I was so used to what I considered my bad luck – and which was largely ignorance and the lack of proper direction – that in every case I expected the worst rather than the best. As a point of fact I might add that, when, many years later, I did return to Toronto – as a tourist – I found Mr. Johnson's cafe not only in a flourishing condition, but much enlarged. A second similar restaurant had been opened in a different location and was run by the same management; it, too, flourished like the first. When, at the time of this visit, I spoke to the now aging manager, he recognized me at once; his first question was, "Why did you not come back to us when you wrote me from New York?" "Why did you not answer my letter?" I countered. "Oh," he said, "I thought that was hardly necessary. I expected you any day."

Meanwhile, as I have already said, I gave my evenings and Sundays to reading. And since, in due time, contrary to the reading of most people, mine was destined to influence my life profoundly, I cannot omit saying a few words about it. I have mentioned that I had brought a small collection of books from Europe. The tin-lined box which contained them had not been opened at Toronto. I broke into it now; most of these books went the way of my wardrobe – to second-hand dealers. It was easy to sell them – at great sacrifice, of course – since they had beautiful bindings and were well kept. So, when from time to time I made up a parcel of them for sale, I looked them over carefully. I parted with them as one parts with old friends who have never disappointed him. I felt about them as all who have loved their books a little too well have felt about them the world over since there were any books. Every time a number of them was to leave my room there were a few which I put back into the box in order to postpone their sale. So, very gradually, my little collection dwindled, the price of those that were sacrificed to be converted into fifteen-cent meals and to be used for my room-rent.

Occasionally, after having struck a bargain with the dealer – mostly they went to a shop on 16th Street – I made him throw in a magazine or two.

These magazines I read as my first introduction into American literature. In them I found some reflection of the actualities of modern American life, not in the fiction but in the articles; and though it took quite a while, at last I arrived at something like an understanding sympathy with American views and ideas. Being of anything rather than a frivolous turn of mind, I preferred informational or argumentative articles to the short-stories which even then predominated in the magazines.

By inference, or by a sort of mental reconstruction which seized upon hints and casual references that I ran across in my desultory reading, three great facts were slowly built up in my mind.

Firstly, there was such a thing as American Lettres. There had been writers in America whose works, unlike the general run of them, were not a mere recast of European models. In my still incomplete and distant view of them, they were, for me, soon dominated by three great figures: Lincoln, Lowell, Thoreau. I did not study them directly as yet; but I marked them down for future reading. Still I gleaned enough of their physiognomies to fill me with a rather rueful admiration. Lincoln's homely features, above all, his utter lack of pretence in casually dropping sentences of tremendous import – sentences that seemed at one and the same time to be formulated on the spur of the moment and to give voice to thoughts which had been carefully and slowly prepared through the millenia, so that they now stood, though printed on mere paper, as if carved by superhuman forces in the granite of geologic ages – Lincoln's face made me forget my own puny misery; his final earthly fate filled me with a personal sense of loss and yet with a sense, also, of a vastly superior significance, such as would in the end outrun mere human destinies.

Secondly, there was an America of which so far I did not know anything. New York was a mere bridgehead of Europe in the western hemisphere. The real America was somewhere else; but where? I was still under what I may call the geographical illusion. Had I seen even part of it yet? I did not know. The essential thing was that my education had been woefully incomplete; it had left part of the life of our globe out of the scheme of things – and that a part which was by no means negligible. I felt again as those first explorers must have felt when they began to realize that behind this fringe of coast which the discoverers had found there lay a vast continent, a world unknown. Somehow I felt as if my task were harder than theirs. They merely needed to set out, at the risk of their lives, it is true, to arrive at the physical facts; and they found glory and reward. The unknown world which I had to explore was a spiritual world; it had to be inferred from abstract facts; worst of all, in order to arrive at something which might be of value to me in terms of happiness or despair, it had to be condemned or approved of. "Judge not," said Christ. But, unless I judged, I could not justify myself. Physical facts can be taken as they are; you do not condemn or approve of a river valley or a mountain. But an outlook or a philosophy of life is either good or bad – a doctrine of life, of either death or life: you must side for or against it; in order to make your decision, you must first know. I did not know. Were Lincoln, Lowell, Thoreau accidents? But accidents do not happen. Where, then, was the ground out of which they had grown? Where was the soil that had borne them, so it might bear me? The one thing needful for the seed is to be planted.

And thirdly, there arose out of my casual reading a new insight about myself. I had come to America to "make my pile". But suppose some millionaire had happened to strike up an acquaintance with me; suppose he had taken an interest in my struggles and completely eliminated the economic factor by signing a cheque. What would such a competence have been worth to me? Precisely nothing. It would have left the main problem unsolved. There was consolation in this, but also cause for despair. Here, in this city of millions of people, there were likely only a very few who knew that America offered a problem – a problem which had to be solved if the world, as I saw it, was to be saved. Unless I was content to be a drone, I had to solve this problem for myself and without help. The third great fact, then, that arose from these midnight thoughts was that I could never be content with being a drone.

Yet, all the time, the economic question pressed. Day after day went by. Day after day I worked hard to find some niche into which I could step, whether for good or for a mere make-shift, that did not matter any longer. Just to mark off what may appear to be a low-water mark in the matter of humiliating my self-esteem, I will mention that one day during these last months of the year I happened across the address of an agency which supplied the households of the idle rich with domestic servants. I went there and argued that, though I had never myself been a footman or valet, yet in my father's house footmen and valets had been kept; I knew, therefore, what would be expected of them in the way of service. I need hardly say that my argument was unsuccessful. Not even an aristocrat with high-sounding titles could have broken into such respectable company as that of the liveried crews of the households of Messrs. Vanderlip or Gould, unless he had very good references and ample experience.

Then an incident happened which was to side-track me for a while and to end in a blow-out.

One evening, when I came home, I found a caller waiting for me, a young man of lively manners and neat appearance.

"Mr. Branden?" he greeted me briskly and shook hands. "A friend of yours gave me your name and address . . . "

"Which friend?" I wondered. "Have I friends?"

". . . as that of a person likely to be interested in a proposition which I have the honour to represent."

While he was speaking in a lively, business-like way, he backed me into a corner where an armchair stood into which I allowed myself to drop. For himself he drew up a straight-backed chair, sat down on its edge, and launched himself with amazing eloquence and volubility into a dissertation upon the excellence of Dr. Elliot's Five-Foot Shelf of the Best Books of the World, let me say, for I do not remember what books they were. I sat, fascinated by a display of oratorical and histrionic powers which, I thought, it must have taken years to train. Several times, while he went through his prodigious performance, I tried to interrupt and to tell him that he was wasting his time; that I did not care for the books; that I could not buy them even if I did care for them; he would not let me. He must have talked half an hour.

I marvelled at the accuracy of his information and the extent of his knowledge, and suddenly I saw a personal application; this was something I might be able to do. I watched him, profoundly absorbed. At last he had said as much as could be said about the books without plunging into the intricacies of literary criticism. Without a break, without as much as a transition, he pulled from his hip-pocket a heavy folder, flipped it open, and displayed to my astonished eyes how the whole five feet of leather-backs would look on my bookshelves. He rose, still talking, never stopping for even sufficient time to catch his breath, and put this display on the little table in my room, upright, so it would hold my eye, so I should not for a moment forget that there, within my reach, to be taken up at will and leisure, stood the World's Best Books in a Five-Foot Row.

And presto, prestidigito! I saw myself confronted with a large sheet of formal-looking paper; a fountain pen was persuasively pressed into my hand; a voice which became more and more insistent and imperative went on in an irresistible torrent, "And the best of it, my dear sir, is that we give you this treasure on very easy terms: five dollars down, and five a month."

An impressive pause; then the command of a general in battle: "Sign here!" An accusing finger pointed to a dotted line.

That finger had a nail which was not quite clean; the spell was broken. I did not sign, but burst out laughing.

My caller was inclined to be offended at my mirth; I placated him by explaining with the utmost candour why I could not dream of giving him an order. I seasoned my remarks with sufficient compliments for his great powers of speech and persuasion; and he was satisfied at last when I apologized for having taken up his time.

"Oh," he said, "that's all right; glad to have shown you anyway; we're doing missionary work."

"Missionary work?" I echoed. "Surely you are doing this for commercial reasons?"

"Of course," he replied, "a man has to live. But, at the price, you will realize that the immediate profit cannot be big. The public has to be educated, and the real profit will not come till it turns to the better class of books without being urged."

"Would you mind if I ask you a question?" I said. "Just how much do you make at this work?"

"Oh," he replied, "that depends; and it varies. Sometimes no more than twelve dollars a day."

"Twelve dollars a day!" I thought; I felt dizzy, just as I had felt when Mr. Bennett had casually informed me that his son was receiving ten dollars a week while learning the jeweller's trade.

"How long," I enquired, "do you have to learn before you become as expert as you are now?"

"That, too, depends," he replied. "A week or two. I have been with these people only two weeks myself."

"Is there a demand for more agents at any time?"

"No end of it," he asserted confidently. "You see, it takes appearance and address to get the interviews; it takes brains to master the canvass . . . "

"The canvass?" I repeated blankly.

"Yes, sure, the talk; we call it the canvass."

"Oh," I said, "you are not making the canvass up as you go?"

"Oh, no," he laughed. "They've got it printed. Every publishing house has its canvass ready made. Most of them have some sort of selling scheme besides."

"I see," I said, sobered in my admiration of his performance. "So other houses, too, besides the one which you represent, sell their publications through agents."

"No book worth buying is ever sold in any other way," he replied; "that is to say, no high-priced set. There would be no public for it if we did not bring it into the homes of the country."

"Well," I said, "you surely come like an angel from Heaven. Would you mind giving me an address or two where I might apply for a position myself?"

"Not at all. Got a newspaper here? They are full of their ads."

Obligingly he marked half a dozen of the advertisements for my especial benefit.

THREE

I Go on the Road

THUS I BECAME a book-agent.
  Three of the advertisements marked by my obliging caller were as I found inserted by three different branches of one and the same firm. As it chanced, I called at the three offices in succession. At the first two I was politely refused – again on account of my English accent. When, late in the afternoon, I called at the third office and found that it, too, represented the same publishing house, I was tempted not to enter at all but to pass it up as hopeless without wasting my time. But somehow it seemed different. The other two had occupied large, expensive-looking quarters on the ground-floor of sumptuous business blocks – this one was located in a dingy house, upstairs, filling rooms which seemed to be an apartment converted for its present purpose. I made up my mind to try.

The room I entered after knocking held a single occupant, a powerfully built man with singularly sagging features and a few wisps of stray grey hair. When I had introduced myself and stated my errand, he bade me be seated. In spite of my height I felt strangely slim and insignificant in his presence. His name was Tinker.

I told him at the outset that I had called at the other two offices and had been refused.

He smiled in a superior, disdainful way. "That's nonsense," he said. "Let me reassure you on that point by saying that your English accent will be an advantage to you instead of a drawback. You will be able to interest people all the more readily because you will prick their curiosity."

This way of looking at the matter struck me as at least unprejudiced. I told the man just what my situation was and impressed him with the fact that I had to make money at once.

"That's all right," he said. "It will take you a few days to master the canvass. Most of our agents can start on the road within a week or so. If you enter with us, we shall take care of you after that. We give you a drawing account of fifteen dollars a week which will, of course, be deducted from your later earnings. That much we risk. We usually let it go for three weeks. If an agent has not made good by that time, we dismiss him and write off our loss. It happens rarely, though. In your case I feel so confident of your ultimate success that I offer right now to carry you for five weeks. You will not need it; I tell you this merely to give you confidence. You will easily understand that, as a business man, I should not risk seventy-five dollars of my money unless I felt convinced that it will pay me in the end."

"That stands to reason," I replied.

"Very well," he continued. "You know our proposition?"

"No, sir, I don't."

"Now, then, Mr. Branden, just give me your attention."

And suddenly I felt myself swept off my feet, so to speak, listening to a talk delivered with an eloquence, a power of expression, a command over face and voice, ranging from quiet jestfulness to the very peak of soul-shaking pathos, compared with which the performance of my yesternight's caller paled to the stumbling attempt of a mere beginner. While the talk progressed – taking up about twenty-five minutes – this hulking man produced, out of the recesses of his clothes, as if from nowhere and by magic, a veritable avalanche of prospectuses, illustrations, sample-pages, bindings – so that, when he arrived at a brief discussion of prices and styles, we were surrounded by a litter of things which looked much more voluminous than it really was because he had stacked everything up in the most artful fashion. There were, he said, three styles of bindings in which this phenomenal collection of Travellogues – for such the books turned out to be – were sold: buckram, half-leather, and full morocco. They sold all three on the same terms, two dollars down and two a month, the only difference being in the time required for completing payments. And then he drew the formidable order-blank and directed me to sign on the dotted line.

I gasped with relief when I took the pencil and smiled. "I surely must read the books," I said.

"Never," he thundered. "We have found by experience that it is better for the agent not to know the books themselves but only the canvass. Agents are only human, after all; they are apt, if they read them, to wander in their talk and to speak of themselves or of what has struck them, instead of presenting the work as a whole. You must understand we have sold this book, which is the best book ever written on the subject for more than thirty years; in these thirty years we have worked out a canvass which has proved irresistible in the long-run. You must believe us in this, or we cannot use you. Two things are needed for your success. You must feel convinced that never was there a book offered to the public which gave them more for their money and which was of greater educative value; and you must be letter-perfect in your canvass before I shall let you go out."

I pondered that. "Well," I said, "perhaps you know best. I merely thought, if the book is what you say it is, I, having travelled quite a bit myself, might be all the more convinced of its value if I had read it and, therefore, all the more convincing in my talk."

"Yes," he replied, "I know; you would think so; it does not work out. As for the value of the book, let me show you what people who have bought it say of it."

And he pulled from his pocket a sheaf of typewritten testimonials, all speaking in the most glowing terms of the work, all of them written by men of undoubted standing in the business, scientific, or literary world.

I was amazed. "Well," I said, "if all that is true, as I must assume it to be, I merely wonder why the people don't rush your offices and fight for these volumes?"

"They should," Mr. Tinker said with conviction. "As a matter of fact, the book has sold in millions of copies. But for the last few years we have been reaching out by a house-to-house canvass, all over the United States and Canada, getting at the less well educated classes, the artisans, clerks, mechanics, and even the farmers. You will find that some people still look down upon the book-agent; but you never want to forget that, like the schools, the universities, and the churches, you are doing missionary work."

There was that word again. Missionary work! I smiled. "What is there in it for the agent?" I asked.

"Oh yes," he said and smiled likewise; "I was coming to that. You get a commission on every sale. Eight dollars for a cloth, ten dollars for a half-leather, and twelve dollars for a morocco binding. Every Saturday your orders will be totalled, and every Wednesday after that you will receive your cheque, no matter in what part of the country you may be working."

"And where shall I work?"

"Right here in New York," Mr. Tinker answered promptly. "I will be quite frank with you. Our still very short acquaintance has convinced me that you are a find for the business. You have the appearance and the address to gain interviews with city people. Such agents are rare. The moment I send you out you begin to draw two and a half dollars a day. You run no risks."

"How many calls does a man have to make in order to make a sale?" I enquired.

Mr. Tinker laughed. "That depends on the man."

"On an average," I insisted.

"There is no average," Mr. Tinker said. "I know a lady who sells a set on every third call and has a pleasant time on the other two. But in the beginning it may take you a week, or two weeks, of hard work to make your first sale. It depends on the way in which you get your interview. This is a science, the art of salesmanship; it has to be learned.

I sighed. "I am willing to learn. When can I start?"

"As soon as you know your canvass to the letter."

Another suspicion struck me. "Is there any charge for the outfit?" I asked.

"None whatever," he replied. "This is a legitimate business. Here is a copy of your talk, and here are the various things which you will need. Of course, you must not only know your canvass, but you must also learn to handle your material. You will find the most detailed directions in this little book."

Mr. Tinker made up a neat little parcel for me. "Well," he said at last, "get after the canvass, Mr. Branden. And when you know it thoroughly, come back. You will find me any time from nine to six except for one hour at noon."

"So long," I said.

We shook hands, and I left.

To Mr. Tinker's surprise I returned to his office the next afternoon and, at his request, gave him the canvass, though not with any great dramatic power, yet with a quiet persuasive conviction and an unhesitating knowledge of the lines which delighted him.

"Now, Mr. Branden," he said, "I am going to let you go out at once. But I beg of you, stick to the canvass. It is the everlasting temptation of the agent to put in little pieces of his own; don't you do it. For one reason, we have to guard against misrepresentation. We insist on our agents' not knowing the books, as I have explained before; every word in the canvass is true; so long as you follow it word for word, we can always back you up. Many and many an agent has had to be dropped from our forces because he could not resist the temptation and got himself into trouble where we could not stand behind him. They said things which amounted to misrepresentation. We shall require you from time to time to give us your canvass. We shall help you in all your difficulties and guide you as much as we can; we ask only one thing in return: that you honestly report to us from day to day about your work. For the first two or three weeks I shall ask you to report to me personally every evening at six o'clock."

And he proceeded to give me further directions. He advised me to set myself a definite number of calls for the day, say thirty, never to go outside the territory assigned, so as not to encroach upon the rights of other agents; to relax completely between interviews; always to ask for the lady of the house; never to state my business before I was seated with my interlocutor, nor to let anything of my prospectuses and papers be seen about my person before I had started upon my talk; never to allow the person interviewed to get in a word while I was launched upon the canvass; and so to control my voice and "magnetism" as to be most hypnotic towards the end.

"We have reduced the selling of this book to a science," he repeated. "Do not expect any great success in the beginning; but if you follow directions, you cannot help winning success in the end. It is merely a question of perseverance."

Little needs to be said about the actual work during my beginnings. I started out on a certain straggling street in the upper Bronx – a poor-looking neighbourhood. When I returned to the office after the first day's work, I was completely exhausted and all but hopeless. The reason for this hopelessness will presently appear.

"Well," Mr. Tinker greeted me with a smile, "how many calls did you make to-day?"

"Exactly thirty," I replied, "as you advised."

"Good. And how many interviews did you obtain?"

"Eighteen."

"Excellent," Mr. Tinker praised. "But, of course, you got no orders."

"No," I said; "still, I have two prospects. I talked two ladies into such a pitch of enthusiasm that they asked me to return to-morrow morning. They simply had to persuade their husbands first."

"And they asked you to leave a sample page?"

"Yes," I replied, rather surprised.

Mr. Tinker laughed. "Well," he said,"you can, of course, do as you please if you want to get your own experience. But if you will believe me, don't call back. I've been in this business since I was a mere boy; I yet have to see an order coming from a back-call. Let me explain. Books are among the remote luxuries, according to the views of our middle-class people. Once they start to talk things over, other things seem to be so much more urgently needed, a sewing machine, a gramophone, a carpet-sweeper. While you are there, two dollars a month seems a trifle; as soon as you are gone, they see only the total of sixty dollars."

I was taken aback. "Well, it strikes me that, considering the people I have been calling on, they are right," I said, not without hesitation.

"Nonsense," Mr. Tinker replied with great emphasis. "You could have got those orders. No woman in the United States needs to talk things over with her husband. If you make her want the books badly enough, she will give the order. Never forget that these books mean an education for those people. You know better what is good for them than they do. That is the spirit which you want to get. But I'll tell you. There was another way of getting those orders. Suppose that you feel you have missed the psychological moment of pressing the matter home with the woman and that she has started to talk of her husband. Get the address of the man's business place; let her give you a slip of introduction to him. See him before he has a chance to talk to his wife, and play up to his fondness for her and the children if there are any."

"But, Mr. Tinker," I objected, "quite a few people convinced me to-day that it would be foolish for them to put money into books. Surely you don't want me to press the matter when I can only too clearly see their point of view."

Mr. Tinker laughed; a trifle unpleasantly, I thought. Then he controlled himself. "The affairs of the people you interview are their own outlook. You have nothing to do with them. It is your business to get the order. How they are going to pay for it, that you can safely leave to them and to us."

I got up.

"Stick to your canvass," Mr. Tinker repeated, somewhat more pleasantly; "do as you did to-day, and the orders will come. Above all, do not weaken in closing. Always think of the untold hours of clean, wholesome pleasure you are bringing to people who know nothing but work. Think of the winter evenings around the lamp. There's pleasure and profit for father and mother, and no end of it for the kiddies."

It was only much later that I understood how masterfully and expertly Mr. Tinker played upon me and my sentimental sensibilities. As a matter of fact, his last words left me with something to think over all evening and all night. That very day, though I did not know it, my education had begun; I had had the first look-in upon humble families, striving to do their level best in the fight for a living; I had understood them and sympathized with them. More than once had I felt that I might have succeeded; I had done what to-day I consider the typical thing to do under the conditions of democratic freedom: I had sacrificed my personal advantage to what I considered best for others; I had desisted.

Mr. Tinker did not know that. After what I had heard him say I did not care to speak about the real trouble I had encountered. As a matter of fact, when I went to his office, I had half made up my mind to tell him all about it and to part with him then and there. Only the two prospects which I had kept me from doing so at the outset. In spite of what he had said I was still determined to call back. But his parting shot was a psychological master stroke. Maybe this talk about "missionary work" was not all cant. Maybe there was something in it, after all. I could well imagine how children would delight in looking at the more than eight thousand pictures that the set boasted of; how their pleasure would be reflected upon the parents; how the parents would be beguiled into reading; how the children would listen and take a new interest in their geography! And what were two dollars a month to people who, none of them, so it seemed, were making less than a hundred dollars a month?

So I kept at it. I called back at the two houses to which I had promised to return. Mr. Tinker was right. I was not even asked to come in but told at the door that it would be useless.

A whole week went by, and in spite of hard work I had no order. But still that last vision, summoned by Mr. Tinker at the end of my first report, persisted. Mr. Tinker promptly gave me a cheque for fifteen dollars; and after I had accepted it, I felt under an obligation to stay with him till it was repaid. But I began to think of a change. I felt that I was in the wrong surroundings; that I did not really have a chance to make good where I was working. So, one day during the second week, I broached the matter to Mr. Tinker.

"I wish," I said to him, "you would send me elsewhere."

"But why?" he objected. "You are getting the interviews; you have the approach. Women do not refuse to listen to you. That is where most of our agents are weak. That's why we have to send them into small towns where people are glad to welcome the stranger. You are weak on closing. You have to overcome that."

"I can't," I replied. "Here I see only people who have their own troubles. They tell me about them."

"But you don't want to listen," Mr. Tinker exclaimed, exasperated. "You are there to talk, not to listen. Just give me your canvass. Let me hear how you work."

I did.

"That is excellent," he praised when I finished; "that is exceptionally good. I can't see why you are not getting the orders. I'll tell you what I'll do. I'll go with you to-morrow morning till we land an order. You give the canvass; I'll do the closing."

My eye lighted up. "Very well," I said. "Shall I call for you here?"

Mr. Tinker and I interviewed an old lady. It was a small, a very modest household. We were ushered into a stuffy, little parlour that spoke of desperate efforts at keeping up the appearances of genteel respectability. On one wall I noticed a framed diploma; the rest of the wall-space was scattered over with a multitudinous arrangement of faded photographs.

The old lady, unmistakably Irish – from her speech and her kindly, round, wrinkled face under the crocheted white bonnet – listened to my forceful talk with a wistful, benevolent smile which had something reminiscent in it.

When I finished and was pulling out the folder with the leather-backs of the bindings, she began in an enthusiastic tone, "Oh, how my daughter . . ."

But Mr. Tinker, taking the folder out of my hand, interrupted her. "Just a moment, madam," he said and rose, towering above her. "You have a daughter – a teacher, as I see by the diploma here on the wall . . . "

The old lady beamed.

"It is for her that I am speaking. Now listen. Don't say a word to her till the books are here. I know you will be impatient to get them. Usually it takes a week to deliver a set; but in your case we shall make an extra effort and get them here by to-night. They will come in a box, of course. You open this box and get it out of the way before your daughter comes home. And here, on this little table . . . " He flipped the folder open and set it up while he was towering above her. ". . . Here you place the whole set and let her discover it. Just think of her joy! Every one of these volumes is bound in full morocco. Every one of the twenty volumes contains four hundred pages of delightful reading. Every page contains at least one illustration besides the many full-page plates. There, look at it; that is the way the set will stand. No teacher can afford to be without it. I know, it is quite a task to bring up a young girl to be a teacher." – His voice became a whisper, tender, caressing, confidential. "You have had your many years of struggle to do it. Now you *have* done it, and at last you are going to do for her this last one thing." Beaming, he worked up to a climax, raising his voice. "You are going to give her this set. And I'll tell you, madam." At this point he pulled out the order blanks, laying them down in front of the old lady; and as he went on, he lowered his voice to a whisper again. "The best of it is that I, too, can do something for you. I am going to make you the easiest terms that I am allowed to make; two dollars down and two a month." He did not even tell her the total. "Just put your name down here, please . . . no, on this line. . . . Thank you, madam. And now, if you have two dollars handy . . . "

With trembling fingers she began to count out quarters and dimes, from a worn-out pocketbook, while Mr. Tinker went on talking, talking.

"Oh, believe me, madam, I know what it means to do things for our children; I know the reward, too; the happy smile, the gleaming eye, a tear, and a kiss on the mother's cheek – and never a word! Thanks, madam. Good-by, and congratulations."

With amazing agility he had gathered all our paraphernalia and was pushing me out, ahead of himself, frowning with impatience as I delayed.

As soon as we were in the street, he relaxed; his powerful shoulders sagged; he took a deep breath.

Then he laughed. "Well," he said, "do you see? That was an easy one, of course. Slick as pulling a tooth. We'll split the commission, Branden. Now go and get half a dozen more."

I did not go on that morning. I remember it as if it had been yesterday instead of three decades ago. I went to

Riverside Park, above the Hudson, feeling at outs with myself and the world.

Missionary work, indeed!

I still see myself, stopping for a moment at the huge foundations of the Library of Columbia University which at the time was building. Here was one of America's great institutions, one of its universities, being erected at a cost of millions of dollars; I had just witnessed how money was extracted from the trembling fingers of bashful poverty. I cried with shame and humiliation when I flung myself down on some bench in the park.

My whole life passed in review before my mind. This seemed a time for great, decisive resolutions. What could I do? There seemed to be some external power which shuffled men about as you shuffle a deck of cards. I had left beaten tracks; I was in the control of some merciless, gigantic machine. Useless to fight! If only I could lie down and die! Nobody would miss me, nobody would suffer if I disappeared. On the contrary, I should leave the way clear for others. If I could make a living only by taking it from others, would it not be better not to make that living and to resign myself? But it was not easy to find a way to do even that.

It was late in the year. The last leaves were falling; most of the trees stood still and bare in the clear, sun-saturated December air. But for me, like a veil of dark-coloured mist, there lay gloom over the landscape, over the river, the park, the heights on the opposite bank. All the ostentation of pride and wealth in this great city looked like a hollow show – like the powdered and painted face of a woman of the street who hides despair and shame behind the smile of effrontery.

I thought of what I had witnessed. "Slick as pulling a tooth."

One after another three pictures arose before my mental vision. A cat, crouched low at the edge of a pond in which fishes are playing, glistening in the beams of the sun; the cat reaches out with incredible swiftness of paw;

one of the beautiful creatures flies up, out of the water, on to the bank; the very next moment it wriggles and writhes between the cat's teeth. – A hawk, sweeping down upon a bare spot between bushes and striking its talons into the quivering flesh of a chick which gives the universal cry of agonized death. – A snake, coiled up in a ditch, and a toad hopping inadvertently near; the next moment the toad fights and pulls and strains against the suck in the mouth of the snake; for the snake, changed suddenly into a fury of wiry, writhing lust, has struck and caught its hindfeet. – These sights I had seen on my rambles in Westchester county. Especially vivid was the horror of the toad's fight against the jaws of the snake.

While looking on when Mr. Tinker had "closed' the sale, I had intercepted a little involuntary unconscious motion of helpless revolt on the part of the old lady; and that little twitch of her delicate, trembling, nearly transparent hand had somehow reminded me with a strange, incomprehensible distinctness of the death-fight of fish, chick, toad. Like fish, chick, toad she had given in; she did not stand a chance!

If that was America, then let my curses ring out over America! I was neither cat, hawk, nor snake!

What was America then? Graft and cruelty, nothing else! Frank and Hannan and Howard on one side – Carlton and Tinker with their smug self-sufficiency on the other!

What could I do? Leave Tinker? I owed him fifteen dollars!

"Well," said Mr. Tinker gaily when I entered his office that evening. "How many orders?'

"None, of course," I replied. "Look here, Mr. Tinker. I did not make another call this morning. No, nor this afternoon, either. I cannot do this work. Not in this way. I come, fully determined to leave you right now unless you give me a chance to work where I can see a different class of people. I cannot foist this thing on to helpless women who cannot afford it. Give me a class of people that can afford sixty-dollar sets of books; and I'll undertake to sell them. But here, in the district to which you are sending me, I must refuse to go on with the work."

Mr. Tinker looked at me for some time in silence, a frown on the huge expanse of his fleshy face.

"All right," he said at last. "I shall send you out to White Plains. I have a crew working there, under the direction of a lady-manager, Mrs. McMurchy. Report to her as soon as you get there. I shall write down her address for you. I shall speak to her to-night over the telephone, and she will arrange for lodging and board. After this you will have to report to her and to follow her instructions. You have been a disappointment to me. But maybe it will be for the best that way. You will have company in the evenings, too."

FOUR

I Seek New Fields

WHEN I ARRIVED at White Plains, some time before noon, I looked Mrs. McMurchy up at once and found her at the address which Mr. Tinker had given me.

She received me in the small, dusky parlor of a private house where she and her whole little crew of agents had found accommodation.

The light in the room was bad; it was not easy to form an accurate first impression. Besides, the lady took apparent care to have what light there was fall full on my face and to keep herself in the shade. She struck me, however, as being at least fifty-five years old; she was medium-sized, very dark of complexion, with heavy features which reminded me of Mr. Tinker's sagging facial muscles, and with strangely strong and prominent lips. Her manners were carefully, studiously polite and smooth. No doubt she was expecting me.

"Mr. Branden, I suppose?" she said and gave me a large, bony, and bejewelled hand which for the fraction of a second lay limp in my fingers.

"Mr. Tinker phoned me last night," she said. "Unfortunately, we are just winding up here at White Plains. We intend to move to Pleasantville to-morrow. It is nearly lunch-time. If you will take your meal with us, you will meet the other members of the crew, and we can see after that what to do."

Since the last sentence was spoken with a questioning inflection, I replied, "With pleasure."

"Mr. Tinker told me that you know the canvass, that you have been working, and that you have no difficulty in getting your interviews?"

None whatever," I said.

"In that case," she went on, "it is a pity that you should leave New York. However, I shall be delighted to have you with us. I understand, the difficulty is in closing."

"It is," I said with a slight hesitation. "But permit me to be a trifle more explicit, Mrs. McMurchy. It might save you further disappointments."

"I shall be glad to hear whatever you may have to say," said my interlocutor with a smile.

"My difficulties," I began to explain, "are not so much of a practical as of an ethical nature. When I see that taking an order would submit the person interviewed to hardships, I cannot do it. Mr. Tinker went out with me yesterday and obtained an order which I should not have taken because it seemed morally wrong to take it."

Mrs. McMurchy gasped with horror. "But Mister Branden," she exclaimed, emphasizing every syllable, "how can you say such a thing? Mr. Tinker and doing wrong! Impossible altogether! I see from that what your trouble is. You are not sufficiently convinced of the value of the thing you are selling. You do not feel strongly enough that you are doing missionary work."

I smiled a weary smile. This, I felt, was mere cant.

"I am afraid," I replied, "that nothing can convince me that a set of books, however valuable, can feed a hungry mouth or clothe a shivering body. Nor shall I ever be able to hypnotize anybody into buying what he does not want. I am constitutionally unable to see wherein lies the missionary part of the fact that I am in need of commissions. If I did this work free of charge, it would be different; as it is, I cannot forget that I ask the person interviewed to pay two dollars a month for from four to six months in order to pay me for my trouble."

I looked with inviting frankness into the lady's face. She smiled, but avoided my look.

"Your conscience is of a delicacy which I have never yet found in an agent," she said. "I believe that you will get over that. I am beginning to see why Mr. Tinker said that he believed you to be a find for the business. I hope I shall convince you that the business is a find for you."

At this moment the house-door opened and closed. At once Mrs. McMurchy was on her feet.

"Just a moment," she said, and stepped into the door of the parlour, beckoning to a fat old lady who had just entered the hall.

This old lady, short, stout, white-haired, looked up at me with a seductive smile on a face which was most artfully rouged and powdered. The effect was startling. Every motion of her betrayed her age; she must have been over sixty; her hand trembled as she welcomed me on my being introduced to her; but her face was made up to an appearance of the most innocent youthfulness.

"Mrs. Coldwell," I heard Mrs. McMurchy name her; "one of our most successful agents."

Mrs. Coldwell's face was lighted by a winning smile. Then she turned to Mrs. McMurchy, and her smile, without disappearing, underwent a change; there was cunning in it, now, and triumph, also.

"I have an order," she said, "and a good one, too; for the half-leather set; from Mr. Regan, the banker."

"I'm very glad indeed, on your account, my dear," said Mrs. McMurchy and put her hand caressingly on her shoulder.

I had to suppress a smile; for in spite of the friendly tone in which these two women conversed I could sense a bitter rivalry, yes, animosity, between them.

The door went again.

"And here," continued Mrs. McMurchy, "is the rest of our little crew. Come in, Miss Henders; come in, Mr. Ray. Meet Mr. Branden, a new member of our crowd."

Miss Henders was a pretty little Jewess, neatly, though inexpensively dressed, with forward eyes, a face which could not conceal her emotions, and manners and movements which jarred a little on my sensibilities.

Mr. Ray was a tall and slender young man, hardly out of his boyhood yet, with easy movements and dark, flowing hair. His brown eyes which showed a peculiarly penetrating and cheerful lustre won him my instant sympathies.

All three appraised me with furtive glances while they were exchanging small talk and banter.

"Any luck, child?" asked Mrs. McMurchy patronizingly from the little Jewess.

"No-o," she pouted in a voice which was a trifle loud. "The sun shines too bright; suckers don't bite.'

Everybody laughed, with the exception of Mrs. McMurchy who frowned instead.

"This town has been drained," Mr. Ray threw in. "It's time to move."

"Yes," exclaimed Miss Henders, "we've done this town; let's do the next."

"Miss Henders," gasped Mrs. McMurchy, her indignation becoming vocal, "how can you speak that way! I can well see why you are not getting the orders."

"Nonsense," replied Miss Henders, "I don't get orders because you send me to women. Women antagonize me, and I antagonize them. Give me the business-men whom I can jolly along. I can't sell the books; but I can always sell myself."

"Miss Henders!!" Mrs. McMurchy exclaimed again, this time more sharply, and glancing at me with a significant look.

"Well," Miss Henders broke off, "I hope dinner is ready. I am as hungry as a bear."

And all three bustled upstairs to their rooms.

Mrs. McMurchy turned to me. "I have not been able to make arrangement for a room for you, Mr. Branden. I suppose you will have to stay at the hotel overnight. But your meals you can take with us if you like. As I said, we shall move to Pleasantville to-morrow; and there I have engaged room and board. We shall get there for dinner. I suppose you would prefer not to start work until we have moved?

"On the contrary," I replied; "if you can let me have an address or two, I should like to make a few calls this afternoon, just to see how things are in the smaller town. Provided I do not encroach upon other agents' rights."

"Very well," she replied and followed the others upstairs.

I was anxious to see how the other members of this crew felt about their work and their outlook; and when, after partaking of their lunch, I was ready to go out and – much against Mrs. McMurchy's wishes – fell in at the door with Miss Henders, I joined her.

"If you have some distance to go, Miss Henders," I said in holding the door for her, "and do not dislike a companion . . ."

"Not at all," she said, "come along."

We walked for a while in silence.

"I suppose you are quite an expert in this business, Mr. Branden?" she asked at length.

I laughed. "Not exactly," I said, "I have been trying to get my first order and failed so far."

"Is that so?" she asked with a sidelong glance from her beady black eyes.

"Yes," I said; "I have just arrived in this country; and I am trying to find a way of making a living."

"Is that so?" she repeated. "Well, I don't want to discourage you. But why don't you rather try something else?"

"Nobody, so it seems, has any use for my services. I am going to try this thing out. The trouble is, I can't bring myself to wrest an order from people who should put their money into necessaries rather than into luxuries like books."

She laughed. "That doesn't worry me. I need the money, and if I could see the people, I'd take the orders, no matter how poor they are. They are not as poor as I am."

A short silence ensued.

"Well," I said at last, "at least you don't talk about missionary work."

She laughed. "No," she said; "that's all nonsense. Most of the people to whom we sell get along quite comfortably without the books. I am frank at least. I want the commissions."

"If it is not intruding," I said, hesitating, "might I ask you how many orders the average agent gets in a week?"

"Oh, I don't know," she replied. "I do know that I work as hard as anybody, and that I am always in debt to the Company. I draw ten dollars a week, and though I sometimes take two orders or sell a morocco set, at other times I get no orders at all; and so there is always a balance against me. Fare, board, and laundry cost from seven to eight dollars a week; and I cannot dress for less than two or three, no matter how careful I am."

"And is it the same with Mrs. Coldwell and Mr. Ray?"

"Pretty much," she replied. "The worst of it is, if we do get an extra order now and then, suddenly one of the old orders, taken weeks ago, goes bad; that sets us back again."

"Goes bad?" I repeated.

"Yes," she explained. "When the books arrive, people refuse to take them in. They've got cold feet meanwhile."

"I see," I said pensively; for by intuition I understood the slang expression.

"Still," she went on, "you may have better luck. Mrs. McMurchy is always telling us of agents who buy cars or homes with their commissions. It may not be all hot air."

I did not feel exactly encouraged by what I had learned.

We separated; and I began to look for the addresses at which I was to call. I had three of them; they were all on the same street; three large residences, looking out, with an air of aloofness, over well-kept lawns that were now withered and dried by the onset of winter. I passed them without going in.

The air was crisp and invigorating; the sun, already advanced on the western half of its short winter arc. Something of that spirit which had guided me during my previous rambles in Westchester county came over me.

There was satisfaction in merely stretching my legs and swinging along. I followed the street on which I was till I reached the open country. A slight icy breeze made my cheeks tingle with its frost, and a feeling of health pervaded me, an animal satisfaction, as it were, to the exclusion of all thought. I entered the woods, without knowing where I was, and I walked, drinking in the air, and with it oblivion, till a feeling of happy weariness came over me. Just at the time when the sun which I saw behind the trees, as if through black bars, touched the horizon, I came to a clearing occupied by a well-kept farmyard. The shadows were rising; a smoky haze lay over the buildings. They seemed huddled, as if for warmth and shelter, against the forest. From behind a building the happy shouts and the laughter of children sounded across. In front of myself I saw a well, and suddenly I felt that I was thirsty.

At the well sat a man. His attitude was expressive of the weariness of physical toil. I approached, and he turned. His face radiated satisfaction and glowed from the work he had left.

"Good evening," I greeted; my voice was hushed by the beauty of the scene. "May I get a drink?"

"Certainly, help yourself," he said. "Wait, I'll get a cup."

"This will do," I replied, picking up a rusty tin cup.

"Look at that," the man said suddenly, without turning, waving an arm against the landscape.

Coal-black stood the forest; in the sky beyond, a dark, lustreless red shaded off through purple and amber into green.

I sat down beside the man. A few more words were passed back and forth. We spoke like old acquaintances; there was no need of introductions. We both were men, face to face with Nature.

A silence fell.

At last I smiled at him, and said, "I have something that might interest you."

"That so?" he asked. "What is it?"

"Books," I replied, violating all Mr. Tinker's rules.

"What kind?"

And I began to tell him about the set in my own way, slowly leading over into the regular canvass. I had gone on for five minutes, when he rose. I stopped.

"Come in," he said. "Let's go into the house. I want my wife to hear that."

We entered a large, simply but solidly furnished room, a combined dining and living room. The man lighted a lamp suspended over the large extension table. From the adjoining kitchen came the clatter of dishes. He offered me a chair and went out. In two or three minutes he returned with a tall, bony, but pleasant-looking matron, her face flushed from the heat of the stove.

"Well," said the man with a smile, "shoot, will you? But start it over, please."

And I began the canvass once more, I sitting, husband and wife standing in front of me, bent over the table, their large, hard hands resting on its top. I gave an excellent canvass, quiet, convincing, never hesitating for a second. I had gone half through it when, with a great noise and much laughter, two children burst into the room. A look from the mother, reproving, but not too sternly, silenced them; and they joined the group of listeners. The boy's eyes shone. I saw he devoured the illustrations which I showed with eager eyes. I also noticed that the father began to watch him with a humorous expression, and that the mother smiled.

When I had finished, I did not go on; I produced neither order blanks nor testimonials; I rested my case; I leaned back and looked at the group.

"Gee-whiz!" exclaimed the boy, "That's some book! Daddy, I'd like to have that."

"You kids get out of here," replied the father with mock severity. "Quick! This is business."

Reluctantly the children obeyed.

Man and wife looked at each other.

"Would be nice for the children," said the mother.

"Would be nice for you," the man replied.

"And for you!" she added.

We all three burst out laughing.

The man looked at me. "How much?"

"Sixty dollars," I said, "in full morocco. Easy terms."

"Never mind about the terms," he said. "I'll give you a cheque for ten dollars; balance on delivery. That satisfactory?"

"Entirely," I replied; and while I made the necessary entries in an order blank, he wrote the cheque.

When he had signed the order, I rose to go.

"Won't you stay for supper?" invited the woman.

"Well," I replied, "I did not go out for business; I went for a walk and fell in with your husband. I suppose it's time for me to get back to town."

"That's all right," said the farmer. "I'll hitch up and take you in. Better stay for supper. It's just about ready, I suppose?"

"I was on the point of setting the table," she said.

When, two hours or so later, I entered the parlor where Mrs. McMurchy had received me in the morning, I found her and Mrs. Coldwell ensconced in a rocker and an easy-chair respectively, reading. Young Ray was playing checkers with the little Jewess. I stopped in the door. Mrs. Coldwell had drawn her feet up under her body and sat there, huddled together like the handful of old, comfort-loving humanity which she was; the young pair were laughing and chattering away; and in the stately, presiding manner of Mrs. McMurchy's I could not help seeing, with a smile, something of the watchful attitude of a brood-hen with her flock.

She was the first one to look up, "Ah, Mr. Branden," she said with a searching look, "did you have your supper? It is rather late."

I felt the reproach in her voice, carefully controlled though it was; she did not approve of my late hours.

I smiled. "Yes, thanks. I've had my supper. I'm just coming in from work."

By this time four pairs of eyes were focused on me; I, not without a sense of the dramatic, slowly drew the order from my pocket, with the cheque attached, and laid it down before Mrs. McMurchy.

"No!" shouted Miss Henders petulantly. "Don't tell us you've got an order."

"Why, Mr. Branden," Mrs. McMurchy said, rising as soon as she had perused the blank to shake hands with me, "this is splendid! You put our young people to shame, I must say. A cash-order, too; for the full morocco binding!"

"What's that?" asked Mrs. Coldwell, not without a touch of envy. "Let me see that bird of paradise! You are starting in well, I declare!" With a trembling hand she reached for the order.

Young Ray said nothing; but his eyes smiled at me.

"I suppose, you know," remarked Mrs. McMurchy, "that a cash-order nets you sixteen dollars?"

"I'm glad," I said; "I did not know it."

"That shows you, young people," she said, turning to Miss Henders and Ray; "the orders are there. I gave Mr. Branden only three cards . . ."

"Well," I broke in, "but I called at none of the addresses. I just took a walk; I was thirsty; I met a man at a well, out in the country; I started my canvass, and I sold him."

"He's sold all right!" exclaimed Miss Henders with a harsh laugh. Apparently this young girl could not refrain from giving expression to her cynical views.

Mrs. McMurchy looked at her with the eye of reproof. Then she turned to me again. "And ten dollars down!" she said. "That shows that the order will stand."

"Oh, the order is good," I said; "but that I got it was mere chance."

"Talk of luck!" Miss Henders could not keep herself from addressing the ceiling.

The next day – it was a Saturday – we moved to Pleasantville, and I started to work on the same footing with the three other members of our crew. By Wednesday, when our cheques arrived, I had not taken another order though I probably had made more calls and given a better canvass than any of the rest. My cheque was for fifteen dollars; which left me in debt to the amount of eight dollars. In one way the work was less unpleasant than it had been in the Bronx. At mealtimes and during the long hours of the evening I had company. I doubt whether there is – that of teachers and doctors excepted – any other occupation in the world that is so conducive to "talking shop" as that of the book-agent. I know there is none in which "the blues" are as common.

Strange to say, I soon assumed in this little crew the part of the comforter. The reason lay in the fact that I had no difficulty whatever in obtaining interviews and that, on the whole, they came off pleasantly. That, too, is easily explained. I did not work up to a dramatic closing. I did not feel angry with the people interviewed if they told me, after listening to my canvass, of their own troubles and worries and forgot all about the books. I even remember a case in which I actually refused to accept an order. I had canvassed a young woman who liked the books and longed to have them. But she had listened to me with every now and then an absent-minded look creeping into her eyes as if, against her will, a different, deeper worry kept her occupied. When I wound up, I sat back, as was my custom, and smiled an encouraging smile. I was ready for her side of the matter. And soon it all came out. The little house was neatly and newly furnished. The woman's husband was a printer making good wages; they had been married a couple of years. But the furniture had been bought on the instalment plan, property-rights remaining with the firm that had sold it. Two babies had arrived; sickness had intervened; they had fallen in arrears with their payments and had twice been threatened with the loss of their things unless they settled immediately. But, feeling in the wrong as they did, they had not done anything about it and considered that such a loss would be only what was coming to them as a consequence of their bad luck. They had not even written to the firm. I felt very worldliwise as compared with this little family of nest-builders. I told the woman they must write and fully explain their situation; no doubt their creditors would be reasonable enough, provided they felt that they were dealing with honest people. I even wrote the letter, so her husband would only have to sign it. And when I had done that much for them, she felt that she was under an obligation to add fifty or sixty dollars to the debts of the household by buying my books. I laughed, refused to listen, shook hands, and left.

At the dinner-table I told this story to the crew; and for several minutes I had to submit to all manner of jests, for none of the other agents would have despised the order.

One of the first things I found out at Pleasantville was that we were going over the same territory for the third time. Mrs. McMurchy had a list, supposed to be complete, of those who owned the set. From telephone directories and personal enquiry she made up the new lists of people to be called on. I soon saw that the previous canvasses had pretty well exhausted the number of possible buyers. This, however, instead of discouraging me, made me feel that probably all I needed was the right kind of a new proposition in order to be quite successful at the business. I began to think of leaving the company.

I pondered a good deal about the cases of my colleagues. Mrs. McMurchy, who saw that I became the centre of the little circle – cheering, entertaining, encouraging, and correcting them – withdrew more and more to follow her favourite pastime of resting up. Two or three times I intervened in a quarrel between her and Mrs. Coldwell who accused her of giving her the poorest prospects to call on. More than once I pooled my cards with those of Mrs. Coldwell and asked her to pick whatever she liked, pretending that it did not matter to me on whom I called and that I could take orders whenever I really needed them.

The trouble arose from the fact that Mrs. McMurchy refused to divide the territory by streets, alleging that such a proceeding would involve an injustice to all concerned. One agent might get a good residential neighbourhood, the other, perhaps, a street of poor labourers' huts. If she had really known anything about the people she sent us to, her plan might have been capable of execution. But, owing to her indolence, her knowledge was a mere pretence; which was proved by the fact that at least one-third of the addresses handed out were erroneous; people had moved, in town or out of town; occasionally we hunted a person for hours and hours, only to find in the end that he had been dead for the last year or two – an exasperating experience when you are told that your success depends on the number of calls you make in a day.

But still, even this inconvenience, frequent as the complaints arising from it were, seemed only a trifle.

The real reason for the lack of harmony between the two women lay in that profound, deep-rooted rivalry which I had felt as soon as I had seen them together. It was constitutional; they could not stand each other. I believe if they had met in a desert, both starving, both at the point of death, they would, before lying down for their last rest, have fought each other to their heart's content.

Both these women had once been married; both had been book agents ever since their husbands died. Both had, whether before or after that catastrophe, acquired a certain veneer of manners which covered up their primitive natures; but if it had not been for that and for the fact that they were not alone in the world, they would have flown into each other's faces and scratched each other's eyes out whenever they met.

Mrs. McMurchy was the daughter of a farmer in Virginia; Mrs. Coldwell was the fatherless daughter of an actress. Mrs. McMurchy asserted proudly that her ancestors had been a family of slave-holders – you know the type; most of them came over in the *Mayflower*, too – and to have had a slaveholder among your forebears marks

you as "quality-folk". Mrs. Coldwell, however, said –
secretly, of course, "Look at her lips and her complexion!
She comes from coloured people! Slave-holders, well, I
guess! Slaves, she means!"

On the other hand, Mrs. Coldwell stoutly averred that
her parents had been married, her father having been a
proud but poor Englishman. Mrs. McMurchy whispered –
confidentially, of course – that she knew for a fact that her
mother had been a Miss even when she died.

As for their marriages, Mrs. McMurchy had been living
on her father's farm when she met her future husband;
Mrs. Coldwell admitted that she herself had been an actress, to which Mrs. McMurchy added – sotto voce – "A
chorus-girl."

Mrs. McMurchy vaguely described her deceased lord
and master as a railroad official in a responsible position –
which Mrs. Coldwell interpretated by saying, "A section-
boss." Mr. Coldwell, on the other hand, had been a mining
engineer; and his widow – this was the sorest of all sore
points – could prove it by documentary evidence. Both
husbands had lost their lives in railroad accidents; Mr.
McMurchy – according to Mrs. Coldwell who had never
seen him, neither dead nor alive – being run over in a fog
by a flyer while setting a switch; Mr. Coldwell – and
again, unfortunately for Mrs. McMurchy's peace of mind,
his widow held proof of the fact – having been in his
sleeper when the train on which he travelled ran into a
freight train and telescoped together.

And now Mrs. McMurchy was manager of a crew with
an exclusive territory, a position which vaguely connected
her with the capitalistic and idle class of the upper ten
thousand; and she gave orders to Mrs. Coldwell who re-
venged herself for the crying injustice of it all by hinting
darkly that she and Mr. Tinker had only one soul between
them; and that they were very likely also one flesh.

Mrs. Coldwell, however, had no ambition. She frankly
acknowledged that she could not have managed anything,
not even a dog; whereas Mrs. McMurchy had the matron-

ly, brood-hen dignity which imposes on most people and which – in women – is called executive ability.

Miss Henders, Ray, and myself sided with Mrs. Cold-well. She seemed so helpless, her outlook so hopeless. For me she was a mere child of seventy – wilful, silly, vain, and conceited – yet lovable on the whole. On Miss Henders she made a strong impression with ancient photographs of her husband and the big house which she had owned in California – she had lost it, together with ten thousand dollars of life-insurance, in some wild-cat mining scheme. Even the worthless share-certificates filled Miss Henders with awe.

This seemed to me all the stranger since Miss Henders was not only an American, but, according to her statements, a socialist. She was a curious product of city-slum America. To see her act, you would have thought her a "flirt" of the purest water, and by no means particular about the object of her flirtations. To hear her talk of "free love" and similar things, you would have taken her for a depraved young lady; for, at least intellectually, sullied beyond repair. Yet, as I convinced myself by and by, she was innocence herself, utterly unconscious of the dangers into the midst of which she walked as if she were brazenly exulting in her lack of prejudice. Besides, she was passionately, despairingly in love with young Ray who could not stand her. If he had left the company, as he was always on the point of doing, she would have "gone to pieces" altogether.

As for Ray, he thought he had found in myself a friend from whom he expected great things. He wanted to be an artist, a draughtsman; and he had one of the rarest gifts that I have ever run across. We spent a good many hours in talk; at my advice he read many books; he seemed convinced that I helped him in various ways which remained mysterious to me. I met him again – he has since left his mark in American Art – and later it became clear to me that at the time he was in what I might call his incubation-period. Of him we shall hear more.

Here were three people, strangely assorted; like myself they openly vowed that what they were doing was not of their choosing; and they were Americans!

Christmas came during this first week. Mrs. McMurchy went to New York; she left the management of our crew in my hands, feeling no doubt that in the petty warfare of this little crowd I represented something like a neutral. For two days I handed out the cards, verified an order taken by Mrs. Coldwell – which seemed insecure – resolved difficulties, and decided disputes.

Meanwhile I was just beginning to worry again on my own account when two new orders fell to my share. Again I had one afternoon given up the attempt and walked out of town into the open country. It was after the first big snowfall of the winter, and the glitter and sparkle all over the landscape was more than I could resist. Again I walked on for miles and miles till I felt honestly tired. And at last I reached a big, residential estate – a mansion built on the hillside whence it looked out over the soft contours of the rolling woods. Close to the road stood – old-country fashion – a lodge where probably the caretaker or the gardener lived.

This lodged I resolved to enter.

A pleasant ruddy-cheeked young woman, surrounded by a crowd of children, came to the door to enquire what I wished. I stated that I had been walking, that I was tired and thirsty and begged to be allowed to rest near the fire and to refresh myself. My request was granted as if it were the most natural occurrence.

A young man came in and greeted me.

These people were Germans, immigrated a few years ago, and gardeners by trade. They had acquired a fair knowledge of English and seemed eager to learn and to get ahead.

By and by I told them about the books, gave them the canvass, advised the buckram binding, and made the sale as a matter of course on a basis of five dollars down and five a month.

The second order was taken the next day under similar circumstances. That would leave me seven dollars in debt to the company by the middle of the following week.

The experience with these two orders gave me a new idea .When Mrs. McMurchy returned, a day or two before the end of the year, I spoke to her, telling her that I was going to leave the town entirely to the other agents; I wanted to work in the open country.

She tried to dissuade me; she did not believe I could see enough people to make a real success; she insisted that all I needed was to overcome my repugnance to a forceful closing; and that, unless I did overcome this weakness, I should sooner or later leave the business anyway.

I overrode all her objections. I pointed out that I had taken only three orders so far – all three in the open country – these orders had stood; if I could not see as many people as in a town, in return my percentage of unsuccessful calls in the country had – so far – been zero. I could make people want the books; if they were able to buy them, they would give me the order, not because they saw no other way of getting rid of me, but because I had what they wished to have. I boasted that I was opening up a new field for the company, proving that the books could be sold where apparently nobody had ever tried to sell them before.

Mrs. McMurchy gave in and let me have a free hand.

As gently as she could, she broke to me the news that the order taken by Mr. Tinker and myself in the Bronx had "gone bad". The young lady, the teacher, had first written to the company, trying to cancel her mother's order, and when they sent the books in spite of her protest, she had refused to take them in. Mrs. McMurchy was apologetic about it.

"The house could sue, of course," she said; "but no company likes to do that because it gives them a hard name."

"Of course," I said. "Not that I care about the house, but it would be a crime to force the poor people."

I asked a few questions about these orders which "went bad" and learned that the company always expected prompt payment if the books were taken into the house; if not, they preferred to drop the matter.

That brought my debt back to thirteen dollars.

On Tuesday we moved to Mt. Kisco. My way of working amounted henceforth to roaming the country, with my prospectuses, sample pages, and folders hidden away about my person. There were days when I simply enjoyed myself; there were days when I made fifteen or twenty calls. I never found any difference in the net result. At last I thought that I could see by the mere looks of a place whether I could make a sale or not. And when I made only one or two calls a day, I was simply passing up what I considered to be hopeless cases.

Time flew.

I was probably the most persistently cheerful member of our crew, for my calls were at least not spoiled by outbreaks of temper on the part of the "prospects". We went to Brewster, to Dover-Plains, to Sharon, and thence into Connecticut, via Danbury and Bridgeport, down to the coast. The winter months went in this way. The three other agents made their board, and so did I. The others were older in the business of selling books, but somehow it remained a marvel to them that I did not give it up. The fact was that I did not know what to do. At last, when we were nearing New York again, I began to play with the idea of going over to another company which had what I considered a more promising proposition.

I spoke of it to Ray; and he confided to me that he was going to drop out as soon as I did. He intended to leave the business altogether.

"Just tell me," he said, "where does it lead? Suppose there were no set-backs. Suppose I could make a little more than my board-bill and lay by a trifle – I can't. I've been wearing this suit for fourteen months, and it's the only one I've got; it's wearing out; but let that go – suppose I could lay by a few dollars a week, where does it get me?

A book agent all my life? I want to draw. When I took this up, I had gone hungry rather too much; I thought it would feel good to get three squares a day. Well, I *am* getting three triangles a day . . . " That was a common joke between us.

"And meanwhile Life slips by," I added.

"That's it," he said. "So long as you stay, I feel that I'm getting something – something that I haven't been looking for. Oh, yes," he waved aside a motion of protest, "you've helped me a lot. I've read. I consider that your acquaintance has been worth to me as much as a year or two at college. I see my way now. I'll go and get a job with a sign-painter or something like that. I'll be happy if I can dabble in paints and with pencils. Before I knew you, I felt as if I were degrading myself by doing manual work. I tried to sell sketches. Now I see I can get an education through books. I'll have my leisure; I shall be at peace with myself. This is worry all the time. When I'm not canvassing, I have the blues. I'm too young. People laugh at me in this business; their laugh stings. I am losing my ambition. When I set out in the morning, my highest wish is to bring in an order, and for a morocco set at that."

I laughed. "Well," I said, "I suppose you are right, Ray. At least for yourself. I don't consider it bad to lose my ambition. In fact, I have nothing to lose there. But I'm not ready to quit. I'll join another company; I don't see my way out just yet."

Several things concurred to change my wish into a resolution.

One day, when calling at a country house, I ran across a man who had the books. I even remember his name, which was Turnbull.

He lived in a large, ramshackle house of palatial dimensions, though, apart from its size, there was nothing palatial about it. He was a handsome, unkempt sort of a man, the kind that will play the devil with the girls and that feels aggrieved when anything goes wrong with them.

When, at my knock, he came to the door, he began to talk as soon as he saw me. "Come in," he said; "you'll find the house in a deuce of a shape, though. The women have left, it seems. My wife, I mean, and my daughter." He laughed the laugh of a man with a more or less unsettled mind; but it was half affected. "Damn women anyway; I never *could* understand them. I suppose, I was drunk last night . . . Well, what can I do for you?"

Reluctantly I stated my errand.

"What's that?" he interrupted me, bending forward and looking short-sightedly at my prospectus. "Oh, yes, the Travellogues. I've got them. There they are on the shelf. Want to buy them? Can't sell me anything, my man. But you can buy every dog-gone blessed thing on this hillside. Haven't got a drop of brandy on you, by any chance? Too bad. Hang that headache! Well, as I said, want to buy them? Ten dollars the set."

"Ten dollars?" I said. I had had a windfall in the way of orders, so that I was a little ahead with the company. "Well, yes, I'd buy the books at that price."

"Good," he said and laughed raucously, "fine, splendid! Anything else I could sell you? Nothing is of much use to me any longer. Wife left me, you see. For good, she writes. Left a letter behind. I had just read it when you came. She will no longer share my shameful life. Shameful is good, isn't it? Because I like a drop once in a while, or twice in a while, sometimes. Well, God be with her! That's settled then, is it, eh? Sure I can't sell you anything else? A horse and buggy? The house? Or the farm? You need a horse in that business! Well, come along. I'll tell Jim to hitch up and take you to town, so you can take the damn books along. Sure, no trouble at all. Take them right along. Just excuse me a moment."

And he stepped to the sink in the kitchen, where he dashed cold water over his head before going out.

Thus I acquired the books and read them. And instantly I began to understand that Mr. Tinker had been right in refusing to let me read them. When I had carefully gone through several volumes, I saw that every positive assertion about the work, as it stood in the canvass, was founded on fact; but the whole work was dead, lifeless, without a spark of genius. The author had seen what everybody else sees; he had followed the beaten track of tourist-travel, even though he had gone far and wide. As I see it to-day, it probably was not without its value for people whose intellectual food consists in the daily papers, the gossip and newsmongery of the Press. The child needs a primer; nobody judges that primer by standards of literature. But at that time I was not yet far enough advanced in common, every-day psychology to make concessions.

The long and short of it was that my acquaintance with the work took the "punch" out of my canvass.

Another thing influenced me in the same direction. As soon as I had seen the paper, the print, and the illustrations, I felt convinced that the price charged for the set was quite out of proportion to its actual cost. I discussed this matter with Mr. Tinker, when he ran over on one of his frequent visits – to Mrs. McMurchy, as Mrs. Coldwell insinuated. I did not tell him, of course, that I had a set in my room. He explained that the cost included, on the one hand the actual cost of manufacture, the royalties, the express-charges, the commissions, and the overhead on the books which stayed sold; on the other, bad debts – for only sixty per cent of the sets which were delivered were ever paid for in full – and express charges and so on for all the books which were not even accepted by those who had ordered them. All that went practically without saying; yet it had never entered my mind.

Soon after, the financial status of Mrs. McMurchy and Mr. Tinker became a problem to me. Surely, the house could not pay them a salary out of the limited proceeds of the sales engineered by them? Mr. Tinker had, so I heard, four or five crews at work, all of them turning in, maybe, from six to ten orders a week. Guarded enquiries along this line revealed the fact that Mrs. McMurchy was drawing three dollars on every set sold by a member of her crew, and Mr. Tinker, one. So the total of the commissions alone amounted to sixteen dollars on a full morocco set sold "on time".

These revelations came at a critical moment when an order of my own gave me food for thought and made me view the whole business as none too legitimate.

I had been making a good many calls in a densely settled rural district. It was one of my off-days, when that instinct which led me to pass over hopeless places seemed to have deserted me.

At supper-time, in the last amber glow of daylight, I passed a mere hut of a house. On any other day I should have gone on; this time I knocked.

It held a single room with two occupants. One of them was a young woman, a mere girl, busy at a tiny cook-stove; the other, a young man – he, too, a mere boy – was washing his face in a basin placed on a box. The room contained an iron bedstead with a cheap excelsior mattress; two boxes flanking the bed; the stove in the centre; and, in front of a wooden bench, along the opposite wall, a home-made table covered with oil-cloth. There was not even a chair.

I do not know what possessed me to give these people the canvass; but I did.

They had just been married, not more than two weeks ago; they were, that I could readily see, absurdly in love with each other. The man was a labourer; the woman had been a servant-girl. They were awkward and bashful; they laughed and blushed at everything. It flattered them to have a well-dressed man like myself speak politely to them and solicit their order. To take it was like leading a sheep to slaughter. There was no escape for them. Yet I took it, waiving even the question of a payment with the order.

A few days after that – my conscience having played havoc with my rest – I went back to see them. It was my intention to advise them not to take the books into their house.

I found the woman alone; to my amazement she was sitting at the table and looking at the pictures in the set. An order in a neighbouring town had "gone wrong", and Mr. Tinker, on receiving that of these people, had promptly switched the set over to the new address.

"Well," I said when I entered, "I see the books have arrived. How do you like them?"

Oh," she replied, half embarrassed, "they are lovely! But how are we ever going to pay for them?"

"I began to feel worried about you," I went on. "That's why I came back."

"Oh?" – with a questioning glance.

"You see, if, after talking things over a little more fully, you had not taken the books into your house, the company could not have forced you to take them at all."

"That's what I told my husband," she said; and somehow I knew how glad she was to be able to call him her husband. "But when he heard there was a box for him at the station, he rushed right off and brought them up. Well . . . it's all the same. I guess, we'll pay for them somehow; but we have not the money just now. He hires out, you see."

"All right," I said, "You've got to make the best of it now. I'll tell you what I'll do. You promised to make me your first payment on delivery. It is due. I'll send it in for you. Then, on the first of the month, you make your second payment."

"Oh, we could not accept . . . " she began.

But I interrupted her. "That's all right," I said. "I am making a little commission on the sale; I should feel better about it if you would let it go at that."

"Well . . . " she hesitated. "All the boys were up, last night; and they sat around till – oh, ever so late; all looking at the pictures and reading. We thought, this morning, before he left for work, if they come again, we'll take up a little collection every time they want to look at the books – maybe that way we'll get the money together."

I smiled at her eagerness. "Quite a scheme," I said and rose. "Don't worry about the first payment. And remember me to your husband. I hope you will be a happy couple."

She laughed and blushed.

The fact that these people appreciated the books, even though I did not, made me feel less depressed about this affair which yet, on the whole, confirmed me in my determination to leave the company for which I was working. There was one trouble, however, which kept me from doing so right away. Several orders of mine, rashly taken, had "gone bad"; I was in debt. We talked about it, one evening, and the other agents merely laughed at me.

"That wouldn't keep me," said Miss Henders. "They do us; if I could do them, I'd welcome the opportunity."

I had a vague idea that this little Jewess rather wished me to leave, and, if possible, without paying my debt – not at all for any serious reason or from love of evil, but from that mere love of mischief which prompts us to long for something to happen, especially something dramatic – a fire, an elopement, a little crime – anything which will break and relieve the tedium of a monotonous life.

That something dramatic did happen, for once. One day in early spring, without the slightest provocation, a man on whom I tried to call set his dogs on me. My clothes were torn, and one of my legs was badly lacerated before I reached the road. The case was reported to the company and the company took it up with a lawyer. Two weeks later the matter was settled out of court. On receipt of one hundred and fifty dollars damages I signed a release; forty-five dollars went to the lawyer; I paid my debt, and was free.

FIVE

I Join a New Company

BEFORE MY leg was quite healed and while I was still limping about with the help of a cane, I called on Mr. Wilbur, the president of the North American Historians' Publishing Company, New York City. These people had, so I understood, within recent years placed a composite history of the world on the market which I presumed to be good. The Editor-in-chief was a man of world-wide reputation as an historian and lexicographer. The different periods and nations had been treated by the best modern authorities in all civilized countries; and the work of those who were not Anglo-Saxon had been translated into English by men who themselves were considered authorities in the respective fields. The work was comparatively new; I held high hopes for its prospects.

I found the offices of the company in one of the most fashionable sky-scrapers of the city, where they occupied a whole sumptuously furnished floor. No other offices or branches, so it seemed, were entertained.

On entering the waiting room and stating my wish to see Mr. Wilbur, I was requested to fill out a blank, giving my business, name, and so on. After a few minutes I was told that Mr. Wilbur would receive me. There was an air of importance and exclusiveness about the whole procedure.

Mr. Wilbur was exceedingly polite. I told him what experience I had had and submitted my weekly statements in evidence of my measure of success.

"I'm glad to hear that," said Mr. Wilbur. "The Travel-logues have been canvassed to death. If you can still sell them, your salesmanship is all right."

"I am weak on closing, though," I put in. "I cannot clinch a sale when I see the prospect cannot afford to buy."

"Well," said Mr. Wilbur, appraisingly, "that will not stand in the way of your success, either, if we sign you up. We shall not ask you to call on anybody who cannot afford the price. But it is lunch-time, Mr. Branden. Maybe we had better postpone talking business till we have had a bite to eat. Will you accept an invitation to lunch with me at my club?"

"With pleasure," I said; "provided you do not find it embarrassing to go about with an invalid."

"Not at all."

We went down in the elevator and to the curb where a magnificent limousine was waiting. A liveried chauffeur who touched his cap was holding the door for us and nodded when Mr. Wilbur gave him our destination. A moment later we shot away. During the short ride only commonplace remarks were made.

Soon after, we were sitting in the luxurious dining-room of a fashionable men's luncheon-club. The meal which Mr. Wilbur ordered was simple but exquisitely prepared; the wine which was served with it Mr. Wilbur had ordered to be taken "from my private stock, please". Mr. Wilbur was visibly pleased when, after tasting it, I promptly named the vintage, Romané, from which it proceeded. That was a feat at which I had excelled in my heyday of Europe.

We were surrounded by the "jeunesse dorée" of a very definite fraction of New York's commercial world. I gathered from Mr. Wilbur's remarks that all of them had more or less decided artistic leanings. In their bearing, dress, and manners there was that which Moliere would have called précieux.

Mr. Wilbur himself, as compared with the majority of these guests, showed a quiet, superior, slightly ironic reserve which impressed me favourably. He did not take these people with their mannerisms seriously.

He was a tall, sparely built man with an exceedingly pleasant, clean-shaven face. His clothes were conservative, but of the best style and cut. A thin platinum watch-chain was, apart from a scarf-pin, the only jewellery which he exhibited. His long, slender hands were unencumbered with rings. He spoke with an even, self-possessed voice from which he was at no pains to exclude his marked, but good-natured irony.

When we had finished our lunch, he initialled his check; and we rose.

"Do you smoke, Mr. Branden?"

"I do," I replied, "I'm sorry to say."

"Oh, why?" he smiled. "I am partial to the weed myself. Shall we go into the smoking-room? There we can talk."

When we were ensconced in two leather-chairs, in a corner of the comfortable smoking-room, away from the bustle of the other guests, Mr. Wilbur's first question was, "When can you start work for us, Mr. Branden?"

I don't know why; but this question convinced me by its mere abruptness that the invitation to lunch had been a scheme; I had been on trial during the last half hour; and I had been approved of. I heard later on that Mr. Wilbur never engaged a salesman before he had seen him eat.

"Whenever my shins cease to give me trouble," I replied. "Within a week or so, I suppose."

"Very well," said Mr. Wilbur. "That will give you time to familiarize yourself with our prospectuses and to work out your selling points."

"Could I read a volume or two of the work itself?"

"Certainly," was the reply. "I shall place a complete set of the popular edition at your disposal if you wish it. Though with the people to whom we sell it does not matter what the books themselves may be."

"How is that?" I exclaimed, more than surprised.

Mr. Wilbur smiled. "You see," he said, after a second or so, "we sell a very high-priced, limited edition de luxe. We have printed one thousand copies on hand-made Holland paper. The plates have been taken down. Our bindings are made of hand-embossed leather, the most costly kind; no two bindings are alike. The sets are numbered. Every one of the twenty volumes contains four hand-painted plates by a famous artist. What we sell is not so much the book as the prestige which the possession of a set will confer upon the holder."

He had been speaking with his quiet irony, as if he were making fun of the buyers. I was taken aback, but I smiled at the idea of gaining social prestige by buying expensive books.

"I see," I said. "What is the price of the set?"

"That depends," he replied. "First of all let me say that there are really two editions – ours and a popular print. This merely for your own, private information. We have nothing whatever to do with the popular set. It is not likely, but it is possible, that you may run up against this popular reprint. So I think it better that you know about it; officially you are not to take cognizance of it. We want you to sell the de-luxe edition. Should you ever, among your prospects, run up against anybody who knows of the cheaper set, you treat it with quiet contempt as a pirated print. It is handled under a different firm; that protects you."

I pondered this; but no suspicion entered my mind. Mr. Wilbur paused while I followed my thoughts.

Then he went on. "I shall take pleasure in presenting you with one of the popular sets for your own use if you sign up with us. It sells, by the way, for sixty dollars. As for our edition – I shall show you when we get back to the office some of the original paintings for the illustrations."

"Just a moment," I interrupted. "Did I not understand you to say that the illustrations in the sets themselves are originals?"

"No; they are hand-painted; well-known artists are responsible for them; but, naturally, they are copies, for they are the same in all the sets. . . . Do I make myself clear?"

"Yes," I said, "I understand."

"Now as for the bindings. We use two materials, parchment and pin-grain morocco. The price of the sets in parchment varies from eight hundred to fourteen hundred dollars a set; the price of the sets in morocco, from five to eight hundred dollars. The difference in the price of the various sets is explained by the following fact. All the bindings are imitations of the bindings of famous books of the fifteenth and sixteenth centuries. They vary in difficulty of execution; for every volume a special plate had to be made. You sell individual sets. We shall always keep you supplied with full-sized photographs of four or five different sets which you can sell. Whenever a set is sold, we supply you with the necessary photographs to replace the ones you have disposed of."

I was impressed, not so much by the prices as by the elaborate preparation of these sets.

"What would my commission amount to?" I asked.

"I am coming to that," Mr. Wilbur replied. "Your commission is twenty per cent. Since you spoke about the financial side of it, we might just as well finish that part. Do not expect to sell one or two sets a day. It may sometimes take you a month before you make a sale, but at the lowest price that will net you a hundred dollars, at the highest it will bring you two hundred and eighty. To show you that I am willing to back up my opinion of your success, I shall open for you a drawing account with our house, the very moment you are ready to start your work. Suppose we put it at fifty dollars a week?"

"I did not expect that much," I said.

"Now as to our selling scheme. You will be under quite an expense because we direct you on whom to call; and though we try to keep a man working in a restricted territory, you may be in Boston or in New Haven when we shall have to ask you to run over to Washington or Pittsburg to attend to a prospect there. We authorize you to call on a man to whom you may get a personal introduction from a friend of his; but if you do, we must require you to notify us by wire; or we might meanwhile send somebody else to see him; this other salesman would lose his time and his money. In any case we discourage promiscuous calls. As a rule we sell only to people whom we know to be bibliophiles. We have lists of people who are more or less habitual buyers of high-priced books. These lists are, of course, subject to constant revision and extension by the work of our salesmen. But if we sold only five per cent of the people whose names are already on them, we should be so swamped with orders that we should have to establish a waiting list. We circularize these people for a few weeks, thus arousing their curiosity. Then we offer to send a representative who will explain, without any obligation on their part, just what our proposition is. We enclose a card addressed to ourselves and expressing a desire to be further informed. Whoever returns this card with his signature receives a further letter stating that our representative, Mr. So-and-so, will call on that-and-that date and at such-and-such hour. Thus, when you see him, you have an appointment; your interview is made."

"Why not eliminate the agent altogether?" I asked.

"My dear Mr. Branden," Mr. Wilbur laughed, "I assure you we should gladly do so. The twenty per cent which the salesman gets would look just as good in my pocket as in his."

I, too, laughed.

"Unfortunately," he went on, "the American buyer suffers from two weaknesses which only the pressure of a personal interview will overcome: indecision and procrastination. An order postponed is an order lost. It is easy to lay a letter aside. But it is a different matter to ask an agent to call again when that agent can truthfully say that, at the customer's call, he has come across half a continent to see him. By the way, I should advise you to look as English as you can and to treat your prospective customers with all the arrogance of a superior education. As for your speech, it is pretty good. I should rather affect that lisp and drawl which you possess naturally. The more English you seem, the less will those people dare to refuse you an order."

I laughed again.

Mr. Wilbur dropped his cigar into an ash-bowl. "Well," he said, "if you are ready to go . . . "

We rose.

"My car," Mr. Wilbur said to the attendant who appeared with our hats and coats.

Two minutes later we were being shot back through the crowded avenue to the office.

There we found, talking gaily to some of the young ladies who sat at the typewriters, a florid young man in well-tailored but pronounced attire who greeted the president of the company with a familiar nod and smile.

"Hello, Wilbur, how are you to-day?"

"Hello, Williams," replied Mr. Wilbur, "how are you yourself? Come in."

We entered his private office.

Mr. Wilbur introduced me.

Mr. Williams shook hands with a great show of cordiality. He had a curious way of throwing out his elbows with an angular motion. "Chawmed to meet you," he said with an accent which was a caricature of insular affectation.

"I was just going to show Mr. Branden the paintings," Mr. Wilbur went on. "Do you want to come?"

"Don't mind if I do."

We went into a long corridor whose walls were hung on both sides with historical paintings of large proportions and in the unmistakable manner of Delacroix. Most of them represented battle-scenes or state-occasions. I did not apply any standards of criticism – for which, by the way, in spite of my historical schooling, I was little qualified – and they did not fail to impress me duly.

I admired conservatively.

"Not bad, not bad," said Mr. Williams with a wink of his eye: Mr. Wilbur smiled.

Then he opened a door leading into a large, well-lighted room in which stood half a dozen glass-cases on mahogany bases, displaying samples of the bindings. There was no doubt about these: they were marvellously done. Even age-spots, caused by the handling of the ancient originals were closely imitated from mediæval models. I could not refrain from caressing one or two of the covers, although I could not get rid of the feeling that they, being mere imitations of things that were dead, had something of that exaggerated glitter and polish which attaches to all that is counterfeit. But I tried to tell myself that the thing itself was legitimate enough. Only much later did it strike me that I never saw a bound set, only empty bindings.

"Marvellous!" mocked Mr. Williams. "What an amount of trouble we go to in order to help the rich in our small way to spend their money! These are much too good for the snobs!"

"Too good, indeed," Mr. Wilbur agreed.

He seemed to feel like myself. I could not know at the time which was the difference between his melancholy and my own. I was to find out that, whereas I felt it nearly as a profanation that things of real beauty should be degraded by being fitted into a scheme for making money, he regretted only that he had to spend an appreciable fraction of what he was getting in order to draw the larger sum out of his customers. When I came to see through him, I understood that he would have preferred to take the money outright and not to give even part value in return.

We returned to his private office. I did not account for the fact; but the whole atmosphere had taken possession of me. I was still a recent immigrant. These were things European. Even a text of the work was vouched for by European names. After all, scientific and literary America did seem parasitic; it rooted in the millennia-old culture of Europe. The word of a young friend of mine, a student of Art in the university of Paris, who had introduced some Americans into our circles, came back to me. "Americans," he had said, "are Americans only till they have made their money. After that they go down on their bellies before everything European." Something of the inexpressible contempt for America contained in these words pervaded my whole being. Both Mr. Wilbur and Mr. Williams, Americans themselves, seemed to share it.

"Well," Mr. Wilbur asked when we were again sitting at his desk, "what do you think about it? Will you give us a try-out?"

" I think so," I said, though hesitatingly, "if you believe that I can make a success at it."

"Of that I feel sure," replied Mr. Wilbur, and, turning to Williams, he added, "By the way, Williams, it just strikes me that Branden and you should be able to pull together for a day or two? Of course, he will have to find his own way; but no doubt it would help him to see somebody else at work. We were just going to book you out for Pittsburg, I believe. I'll make sure about it. You were to call on one of our steel magnates, Mr. What's-his-name – Kirsty, I think. How would it be if Mr. Branden accompanied you on the trip? Should you lose your order, we'll credit you with a week's allowance anyway. That satisfactory?

"Sure," said Mr. Williams, "quite."

"All right," said Mr. Wilbur, and pressed a button.

A trim young lady entered.

"Bring me a salesman's contract, Miss Donahue," he addressed her. "And do you remember for whom we were going to book Mr. Williams?"

"For Mr. Kirsty, Pittsburg."

"Well," Mr. Wilbur pondered aloud, "suppose you make the date a week from day after to-morrow at eleven o'clock, in his office. You think you will be ready to go out by that time, Mr. Branden?"

"I think so, yes," I replied.

"All right, we'll leave it at that. Just include Mr. Branden, B-r-a-n-d-e-n, in your announcement. Thanks Miss Donahue."

A few minutes later I had signed a contract in duplicate binding me for one month; and Mr. Wilbur dismissed me, saying, "Please drop in at this office a week from to-day. We shall book you for your train and supply you with funds. Miss Donahue will address a set and all the material for study to you."

On the appointed day I presented myself at the office. I had carefully studied the "literature" with which I had been provided, a little booklet entitled "Hints for our Salesmen," and had read two or three volumes of the work itself. I was thoroughly convinced of the intrinsic value of the set and declared to Mr. Wilbur when he received me that I should be willing to go on the road in order to sell the popular edition on a straight canvass.

"That's all right," he said with his usual good-humour. "The point is, we can get a hundred canvassers for the popular edition where we get one who can sell the high-priced set. Besides, as I have said, we have nothing to do with the other print. I should like to try you out on our proposition."

He pushed an envelope across the desk. I opened it and found a cheque for fifty dollars, a return-ticket to Pittsburg over the Pennsylvania railroad, a sleeping-car reservation, and a receipt for these three items which I signed.

"As soon as you get through at Pittsburg, please report again at this office," Mr. Wilbur said as I rose.

I met Mr. Williams at the station in Jersey City. Since I did not know what else to do with the remainder of my baggage, two suitcases and a large steamer trunk, I took them along.

"Hope you've had your supper?" Mr. Williams asked when we boarded our car.

"Yes," I replied.

"Well, let's turn in," he said and led the way to our berths.

I lay awake for the greater part of the night. I felt sorry that we did not travel by a day-train; everything that I might see had a bearing upon my one great problem, America. Now I was flying along again, through one of the richest and most famous states of the Union, and I was passing through it as if I were rolling along through an underground corridor. Such was the effect of the night. And what a change! Here I was travelling with all the appurtenances of wealth. If a few months ago my appearance and my clothes had stood in the way of success, suddenly they had become my greatest asset. Even my brogue, which had cost me more than one position, I was now advised to accentuate rather than to get rid of. A few weeks ago I had been selling a work which I should not have cared to put into my own library – I had given my set to Mrs. Coldwell – which the people, however, wanted and could not afford to buy. Now I was going to sell a work which I valued highly – to people who never read what they bought! This book, I felt sure, I could make people want much more strongly because I knew it: its intrinsic merit was to count for nothing! I did not feel very comfortable over that point; but I could not afford to indulge in such thoughts. If this business proved to be a money-maker for me, I was going to stay with it; I needed money. And there was another alluring prospect. I was going to see – at my leisure – a good deal of the country into which I had come. True, it was a superficial, a sight-seeing only; but even that was necessary. I could not but marvel at the opportunity which had unexpectedly opened up for me. I could not help wondering, either, how it was that people trusted me. The amount advanced to me totalled over sixty-five dollars. I did not know at the time that Mr. Wilbur, after my first interview with him, had telephoned to the other house and verified what I had told him. Above all, he had learned that I had actually squared up the advances which I had received. He probably thought that he could trust a man who would do a thing considered so Quixotic by most of the agents who sold books.

Some time during the night I started up from my half-sleep, wakened by piercing darts of light at the very edge of the window-curtain. Soon after, voices shouted, the train slowed down and finally stopped. I raised the blind; and there, just in front of my window, I read the name of the station in the glare of an arc-light. It was Harrisburg. This name brought to my mind that of the river on whose banks the city stands: Susquehanna. I rolled the word in my mouth: soon we were going to follow the course of the Juniata, famed in song; and again a poignant regret came over me, a desire to swing my legs, walking along its banks, to be free, free, like the bird, to go where I listed.

A strange feeling came over me, a suspicion, an anxiety. Frank, Hannan, Howard: graft, I thought; the manager of the Telegraph and Cable Company, the Captain at the Belmont, Mr. Tinker: cruelty; Mrs. Coldwell, Turnbull, and others whom I had met in my canvasses: failure! Were these the three sides of America? Did graft and cruelty prey on weakness only? The two police-officials whom I had met, the captain at the central station in New York and Mr. Mulligan, the detective, seemed to look at me out of the dark; but I dismissed the thought of them; they did not fit into this ready-made scheme of condemnation. Bennett, too, raised his head in my half-dream; and then the pleasant young captain at the King Street restaurant in Toronto. Nor did young Ray fit in; nor the couple from whom I had taken the order of which I repented. Well, how about Mr. Wilbur and those I was going to meet in my new position? I did not know. But had not he himself given me the clue? Contempt for his compatriots, was not that the very essence of his business? What he sold, was social prestige! I felt half sorry for having met him. Yet, even this was knowledge which I was acquiring. I had to go through with it, now.

When daylight came, I got up. We were nearing Johnstown, on the west-slope of the Alleghenies. There was a commotion in our car as we approached the city of the Cambria Steel Works. A good many passengers were preparing to get off the train. More and more people were dressing behind their curtains. The porter began to knock down the berths.

It seemed as if we were dropping into a black pit of smoke, an underground hell of ferocious activity. Only a few minutes ago we had been on green hillsides, crossing, re-crossing the swift, alluring waters of Conemaugh Creek. Now dingy huts and smoke-blackened houses made up the scenery, as with a grinding of brakes we came to a stop. And then we pulled out again; the mountains rose; trees just budding out into a green haze of foliage, spoke of spring in the world, of hope, of innocent life.

We crossed through the Chestunut Range, beloved scene for me of many a later ramble. Then again the pit. Black sores broke out on Nature's beautiful skin; steaming scars lay across the landscape; smoke-and-flame-belching furnaces wove the black cloak which covers the Iron City with its outforts, Braddock and Duquesne, Homestead and Bessemer. An incomprehensible world.

Just before we reached Pittsburg, Mr. Williams emerged, smiling, in the best of conditions and humours.

"I'm glad I slept through the trip," he said, "I don't like to have breakfast on the train. Give me your checks. There's the conductor now."

He gave the necessary directions with regard to our baggage.

A few minutes later we boarded a cab in front of Union Station and rode to the Fort Pitt Hotel.

"At least," I thought to myself, "these agents travel in style. It is less tiring, anyway."

While we had our breakfast, I remarked upon it.

"Damn it all," said Mr. Williams, "that is the least they can do for us who do their dirty work, I should think."

I looked up, rather astonished at the bitterness in his words. He laughed.

"Don't mind me, Branden," he said. "I always feel out of sorts when I am going to call on one of these suckers. But I do my best work when I'm in that frame of mind."

For the day we had nothing to do except to make sure of our arrangements. The interview was provided for; but Mr. Williams explained that we might meet with foreseen and unforeseen difficulties unless we changed the mere announcement of our visit into a definite appointment. He did that over the telephone while I stood by.

"That Mr. Kirsty?" he asked when the connection had been made. "This is Mr. Williams, from New York. You had a letter from my house announcing my call. What time do you wish me to come? Ten, you say? Well, all right, make it ten sharp. Try to be disengaged when we come. Yes, we'll be there at ten sharp."

"The fish is hooked," he said, hanging the receiver up. "Suppose we'll land him."

He yawned and stretched.

"Well, Branden," he went on, "I'm going to see friends. Want to come along?"

"If you don't mind," I replied, "I should prefer to see something of the city and its surroundings."

"Not at all," he said briefly; "suit yourself. See you some time to-day. If not, to-morrow morning at breakfast. I'll be down at eight thirty. So long."

I explored the city for the rest of the day.

Just a word about the man on whom we were going to call. His name was a synonym for enormous wealth. Mr. Kirsty was one of those Americans who, by the ruthless exploitation of preempted natural resources and of basic inventions which were useless to their inventors because they lacked the capital to exploit them had obtained a position of power and influence, such that for a while their say-so counted in certain matters for more than the voice of the commonwealth. I met a number of them in my peregrinations; and though I did not see them at their best – nor at their worst – I found that the interview which I am going to describe was typical in one respect: it shows their personal insignificance. We are apt, in our thoughts, to associate immense wealth with some nearly superhuman mental endowment. I found them to be middle-class people, in most things of no greater intelligence than the next one, and remarkable only by a certain blind, unfaltering calculation of what is to their profit. Morally they seemed neither better nor worse than the average. They were adept in seeing their advantage, and very indifferent to the higher ethics in going after it, just as most of us are, on a smaller scale. Yet, being only average people, with an average conscience, and by no means Napoleons, they had a sore soul; at heart they could not understand, nor be reconciled to, their own success. They attributed it to some form of genius before which they themselves stood in awe as if it were something imposed upon them by destiny. With most of them there was added to this a certain uneasiness which drove them to devoting millions to what they considered worthy causes – enterprises which in the opinion of any sane person should be exclusively reserved to the state. During the time that has elapsed since these things happened the Mr. Kirstys have multiplied and fattened to an amazing degree; large-scale "philanthropy" has become the fashion among multi-millionaires. I suppose, John's "Repent ye" has penetrated even the gates of gold.

When, on the decisive morning, Mr. Williams appeared for breakfast, he astonished me by the elaborate toilette he had made. He was visibly nervous and tried to hide the fact under an all-embracing, artificial jocularity. It reminded me of Mr. Tinker's nervous tension when he closed the sale to the old Irish lady. As for Mr. Williams' appearance, only a slang-word will describe it briefly: he was "dolled-up"; another slang-word will describe his frame of mind: "he was keyed up to a high pitch." Under his jocularity I sensed an irritability which was always on the point of eruption. I could not but marvel at my own calmly observant mood.

A cab was waiting outside – cars were still rare at the time and none too reliable. Watch in hand, Mr. Williams paced the lobby, stooping now and then to finger the Gladstone bag in which he carried his materials. I could not help contrasting the calm insolence in his tone when he had spoken to Mr. Kirsty over the telephone with his nervous excitement before the battle. After all there was nothing at stake beyond a commission!

At last he judged that the moment had come; picking up his bag, he nearly snarled, "Time; come on."

A few minutes later the cab stopped in front of a tall office building. We shot up to one of the upper floors.

The master of the forge seemed to roost like a bird of prey above that vast army of workers who directed the activities at the mills.

A stern-looking, simply but expensively dressed young lady of thirty received us with a questioning glace when we left the elevator and stepped into a large reception room.

Mr. Williams flicked a calling card out of his vest-pocket and said, "Mr. Kirsty expects us. I hope he is disengaged."

The young lady looked at a clock in the southern wall, between two high windows. My eyes followed hers. It was exactly ten o'clock.

The view from the windows was superb. It flew out over a veritable sea of roofs to the Monongahela River and rested beyond on the southern bank.

"If you will wait a moment," she said and turned to a tall, distinguished-looking young man who, some papers in his hand, entered the room from the east.

He glanced at the card and nodded.

The lady made a motion inviting us to follow her. We entered a long and wide corridor in which three or four more young ladies were sitting at small desks from which they operated little gates barring the way. I could not suppress a smile and an ironical thought: "Royalty is hedged about with guards!" We passed them all, the presence of our guide acting as an "Open, Sesame."

Then we entered the presence.

The room was large, fitted with rose-mahogany bookcases which completely concealed the walls. Two leather reclining chairs offered the only sitting accommodation, besides one straight-backed chair by the side of, and a swivel-chair behind, the huge, flat-topped desk in the centre of the room. The floor was covered with a deep-napped, dark-red carpet.

Behind the desk, a small, rotund man was busy. I search my brain in vain for a word to describe his activity. What he was doing seemed commonplace enough. He was bending down and impatiently opening drawer after drawer and pushing them shut again, as if searching for something that had been mislaid. But when he pushed the drawers back into place, he did it with such unnecessary energy that his movements looked as if he were, monkey-fashion, furiously jumping up and down.

Then I saw his pale, flat-featured face with the small, knob-like nose, framed in carefully brushed, perfumed, and yet straggling grey whiskers.

The expensive clothes, though freshly pressed, were hanging about him as if carelessly dropped in a pile and by chance caught up on something resembling the ill-shaped figure of a man. There was something shaggy about his appearance. That was a multi-millionaire.

When he raised himself, he shot a glance at the young lady who had been standing in front of us, in the attitude of quiet, expectant deference.

She stepped forward and, without a word, laid our cards on the desk before him.

He nodded and bent down again, without paying the slightest attention to us.

The young lady left the room.

Mr. Williams, with an air of self-possessed insolence, stepped up to the desk, put his bag on the straight-backed chair, opened it and straightened. He looked back at me and winked.

I, too, approached; we waited.

At last Mr. Kirsty seemed to give up his search. He pulled his watch from his vest-pocket – it did not come quite readily, and I could hardly keep from smiling at his impatient jerk. Then we heard his singularly high-pitched, querulous voice.

"Well," he said, "I can give you just five minutes."

But Williams cut in with a note of indignant protest. "Mr. Kirsty," he said, "we have come from New York in order to give you the privilege of acquiring one of the remaining four sets of a work which some of your friends considered it an honour to possess."

"Well, what is it?" asked Mr. Kirsty ill-humouredly.

"If you cannot devote more than five minutes to a proposition like ours," Mr. Williams continued, "I prefer to take the next train home."

"Well, well," Mr. Kirsty said as if speaking to a child, but still with that querulous note, "you know I am a very busy man."

"So am I," Mr. Williams rejoined; "I cannot afford deliberately to waste five minutes of my time and energy."

"How if you saw my secretary?" Mr. Kirsty tried to evade.

"Your secretary," Mr. Williams said, this time with a smile and a bow, "unfortunately is not on the list of persons to whom we offer this work."

No smile on Mr. Kirsty's face betrayed the conquest which these words had made. He dropped into his swivel-chair and made a motion to Mr. Williams to be seated; to me no attention was paid.

"It is not necessary, of course," Mr. Williams began, "to speak of the work itself. The names of the men who are responsible for it are sufficient."

He laid down a list of the authors.

"I will briefly explain how it is got up. The text is printed in one thousand copies, strictly limited. The sets are numbered. When the work appeared, there was a natural rush upon it. We held on to the first impressions and are, therefore, able to offer you number eight in a binding selected by yourself. It goes without saying that hand-made paper is used; the illustrations are hand-painted, the print a beautiful Aldine type with hand-illuminated capitals at the beginning of each chapter."

Sample pages were spread out in front of the prospect.

"As to the bindings, no two sets, and in a set no two volumes are bound alike. The higher numbers are bound in morocco; about twenty sets were held for parchment bindings, gold-embossed. Each binding is an exact reproduction of some famous book-cover from the middle-ages, copied by artists whom we have sent abroad expressly for this work."

He spread out a number of cuts.

"These are the photographs of the bindings which are available. As I said, four sets remain unsold. We shall take pleasure in binding the set which we are holding for you, number eight, in whatever covers you may select."

Mr. Kirsty did not touch the sheets; but he shot an occasional glance at them while he listened.

"Nine hundred and ninety-six sets have been disposed of," Mr. Williams went on. "I have a complete list of the subscribers before me. The buyers of the higher numbers would, of course, not interest you. Here is the list of the one hundred first sets with the names of their holders."

For the first time Mr. Kirsty reached out for what was offered to his inspection. He scanned the list not without interest. "These people," he said in his high-pitched voice which lost its querulous note, "you say have the set? An interesting list. How long have the books been on the market?"

"Six months, I should say," Mr. Williams replied.

"How is it," Mr. Kirsty complained, the querulous note creeping back into his accents, "that I receive this offer only after the greater number of the sets have been sold?"

"You own fault, Mr. Kirsty," smiled Mr. Williams in an amiable tone; "we wrote you about it before number one was off the press. It is our rule never to call except on appointment. At the same time, you see, we were holding this set for you because we knew you for a connoisseur and a lover of rare prints. The moment we received your card we also made bold to reserve for you what we considered the finest of all our bindings. If I may offer a suggestion on a point or two, I shall lay out for your approval what Mr. Wilbur and myself were thinking of when we had your call."

He laid out a set of twenty photographs which covered the desk.

Mr. Kirsty meanwhile went back once more to a careful scrutiny of the list of subscribers. The thought in his mind, though no doubt it remained unconscious, interpreted itself to me in about these terms, "It is a comfort, after all, if I am going to be taken in, to be in such company. I wonder whether this list is according to facts? There is the name of my friend, Mrs. So-and-so. I might call her up over the wire; but it is not necessary, these fellows know that I might do that; they would not dare to put her name down unless she had bought the books."

What he said, was, "How about the price?"

"Fourteen," Mr. Williams replied with an accent of apology as if ashamed that it was not more. "You see," he went on, "the cost is, of course, quite out of proportion to the intrinsic and the rarity value of the set. We are not dealers. We are craftsmen. We do not raise the price according to the demand. We could actually make money by selling to speculators. That is not our way of doing business."

"You say this set will have to be bound for me?" Mr. Kirsty asked; and at last he was actually looking at the photographs.

"Yes," Mr. Williams replied, laying down an order blank.

Mr. Kirsty got to his feet. "Well," he said, once more in his querulous and impatient tone, and beginning to work at his drawers again, "I suppose it is all right. Send the set along. What is this?" he added, picking up the order sheet and glancing at it. He handed it back to Mr. Williams "My word is as good as my bond," he said, not without the punctilio of the small mind.

"Of course," Mr. Williams agreed with a bow of apology.

He quickly gathered his belongings, except the photographs and the partial list of subscribers which Mr. Kirsty seemed to hang on to, bowed once more, and left the office, with me following on his heels.

The cab was waiting. The interview had taken half an hour. It had filled me with scruples and puzzling thoughts. But I could see at a glance that Mr. Williams was not in a mood to resolve my difficulties. He was in that state of complete relaxation which I had observed once before, though to a lesser degree, in Mr. Tinker. When we got back to the hotel, he hurried up to his room and threw himself on a lounge.

At dinner-time, however, I could not repress one question.

"How is it," I asked, "that the house is still engaging agents when only four more sets remain to be sold?"

Mr. Williams gave me a look of dumbfounded surprise and then laughed for a moment so uproariously that I felt the colour rising to the roots of my hair.

Then he turned to the waiter and ordered a glass of milk. When the waiter brought it, he pushed it over to me. "Want a bottle," he asked, "with nipple attached?"

I reined in my anger. Mr. Williams was beneath my resentment.

When we boarded the night-train, Mr. Williams was in a state of complete intoxication.

SIX

I Land Somewhere

M R. WILBUR," I said earnestly when I faced him for the third time in his office, "will you let me go out selling the popular edition?"

"Well," he said hesitatingly, "I have nothing to do with the sale of that edition. I suppose you could easily enough get in with those people. But what are your reasons for wishing to drop the de-luxe set?"

"I do not know whether I can discuss that with you," I replied. "What I do know is that I can sell the book on its merits, quite apart from any bibliophile considerations."

"Certainly," Mr. Wilbur agreed. "But you can sell the de-luxe edition on its merits just as well, in spite of all the bibliophile considerations." He smiled at my quaint wording while repeating it. "The point is this: can you sell the books to people who have more money than is good for them? I think you can; if I am right, you should do so; for your own good as well as ours." He looked at me, searchingly, it seemed; and puzzled, too. "Let me clear up a point," he went on. "I suppose it was a mistake to send you out with Williams. He happened to be handy, that is all. Williams is a good enough fellow as they go; but I am afraid he is rather a snob, and apparently he has displeased you."

"It isn't Mr. Williams," I replied. "I should not choose him for my friend, no matter what he might be doing. But

I do not expect to find on your staff only men who are congenial to me."

'Well," said Mr. Wilbur, "what is it?"

"If you must know," I yielded to his insistence, though it exasperated me, "it's the method. I'll give you one example. Mr. Williams stated to Mr. Kirsty that there were just four sets of the edition left."

Mr. Wilbur laughed; then he frowned. "But permit me, my dear Mr. Branden," he said; "we are not responsible for what one of our agents says in order to clinch a sale. Mr. Williams directed us to ship a set to Mr. Kirsty, at fourteen hundred dollars. We do so because we have no reason to doubt that the sale was made in a perfectly regular way. There, as far as we are concerned, the matter ends, provided we receive, in due time, a cheque for the amount. Do not for a moment believe that I countenance sharp practice. We want you to sell the books. We pay you a very liberal commission for doing so. In return you have to work out your own plans. This is a different proposition from the Travellogues. We do not ask you to memorize a canvass and to deliver it letter-perfect. Our customers would not stand for such crude methods. I am sure you can sell the books. If you do not think so, that is entirely your own business. I do not ask you to say anything that is not strictly conformable to your own standards of honesty. We have never yet heard a complaint from a customer who bought the books from Mr. Williams. He is one of our most successful salesmen. I know he is making a fortune. I do not enquire into his selling methods, though what you tell me shocks me greatly. But I have nothing whatever to do with that end of it. Should a customer complain, on the grounds of misrepresentation, we should simply ask him to return the set at our expense; and we should refund the money. That seems perfectly fair, does it not? You say you can sell the books on its merits. Very well, do so. I think you have the appearance and the approach, the tact, let me say, to sell to a class of people who, as a rule, do not buy

books in order to read them. They buy as collectors, probably as collectors who do not know very much about what
they are collecting. They do it because it is fashionable.
Others buy rare etchings, paintings, or precious stones.
We merely give you, if you want to look at it that way, an
additional selling-point. But we do not object at all to
selling the books for the purpose of being read. They are
good enough to be read; that is more than can be said of a
great many other books sold in the same way. I am in this
business in order to make money; I am glad to say that I
am making it. I sell a high-priced de-luxe edition for one
reason only; there is more money in doing so than there is
in selling a popular set. There is nothing unethical in
supplying a demand, is there, now?"

"I suppose not," I sighed. I could see no flaw in Mr.
Wilbur's reasoning. "You make me feel as if I owed you an
apology."

"Not at all," Mr. Wilbur replied. "I understand your
attitude perfectly. As I said, it was a mistake to send you
out with Mr. Williams. But I did not know it myself."

"When do you want me to start?" I asked.

Mr. Wilbur smiled good-naturedly. "That sounds better,"
he said and pressed a button, waiting for his secretary.

"Miss Donahue," he said when she entered, "what was
that enquiry we had from a New England doctor?"

"Oh," she said, "Dr. Watson, Willowtown, Connecticut."

"That's the man. Please announce Mr. Branden's visit to
him. For Thursday, let me say. Will that suit you, Mr.
Branden?"

"Certainly," I said, "if I can reach him by that time."

"Yes; you run down to New Haven and make connections there. All right then, Miss Donahue. Better send the
letter at once."

There the matter of my scruples ended for the time
being. I spent the night in New Haven, and the next day
made a small manufacturing town in central Connecticut.

The following morning I engaged a team and had myself driven out to a small residential village which had all the charms of a New England hillside.

I found the doctor in, though he did not expect me.

"You did not get my wire?" he asked when I gave him my name.

He was a tall, strong, active man with the pleasantest face and a brilliant smile which bared gold-glittering teeth.

"Too bad," he said. "The day after I wrote to your house I bought a farm. That ties me up. I could not think of buying books at the present time; much as my fingers itch for them. I did not think either that they would send a man expressly to see me."

"Don't let that worry you, doctor," I replied. "It does not matter. But since I am here, I should like to show you what I have got."

He looked at his watch. "Why yes," he said. "I'll be glad to listen. Come in."

I gave him a strong canvass on the work itself.

"That is the gem," I said at last, "now comes the setting. But I don't know whether to go on. Maybe I am taking up your time?"

He laughed. "Seems to me I'm taking up yours," he said. "I like to listen to you. You know the books."

He followed my explanations like a child, frequently stopping me to look again at a photograph or a sample page, and exclaiming delightedly whenever something struck his fancy.

"How much of a fortune does that thing cost?" he enquired at last.

I stated the prices of the various bindings.

He was full of regret. "Too bad," he repeated. "Too bad. But I can't think of it. Not at present."

"Maybe at some future time," I suggested; "if we are not sold out by then."

"Yes, yes," he said. "They won't let a book like that run out of print. They'll get up a cheap edition when this one is exhausted. I must have another chance at it." He was pensive for a few seconds. "Say," he went on, "can you offer a set to anybody else? A college-friend of mine happens to be in town. You know him by name; Mr. ———— " He named a member of Mr. Harrison's entourage who stood even then rather high in Federal politics and who has since been directing the nation's destinies. "I should like to give him a chance to look at this. Would you show it to him?"

"I might," I said.

"Good. Wait a moment. I'll call him up and tell him about it."

"Sure," he said when he came back. "He wants you to come right up. It will be noon when you get through. Come back here and have dinner at the house. I know Mrs. Watson will be delighted. I'll put you on the road. Meanwhile I shall have to make a call myself."

He reached for his hat and satchel, and we went out.

I had a most pleasant interview with the young statesman. I gave him the same talk as Dr. Watson and showed him the different bindings more as the appropriate setting of something which was worthy of being set well, than as the thing which in itself constituted what I had to sell. Nor did I, when I had finished, press a sale.

The young statesman's brother, with whom he visited, came in, a tall man in the prime of life whose sparse body contrasted strangely with that of my prospect who was even then inclined to obesity. This brother was a scholar, a member of one of the leading universities.

The conversation at once became general, with European conditions for its theme.

When I rose, stating that the Watsons expected me for dinner, the statesman asked me a few questions about the work and finally requested me to have one of the five hundred dollar sets forwarded to his brother's address, signing a contract by which he agreed to pay for it in five instalments of one hundred dollars each. I was not prepared for any such arrangement but judged that I could safely accept it on my own responsibility.

An equally pleasant dinner-hour followed at Dr. Watson's. When, there, too, I rose to go, the doctor asked me whether I could show the prospectus to still another friend of his, the station agent of the village. I hesitated this time, but agreed that no harm could come from showing him.

I went to see the agent.

A tall, elderly man received me, saying with a laugh that Dr. Watson had set his ears atingle with talking of the books.

I told him I was transgressing my authority in showing him the set; but, since I had done so already in selling the young statesman, I thought it only right to repeat the offence.

"You sold him, eh?" he said. And when I had given him my canvass, he jumped up and exclaimed, "I must have that thing. Excuse me a moment, will you?" and disappeared into the rooms beyond.

When he returned, he stated that he had talked it over with his wife.

"Tell you what I'll do," he said. "I take the cheapest set, of course. It's the books I want, not the bindings. I'll give you a cheque for fifty dollars now, one hundred on delivery, and the balance when it suits me within ninety days. That should be satisfactory."

I thought so; the sale was closed.

I sent a wire to Mr. Wilbur, and set out for New York, which I reached the following day.

I felt a trifle uneasy about these sales. The question of partial payments had never been mentioned.

To my astonishment Mr. Wilbur did not waste a word on that side of the question. He simply congratulated me on my success. But he disapproved of my having sold at the lowest figure.

"It is just as easy," he kept repeating, "to sell an eight or nine hundred dollar set as a five hundred dollar one. There is a weakness. The edition being limited, it means a loss to us if we have to part with a set at the lowest figure. I suppose you will get over that. You have made no promise with regard to the numbers?"

"None," I said laughingly, for I could not remember having said a word about the limited nature of the edition.

I was immediately sent out again, this time with three addresses, in Cleveland, Lansing, and Grand Rapids. Within a week I returned, having wasted my time, energy and money, for I did not bring an order. When I set out on this trip, I had a little over a hundred and fifty dollars; when I came back I had less than fifty.

Mr. Wilbur was perfectly polite about it.

"You can't always sell, that goes without saying. Don't worry. We have to find out what class of people contains your customers."

"Scholars," I said promptly.

Mr. Wilbur rubbed his forehead with a rueful smile. "The trouble is, few scholars will buy our set. They are, as a rule, not blessed with worldly goods."

"Have you any calls for me on hand?" I enquired.

"I don't know," he answered. "We have a number of cards; but I believe they are more in the line of some of our other agents. We better wait a day or so."

I took courage. "Mr. Wilbur," I said, leaning forward. "Suppose I strike out for myself?"

"What do you mean? Work on a straight canvass?"

"Yes," I replied. "The only two orders which I have brought in so far were obtained on a straight canvass."

"I don't believe you'd get the orders."

"I feel sure of it."

"People have learned to distrust the agent who comes around and offers expensive things."

"They do not mistrust me."

"Where would you want to go?"

"New England," I said. "Let me try. I'll go out for two weeks. I shall not ask you for any money beyond my commissions. If I do not land an order within two weeks, I'll come in and acknowledge defeat."

"Very well," he agreed; "we'll try."

Accordingly I ran down to New Haven again.

Spring was advancing; my feeling of insecurity was submerged in the enjoyment of landscape and salt-air. I took long trolley-rides and cross-country drives. I was nearly at the end of my funds when I took quarters at Waterbury, the city of watches. I even remember the Elton Hotel at which I stopped.

Again I made two sales in one day; one to a young, rising manufacturer in the city; the other to a school-superintendent somewhere in the Naugatuck Valley. The latter was an approval-sale; but it stood. Again both orders were for the cheapest set; and both were obtained strictly on the merits of the work. The commissions pulled me out of a difficulty, for I could not have liquidated my bill at the hotel without selling the remainder of my wardrobe had I not made a sale in the nick of time.

There was really no necessity for me to patronize the best hotels. There was no reason either why I should have taken a Pullman-seat for every train-ride. But such is the power of suggestion in this land of waste that it never occurred to me to do otherwise. Mr. Williams had succeeded in linking the work up with high living.

Thus, for the time being, Mr. Wilbur acquiescing in my ways, I settled down once more into something of a routine. Orders came, but they came sparingly; they paid for my living. Thus I explain the fact that details of my work are lacking henceforth in my memory of the season's activities.

Again I read a good deal; and, since my income seemed to keep pace with my expenditures, no matter how much or how little I spent – I simply lived up to my income – I began to read, not only magazines, but books.

I roamed the New England coast. I remember summer days at Old Orchard Beach, a cruise or so in Casco Bay, drowsy mornings in Cape Cod fishing-hamlets; altogether a summer which resembled a holiday of my old days in Europe more than American "hustling". I was due for an awakening.

The time of the first anniversary of my immigration came around. This occasion brought with it retrospection and the onlooker's criticism. What had I gained? A little knowledge beyond the lines of that book-learning with which I had been equipped before I came. Graft and Sharp Practice I had become familiar with. To the types of Hannan and Howard and to that of Tinker, a third one had been added and stood out in sharp relief; that of the snob, of the newly-rich. And he, take it all-in-all, was merely one of the dupes of the former two. The immigrant sees only that which strikes him forcibly.

Where did I stand, I personally? I closed my eyes to this question. I felt a curious world-weariness from which I tried to escape by immerging myself in a languid sort of sympathy with nature. This sentimental response to Nature's moods, however, could not last; it might do in summer-time; but winter was going to come. Then I should be thrown again with men, living men or man embalmed in books.

I must record an adventure which was entirely an adventure with books.

I have already mentioned that I had conceived a great love for Lincoln. There is nothing strange about a young man's enthusiasm for a hero of history. It was not that. My enthusiasm had little to do with the man's achievements; it had little in common with the American boy's school-fostered hero-worship. It was a passion which took hold of me, a passion which longed for self-effacement. Had Lincoln been among the living, I should have been glad to walk across a continent in order to be near him, to serve him, unbeknown to himself. The fact that he had been assassinated seemed an enormity far beyond the mere enormity of an ordinary murder, such as in itself to make the idea of a Providence a mere mockery. The smallest of his words seemed pregnant with the innermost being of the man. There was a truth and a simplicity about every statement of his, far beyond the powers of any statesman of Europe; all others seemed to be fops as compared with him. His speeches I knew by heart; his features were as familiar and present to me as the reflection of my face in the glass. To him I applied what Wordsworth had said of Milton.

Was Lincoln an accident? Was there in this America a soil from which he had grown? I had not found it. If there was, to find it should be the task of my life.

One day something terrible happened; that is to say, it seemed terrible to me. In my miscellaneous reading I ran across an account of Matthew Arnold's visit to America. Arnold had called at the White House in Washington; and, from the great height of his European "culture" had coolly broken the staff over Lincoln by calling him "crude". A horror seized me when I read that, a horror as may seize a man, a clean, honest, straight-thinking man, when he listens in while some grotesque miscarriage of justice is being enacted. I remember how I got up, searched for Arnold's "Essays in Criticism", and threw them into the fire-place of my hotel-room after touching a match to it. By this word, by this judgment Arnold had broken the staff, not over Lincoln, but over himself; and not only over himself, but over that whole culture-medium from which he came; and quite consciously I took the word "culture-medium" in its bacteriological sense as a name for Europe's spiritual atmosphere; it seemed to express so well what I thought of Europe at the moment.

This afternoon marked an epoch in my life. Like a flash-light, suddenly turned on some figure standing veiled in the dark, it illuminated for me that which I was searching for: the real America. In its light my whole past and present stood condemned.

I remember also that I thought ruefully of the fact that only a few months ago I had used Arnold's very word in condemnation of what I had seen of this New World. I am afraid there was still a good deal of spiritual pride even in this attitude. Unconsciously I was classing myself side by side with Lincoln, as opposed to that part of America which had wounded and hurt me. I looked down at my clothes; I looked at my present life; I longed to be on the hills and the plains, clad in rags, feeling at one with the clouds and the stars, with beetling mountain-cliff and hollow in the ground.

This day changed my aims; though not with any immediate effect; it cut me loose from Europe.

By a sort of inertia I went on for some time longer. My moorings were loosened, it is true; but it took the riving thunderbolt to sever them completely.

A more or less immediate effect of my mental preoccupations was that my sales fell off. At last, in the height of summer, I was in debt again. For a week or two I had to use my drawing account to tide me over.

I went to New York to talk matters over.

Mr. Wilbur received me. He seemed a changed man, nervous, exhausted; I attributed it to my bad record.

"You seem to be going to pieces," he said. "We'll have to look into that. For the moment I want you to go north with Mr. Williams once more."

"The fact is, I have troubles and worries of my own," I said. "My work will pick up again."

"Your work has been good on the whole," Mr. Wilbur replied. "I believe you are too much alone. So long as a salesman averages one or two orders a month, we have nothing to complain of. As it happens, we have three enquiries from up-state. I have special reasons why I want you to go with Williams. I can't explain. A situation may arise with which one man alone may not be able to cope."

"I'm willing, of course," I said. "I'll do anything you wish me to do. But might it not be better to give us full details?"

"No," he replied. "I prefer not to explain."

Williams and I took a day-train for the ten-hours' run. Mostly we read; occasionally we talked. Naturally, when we conversed, we "talked shop". To my surprise, Mr. Williams intimated his intention of leaving Mr. Wilbur and going into business on his own account. He, too, seemed nervous and apprehensive. I could not understand it at all.

"This scheme has been overworked," he said. "It's time to quit."

"Do you mean to say that there is no market any longer?"

Mr. Williams laughed that contemptuous laugh whose sting I knew so well. "Market? There's no end of the market in sight. There's one born every minute, you know. But I think it's getting dangerous to plant three sets in one small town. Wilbur is getting gay; it's time to cut loose."

A sinking feeling took hold of me. Thus, I suppose, the aviator feels when he realizes that he has lost control of his plane.

"I have an idea," Williams went on, pensively, "that Wilbur knows it, too; he wants to grab what is in sight and to retire. He's made a pretty penny, God knows. I have an idea that I can do as well; and I want to do it on the level. I'm not afraid of work, as Wilbur has always been."

"Just a moment," I said, "Do you mean to say that this thing is not on the level?"

"This? What? Wilbur's scheme?" he asked and chuckled. "You're green, Branden. But I do like your innocence. I'll tell you. Just listen to this. Wilbur sells through agents; he prefers such as you. If he sold through the mails, the Post-office authorities would get him. He probably gave you a lot of hot air about his unwillingness to let you go out on a straight canvass. You mustn't believe all he says. He wants the innocent ones. He's got half a dozen or more like yourself; don't think for a moment you are the only one; you're not. He's glad when he gets your kind. He'd drop me like a red-hot poker if I didn't know too much about him. More than that, I've been thinking he must be up to some trick since he sends you out with me again. He says of course, you've gone to pieces and need jacking-up. But three calls from one town, that seems fishy. I had half a mind to give him the slip and not run up at all."

"Mr. Williams," I said, "I am dense, I suppose. Would you mind telling me just where the trick in all this lies?"

I feel sure it was merely pity with my lack of experience which induced Mr. Williams to vouchsafe the desired information. I give him credit for being more kind-hearted than I had thought him to be.

He gave a short laugh and went on, "Not at all. In the first place, the so-called de-luxe edition is nothing but the so-called popular set. Wilbur merely buys, at wholesale prices – at twenty-four dollars, to be exact – some one or two hundred sets of that edition, whatever he may think he needs. He tears the buckram bindings off and sticks his bindings on, after having added a flyleaf with the famous number."

"But the Holland paper?" I broke in, incredulous in the face of such a revelation.

Mr. Williams sat up and looked reproachfully across at me. "Ever seen a set?" he asked.

"No," I replied; "come to think of it, I never have. I've seen only empty bindings."

"Of course," Mr. Williams nodded. "The paper is deckle-edged; but it is machine-made right here in this state of New York. Do you know Van Geldern when you see it?"

"I do," I said.

"Well," he went on; "this looks like it. But search for the water-mark, and you won't find it. Anybody who really knows paper feels the difference on the spot. He has never yet sold to a paper-man."

"And the hand-painted illustrations?"

"Down there, at their office, they have some fifty young ladies sitting who colour the half-tones at the rate of twenty an hour, or the boss wants to know the reason why. Water-colours, same as coloured picture-cards."

I was speechless and did not dare to enquire about the bindings, for fear of having to listen to more such revelations. But Mr. Williams was heartless now.

"The whole thing is a con-game on a gigantic scale, operated with the help of two factors," he said, "the gullibility of the well-to-do, and the innocence of milk-sops as yourself. Of course, there's something genuine about it, or you poor fish would not bite. Why, he's been selling this thing through such as yourself for six or ten years, at all kinds of prices, getting rich on the fat of the land. He shows you the bindings, and they are the only thing that's worth a tinker's damn in the whole get-up. He has to spend some fifty dollars or so a set on that. As for myself, I've been in it so long I've got used to it; while I'm making money, I have no kick. The public seems satisfied to be bled. Only, I can't understand why he is getting so darn careless. Three sets in a small town, that's more than I should risk, with the whole U.S. full of suckers to choose from . At least, when you're screwing the prices up so that it amounts to wholesale robbery."

"Well," I objected, "if the thing were honest otherwise, I could not see anything wrong in it if he sold every citizen in a one-horse town of five hundred."

"Greed I call it," exclaimed Mr. Williams. "People are bound to get together in the long run and compare notes. Duplications in numbers are apt to crop out."

"Duplications?" I asked stupidly.

"Of course," he said. "You don't for a moment fall for that gaff about a limited edition, do you? The thing has been sold, as I said, for more than six years. The swallowing capacity of the public is its only limit. At first Wilbur may not have thought of going beyond a thousand copies at a hundred and fifty per. But the first fifty thousand which he cleared came too easily. He branched out, got a sumptuous office, a car, and so on. He actually seemed to fill a demand. I tell you, whenever he steps out, he'll first salt down a cool million or so."

After this, we did not talk any longer. I felt as if the earth under my feet had given way. I could have cried with blind fury.

We were passing through the landscape of the upper part of the state. A year ago I had passed through it, too, on my first, ill-fated trip to New York. I thought of that trip and of what the interval had brought. Sometimes to-day, in thinking back, over the gulf of the years, of the days of my childhood, I feel a similar contrast. Joy, innocence, the length of days, the unbounded confidence in myself, all that is gone. Weariness, the rapid succession of seasons, a doubtful appraisal of myself – that is what has taken its place. I had no eyes for the Adirondacks, none for river-valley and gorge. Again there was a veil of gloom over everything, that smoky haze which had lain over Hudson River and Palisades, that morning in Riverside Park. Where did I stand? What was I to do?

I thought of the orders which I had taken during the spring and early summer. The enjoyment of those rambles through the New England hills was spoiled even in memory. I could not think of Dr. Watson and his friends but with shame. Why was it that the memory of pleasant encounters had to be soiled and sullied for me through none of my fault? Was I indeed destined to be ground to pieces?

I was not going to partake in the business at our destination. But I had a return-ticket and, therefore, might just as well go on and sit in the train as anywhere else. It was just that: I did no longer dare to touch anything. If with my best intentions I had succeeded only in becoming the involuntary accomplice of a swindler, what was I to do? Already a year and more of my life on American soil had been hopelessly wasted!

We arrived in our town and registered in the best hotel.

Strange to say, after supper even Williams seemed to be in a softer mood than was usual with him. I told him I was not going to go on with it.

"I don't know as I blame you," he said. "But listen here, Branden. Come along with me to-morrow. I feel shaky myself. I'll consider it as a favour. Since you've come along so far, don't leave me just now. I was a fool to come out. Hunches are nonsense of course. But I'm unnerved. To you nothing can happen, you know."

"If it's any help to you," I said, "I'll see you through."

"Thanks," he replied.

Nobody could have said that I had had no warning.

Next morning Mr. Williams arranged for an interview with one of our three prospects. The hour named was three o'clock in the afternoon.

When we arrived at the address, a stenographer took our cards into an inner office. We were told to enter.

The room into which we came was a small, private office, the greater part of the floor-space being taken up by a large flat-topped desk in golden oak. At the centre of one side of it sat a heavy man with clean-shaven face and short-cropped grey hair. Opposite him sat two men, one tall and slender, the other medium-sized and somewhat stout; both were reclining in arm-chairs; the taller of the two was smoking.

I felt at once that a storm was in the air when I saw the three pairs of eyes which were fixed upon us as we entered.

"Mr. Williams?" the one who sat by himself enquired, rising.

Mr. Williams acknowledged his identity by shaking hands.

"And Mr. Branden?" the man went on turning to me. Then he named his two friends by way of introduction.

The three men on whom we were to call were assembled here! That could not possibly be without significance.

"Whom of you two am I to address?" the man at the desk asked with a smile. "Or do you both represent the North American Historians?"

I noticed that the taller one of the other two had drawn a sheet of foolscap towards himself; he was ready to take notes.

"I am responsible here," said Mr. Williams, turning pale; "Mr. Branden has just severed his connection with the house. He came along as my friend."

"Well, Mr. Williams," the stranger went on, "will you be kind enough to answer a few questions?"

"I don't understand," said Williams. "I came to give you particulars about a set of books you were supposed to be interested in."

The stranger laughed. "I have the books," he said. "We all three have the books, and you know it." A motion of his hand embraced his two friends on the opposite side of the desk.

"That so?" said Mr. Williams with remarkable coolness. "I hope you like them."

The three men laughed.

"We do," the spokesman replied. "But, as I have said before, I have a question or two which I should like to have answered."

"Shoot," said Williams.

"You are selling a limited edition, are you not?"

"We are, of sorts,"

"The sets are numbered?"

"They are."

"A strange thing has cropped out; quite by chance, as such things are apt to do."

"What is it?" Williams was getting impatient.

"This gentleman there and myself we have both the same number."

"What is the number?" Williams shot back.

"Fourteen," came the answer.

Williams laughed lightly. "But, gentlemen," he said, "perhaps you are aware of the fact that quite a few people are superstitious and would not accept a set with the number thirteen. So it is our rule, in limited editions, to duplicate either the twelve or the fourteen."

The three men laughed again.

"You've got your nerve with you," the spokesman said at last. "If you can explain the other difficulties away as slickly as you did this one, we'll let you off; just for the fun of it. It was rather a mistake," he went on, turning to his friends, "to let these fellows know beforehand what it was about. They've had plenty of time to prepare their excuses."

When Williams heard this remark, he sat up.

"What's that?" he snapped. "Did you write in to head-quarters about your complaints?"

Again the three men laughed.

"Did we?" asked one of them.

But Williams was on his feet now. He bent forward with such an expression of earnestness on his face that their laughter died out.

"Gentlemen," he said, "I'll be brief. You have been the victims of a crooked game. I am only an agent. You don't want to get me; you want to get the crook."

"And let you skip? Not much. You sell the books. It's you we've got. We'll trace the rest of the gang through you."

"Never mind about me," Williams shouted. "I'll turn state's evidence. I'll help you all I can. I was willing enough to shield the fellow; but now I tell you, get Wilbur before it's too late."

"How too late?"

"Don't you see that he is making his get-away?"

"How can you know unless you're in with him yourself?"

"By putting two and two together, gentlemen. For God's sake, don't waste time. Don't you see?" He spoke faster and faster. "Neither I nor Branden here were told anything at the New York office except that there were three prospects in this town. He sent us out because by doing so he kept you from going right after him and at the same time he got rid of us at New York. The dirty beggar tried to play us off for a chance to skip and to cover his tracks. He uses his agents and gets them into a beastly mess and expects them besides to go to jail for him. Take Branden here. Why did he send him up? Because he is innocent. Till yesterday he did not know that every word in the gaff he gives the suckers isn't gospel-truth. When I told him, he refused to go on with the work. I had a hunch that we should have trouble, and I begged him to come along, or he wouldn't be here. I'll turn state's evidence. But get him, Wilbur, the tricky skunk!"

He had spoken with such convincing vehemence that, when he finished, every one in the room was on his feet.

"I'll go," said the taller one of the friends and reached for his hat. "Wait for me here."

An anticlimax followed. Williams explained in detail how the scheme was worked. When the tall man returned they told me, after a short discussion conducted in a whisper, that they had agreed to leave me out of the proceedings. But for the time being I remained with them, for I was curious how things would develop.

Two hours later a messenger-boy appeared and handed the tall man a yellow envelope.

He tore it open, shrugged, and said, "Williams was right. The bird is flown."

SEVEN

I Wind Things Up

IF I HAD REMAINED cool under the blow received, or if I had naturally possessed a great presence of mind, I should not have returned to New York; my whole future life might have run along different lines. But I was – and still am – of that slow-moving type to whom the good repartees occur when the conversation is over and who, after the debate, think of all the clever things they might have said. I was the very antipode of Mr. Williams.

So, on the morning following the crash, I took the train back to New York.

The trip was a fiery ordeal. I was in Purgatory or in worse than that. If I call it by the milder name, it is because I have lived through and beyond it, though I have not risen to Heaven yet.

I kept repeating this one question: "Why?" There were the Bennetts, the Watsons, and many others. Why did not I stand on their side? Why was it that everlastingly I remained the outcast? "Why?"

The question offered no comfort. The answer might do that.

I had been trying to cast anchor somewhere; and whenever I thought I had done so, I was cut adrift again.

People who are born and raised and grow up and run their course of life in the same community or at least in the same country are borne along by the current of a river. They may cut slantways across the current, changing their position relatively to the banks. Still the current of the general activities carries them on and forward. Only the criminal classes strive against the current. I, the immigrant, was trying to cut straight across. *I was cross-sectioning the life of a nation.* The current was not a helping, it was an impeding factor. A submerged rock or an eddy, the anomalous conditions in the current, offered the only help: they were the anomalous conditions in society. I, cross-sectioning it, got caught in the eddy, held on to the rocks obstructing the flow.

If I had not found something like this rhetorical figure, some simile for my experience, I should have mistaken for the current itself what was merely a ripple on its surface.

I did not arrive at any very definite conclusion during that trip in the train. Yet, I remember, there was some vague idea of "breaking away" which seemed to give comfort by holding out possibilities. This idea was linked up with my reading. The magazines of that time – they were neither so numerous nor so clearly differentiated as they are now – were full of the realization of a great change coming over the country. America was fast changing from an agricultural country into an industrial one. I read a good deal about abandoned farms. The development was viewed with alarm by many. But over against that movement towards the industrial centres – with its mad rush for wealth – there was being born another movement which I can probably best characterize by stating a fact of literary history: John Burroughs was coming into his own. I was a young man, not yet twenty-six. My knowledge of American lettres was neither deep nor extended enough for me to form a clear view of the significance of these synchronous counter-currents. But it was the time when you went "out west". I had only a hazy idea of what that meant, especially in a non-geographical sense; or I might have gone "out west" in the east.

Underlying this western exodus, this phenomenal growth of western communities, and also that literary movement which for me crystallized in Burroughs' name there was a movement of vastly greater significance which has not yet, not nearly, reached its peak. It was the movement away from the accidentals of life and towards the essentials. It was a desire for a simplification of issues. Modern life is not essentially more complicated than the life of old. It is nonsense to assert such a thing. But, what is commonly called civilization is indeed a movement from the essentials to the accidentals. To hear modern economists talk, you would think that the problem of transportation were the problem of life. Through too rapid progress along one line we have lost the real perspective, that is all. In that mistaken sense I consider "Civilization" as a chronic disease of mankind which every now and then breaks out into some such acute insanity as the late war. I saw these things by no means as clearly then as I see them to-day; which may not be any too clearly yet, even though I have stripped myself pretty well of that encumbrance which is commonly called learning and which would be more accurately defined as Thinking-in-Ruts. I dimly felt a desire to do something, to get away from things, to simplify them, to remodel myself and my life. The question of that soil which I had for the first time clearly formulated for myself when I felt at outs with the world, at Niagara, assumed such proportions that I felt I had to do something very definite about it. Still, and that is typical for the immigrant as well as for the young, the search remained a geographical search.

Before I got back to the city, I had another adventure with books. It is significant for my state of mind, for my utter loneliness and my mental dependency, that so often my most vital decisions arose from what I read rather than from things which grew out of the personal contact with living men and women.

When I had started up-state, I had picked at random one of my few remaining books and slipped it into my pocket. In going, I had bought a magazine; in returning I had not done so because I no longer dared to spend even that much money unnecessarily.

At last, when I was weary of following my own thoughts, I took this book out of my pocket. It happened to be Carlyle's Sartor Resartus. I felt half annoyed to find that what I had taken along was something so well known to me that it could hardly contain a line with a new message. Yet, when I opened it, much as our forefathers or foremothers used to open their bibles with a pin, to find a guiding word to help them in their perplexities, a sentence seemed to leap out of the page, of such import to me, of such personal application to my very needs, that it came like a revelation.

The sentence was this:

"The fraction of Life can be increased in value not so much by increasing your numerator as by lessening your denominator."

Here was said what interpreted for me the phrase "going out west". It seemed uncanny. I was looking for guidance, and guidance had been vouchsafed. I was going to lessen my denominator.

What I found by way of interpretation was this –

In elementary physics the efficiency of a machine is often defined as a fraction: Work out over work in. This fraction can be raised in value by increasing the "work out" while the "work in" remains unchanged: or, by lessening the "work in" while the "work out" is kept at the same level.

The personal satisfaction, the amount of contentment, the ratio of joy to suffering which you manage to extract out of your life – that corresponds to the efficiency of the machine. Well, then; the value of your own life to yourself is this fraction: "What you obtain over what you wish for."

Wish for nothing; your denominator is zero; the value of the fraction, therefore, infinity, no matter what its numerator may be, short of nothing.

I did not see at once, that goes without saying, how this result could be worked out in practice. But even as a theoretical proposition, as a theorem, or better still, as the mere definition of a final aim it held forth hope, it was full of promise. I suddenly seemed to understand three great historical figures that had been enigmas: Sulla, Diocletian, Charles the Fifth.

When we came to New York and the train slowed down for the stop at 125th Street, I felt suddenly moved to accentuate the new departure in my life by getting off there, in the cheap Harlem neighbourhood, instead of going on to the expensive district of 42nd Street.

When I ran down the steps of the elevated station, carrying my suit-case, whom should I catch sight of but young Ray! He was crossing the avenue, clad in blue, paint-bespattered overalls, an oil-tin and several brushes in his hand.

I shouted his name; he stopped in his tracks.

A joyous smile lighted up his face when he saw me coming. Then he grinned sheepishly and looked down at himself and back to me as if to call my attention to his attire.

"My, you look prosperous!" he sang out as soon as I came into hailing-distance.

"Look," I said, "but am not. Well, how are you?"

We shook hands in a way which convinced me entirely of the sincerity of his feelings.

"Say," I said, "I must see more of you during the next few days. Where is the cheapest joint around here to put up in for the night?"

"Well," he said, "the Plaza isn't exactly around here, but it's the nearest of the joints which you call cheap."

I laughed. "Listen; and get this. I'm down to rock-bottom, out of a job, and in a day or so going to leave the city. Got it? All right, where is the cheapest joint?"

"Well," he replied, "I've got only a small hall bed-room and no hot or cold water on tap there, but, if it's cheapness you're after, nothing cheaper than to share my bed."

"Good," I said, "I accept. Are you through for the day?"

"Apart from bringing this pot of juice and these brushes home to their rightful owner. I've just been painting the finest Bull Durham sign in the city limits. And then for a wash and the merry life!" he rattled in irresistible good-humour.

"Going in the direction of your roost?" I asked.

"Exactly opposite."

"Then I'll wait for you here at the station."

When we had washed up, we went down-town to have my trunk brought up from the hotel where I had left it. Our supper we had in one of those numerous restaurants which cater to people of cleanly tastes and slender purses.

Then we went home and settled down to what Ray was pleased to call a "pow-wow" of gossip.

I told him of my adventures, and he repaid me by giving me all the news of the "Travellogue-crowd". Mr. Tinker had gone bankrupt as a manager; he and Mrs. McMurchy, having at last thrown their fortunes together, were themselves out on the road again. Miss Henders was working in some capacity in the employ of the Socialist party; Mrs. Coldwell, poor old soul, was canvassing for magazine subscribers.

"How about yourself?" I asked.

"Oh, I'm fine," he said. "Nothing to be proud of, I suppose. But when I go out in the morning, I know that I can do what I'm asked to do. I have my definite work; and when it's done, I'm free to read or to draw. In a few years' time I feel sure I'll come into my own. Meanwhile I get quite a little fun out of this sign-painting business. The fellow I work for thinks I've a natural gift for that sort of thing. Sometimes I feel quite an artist when I paint the cows and meadows for Horlick's Malted Milk, or the Injuns for Round Oak Stoves."

We both laughed more, that night, I believe, than either one of us had laughed in months together. We were the silliest of silly boys; there was nothing that refused itself to being travestied and laughed at.

Young Ray took it for granted and prevailed upon me to promise him that I should stay with him for at least a few days. He asked for my plans; I did not have any plans. I disposed of the rest of my wardrobe, having picked out one single, brown, English riding suite with breeches – soft-leather-lined – and a raincoat to keep. All I knew myself about my intentions was that I was going to "go out west".

The rest of my books I gave to Ray, picking out only two slender volumes, one a New Testament, bound in pliable leather, the other a Greek Odyssey in rather stiff cloth, but both narrow enough to slip easily into the hip-pockets of my breeches. My suitcase I filled with some cherished trifles, ivory nail-files, military brushes, and similar things, keeping, to fill my pockets with, only such toilet-articles as seemed indispensable, razor, tooth-brush, comb, and so on.

On the third day after my return to New York I was ready to start. My cash, I remember, amounted to seventeen dollars and a little silver. Ray begged me to accept some money for the books which I had given him, but I refused.

"Sooner or later," I explained, "whatever I take along, will come to an end, no matter whether it is ten or a hundred dollars. The sooner the inevitable happens, the better. It will be a crisis which is bound to come. We'll see what will follow in its wake. I wonder whether a man can starve in this country? I have no doubt I can do so in the city. There is a condition here which is probably the same with regard to all immigrants except those that have the strong arm. If I were still in a bitter mood, I should call it the conspiracy of indifference. But the bitterness is gone. There is nothing left but curiosity."

And after a short silence I bent forward and went on, "I'll tell you a secret, Ray. Don't think I'm crazy. Don't ask any questions about it. You'll understand it one day, provided I can still get hold of you then. You'll understand it whenever I shall ask you to forward that suitcase of mine. The secret is this: I am going in search of Abraham Lincoln."

A day or so later, of an early Sunday morning, Ray said good-by to me at the ferry station of 23rd Street, where I had entered New York a year ago, and I was off, walking, a tramp.

BOOK THREE

The Depths

"The fraction of Life can be increased in value not so much by increasing your Numerator as by lessening your Denominator."

— Thomas Carlyle

I Go Exploring

AT THIS POINT, where I begin to tell of the adventures during the second year of my apprenticeship on American soil, I find myself confronted with a difficulty.

I had become an onlooker again. For quite a while, after I left the city of New York, nothing of what I went through stirred me very deeply. I had tried to meddle with the affairs of American life; I had burned my fingers. I felt no temptation to try again before I had regained an inner equilibrium and a maturity from which I felt myself to be separated by a great distance. I was engaged in a search.

One consequence is that memories have become dulled. Only what moves us deeply do we remember across the gulf of time. Above all, the chronology of events is confused. Many impressions refuse to fall back into their proper places. The only help I can get is from associations of locality. Where an impression or an event is indissolubly linked up with the scenery in which it arose or took place, I can fit it back by putting it into the proper point of my itinerary. Where I have not succeeded in doing so, I have preferred to treat it as negligible and to leave it out. The narrative must thus lose some of its connections; transitions will be missing; apparent contradictions will crop up; feelings, thoughts which are hard to reconcile. And there are, especially in the beginning, detached scenes, disconnected visions, like mere pictures flashed upon the screen of memory, seemingly quite meaningless; and yet they belong into the tale of my tramps.

The very first memories are a series of mere visions.

To the left arises a railroad embankment, twenty feet high, with a cinder slope from which here and there a cloud of sharp, cutting dust whirls up in a playful breeze. To the right runs something like an aqueduct or a large watermain – if I interpret the picture in my mind correctly – which shuts out the view. Underfoot the road, smooth, tarry, soft to the touch, tremendously hot from the sun which beats mercilessly down on everything. The whole road, running for miles between embankment and aqueduct, is alive with hordes of winged locusts which, jumping and flying, stir up an exceedingly fine, oily dust. So densely do these insects cover the road that it is impossible not to crush them at every step. When the breath of the breeze sweeps the ground, they fly up to the height of my face, hitting my cheeks, my ears, my neck with the sharp impact of their mandibles as with blunt needle-points. In spite of the tar on the road, which pervades the whole atmosphere with its tiring smell, the main feature of the landscape is dust, dust. The perspiration runs down my face, cutting runnels into the black coating which begins to cover it. The wide leaves of False Ragweed plants on the embankment are also grey with dust; their stems are covered with locusts. The dreariness of it all is accentuated when, at a bend in the road, those huge pipes to the right come quite close to the driveway before they form their angle; I stand and listen to the swish of swift-moving water within. The sound seems so cool. The sleeve of my coat on the arm which carries the waterproof is crumpled and creased as if pressed and ironed that way; the skin of my arm is beady with sweat.

Locusts, tar-smell, dust and heat; for miles and miles.

In the afternoon I come to Newark. I have never been back there. A gulf of many years separates me from that Sunday afternoon. But I see a raised railway station, some twenty-five to thirty feet above the level of the road. I am in the grateful shade of dusty trees – their leaves coated with the deposits of smoke – and look up at that station where light, washable summer-dresses flit about as if they had a life of their own – a weird impression of unreality attaches to it all. The wearers of those dresses are beings in a different world from my own – they seem like marionettes – they live in a world of make-believe and pretence – a world that resembles the painted wings on a stage – the reality is dust and tar-smell. I cross a street and get a drink at a public fountain. People glance at me as if they were seeing an apparition. Their movements in the street look as if they were trying to hurry past – as if my sight looked like a threat.

But the shade is grateful.

I walk at the chance of the road. It does not matter where it leads.

At last I have crossed the city and swing out again into its outskirts. Houses become an episode. In the cooling air of lengthening shadows I step along at a brisker rate. Deeper and more refreshing becomes every single breath I take.

A little bridge leaps over a brook. Verdure clothes its banks right down to the water which merrily scampers along. I leave the road to the left, eagerly hurrying over the meadow, and reach a willow-clump at the water's edge. Cap and coat are thrown off, the sleeves of my shirt rolled back to the arm-pits. I plunge forward, submerging head and arms in the cooling flood. If Ray were with me, we should now start romping and splashing, shouting and laughing the while. But every noise sounds strange, since I am alone, alone. I feel hushed.

I am on the road again and suddenly realize that all day long I have not eaten. There are buns in the pocket of my raincoat. I find a bottle, a perfectly good, sound bottle by the roadside. It seems a treasure; I pick it up.

The road rises over the shoulder of a hill. As I climb it, the feeling in my legs which keep swinging along mechanically is that of a man who for the first time in his life

shoots up in an elevator; the ground seems to press upward. Rail-fences appear on both sides. A desire overcomes me to whistle as I march; but I am shy under the
eye of nature. Dusk is rising.

Simultaneously I see in front the white slice of the moon
floating in the deepening blue, and in a straight line with
it, above the crest of the hill, the black shape of a building.
When I approach, I find it to be a crossroads store. Forget-
ful of its being Sunday, I stop and ask a man who sits on
the stoop for a can of condensed milk. He mutters something; but he gets up, walks in, and returns with the tin.

A little farther along the road a car lurches past me, the
exhaust ringing like so many pistol-shots through the
quiet air. I pass a farm huddled by the roadside in a cluster
of trees.

My purchase at the store has set my thoughts on milk.
My throat seems to cry out for milk.

I stop and turn.

"Yes," says the woman who is working at the stove in
the dusky kitchen at the back of the farm-house – no
lamps being lit yet – "yes, I guess I can let you have
some."

And while she fills my bottle, out of the shadows beyond
a man steps forward into the frame of the door. "Had a
breakdown?" he asks.

For a moment I fail to understand. Then it flashes upon
me that he takes me for the driver of the car which has
just shot by – cars were still scarce at the time, still something to be commented upon. And, strange to say, nearly
against my will, certainly without any intention of decep-
tion, simply as the easiest way of avoiding further queries,
my mouth answers, "Yes, rather."

But I feel the colour mantling my face which is merci-
fully hidden by the darkness. I take the bottle from the
woman's hands and ask for the charge.

"Oh," she says pleasantly, "I don't think we'll miss it."

"Thanks," I say and walk off.

Out on the road, away from the shadows of buildings and trees, there is still the light of the heavenly sickle. I feel strangely weightless.

I am cut loose, adrift on the world.

The ribbon of the road still rises; but it reaches the crest, and I top the hill. Like a pair of weights suspended from my body my feet swing on, downhill now. Below lies a shallow valley, filled with the shadow of trees. As I move on with large strides, my body seems to gather weight, my knees begin to bend at every step.

Not a single, solitary thought is in my head. But my teeth seem to be on edge for the bite into those buns; my throat seems to anticipate the gurgling flow of the milk.

Thus I reach the bottom of the valley – there is a tiny trickling stream which crosses the road under a culvert. I step aside, on the meadow and bend to the ground – the grass is wet with dew; but that does not matter. I spread my raincoat out, sit down, and eat. Half my bread I put back into the pockets, half my milk I leave in the bottle. I rest.

I seem to be weighing the time, as if I held a certain mass of it in my hand.

At last I get up to proceed. But an unearthly load presses on my shoulders; the ground seems to heave under my step; I notice that I stagger.

I do not reason or think; instinctively I strike to the left, into the forest, on rising ground. Dry leaves rustle under my feet. The failing light of the moon only half illuminates the roots in which my feet get caught. At last I spread my raincoat on the ground and lie down.

The air is still warm; but everything around is hung with beads of dew. The clean smell of humus, mixed with the smoky haze of the lower air, has something heady; it affects me like new wine. Strange noises are alive among the trees, rustlings and whirrings of the creatures of the wild. The very stillness which is underlined by these noises has something exciting. Long, long I lie awake. And when at last I doze, I still toss restlessly about. An uncanny, mocking laughter close at hand makes me sit up; I do not recall where I am, I do not awake to full consciousness. I feel chilly; my clothes are damp; I curl up, pull my raincoat closer about my body, sink back, and sleep.

And then: all kinds of sounds are astir: a dog barks, a cock crows, a cow lows in the meadow. Birds begin to twitter and to chirp. I am lifted out of the depths of sleep. A lassitude which is nearly voluptuous pervades limbs and body. Awakening is like a resurrection; but I do not move.

Gradually the sky begins to whiten, the canopy of the leaves overhead turns into a black etching. Slowly, slowly the light of day steals into all things around. I lie still, I do not even look. But the consciousness that another day has risen soaks into me by never-suspected senses. I am still alive.

By and by the consciousness of what I have done obtrudes. I laugh; but a sob mingles into the laugh. It seems so simple – all I have done is to walk out of a great city. But it means that I have left the society of man. I am an outcast – something closely resembling those dreaded beings which I have thought of with a shudder: anarchists. I am alone; I stand against the world.

This thought sends me into a sitting posture; but I fall back with a groan; a wild, stabbing pain has flashed across my back. A sob convulses my whole body; tears, unreasoning tears seem a relief. Again I try to rise, this time slowly, cautiously. I am very stiff, every movement seems to hurt.

At last I stand. My foot-joints, my ankles, my knees, my hips, and my back – all hurt. But I pick my raincoat up and start a descent from tree to tree.

Meanwhile the sun has risen in the east, and its orange-coloured rays send golden flashes along the leaves overhead. I have to get out of the woods to dry, to shake off the cloak of misty dampness that covers the world.

I reach the road in the valley-bottom where the little stream hurries towards the east. White mist still floats; I shiver as I step over the deep-napped carpet of the meadow. I stand and listen. There is no human sound. So, slowly, painfully, I strip and wash. Then I bend down and drink deep at the nearest pool. Again I shiver; and when I have sat and eaten, I rise and limp back to the road, to a point where a dry, mossy spot in the western hillside catches the light and heat from the sun. There I sit down once more to gather warmth.

This second day there was a new quality to the rays of the sun, something I could not define as yet; but for the moment it felt good. It was what we realize when we say, "It is going to be a hot day." Not an air seemed to stir; I did not move, but lay there for hours.

I do not know how far or in what direction I walked that day. But I remember how more and more that strange feeling in the air predominated which forebodes a storm. I also remember that my progress was slow and halting. The stiffness in my body and limbs did not disappear altogether, though I finally settled down into a definite routine of motion. The slightest departure from this routine brought pain. The atmosphere took on that breathless, brooding concentration which causes us to look into the sky for thunderheads.

My vision clears towards the afternoon when I was slowly plodding along a road which was more and more densely flanked by farms and residences, till it changed into something like a wide and spacious street; but there were no trees to give shade.

I looked up again and saw vast threatening clouds with edges of a ghostly white.

I scanned the street and caught sight of a large, unpainted building ahead which resembled a store. I went on; a sidewalk sprang up out of the edge of the road. The building was indeed a store. Connected with it was something like a little inn which did not look as if it were doing a flourishing business.

I entered the store, bought ten cents' worth of bacon and a loaf of bread, and turned back into the street.

Again I looked at the sky and hesitated. Then I entered the hall of the inn and waited. Nobody came, and at last I sat down.

Heavy drops began to knock at the building like finger-knuckles. I thought of the city, of Ray, and brushed the thought away because it sent a sob rising into my throat.

A short, fat woman entered. I rose to my feet.

"You take in guests for the night?" I asked.

"Sometimes," she said and looked me up and down, coolly, with insolent appraisal.

"What do you charge for a room?"

"With meals?"

"No."

"Fifty cents," she replied, ". . . in advance."

I laid down a dollar bill, and she gave me the change.

This interview proved that I was indeed on the other side of the line which demarcates society.

She showed me my room, and I laid my parcels on a table there. The air in the room was witness that it had not been occupied for a long, long time. There was no dirt; on the contrary, everything was painfully clean; but it smelt of damp sheets and lowered blinds; to this very day, when I catch the smell, I see the room.

I raised the window and went out.

In front of the store the sidewalk was roofed over, and in this shelter stood a chair. When I sat down, a wind sprang up, suddenly, furiously, with a whirl preceding it; and then it settled down into a roaring blow. The rain lashed the road and gathered into brooks on both sides, shooting down the gently sloping hillside. It was a soaking, gushing, drowning rain, as if the gates of some lock had been opened and a flood were sweeping over the dusty stretches below. I looked on, unmoved; and as suddenly as it had started, it ceased. The sun broke forth again; I breathed more freely; and only the little brooks on both sides of the road, yellow with the washings of clay, told of the short and vehement fury of the storm.

It was still daylight when I turned in. I was paying precious money for this room; I was going to get my money's worth of the luxury. No mere eight or ten hours of sleep would have seemed adequate; I meant to have six-teen at least and had them.

As for the next day, or the one after that, and probably quite a few more that followed, my memory is a blank. I do remember, though, that the experience of the nights in the open was more than once similar to that of the first night. It took me two weeks or longer to learn that I had to get under some kind of cover, straw or hay, to protect myself from the dew. I also remember how I got used to being silent for days and days at a stretch. When I entered a store – I preferred little crossroads places to those in towns – my voice sounded husky to me, unfamiliar like that of a stranger.

Gradually I became hardened to this life.

One day, after a week or so, I found that I was nearing the city of Philadelphia. Promptly I struck off for the west. I did not care to go even near a city.

I also settled down to a certain routine in my habits, a routine rather unusual for a tramp, I suppose. Every sec-ond day I shaved, carefully, painstakingly, with the help of a little disk-mirror which I carried in the pocket of my vest. Every third day I washed my underwear and my shirt – they were of the best that money could buy – in some brook or stream, provided the sun shone brightly or the wind blew briskly enough to dry things within an hour or so.

As for the two little books which I carried, I tried to read the New Testament; but it seemed irrelevant. I must confess that, up to that time, I had – like most people, ministers not excluded – never read it with an open mind; I found that I could not do so now; but I kept the booklet. Now and then I looked into the Odyssey, and I liked it better; I suppose, because I was much more familiar with it; and if I picked out a line or two, I did not need to feel that I was perverting their meaning by taking them out of their context. Their meaning did not greatly matter, anyway; there was a sadness about the whole which chimed in with my mood; there was a soothing melody in its rhythm which made me forget my feeling of loneliness.

I was in Pennsylvania now; and once more a vision arises of my staying at an inn over night – the last time during that season as far as I remember.

I had been swinging along vigourously all day, topping bare and barren-looking hills, down into shallow valleys and over hills again. Here and there I had seen a needy-looking farmstead in the distance; but I had not passed a single one close by.

Then, somehow, in the dusk of evening, the road I followed gave out; it was on a marshy plain in the hills; it became less and less well marked and finally ended in a number of diverging water-soaked wheel-tracks, not far from a cluster of half-decaying, storm-battered, lightning-rived remnants of trees.

Thus I struck out at random, going west.

I came to a steep ridge and climbed it. Night began to wrap the world. But when I reached the summit, I looked down upon a long, winding valley, filled with the shadow of trees. Darkness lay huddled down there, in the fold of the hills, as if it, too, had coiled up for the night.

Compared with this darkness, the heights and summits seemed to reach up into a thinner, less opaque air, into a region of indistinct, grey visibility which seemed pregnant with danger, threatened with the invasion of incomprehensible, cosmic things sweeping along over the universe.

The valley in its inky blackness seemed infinitely sheltered, cosy, homelike. Right in its centre gleamed, ruddily, a light. I greeted that light like a message from the sane, quiet, well-ordered world of man. Up here on the heights perched insanity.

As if I were fleeing from the threat of the inanimate world above, from the terrible things that lurked and flitted through the grey of the upper air, I started to plunge down the hillside, stumbling over rocks, falling headlong over roots, running up against rail-fences, scaling them, rushing forward again.

Then, having once more brought up against a rail-fence, I suddenly heard human voices close by; I stopped short, a lump in my throat. The night was so dark by this time that I could not have seen my own hand, even though I had held it up close to my eyes. As I stood there, blotted into the dark shadows of the trees behind, I saw two glowing spots glide down upon myself; the voices became louder; and from the ground, close at hand, the reverberating tramp of two men walking downhill arose. They were talking and laughing and smoking. They seemed to be coming straight on; but at the last moment they swung off and passed me, not more than two or three feet from where I stood, unsuspected by them in the dark.

I realized that only the fence in front of me separated me from a road which led along the bottom of the sloping valley to the light.

I waited so as to give the men time to get beyond earshot. Then I climbed out on the road and settled down to the rhythm of their steady swing which I still heard.

After a while I became aware of a widening of the road. Without seeing a thing I was conscious of the fact that there were houses on both sides; at last one of the houses showed a mild, ruddy light through two or three windows. This was the inn; I had escaped . . .

I was a wanderer in the hills. Soon after I became a wanderer in the valleys. But before I reached those valleys, one more picture engraved itself on my brain so that it stands in sharp outline to this very day.

Again, in a steady tramp, I was winding up a hill. The sun shone brightly from the western sky; a clear, blue breeze came rambling across from the east. I stopped now and then and turned to let it blow through my heated body. I was young, and the world was young.

I have a picture in my mind even of the looks of the soil to both sides of the road. It was a bare, heavy clay with marly patches here and there, a poor soil for farms, washed into gullies by many rains.

Yet, at last I saw a cluster of little buildings ahead, right on the summit of the pass in the hills. It seemed to bar the road; but as I approached, I found that the road turned aside in a double bend for this cluster of poverty-stricken hovels. As I turned, I saw beyond the rail-fence the scaffolding of a well which had a pole-lift. I had not met with water for some time; and so, at the sight of the well, I realized that I was thirsty. I followed the second bend of the road, and it brought me alongside the unpainted, rain-washed house.

There was a gap without a gate in the fence, and I entered. I looked about in the yard, but I saw no one, nor any sign of human occupancy. I went to the back door and knocked, but received no answer.

I went around to the front; and there, on a rough, wooden bench, leaning against the house, sat two old people, a man and a woman. They were old indeed, hollow-eyed and hollow-cheeked. And when I turned the corner of the house, the old man was holding one of the woman's hands between his two; and she was leaning against his shoulder, crooning some old song. Their hair was white and soft and smooth; the man's long, flowing beard as lightly grey as the rain-bleached lumber of the house. In their watery, light-blue eyes was a far-away look.

I wanted to steal back as I had come; but I had been seen, and both of them started.

"Hello," sang the man in a childish treble.

"Hello," I replied shamefacedly; and I made known my want.

The woman bustled away with astounding activity and got a cup; the man drew water from the well and would not let me help.

Somehow I felt the need of furnishing a pretext for my presence, and I enquired for the road to some nearby town. They pointed it out but thought I could never reach my destination by nightfall. Again I fenced. Was there a farm somewhere along the road where I might stop in case the dark should overtake me? I was thinking of some straw or haystack to crawl into. No, they replied; most of the rare travellers along this trail stopped with them; they had a cot, not much of a bed, to be sure; but they kept it set up against the home-coming of their son; might I want to stay for the night? Hardly. I could not afford to pay for a night's rest anywhere; I might snatch an hour's sleep by the roadside. And catch my death of cold, to be sure! That would not do! As for pay, they never took any, for their son's sake; and had they ever done so, they would not take it from me; I reminded them of their son so. That son, I must know, had gone off, along that very road, twenty or twenty-five years ago – yes, twenty-four it would be, come next Easter; the farm had not paid a living for the three any longer; he had gone out west; and there, on the hill which I could just see over yonder, he had stopped and waved his hat for the last time back home; and that was all they had ever seen or heard of him; was he alive still, did I think? But surely, he must! And both wiped a tear from their eyes.

I stayed over night; and, oh, how I wished I could leave a "wonderful pitcher" behind!

One day, I looked down upon Harrisburg.

I remembered, of course, the night when I had looked out at the station, from the window of the sleeping-car; but I banished the thought. I banished many thoughts those days.

I turned to the north to avoid the city.

I came down into the Susquehanna valley. I do not remember a great deal of this part of my tramps. But I still feel how my blood was quickened by the sight of the swift-shooting river. I have a vision of a wide, flat-bottomed valley with large slabs of rock under shallow, smoothly gliding sheets of water; of little islets with tufts of long, waving grass nearly choking the current; of a good road along the bank. I have often longed for a second sight; but it has been my fate not to see these parts again. Nothing remains in my memory but the impression of an inner and unconscious development of myself.

The first factors in the complex fraction of my life at the time which I will enumerate are, as it were, positive ones; or, to borrow Carlyle's figure once more, they must be put down in the Numerator.

For one thing, I established a mood which eliminated the feeling of loneliness. It may have been because I got used to being alone. That terrible need for communication, for imparting to others what I garnered in impressions, moods, thoughts was on the wane. My body had become adjusted to the conditions of the tramp and left my mind free to commune with itself. Things that I felt or thought began to crystallize into short statements, sometimes into brief lines of verse. I obtained a pencil and a little note-book and occasionally jotted observations down. But I did not date them; nor did I attach to them the names of localities. Nothing was further from my mind than to keep a journal or a record. What I wrote down fulfilled its purpose right then and there, in affording me that satisfaction which we find in formulating elusive things. So, when among my papers I ran across this little note-book, several years ago, it helped me to realize in remembrance the general mood of the days; but it did not reconstruct definite scenes and events in the album of mental photographs. To-day, when at last I am trying to write this record, even that little help is no longer available; the note-book seems to have been lost.

Further, there stands out another fact, an external one this time. All my life I have been a lover of water – rivers, lakes, the sea. I had made many an inland and outland voyage. Water is nothing inanimate. It responds to the moods of sky and cloud as we do. The mere fact that water is rarely silent has something to do with it. Water is company. Instinctively I clung for a large part of my tramps to the courses of rivers. Here it was, first, the Susquehanna, then the Juniata; later, Conemaugh, Allegheny, Ohio, Missouri. There were other reasons for this, of course. So long as I followed a river, I was sure I could not stray. I had one of the prime essentials for sustaining life without ever approaching human habitations which I shunned. Shade and privacy were available whenever I needed them – for my ablutions, for instance. When the time came, as now it did, that I needed a fire at night, I was never at a loss for fuel; and soon I learned that a river is also a bountiful giver of other things which were no longer – to me – necessities. All this, however, was secondary; for even in cutting across the streams, so long as I was within the mountains, I should have met enough of them to minister to all my wants. The river, whether large or small, relieved the feeling that I was alone and an outcast.

Among the negative factors – or those that went down in the ever-lessening Denominator – the most important one was the habit of utter frugality which became established. I learned to expect less and less. Wild fruit – blackberries above all – the bark of certain trees which I began to be familiar with, and nuts played an ever-increasing part in my daily fare. Less and less did I spend money. Against such days as proved barren of finds I carried a bundle. I learned to pick up tin-cans for cooking-utensils. I eliminated bread from my diet as too expensive and substituted oatmeal which I cooked in those tin-cans. I carried salt and, as the rarest treat on chilly nights, a little tea. There was no longer any need for my entering stores except once a fortnight or so; less than half a dollar bought all I needed for the interval. I might mention that I also learned to eat roots and tubers – parsnips, turnips, potatoes – raw with great relish. These I did not scruple to purloin from occasional fields.

Since I avoided men, they being what above all was to be feared, I escaped importune questions and the discomfort of prevarication.

My body lost its last vestige of fat. I was a bundle of bones, sinews, muscles. I doubt whether my health has ever been what it was during this tramp in the valleys of the Appalachians. I did no longer flee from sudden drenching showers. I merely rolled my provisions, my watch, my matches in my waterproof and protected them as best I could, letting the rain soak my clothes as it listed. Nothing seemed to do me any harm. I felt fit and able to cope with any difficulty, amply equal to any feat of athletics. I prided myself on strength and endurance.

The woods began to flame on the east sides of the ridges. But on the west side of the divide, beyond Altoona, where the waters drain into the Mississippi basin, they were still green. To pass to the west slope seemed like experiencing a resurrection of summer after fall had come. The waters seemed warmer there, and so did the air.

And now, to close this chapter of dim reminiscences, I have to explain a general attitude towards things and scenes which I find it hard to grasp in thought and harder still to formulate in a medium as coarse and lacking in delicacy, and as unfamiliar to myself as language is.

Every morning I awoke as to a feast.

I was young, in the early years of manhood. My whole body and soul were astir with the possibilities of passion. Love was not only a potentiality; it was a prime need, it was a craving, a cry of my innermost being.

And this love had no object except the woods, the mountains, the streams; bird, insect, beast, gossamer threads, smoky haze, the smell of the earth. These, or more briefly, the country, I loved.

My love for it was not the love for a friend – which is the love for that which is not; it idealizes, substitutes, omits, redraws. It was not the love for the mother – which is the love for origins, help, food, shelter, care, guidance, akin to gratitude. It was the love for the bride, full of desires, seeking all things, accepting them, craving fulfilment of higher destinies. Forgotten was where I came from; forgotten what I had gone through; forgiven in advance what I might rush into and still have to suffer. Every fibre of my being yearned. And though what lured me was nature, yet it was also America.

TWO

I Lose Sight of Mankind

I HAD REACHED the Ohio River, with the state of Ohio to the right and West Virginia to the left. The river ran shallow between great, rolling hills. Farms dotted the rich bottom-lands of the flood-plain. The huge scaffoldings of oil-wells began to obtrude. The nights began to be cooler; rainy spells were apt to be cold spells now and to last for days. My capital had melted to two or three dollars.

It was somewhere in Ohio, with the town of Wheeling not far off across the river. Never did I go out on the road; I followed the river exclusively. Sometimes great paddle-steamers lay stranded in mid-current; big timber-rafts were anchored or drifted past with their crews. To see men who followed such occupations seemed to bridge the chasm between myself, the nomad who lived off the land, and the settled portion of mankind for whom I still had nothing but aversion. I looked at those men on the rafts with longing and curiosity.

Progress along the river was sometimes difficult, sometimes dangerous. I had to climb over the rocks on the throw-side; to wade through the mud of the flats on the inside of curves. By this time I had discarded my shoes, which I carried in my bundle, together with gaiters, stockings, and coat. I began to notice the wear and tear on my clothes, and it worried me. I began to feel that the time

was bound to come when I should have to fit myself again
into the great machinery of civilization; I dreaded its
approach.

One morning I awoke to a sunless sky. A raw wind was
blowing, lashing the river into short, angry waves which
ran against the current. I was on the inner side of a long,
flat curve, the bank being filled in with fine, alluvial deposits of the river. Every step which I took made a hole in
this soft mud which instantly filled with water as I withdrew my foot.

I was coughing when I started out.

I knew I was near some industrial centre – Wheeling, I
suppose – and I wanted to get past it that day. It was hard
to walk with fair speed. But I hurried on. I remember how
I worked myself into a sweat while I plodded along in the
shelter of some vast, low ridge of gravel running out into
the angry river. When I rounded it, the raw, bleak blast of
the wind felt grateful for a moment; I sat down on a block
of stone.

By noon I felt there was something wrong with me. I
counted the beats of my pulse and found it careering
along at fever-rate. A dread seized me that I might break
down and be found by men who might want to take care
of me. It did not matter to me what happened; I could have
dragged myself into some cave to stay there and to die; but
I did not want charity. The district in which I was seemed
densely populated; the farther I went, the more so it was.
There seemed to be no other way; I had to get through,
past those towns which lay ahead. But the more I exerted
myself, the harder it became to keep moving, and the
oftener I had to sit down and to rest. At last I saw a bridge
which crossed the river ahead. To the right, on my side of
the water, there was a large mill, some iron-works, as I
conclude from the outline of the picture in my memory.

A fine drizzling rain began to fall, lashed and driven
home by the wind. I began to sneeze and to cough in
ever more violent attacks. My head was a whirl; but I
plodded on.

It was late; I began to see that at best I could not get far beyond the town. Still, I rested and dragged myself forward again. To the last I had only one thought; to escape observation.

By the time that I saw the bridge looming overhead, lights were burning on both sides of the river. From behind, where the mill towered, the clangour and roar of big industry sounded down. I was sitting on a rock again; the rain was coming down through my thin clothes. I had no thought any longer; I did not even realize my misery, which was merely physical. When I tried to rise and proceed, my knees gave out under me; I fell to the ground.

I groped for a spot that might be smooth. I found a mound of sand and lay down. Thus I remained for an hour or so, soaked to the skin by the rain. Then I proceeded to make myself as comfortable as I could. I worked my body into the moist sand, making a mould of it which hugged half my body and half the legs which I had drawn up. Without rising I untied my bundle, took my coat out, wrapped my provisions again in the waterproof, stowed the bundle away in the angle between body and thighs, pulled the coat over my shoulders, and lay back again. My head was lying towards the river; my back turned to the wind. The rain was increasing in force and in quantity; but gradually I became aware that by some freak of chance I had blindly picked on a spot that was, as far as the rain went, largely sheltered by the great span of the bridge overhead.

Long, long lay I awake there, watching the lights move about on the high bank where the mill stood. Green lights and red lights they were, and occasionally the white glare of a shunting engine.

I was glad that the bank was so high; it lessened the danger of being detected. I was grateful for the shelter which the bridge afforded. And I was not without a feeling of comfort, for I was warming the sand that formed the mould in which I lay; I never stirred, instinctively conserving all the heat of my body.

I fell asleep. And I lay awake again; I was awake all through the fitful dawn. I was conscious – over and above, or maybe below that clangour and roar of the mill – of a strange sound, as if water were tearing and rushing along at an unusual speed; and when I had adjusted my ear, so it would pick out these sounds and neglect the louder ones which proceeded from the mill, I heard, lifted above the subdued swish, set off against it, the short, playful lapping of eager little wavelets, very close at hand, yes, coming nearer as I listened.

I lay thus for hours.

Great white clouds were sailing in a blue sky. The wind was gusty; I was wet all though. But so long as I did not stir, I did not feel cold. Only when I moved the least little bit, just my feet, or my leg, for the smallest fraction of an inch, a cold wave seemed to run into my body in unexpected places. Slowly I realized that I was lying in water; the water came up from below; but I did not care. Although it came to be torture not to move, I forced myself to a strict rigidity; I concentrated my attention and a passionate effort on this one thing: not to move. I must have fallen asleep again over that.

Then I felt a touch in my back; it was repeated; it was a rough touch; I lifted myself in sudden anger.

There, towering above me, stood a huge, hulking man with one or two things – the cap, maybe, or a badge – suggesting the policeman.

He was kicking me with his foot, not violently, but insistently. He said, "Move on, there! Or I'll have to run you in. No vagrants wanted."

I gathered myself together and staggered to my feet – swaying like a man in his liquor. I did not say a word, picked my bundle up, and stumbled away with a supreme effort, reeling.

The river had changed overnight. It had risen several feet and increased tremendously in width. Its floods were yellow and gurgled along, carrying a strange assortment of drift.

Once I got over the first shock of moving it was not bad. I felt that I was still feverish; but I was rested; and for the moment the problem was to establish a routine of movements which might proceed automatically. That was a problem not so easy of solution on ground which was soft, with an infinitude of various-sized pebbles and stones embedded in it. But I got away from the town.

The morning was showery, the wind blew in squalls; the air was not warm; but whenever the sun came out, it shone with great power. I plodded on for several hours. Then I began to feel that it was imperative for me to partake of some food.

At last I came to a point where the river bent to the south. That made my, the northern, bank the throw-side of the current. Consequently it was steep and rocky, all movable sediments having been washed away by previous floods.

In one place rocky ledges jutted out over the river, like platforms arranged in a succession of steps, the lowest one being just a few inches above the water, the higher ones receding more and more. One of these upper platforms consisted of a rock-ledge six inches thick and protruding over the lower one for a distance of two or three feet, thus leaving a roofed-over space some three feet high. The yellow river shot by with great speed.

I stopped for the day; I had all I needed and all I could expect: a smooth, dry, rocky floor, shelter from the wind, a roof to ward off the rain, and a natural nook in the rocky shore which caught and held the heat of the sun. It was quite a find.

I unwrapped my bundle. It was moist inside, but not wet. The matches would not strike right away, but they were not completely spoiled. The oatmeal needed drying, too; but things looked pretty cheerful. A sharp pain in my side, however, warned me that I had a touch of pleurisy. I took my water-soaked clothes off and shrugged my bare body into my raincoat. Then I caught water from the river and let it stand for the mud to settle while I prepared a fire. My clothes I spread over the ledges to dry them; and whenever a shower came, I stowed them away under the platform to protect them from further wettings. Then I went into the willow-brush higher up on the bank to lay in a store of firewood; and by two or three in the afternoon I felt quite comfortable.

But the showers began to be more frequent and threatening again. They were thunder-showers now, bringing swift and violent outbursts under which the rocks quaked and shivered. I lay under my ledge, having spread a bed of willow-boughs, and using my clothes as covers.

The world seemed to belong to me.

Sheet-lightning and sudden thunderstorms kept up all night; and even the following day, when the river had risen so as to cover the lowest rock-ledge, the weather looked still so threatening that I resolved not to quit my camp. The pain in my side was gone; once more I felt the exuberance of youthful spirits.

This day was memorable for me because I learned to watch the drift of the river for things that might be useful. I went half a mile upstream; and whenever I saw something coming which caught my eye, I swam out.

One of the first things which I brought to shore was a large teakettle. True, after I had washed out the mud it contained, I found it leaked a little; but that hardly mattered, the leak was not big enough to let the kettle run empty in less than half an hour. This teakettle which I carried henceforth for eight or ten weeks became one of my most highly prized possessions; it solved a problem which I had long been pondering. Beyond the realm of the river, on the higher bottom-lands of the ancient flood-plains, stretched vast fields of corn. I did not reflect on the moral aspect of the matter – I simply levied my toll henceforth, picking a few ears here and a few ears there. It was fodder corn, of the flint variety; and it soon needed anywhere from one to six hours boiling to soften it enough for profitable digestion in a human stomach; but it did away with the irksome buying of oatmeal which threatened to exhaust my funds.

Few people have an idea of the value and the variety of the river-drift after heavy rains. The next thing that attracted my attention on this day was a round, shiny, yellow object that bobbed up and down, looking for all the world like the bald skull of a human being. I was half afraid of going near it when I swam out. It proved to be a pumpkin; I brought it in.

Along towards evening I made my biggest find: a box containing a perfectly well-preserved ham of a well-known packer's brand. This ham taught me the first of a series of lessons which I was slow to profit by. You must not forget that this was not altogether a pleasure outing. It goes without saying that I tried to palm it off as such to myself as well as to the rare people who spoke to me – a clam-fisher here and there, or the attendant of a lock. I never took food any longer more than twice a day; and often it was not very satisfying. In fact, I do not think that I am going beyond the limits of the truth if I state that I had accustomed myself to a perpetual feeling of hunger. This evening I carved, with a pocket-knife, a pretty little corner off this ham; I boiled it, together with a quarter of the pumpkin, in a tin-can. I boiled it till it was deliciously tender. And then, not having partaken of meat for the last six weeks or so, I devoured it like a cannibal. Half an hour later I was violently ill; I found I could not retain the food I had eaten.

Another trifle had gone wrong in connection with this ham. When I brought it in, the current had swept me too far downstream, and I attempted a landing at my ledges. The speed of the current was considerable there, fifteen miles to the hour, I should say. And in my attempt to reach out for the ledge while I was being carried by I had grazed a submerged rock with my knee. When I was ashore again, I found that the point of the rock had cut a bad gash across it, two and a half inches long and as deep as the bone underneath allowed.

Next morning my leg was sore and stiff, and since I did not feel overly fit – a consequence of my indigestion – I resolved to stay in camp for another day.

The whole previous day it had been raining off and on, in violent, fitful showers; often I had been forced to retire under my rock-ledge for shelter. The river had still continued to rise. But this third day at the camp proved to be one of those glorious days of the fall when time seems to stop and to stand still.

Downstream lay a wooded island, dividing the river into two broad arms. The huge domes of the trees on this island seemed, in the sunlight of the early morning, to be fashioned of dark-green gold. The arms of the river to both sides looked like gates into a beyond which called and beckoned: Come, oh come! I fretted at being held.

There is a distinct gradation in the things the river picks up when it rises. I have seen a creek take all the breakfast paraphernalia from a roofed-over porch on which a coloured household had been sitting when the rainstorm started. The rise of the waters in the steep little creek was so sudden that, when they rushed away to secure other things about their yard, chairs, table and dishes had been swept off that porch before they had thought of their being in danger. Large logs, meanwhile, which they had felled for their winter's fuel, got caught in the brush surrounding the farm and settled down with only a slight dislocation when the flood ran out without going beyond a certain level. But from the opposite bank, helpless to interfere, I had watched the sugarbowl, from among their dishes, set out on its merry jaunt to the Gulf of Mexico, going at an amazing rate.

On this third day of the rising river hewn timbers, large logs and similar heavy freight began to travel downstream.

And they gave rise to, nursed, and finally launched a new idea. Why not make a raft and embark and let the river carry me on its patient back?

Nor did it take me long to suit my actions to the thought. I was on the throw-side of the current; heavy things swept very close along that last, submerged ledge, sometimes

touching it and rebounding. The ham had been abundantly tied with a fairly stout cord. The little box furnished
boards with nails which were short, but sufficient, I
thought, to hold the two or three logs together, which I
needed to carry me.

I lay down at the edge of the lowest platform, pocket-
knife in hand to use as a grappling-hook. I made my first
catch, a log which came floating down crossways to the
current. I buried my knife into its one end with such force
that, when it gave under the impact, I nearly followed it,
head first. I had to strain every muscle in order not to let
go of both knife and log; but when it swung around, into
the current, its pull eased off, and I guided it into the
sheltered pool below the ledges where I tied it with my
cord to a projection of the rock. Soon I had three logs
which promised well. Then I saw a board floating by; and
I remember distinctly what a feeling of anticipation of
pain it gave me to see large nails sticking out of them; I
could not help imagining vividly how it would feel to step
on them with bare feet. But I wanted some of those boards
for the top of my raft. To swim out after them was out of
the question, on account of my sore and swollen knee. Yet
I set out, limping upstream to where the bank sloped
down more gently and evenly. And then I saw something
which sent me rushing into the water: a wide board or
plank or whatever it might be. I could nearly reach it
before I had to relinquish my toe-hold on the river-bot-
tom. I was swept off my feet for a second or so. But I had
the precious thing, and I threw myself back, holding on to
it, pulling with all my strength, striking out with one foot.
My whole body floated under that plank or whatever it
was. My toe hit something there; I gave a yell of pain; but I
did not let go; and the next second I came to with a terrific
jolt and crash: we had brought up against the ledge of
rock. Already the force of the current was swinging me
out into the river; but with a twist of my body I threw
myself on that lowest, submerged ledge and found myself

lifting the whole thing bodily out of the water: a long, wide kitchen-table. God knew where the river might have picked up such loot; I laughed and danced about on the ledge, pulling the thing up and setting it on my platform. I went all around it and examined it carefully. The top was warped, but that was nothing; one of the legs had nearly been broken off by the impact on the ledge, and it stood sadly awry, but what did that matter? Here was what I needed: this table was going to ride astraddle over my logs; it was going to be the top of my raft.

I looked myself over. I had acquired quite a new crop of bruises and scratches; but what was that? I was going to ride along henceforth; I did not need to walk any longer.

I went upstream to get my raincoat which I had thrown off when I dashed into the water. I was exulting over my find, and I was half tempted to set out at once.

That night I ate carefully, cutting the thinnest possible slice off my ham, and chewing it carefully and long. But the mere taste of meat nauseated me.

The story of my trip on the raft stands out with great clearness in my memory. There were fun and disaster, comedy and quasi-tragedy enough in those two weeks to fill a book by themselves. But all that has little bearing upon the present story; I must skip. I shall, after a few brief hints, explain only how my raft came to harm.

For a day or two it kept increasing in size; I soon caught more logs and set the table over them crosswise. That did not increase the area of my deck – sixty by thirty inches – but, since there was a greater buoyancy underneath, it lifted it higher above the water. That I found desirable after I, with my whole outfit, had once or twice been swept off by the wingwaves of passing tugs. Another improvement I introduced when I had lost that one leg which was already badly loosened by my first collision with the ledge at the camp. The remaining legs would catch at snags and sandbars in shallow water. If I happened to be standing, I was shot overboard by the sudden jolt. One evening, while camping on a huge sandbar pushed out by a tributary of the river, I removed them and, swinging them aloft and bringing them down on the sharp edge of an upended rock-slab, I broke them off short, leaving mere stubs to slip over the logs and to hold them together.

I weathered another three or four days of rain – a slashing, driving rain it was – with the table-top set up slantways as a roof, covered on the outside with my raincoat.

At first I always landed for the night. Then, tentatively, I began to sleep on the raft, drawing my legs up and lying on my side, with a layer of willow-boughs for a mattress, the whole craft being tied to some overhanging tree. That eventually led to the loss of the raft.

One evening I discovered, just before it was time to land and to do my cooking, the trumpet-shaped mouth of a creek which emptied into the river. The river being still high, though falling, this creek-mouth resembled a drowned valley. There was no current; the water stood perfectly still and clear. I at once poled into it and found it delightfully sheltered and calm. At the mouth, this estuary measured some sixty to seventy-five feet across, with high banks rough with the underwashed roots of great willows, the peach-leaved kind; inland it narrowed down, in the form of an isosceles triangle, the perpendicular of which measured about a hundred feet. There, at the apex, a miniature valley or chasm opened, ten feet wide, with shallow, limpid, ice-cool water trickling down.

I resolved to tie up and to spend the night on the raft. All went to perfection, and by eight or so I was asleep.

Then, about midnight, a great commotion arose. I awoke and sat up. It was a dark night, but the stars stood out brightly. All around I heard the wild swishing and sucking of tearing water. I noticed that I was adrift; the thin cord had been torn. I also noticed that, for a few seconds, I was being shot, at great speed, out to the open river. I saw lights ahead – a chain of big river-scows went upstream, the steam-tug labouring painfully against the current. I saw it all in a flash. I expected the wingwave and grabbed for my things so as to hold on to them. Already, in front, a black wall rose out of the water, rushing on, towards me. The next second my raft was uptilted and thrown over, upside down; and it and I were racing along at tremendous speed, back to the land, and into the creek, and on and on. At last, after having scraped and knocked along and against a hundred obstacles, I was violently deposited against the upper side of a rock, for the water was running out again. There I sat, stunned into insensibility by the rough handling I had experienced. All this had taken considerably less time than it takes to tell it. When I could think again, I saw clearly what had happened and blessed myself for a fool.

All large river-craft, especially that going upstream, is, since it throws the water back with its paddles, preceded by a powerful suck; in front and abreast of it, the water, being churned into swifter motion behind, starts to race downstream to fill up the valley created there. Then the big wingwave comes in which all these waters mass together. When this wingwave struck my trumpet-shaped creek-mouth, a certain mass of water, measured by the height and length of the wave and by the width of the trumpet at the river-line, entered it with a given momentum. Since the mouth narrowed down towards its apex, the big wave was compressed from both sides, and, since the mass of the water could not escape, the wave rose in height, and its motion became swifter and swifter, till it reached the chasm of the creek. Its width being only a sixth or so of the trumpet where it had first caught the wave, it is a simple problem in mathematics to calculate the height and speed of this "bore", as geographers call it.

It was a cold night, clear and cold; and, of course, I was drenched to the skin and dripping. I found that I was still holding on to my coats; but where the rest of my things might be, I had no idea. There was nothing to do but to make the best of it and to wait for daylight. Painfully I climbed the bank of the creek and emerged in a cornfield; at last I came to a place where the huge stalks had been cut and put up in shocks. I crawled into one of these and was grateful for the warmth it retained.

Next morning, with the first of the sun, I limped back to the creek and found that my raft had been shattered into its component parts, all of which lay high and dry where I could not move them. I found my kettle, badly battered, but still serviceable. I found my bag of oatmeal, none the better for a night's soaking, but still to be dried and hoarded against a day of need. I found my tea-tin in perfect condition; and, after much searching, I found my watch – a bequest of my grandfather's on the maternal side – smashed and useless henceforth; but it, too, I picked up, of course. I did not find the remainder of my precious ham.

There was nothing to it – I dried everything and took to my feet again; the idyll on the river was ended.

I had had a warning, too; the cornfields were being harvested. When that source of food gave out, what was I to do? The loss of my raft was rather a disaster – a shipwreck in little.

My progress was slow and painful; but I kept going.

The nights were getting colder; everywhere the corn was being husked; the leaves on the trees took on a dry rustle. One morning, when I awoke, I found the sparse vegetation on the river-sands white with frost. I did not mind the slight suffering caused by the chilly nights – the days were still pleasant enough, as a rule. But there was a threat in this coming of winter: what was I to do?

THREE

I Come Into Contact With Humanity Again

T HE VALLEY of the river widened out; the islands which divided it were larger now; sometimes one of the two arms was closed by a weir, the other, by a lock.

I was more and more getting used to going hungry. Sometimes I felt a weird intoxication with hunger; at other times my mind seemed to see things with extraordinary clearness and logic.

One day, about noon, I came to a place where a large island, in outline like a pear, densely wooded, was connected at its upper end by a narrow strip of sandbank with the shore along which I travelled.

An impulse of exploration made me cross over to the island. Below the sandbank which I followed, there was a dead arm of the river. No doubt the sandbank was flooded after heavy rains, and the water in this dead arm was swept out. But the river was low at the time, and with the big trees – sycamores mostly – overhanging the stagnant water in the autumn sun, there was something infinitely quiet, soothing, sadly reminiscent about the place. I felt a desire to linger. The island proved a veritable trap for driftwood which I had to climb over in order to penetrate into the sanctuary of its recesses.

Suddenly I heard a noise, the cracking of a dry limb, or the snapping of a dead sapling. I stopped and listened. Not a breath seemed to stir. It was a perfect day for the season – clear, cool, crisp, yet gratefully warm. I felt as if I were confronted with a great, decisive leave-taking. Soon, soon I had to go back to the world of man. I wanted to drink to the dregs the last cup of freedom vouchsafed.

The noise was repeated; and when I carefully scanned the trees, I became aware of a man who was gathering wood, breaking dry limbs and picking up drift. I did not care to be interfered with in my present mood; so I started on a silent, infinitely cautious retreat.

I returned to the northern river-bank and continued my way downstream. By the time I reached the lower end of the island it was late in the afternoon; and I was watching the way the current on the far side broke into an eddy where it touched the stagnant water of the dead arm when a strange sight caught my eye.

From under the overhanging trees of the island a boat detached itself. It was loaded with brushwood. The sticks had been laid crosswise over the boat – making a load twelve to sixteen feet wide; they were piled across its whole length, to a height of three feet or more above the gunnel. The load was so heavy that, where the gunnel of the boat ran lowest, in the centre, there was not more than one or two inches of freeboard above the water, the ends of the lower sticks on both sides dipping into it. On top of this load stood, gingerly poised in midair, a tall, gaunt man who held a long, straight pole with a boathook fastened to its end. With this pole which he moved slowly and carefully – balancing the while – he guided the craft. It looked as if he were performing a feat on the tight-rope. Fascinated, I watched.

He pushed out into the dead arm of the river, guiding his boat by the lightest and deftest touches of the pole on limbs and trunks of trees. I marvelled at this exhibition of skill and strength required for handling the enormously long pole without disturbing the equilibrium of the over-loaded boat.

All went well till he reached the end of the island. But there he miscalculated a motion. The sticks of wood, where they reached out on the far side, just dipped into the furious current that shot out from beyond the point of the island; the next second his craft gave a lurch, settled down, was caught in the eddy. In order to recover his balance, the man made a step to the side; the whole load tilted over, and with a curious, grotesque twist of his body, he slipped down into the water which splashed up high. It looked so funny that I burst out laughing.

But my laugh changed into a gasp: the man had gone down like a stone. Then his head bobbed up again – he was in the quiet water of the dead arm; his boat had gone off, careering, with the current. When he appeared at the surface, I saw that he was fighting wildly. He went down again, a burst of bubbles showed the exact spot where he was: he could not swim!

The weird feature of this life-and-death struggle was the absolute silence in which it proceeded. There had been no shout, no sound beyond that of the splashing water.

Now I am – or was – by nature nearly amphibious, swimming and diving being my favourite pastimes. So, the moment I realized his danger, I dropped what I was carrying, stripped off my coat, and plunged in.

When I got him, he seemed to have given up; but as soon as I jerked him to the surface, he started to fight, grabbing wildly, impeding my arms. I shouted at him, but he did not cease. So I whirled him around, getting one hand under his chin and forcing his head back; and simultaneously I lifted the other hand and brought it down, edgewise, on the root of his nose. He hung limp for a minute, long enough for me to reach shallow water. I hauled him ashore. He sat up, in a dazed, half unconscious way. I left him.

This was an adventure for me, and I was pleasurably excited. I did not mean to leave my work half done. I ran downstream, caught up with the boat which had capsized, swam out, found its rope, took it ashore, and tied it.

Then I returned to the man. He got to his feet and shook himself in a strange way, just as a dog would shake himself after a wetting, or a horse when you pull his harness off after a hard day's work. I had never seen a man shake the water out of his artificial pelt in just that way. It had something contagious; I found myself rehearsing the thing in anticipatory impulses; I came near trying to imitate him.

There were other queer things about him. His hair was long, like that of a woman, grey; it was braided into a stout, long braid which was twice laid around his head, like a turban. His face, as I see it very clearly in my memory, closely resembled the face of Mark Twain in Carroll Beckwith's portrait, only that moustache and eyes and shaggy brows were grey, and there was absolutely no expression in his features. He was fully as tall as I was – and I am over six feet.

Again and again he shook himself, but when he stood still there was something of the stiff and silent dignity of the turkey-buzzard about him. His expressionless face had an albino-like look.

You would expect a man to say a word or so when you have just saved his life – "Much obliged, old chap" – or, "Thanks for going to all the trouble" – but this man didn't. He merely looked me over and allowed his dead eagle-eye to rest for a moment on my things, the kettle, the tin-cans, my bundle, all which I had been carrying slung to a stick which rested on my shoulder.

His glance made me look down at myself. His eye had been halting for the fraction of a second on my knees. They were shaking violently. I became aware that I was sick with hunger and weak with fatigue from my exertion. Also, of course, I was wet through; and the evening was turning chilly.

The man walked off, up the bank, stepping with a strange leg-action and an uncanny, nearly supernatural dignity. Never a word he said. I looked after him, dumbfounded. But neither did I say a word.

Then, just as he was about to disappear in the willow-brush of the upper bank, he looked back for a moment before he went on. There was no expression in his vacant, bold eye even then. I could take that look or leave it, just as I pleased. I might interpret it as a look of fear or as a summons.

I chose to take it for a summons. I quickly picked up the shoulder-stick with my things attached, threw my coat over its end and followed him.

There was a wide band of shore-brush; through it led a narrow path which I followed in the wake of the man. The brush changed in character: from the willows of the bank to the thickets of the hillside – honey-locust predominating.

At last, half way up the hill, we came to a shoulder in the rising ground which was cleared. The path now led through a tiny corn-patch to a hut beyond. I could look out here to right and left, for the corn had been cut and shocked. There was no other human habitation within miles on either side. The sun was touching the horizon exactly in the river-gap.

We entered the house. It was built of lumber, unpainted, with that silky-grey appearance which testified to the weather and the rains of many years. A large slab of stone served for a doorstep.

The arrangement of the room into which we came was as follows. The wall opposite the entrance held a small window, one and a half feet square. To the right there was a fireplace, built of the rough stones of the hillside embedded in mortar. Beyond it, a home-made door of thin boards led into an adjoining room. Along the wall to the left stood a home-made table; for a seat, in front of it, an upended box. In the corner, behind the door through which we entered, a rough bed was strewn on the floor: straw, covered with a rag-blanket: at its foot two or three more blankets lay in a crumpled pile. At a glance you knew it for a bachelor's establishment.

My host crouched down, squatting stiffly on his heels and built a pyre of woodsticks in the grateless fireplace. Then he stood again, whittled a small piece of soft, white wood into a fan-shaped flowerhead of shavings, disappeared through the door into the adjoining room, and reappeared in a minute or so with his stick ablaze. He applied it to the wood in the fireplace; the flame licked upward.

He took his smock off and hung it on a nail. His shoes and coarse cotton socks he removed, too, and laid them on the floor, close to the fireplace, along the wall. He did not pay the slightest attention to me. He moved about in a sober, grave way, slow and deliberate, with no unnecessary flourishes or bendings.

Thus he squatted down again, in front of the fire, but this time with his back to it, warming himself. His shirt began to steam over his shoulders; then he turned and sat a while longer. At last he got up and went out.

I began to feel "creepy".

But, while he was outside, I stripped my wet clothes off and slipped into my raincoat which was dry. I looked out of the window. The tiny yard of this hermitage contained a well and a large pile of just such wood as the man had lost. It was closed on the far side by a low building which seemed to serve for a pig-pen; I saw the man throwing feed into its rail-enclosure and heard the grunting of swine.

The man returned into the house and room before I had had time to pick up my wet clothes. He bent down and carefully hung them on nails in the fireplace wall. That was the first indication of the fact that he was aware of my presence.

Next he busied himself at the table, pushing things about and rearranging them. He reached up somewhere into the now dark corner over the bed and brought down a mug, knife, and fork. It seemed so much like a conjurer's trick that I nearly jumped. But when I looked closely, I saw that a box was nailed to the wall there, serving for a cupboard. Then he took a tin kettle from the table, shook it – I heard the swish of water – took it to the window, peered into it, and, finding the contents satisfactory, placed it on top of the blazing wood in the fireplace, pressing it down to keep it from tilting.

Then he went out again.

I felt strange. Had I saved a lunatic from drowning? His actions were sane enough. As for his head-gear, that hair when unrolled must have reached down to his knees! It looked as if he took care of it; but that might be because it was wet. There was a reddish glint in his eye which was not really grey but whitish. It reminded me somehow, when at rest, of the eye of white rabbits; when it moved, of that of an eagle; it was so imperious.

When he came in again, this time, he dropped something large and light which rustled in the adjoining room and kicked the door open. He carried a sooty lantern and an empty box. The lantern he suspended from a hook in the ceiling; the box he dropped close to the door. Then he pulled the table out from the wall, put his box on one side of it, pushed the other with his foot to the opposite side, and lifted the tin kettle which was spouting steam, with the help of a stick passed through its handle. At last he sat down on his box.

Again he looked at me with a brief glance: take it or leave it; again I took it and sat down. He poured some of the contents of the little kettle into a mug and pushed it as well as a pan of unraised corn-bread and a tin of molasses across the table to my place. The beverage was tea, bitter with many stewings. He started to eat; and I, too, ate a little, very carefully, for I was no longer used to such sumptuous fare, and more from courtesy than from appetite, though I was hungry.

I concluded that the man was deaf and dumb.

When he had satisfied his hunger with great bites of corn-bread soaked in molasses – he had a splendid set of teeth – he got up; and, passing into the darkness of the adjoining room, gathered what he had dropped there before. It proved to be an armful of straw, good, clean oat-straw too.

This he threw into the corner opposite his own bed, spreading it out with a kick or so of his foot. On it he dropped one of the blankets which he picked up from the crumpled heap on his own side; and he stood and looked thoughtfully at me.

Suddenly he reached up and took the lantern from its hook. When he entered the adjoining room, leaving the door open, I saw for the first time that from its ceiling there were hanging down great bunches of half dried and entirely wilted "hands" of tobacco. So I was in the tobacco-belt! It also proved to be tobacco that he went after; for when he came back, he held a large "braid" of it in his hand; from which, after disposing of the lantern, he cut a generous chew.

Again we sat for a while in utter silence. I had found some cigarette paper in a pocket of my raincoat, had rubbed some of his "long-green" into granules and was smoking. I pondered a problem. I wished to speak, to say something. But, after having been silent so long, it seemed inconsiderate to start speaking now; there was something indelicate about words; I gave it up.

His large, heavy hands were resting on his knees; his shoulders were bent forward; he was staring into the fire which he fed from time to time. Suddenly I became aware that he was going to sleep. His eyelids fell; he began to nod; his head shot forward; and he pulled himself back, aroused.

As I got up, a sudden temptation was too strong for me.

"Suppose I'll turn in," I said.

I repented at once; the colour mantled my face; but not a flicker in his features betrayed that he had heard.

Yet, seeing my motion, he, too, got up, slowly, stiffly, reached for the lantern, and waited for my next move. When he saw that I turned to the litter of straw, he gave the lantern an expert jerk which extinguished its flame. Thus he deposited it on the floor and rolled in. There was enough light from the fire for me to lie down by.

You can imagine that I lay awake a long while. The mere fact that I was under a roof was exciting. Here I lay in the same room with this man of sixty or more who looked like an oaktree, lived like a hermit, and was either

a lunatic or a deaf-and-dumb cripple. Even now he was
weirdly silent. He lay like a log, without stirring. I had
expected to hear him snoring; I did not even hear him
breathe. Instead I heard mice and rats go through a veritable carnival of running and jumping, capering and dancing. At first I had pulled the patch-blanket merely over my
knees; but it turned pretty cold; and when I did get drowsy,
I forgot all squeamishness and rolled up.

I awoke with a start, becoming conscious of the fact
that somebody was moving about in the room.

The man had relighted the fire and was leaving through
the door when I opened my eyes. I jumped up and felt my
clothes which I found dry. While dressing, I looked around
and wondered no longer that I had been cold overnight.
There were large cracks in the single boarding of the
walls; lack of fresh air was no vice of this habitation. The
wood used in the building was sycamore lumber; it warps
and twists when exposed to the weather.

The man gave no sign of recognition when he entered.
He had two eggs in one hand, which he put on the table. In
the other he held the little kettle, apparently freshly filled,
for it dripped with water; it he placed on the fire.

He went out again, and this time I noticed a peculiarity
of his footfall. I found that, whenever he put his foot down,
his heel touched the floor first; and, after lifting it again, he
brought his whole sole down with a thump, walking in a
knock-kneed way; he was a high-stepper.

After breakfast he seemed in doubt what to do. He
moved aimlessly about. At last he went to the front-door,
opened it as if to go out, hesitated for a second, and waited
for something to be said or done.

I was going to hang on to him. He was not going to get
off as lightly as all that! I had saved him from drowning,
he was going to keep me for a day or two!

So I made as if to follow him; and he held the door till I
took hold of it.

In the open, a subtle change in the landscape struck me
very forcibly. There had been hoar-frost on the ground

before; but to-day the crust of the ground itself was frozen. In the corn-patch the stalks and weeds north and west of the shocks were still furred with white. The leaves of the honey-locust and the great sycamores in the distant river valley were tinged with yellow. Overnight the season had changed from late fall to early winter. The next storm would bring snow!

My host wended his way down to the river and, beyond the willows, along the pebbly shelf of the beach.

We went down to his boat. He first pulled it up quite a piece on the sandy shore. It was a strong, heavy boat. Then, with a powerful heave, he turned it on its keel. He, I say; for though I made a pretence at helping him, I was so weakened by my late mode of life that my efforts, had they been needed, would not have counted for much. Then he launched the boat back into the water, took the rope in, and laid it down in the bow. For a moment he stood helpless, looking around. Apparently he was baffled because the pole was lost, which he had not realized so far. He went up to the edge of the beach, where the ribbon of the high-water drift was deposited, and selected a pole there. When he came back, he climbed into the boat.

Again, as at the door, he hesitated awkwardly. I climbed in after him; and at once he began poling upstream.

When we came to the quiet water in the dead arm, he landed; but since he did not fasten the boat beyond running it on to the sand, I did not follow him. He disappeared into the willow-brush; and after a short interval he returned, carrying another long pole and a tin dipper. He tilted the boat, climbed in and bailed the water out.

Then we went for a load of wood. He piled it just as high as the day before, possibly feeling safe in my presence, but he pushed across the dead arm before we reached the point of the island. This dead arm was strangely deep.

I stayed all day, and the next day, too. We kept at work; he carried the wood up with the help of a rope, slinging it on his back in huge bundles.

The third morning, while we had our breakfast, I thought I saw a change, an ever so slight change in his manner. I cannot define it in detail. One trifle lingers in my memory.

When I had helped myself to molasses, he took the tin and, before helping himself, he looked into it, hesitating.

Maybe he considered that by two days and three nights of hospitality he had paid for the slight service I had been able to do him. It is true, I helped him with his work; but when a person can do a piece of work by himself, he cannot afford to hire help at the expense of a diminishing supply of molasses in the tin. I agreed with this unspoken argument and made up my mind to leave.

When, after breakfast, he went to feed his pig, I rolled my bundle and tied my things to the stick.

H returned after a while but did not pay any attention to my preparations beyond a casual glance at the bundle on the floor. I sat for a while longer. Apparently he was getting ready to bring in another boat-load of firewood against the winter. At last he opened the door and stepped out, holding it for a moment, as was his custom, till I made a move. I picked the shoulder-stick up and followed. And down we wended our way to the river.

I felt soft in my heart. We had not made friends, but I had enjoyed his quiet, matter-of-fact hospitality. I should have liked to shake hands, to say a word of thanks to this man with the braided hair whose life I had saved.

When we reached the boat, we stood for a moment, awkwardly, he holding the pole in one hand, the rope of his craft in the other, and looking out to the water, as if waiting. I did not know what to do; with a shrug of my shoulders I turned.

Then I stopped and said, "I suppose, it's about time for me to be moving."

And something startling happened. The man spoke. He spoke with an effort, twisting his whole body in the act, the words sounding like those of an overgrown boy when he is changing his voice, hoarse, unexpectedly loud and husky. It looked and sounded as if he were heaving the words up from, let me say, his abdomen and ejecting them forcibly.

What he said, was, "I reckon."

Then he climbed into his boat and pushed off without as much as once looking back.

That was my first encounter with a human being in more than three months.

It affected me profoundly, probably because it came at a critical moment. As for the peculiarities of this representative of the genus homo, I did not feel called upon to judge him. I did no longer forget that possibly my own mentality would seem abnormal to most people with whom I might come into contact. Certain conceptions which were dimly forming in my mental recesses made me question the value of much that was highly prized by other men. I had found, for instance, that talking largely keeps you from thinking. Without reading as yet, certain passages in the story of Jesus had taken on a profound and new significance for me. A deep-rooted suspicion of all that is called learning, progress, culture pervaded all my thinking. I was no longer so sure of my superiority over those who had not received my "education." I had come to regard education as pretty much the opposite of what, in a sane world, it should be. It seemed to me to be a process of filling old wine into new skins. I began to suspect that there might be more wisdom in this "hermit's" mode of life than in that of the most refined and cultured scholar. Yes, I sometimes doubted whether he might not have deeper, truer thoughts than any one I had ever met before. Certain sayings of Christ's – in the sermon of the Mount, during the last supper – sayings which in the common interpretation were just words without meaning – gradually grew upon me. More and more my thoughts began to circle around Jesus.

But I had gone out on a search when I started these tramps; I began to see that the search had been beside the point. So long as my search remained geographical, it must of necessity be a failure; at the same time this geo-graphical search, though it might not bring me nearer to the thing sought for, was slowly fitting me to undertake the real search. Also, it taught me toleration.

Still, the give-and-take of the world was not to be for-gotten. I should have to give as well as to take. These three days at the hermit's house were earned. What I had done for him was in my own estimation worth what he had done for me – though, what I had done for him seemed trifling indeed because it had been so easy for me. But I came to the conclusion that in the long run only one kind of work would do for me – and that was precisely work which did come easy: work which I should choose as play, as a pastime if I were not driven to it by necessity. If I could have earned a permanent living by pulling out of the river a dozen drowning people a day, I should have been glad to go to work right then. Unfortunately people were not reckless enough to risk their lives in order to provide a living for somebody else. So I could not rely on finding off-handedly what I was looking for.

On the other hand, once the problem was clearly grasped, makeshifts lost some of their repulsiveness. If it was understood that, no matter what I might undertake to do, provided it was useful, provided it was in some way productive, even though it went against my nature and could not in the long-run result in that profound satisfac-tion which we all crave – in the "abundance of life", in Jesu words – if it was understood that I could drop it whenever it became irksome, then, I believed, there were a great many things which I could do. Why not, for in-stance, help a farmer with his work? Why not go into some office and add up figures? One thing only was de-barred from all my thoughts: selling in any form whatever. All selling at a profit was, for me, tinged with that taint attaching to Mr. Wilbur's game.

I began to feel more cheerful about my outlook. I began to see things not without a sense of humour. I even rea-soned this way. Suppose I undertook to do what I did not know the first thing about: was I not eminently adaptable? Might I not quickly pick up the tricks of almost any trade and give an employer complete satisfaction even though, without knowing it, he had to teach me first how to do it? I did not care to get something for nothing; but if a man insisted on experience, well, might I not humour him for a while and later tell him that, when I started, I had had no experience whatever? I began to rehearse imaginary interviews which sometimes made me laugh.

The river banks and the hills beyond had donned their most gorgeous garb. Yellow and orange tints prevailed; but here and there the scarlet of an oak or a hard maple was embedded in it like a softly glowing flame.

Night-frosts were the rule now rather than the exception. The river itself, though during the noon-hours the waters still seemed warm, especially in shallow bights, took on a look of chill, particularly in the early morning when white, thready mists sometimes filled the whole valley and sometimes merely covered the surface of the water with curling veils.

A railroad ran close to the river for a while; it seemed sent by Providence for my especial benefit; for I found it easy to discover some culvert or short viaduct bridging a creek or a gully and yielding shelter for the night. A little fire goes far to heat even the out-of-doors if it is built so as to have its heat reflected from a wall behind or a roof overhead. I was careful to extinguish even the last spark of the glow in the morning, carrying a kettle of water from the river and pouring it over the ashes if they were still warm when I left.

It was under such a culvert that I had my next encounter with humanity.

One afternoon it began to rain; soon snow was mixed with the falling drops; and since a raw wind was blowing, this mixture became increasingly disagreeable. The drops struck through my thin clothing; they were cold, chilling me to the bone. I began to look for shelter, going up to the track and following it. I was out of luck, for I had to go a long while before I found what I wanted. It was dusk when I saw a cross-valley ahead. When I neared it, I went out on the cinder-slope; and I was just jumping down into the bushy hollow below when I caught the gleam of a light.

At once I stood rigid; I still had the instinct to withdraw when I expected to meet man or woman. For half a minute silence prevailed.

Then a pleasant though rough voice called out, "Come in!" and laughed at its own joke.

I jumped across the little brook bridged by the culvert and stepped out into the light of the fire.

"Hello, pal," the same voice said; "come on; supper's ready."

I saw a little man, round-faced, round-bellied, with a week's stubble on cheeks and chin and the pleasantest laugh on his features which I had seen for a long while. He was squatting behind the fire over which a kettle hung suspended; the appetizing odour of broth struck my nostrils; I threw my bundles down.

"Coming far?" he asked.

"Not very."

"Kind of cold out-doors to-night," he went on, laughing. "Want a roof overhead."

He looked me over with open scrutiny. I was not sure whether to stay or to proceed; but I wanted to get warm first.

So, while he rambled on, I squatted down.

"Got a cup?" he asked.

"No," I said; "I have some tins."

"Just as good," he nodded, "just as good. Help yourself. Squirrel-stew. Mighty nice."

I complied; and meanwhile my eyes began to roam. It was clear at a glance that this was a more or less permanent camp. There was straw tucked away in the angle between creek-bank and culvert; there was quite an outfit of dishes; overhead a large sheet of tar-paper was carefully stretched across the joists.

"Been here long?" I asked.

"Quite a while," he said, "quite a while. Nice place too; but you've got to watch out for the section-gang. They steal like rats. I always break camp in daytime."

The stew was very good indeed; but I did not dare to do much beyond tasting it; I knew the danger that lurked in too-nourishing food.

The little man kept up a rambling, inconsequential talk.

"Well," I said at last, "I suppose I'll be moving along."

"Moving?" he asked, offended. "I guessed you were booked for the night."

"I was," I said truthfully; "but . . . "

"Don't let me push you out," he said; "I don't pay rent here. Say," he added animatedly, "yez aren't afraid of me company, eh?" He chuckled. "Afeard of me! Say, pal, I'm the harmlessest feller on earth, even though I'm wanted."

"Wanted?" I asked blankly.

"Yes," he said.

"Where?"

"Cincinnata."

He pulled a crumpled sheet of paper out of his pocket, carefully spread it on his knee, and smoothed it with a rough hand.

It was one of those sheets sent out by the police of the larger centres to rural authorities, containing pictures and descriptions of people who are "wanted".

He pointed to one of the portraits and said, not without a touch of pride, "That's me."

"But what do they want you for?"

"Bravery."

"Bravery?" I repeated, puzzled.

"Yea," he said. "I skipped. Knocked a guard on the bean and walked out."

"Oh," I said, "I see. You have broken jail?"

"That's it," he nodded. "Didn't really mean to. Only I didn't want to let them turn me out in winter. Shouldn't have minded if it had been summer. Too much trouble to get back again. Don't mind it yet. Still nice outside. But in winter you want a roof over your head."

"Well," I said at last, "running away from the roof does not exactly seem the way to get under it."

"It doesn't?" he countered. "Shows what you know about it. I'm going to get caught after a while," he elucidated. "Pal of mine – lives up there," and he pointed up the bank, "he's going to catch me and make two hundred bucks out of it, too." He chuckled again.

"How about myself? Aren't you afraid I might betray you?"

"You?" he laughed contemptuously. "I'll trust ye."

I wondered why. He looked at me, appraisingly.

"Hiding?"

"What do you mean? I? No, I'm looking for work."

"Work?" he exclaimed and laughed again. "I wouldn't pick it up if I found it. What kind of work?"

"Any kind," I said. "Want a roof overhead in winter." I grinned at him.

"Wall-l," he said, "mebbe I c'n help ye."

And he told me of a large farm, a little to the north and the west along the main road to Cincinnati, a company-farm, as he called it, where help was always wanted, so he said.

After a while he spread his straw, and we rolled in.

I had been lying for some time, trying to go to sleep when a thought struck me.

"Sleeping?" I asked.

"No," he replied.

"I was wondering what you had gone to jail in the first place for?"

"Punched an officer on the jaw."

"What did you do that for?"

"Cause I wanted to go to jail."

I pondered that. I began to see light. But I wanted to make quite sure.

"Why?" I asked at last.

"Cause I like it there. That's why."

At that we left it.

Next morning I thanked him for his hospitality and struck out for the road to the company-farm.

FOUR

I Try to Find Work for the Winter

THE "COMPANY-FARM" was easily found. Its
gigantic barns showed from a great distance; I approached it about noon. The barns occupied the eastern
third of the yard. To the north there stood a pleasant-
looking, white-painted dwelling with a little lawn in front.
To the west, a small, white house stood next to the road;
behind it stretched a long, low building painted red, the
purpose of which I could not make out but to which some
men whom I overheard later referred as the "bunk-house."

I stopped at the gate and dropped my bundle.

A number of men, some of them coloured, but most of
them white, came in from behind with heavy teams. They
stopped at the barns, tied the lines up, and led the horses
into the buildings. One team was a mule-team. I had never
seen mules outside of the circus. I remember that I admired the careless way in which the driver handled the
slick and elegant-looking little beasts; I had heard that
mules kick. I had always loved horses, and though I had
handled only drivers and saddle-mounts, I had no doubt
but that I could easily catch on to the intricacies of any
work-harness and establish a friendly relation between
draft-horses and myself. I resolved to make that my "talking-point." I was going to offer myself as an experienced
teamster. I noticed that, after a while, every man who had
entered the stables came out again and, crossing the yard,
entered the little house on the west side, close to the road.

Then I saw a heavily built, tall man leaving the dwelling in the background and crossing the yard to the barns. He had an air of authority about him and spoke to several men whom he met, apparently giving orders or receiving reports.

I entered the yard.

The man disappeared behind one of the buildings; but in a short while he appeared again in the door of the southernmost barn. He was talking to an undersized fellow who looked strangely dwarfed by his side. Then he nodded and started back towards the house from which he had come. He saw me lingering in the centre of the yard and changed his direction. When he approached, he looked at me with a questioning glance.

"Are you the superintendent?" I asked.

"I am," he replied, briefly but not unpleasantly.

"I heard you are in need of help?"

He laughed and looked me over. "No," he said. "I have more hands now than I can keep busy. Harvest is over. I'm thinking of laying off rather than of hiring. Had your dinner?"

"No."

"Well, there's the cook-house. Better take a bite before you go on. I'll send word over. New in this country?"

"Yes," I said.

"Tell you," he went on; "better hit the town. Some factory or so. No more work on farms this winter – unless you find one where they keep stock." He nodded. "Go in with the men," he repeated. "Have your dinner."

And he walked off, calling to another man to let the cook know he had sent me.

This other man fell into step at my side.

"Did he hire you?" he asked when we reached the cook-house.

"No," I replied monosyllabically. I was thinking of my "talking-point" which I had not even had an opportunity to use. But I did not feel depressed by my lack of success. Against my expectations I had been treated courteously.

We entered a large room with two long tables. On both sides of the tables a miscellaneous crowd was seated on benches. Never, not even in my days as a waiter, had I seen a number of men so completely given over to the task or the sensuous pleasure of eating. "Pass the taters," "Soup, please," and similar exclamations were the only words I heard.

My companion and I found seats. He, too, devoted himself immediately body and soul to the task in hand. Everybody seemed to be in a hurry. Though several of the men looked at me, they did not speak. When a "flunkey" passed, my companion gave him the message of the superintendent.

The food was good; there was plenty of it. Soup, sweet corn and cabbage in large dishes, potatoes, meat, and pie: it was the first "square" meal I had seen since I had left New York in summer. I could not resist the temptation. Though I ate sparingly at first, towards the end I began to "fill up". Most of the men drifted out again, some lighting their corncob pipes; the smell of the burning tobacco was sweet to my nostrils.

When I, too, got up, I felt drowsy.

Outside, north of the building, lay a huge pile of sawed wood. An axe was leaning against the pile; and with the impulse to pay for the meal I had had I crossed over, picked it up, and started to split the sticks.

Suddenly I felt faint; the world seemed to turn; a cramp convulsed my stomach. I had to rush behind the house; I could no longer retain decent food.

But I returned to the woodpile.

Shortly after, I saw the superintendent in the yard again. He, too, saw me and came over.

"Don't waste you time," he said. "Move on."

"I thought . . . "

"Yes, I know," he interrupted. "Never mind. That's nothing. Where we feed a hundred, we can feed a hundred and one. You can't afford to stop where they've no work for you. Get to the next place."

"Thanks," I said, dropped the axe, and walked off, though I could not see any call for hurry.

That evening, I am afraid, I succumbed to self-pity. I looked at my thin arms and shook my head. The worst of it was the realization that in my present condition I had no right to ask for work. I feared that my digestive powers were permanently impaired; that, to put it technically, I had lost the power to saponify fats.

I had delayed too long. It was too late, too late! Just when I had begun to see light, when I wanted to live again because there was a life's work to be done somewhere! What that lifework was I did not know; but it was there, somewhere, waiting for me; I should find it; once found, it would put me entirely beyond all troubles of an economic nature. I had been sorely in need of this tramp. I felt forcibly that, as I was at the time, it constituted the most important part in my education. Nor was it ended; I felt sure of that, too. My education was proceeding apace. But I had to interrupt it for the time being; life seemed precious again, and I could not winter on the trail.

I had delayed too long; and yet I delayed still longer. There were two reasons for that. Firstly, the advice received from the superintendent of the farm kept me from visiting other farms – it withdrew the open country as a field for my endeavours; the city which I was nearing now I did not want to try. Remained the small town; and the small town was terra incognita to me. I did not know how to approach it. The second reason was that I fell in with a man who was moving to Indiana. He moved in a large, flat-bottomed boat in which he offered me a ride provided I would act as pilot. I accepted readily, for thus I could avoid Cincinnati. Of this boat-trip I remember little, except the river-view of the city and comfortable nights in the open. The first few days' tramp below Vevay, where my companion landed, is also a blank in my memory. But, if going "out west" could help me, this ride surely furthered my plans.

Now, one chilly night, I had built a large fire on the beach-shelf of the river. I remember well how inky black the night was. I had been busy to the last, gathering a pile of dry drift to feed my fire with overnight.

At last I sat down and toasted myself in the radiating heat. I had not been sitting very long when, out of the surrounding darkness, a man stepped into the dome of light thrown up by my fire. I was startled; I had not heard him approach.

"Good evening," he said.

He was medium-sized, middle-aged, in decent work-day clothes; a mechanic, I judged, or a blacksmith.

I returned the greeting.

"Camping?" he asked.

"Looks that way, doesn't it?"

"Mind if I sit down?"

"Not at all. Travelling?"

"No," he said. "I live here; up in the house on the bank, this side the town. I saw your fire and wondered."

"Is there a town close by?" I was none too well pleased.

"Yes," he said. "Quite a little town, too. Have a mill there." He stated what kind of a mill it was; but I have forgotten.

"Getting to be pretty chilly for that sort of thing," he went on, "isn't it?"

"Yes," I said, rather peeved at his obvious curiosity.

But he was not to be rebutted. "Just out for pleasure?"

"No," I replied, "looking for work."

"That so? What kind of work?"

I had a sharp rejoinder on the tip of my tongue and looked up. The expression in his face reminded me of Bennett, the first man who had spoken to me in a friendly tone on American soil.

I withheld my rejoinder and said, "Any kind. Anything I can do."

He looked at me for a while. Then, "You don't look like an ordinary tramp. Don't talk like one, either. Sounds as if you had seen better days."

"The days are good enough right now," I said in order to evade the question implied. "It's the nights I mind."

He laughed. "Guess you're right."

Again we sat in silence for some time.

"Ever worked in an office?"

"No," I replied, "not exactly. Been a salesman, though, out on the road."

"Well, how did you ever . . . "

"Never mind," I interrupted him, not bad-naturedly, "that is a long story."

"Good at figures?"

I grinned.

He became eager. "I knew it. You've had an education." He pronounced it "eddication". "I've never had much schooling myself. Had to go out and earn my living when I was twelve. But I can tell."

"Well," I sighed, "education be hanged! You're better off than I am."

"That's so," he agreed, "but if I had had an education, I shouldn't be where I am."

"Maybe not. You might be on the tramp."

"Yes," he laughed. "I guess I should be satisfied as it is." After a while he added, "We've got a mill in town. I work there. The boss needs a man for the office. Must be good at figures, he says. You might suit him. He's a funny fellow, kind of. But if you know how to take him, he's easy enough to get along with. I've been working for him going on fifteen years now."

"Well," I said, "I might try."

"Sure, do," he said; "if you don't hit it off with him, there's Heini, the miller. He runs a coal-yard. Can you handle horses?"

"I suppose so."

"Well, he's looking for a fellow to deliver coal."

And so the talk drifted on a while longer.

At last my caller got up. He hesitated.

"Say," he said, "makes me feel kinda bad to lie down in a warm house and think of you out here. Wish I could do something."

"Oh, I'm used to it."

"I can't take ye into the house," he mused, "the old woman is awful perticular. Ye wouldn't like it yerself."

"Don't bother."

"I've got a stable," he persisted, "with no horse or cow in it. There's a hayloft upstairs. It's clean, you know."

"Well . . . " I hesitated.

"You can just slip out in the morning," he urged.

"All right," I said, getting up. " I won't need to bother about the fire."

"No, that's right, too," he agreed, evidently pleased.

I threw sand on the coals of the glowing wood and scattered them about. When I followed him through the brush of the bank, we came to a building.

"That's the stable," he whispered while he quietly opened the door. "Wait. Don't make any noise. I'll get a lantern from the kitchen."

He disappeared in the direction of the house.

Soon after, he returned with a burning lantern. He chuckled. "She was setting in the kitchen," he whispered, half choked with subdued laughter. "Sound asleep. I took the lantern away right under her nose."

I smiled.

He showed me the ladder into the loft and another door through which I was to leave in the morning.

"And say," he added; "if you've no luck and are still around to-morrow night, I'll leave the lantern here by the door. Come back. I'll look some time in the evening. If it's not there, I'll know you're upstairs."

"All right," I whispered. "And thanks."

Before long I heard the door once more, and I held my breath. But it was the man again. His head appeared in the opening.

"Still sound asleep," he chuckled. "Thought you might like a bite. I can tell her I had the snack myself."

He put a plate on the floor of the hayloft.

"Well . . . thanks awfully," I said while he retreated.

The plate held the leg of a chicken and a few buns.

I thought of the couple in the house while I ate one of the buns and chewed just one single bite of the chicken. Some men, I thought, have the instincts of mothers; their wives are like dragoons! I fairly saw a large-bosomed, big-boned woman sitting on a straight-backed chair, arms folded, spectacles pushed up on her forehead, very erect and sound asleep.

Next morning I was late, and I had a headache – from sleeping in the hay, I judged. A cat or rat had carried off the remainder of the chicken-leg; I ate another bun and slipped out.

I went down to the river. There was a thin shelf of ice along the beach, the first ice I had seen on the water. If I had needed a reminder, here it was!

I shaved carefully that morning, and I spent an hour cleaning my coat and shoes.

Then I hid my bundles in the willows and went to town. For ever so long I had not been in the streets of a town, and things looked strange to me. The houses seemed so small and so crowded.

There was a business square, and the stores – one of them called itself a Department-Store – looked quaint in their provincialism. I felt greatly out of place. More than by anything else this feeling of awkwardness was caused by the fact that my hair had grown so long as to be conspicuous; it curled in locks behind my ear. It is characteristic for the gregarian nature of our civilization that such a trifle should put a man out.

I dug about in my pockets for the two or three small coins which I still retained; there were seventeen cents altogether. Then I found a barber-shop, a tiny box of a house with the traditional badge in front.

When I slipped in, I found it empty of customers, much to my relief. The barber proved willing to cut my hair for fifteen cents; and I indulged in the luxury. But I paid him many times fifteen cents if I charge him for the trouble it cost me to evade his many questions as to my aim in life,

origin, and present purpose. He was as itching with curiosity as an income-tax report-form. When he finished
with me, I looked at myself in the mirror. My cheeks were
thin; I was tanned to an astonishing depth; but my clothes
had stood up under my mode of life in the most wonderful
way. I looked quite civilized now that my hair was cut. I
did not realize how unmistakably foreign my breeches
made me appear; it took the war to make the average
American accept breeches as sensible leg-wear.

I enquired for the road to the factory. Was I going to
work there? No, but I could find the superintendent there,
could I not? The superintendent? No, indeedy! Not this
time of the day! He'd be at the office. And where might the
office be? He gasped, as if to say, Truly, I did not seem to
know anything at all! The office was down the street, a
block or so; a little red building; I could not miss it.

Well then, I went. The office was found, and I entered.
There was a front-room, with a young lady and a young
man standing at high desks in a grilled-off space to the
right. Beyond, a door with frosted glass panels marked
"Private" led into another room.

"Good morning," I said jauntily. And, pointing to the
glass door, I raised my voice to a questioning inflection,
"The superintendent?"

The young lady nodded.

I knocked.

"Come."

I entered and found, sitting in a back-tilted swivel-chair
at a desk and smoking a cigar, a man of medium size,
with a grey moustache and a puzzled, dissatisfied look on
his face.

"Name's Branden," I said cheerfully. "I hear you are
looking for somebody who is good at figures?"

"Mebbe," he replied in an absent-minded, preoccupied
way, busying himself with papers on his desk.

"I am," I said confidently.

"You're what?" He looked up.

"Good at figures," I smiled.

"Where'd you come from?"

"Down the river."

He drew his brows up, so that the skin of his forehead was pushed together into innumerable folds.

I thought it was time to be serious. I gave him a brief talk about myself. I had recently come into the country; had tried to find work; had not been able to find anything congenial; had started out west, on foot, since I had no money; I had had what is commonly called a good education and felt able and was willing to do any work that might have to be done around an office; as for remuneration, I was prepared to start at any figure that would pay my board. It was quite a good little talk.

He listened patiently enough. He even seemed still to be listening when I had finished. Then he sighed and settled back.

"Know a time-sheet?" he asked.

"No," I said, very earnestly now; "but I feel sure it will not take me very long to find my way through it."

He looked up again. "Feel pretty sure of yourself, don't you?"

"Not at all sir," I said. "But I do feel sure that there can be no great mysteries about the routine of an office. I am willing to work hard. All I ask is to be given a chance. Let me try for a day or so. If I find out that I cannot do your work, I shall be the first to tell you so, and I shall not ask you for a cent."

"Let you try right now," he said with a smirk, cigar in mouth. He picked up a sheet of paper which lay on his desk and flipped it over to me. "I've been puzzling about a problem in 'rithmetic," he said. "Sit down. Solve it."

I sat down and read it over. I remember the problem, though not the figures involved. It was this:

"A pole 98 feet high breaks off, and the top strikes the ground 84 feet from the centre of the pole. Where did the pole break?"

I reached for a pencil and wrote as follows:

"Let *a* be the distance from the ground.

Then $(98 - a)^2 = a^2 + 84^2$
$$9604 - 196a + a^2 = a^2 + 7056$$
$$196a = 2548$$
$$a = 2548/196 = 13$$

The pole broke 13 feet from the ground."

This solution I pushed back to him across the desk.

He looked it over in a careless way, glancing at it sideways, past his up-tilted cigar.

"Hm," he snorted. "That's algebra! I want 'rithmetic."

"Pardon me, sir," I said. "The problem, as it stands, cannot be solved in a purely arithmetical way. It is a problem in elementary algebra."

He frowned. "What?"

I repeated. "The problem cannot be solved without the use of an equation."

He laughed. "We've got a principal in our school here," he said, "who is a mathematical expert. He gave this problem to my boy as an exercise in 'rithmetic. The boy has never had any algebra. Do you mean to tell me that you know more mathematics than our principal of the school?" He had spoken with a strongly rising inflection in his voice.

I shrugged my shoulders. "I don't mean to say anything except what I said."

The man was on his feet now; both his hands came down on the desk with a thump; the veins on his temples seemed to swell to the bursting point; his voice was a roar.

"You know everything," he shouted, "don't you? You know everything better than anybody else? You tramp! Get out!"

I stood and laughed in his face. Then, with another shrug of my shoulders, I turned and left him.

In the grilled-off space of the front-room the young man and the young lady were looking at each other, smiling furtively. I saw that they had heard.

When I closed the door of the private office, they craned their necks to look at me. Both smiled when I nodded across to them.

"Good morning," I said.

"Good morning," both replied and ducked guiltily down into their books.

I went back to the river. The river was a great friend of mine those days. The river did not call me a tramp. It did not bellow at me. It bore with me patiently.

A tramp! Jesus had been a tramp! There was nothing in the word to cause pain. If somebody had called me a swindler or a crook with as much truth as this man had called me a tramp, it would have hurt. But a tramp? What, then, was the discouraging thing about it? It was the intention behind the word. The word was used with intent to hurt. Where did that intention come from?

I sat on the riverbank, head between knees.

Was this man "no good"? I could not say that. He might be a good citizen, a good husband. I even had some ground for the assumption that he was a good father. My friend of the night before had called him a funny fellow; but he had added that he was easy enough to get along with. I must have antagonized him. I had antagonized people before. What in me was it that did it? I came to the conclusion that it was the fact of my recent immigration.

What did it come to? America had worried along without me. There seemed no reason why I should press myself upon her. My life-work! How could I ask these people to help me in order that I might be preserved for some purpose which certainly would not benefit them? It was easier to give in.

Jesus – Abraham Lincoln! What nonsense to search! The Lincolns were living all about me, of course; there were thousands of them, hundreds of thousands, millions! If there were not, what with graft, "con", politics, and bossdom the country would long since have collapsed! The very disease of the bodies politic and social proved their fundamental health. Who was I to think that anybody in this country needed me? And unless I was needed, I did not want to stay. I was not a parasite!

And yet I felt sure that, if I could only find them, the Lincolns in this great commonwealth, the small ones and great ones, would gladly stretch forth a helping hand; they would point out some nook, some hidden valley maybe, where I, too, might help in fighting back disease, be it on ever so small a scale. They would not call me a tramp, with intent to hurt.

And gradually, by the time the sun had reached the middle of the western sky, I reasoned myself back into a different frame of mind. I laughed at this manufacturer who was a victim of his own dyspepsia. How easy it would have been to answer yes instead of no when he asked me about the time-sheet! Such an answer might have given the whole interview a different turn. What did it amount to? There could not be any great mystery about such a thing. That pleasant young lady would have been glad to point out its meaning to me; and the young man, too.

I determined to make another attempt, to go uptown once more, to see Heini, the miller.

I found the flourmill and entered the little office. A counter separated the front from the realm beyond. Again there was a little box of a private office partitioned off to the left; a second door, behind the counter, apparently led into the mill.

It was through this second door that the miller entered.

He was a small, round little ball of a man, with a greying beard and shoe-button eyes, a man of quick, soft movements, apologetic in manner, pleasant-faced, pleasant-spoken – a German-American. I do not remember his name; for simplicity's sake I shall call him Mr. Miller.

"How do you do, Mr. Miller," I greeted him with a smile.

"No, no, no," he said with exaggerated energy, raising both his hands. "I don't want anything. I no can use anything. Nothing at all! Business is bad. I don't know what we are coming to! Chust look out. Look out through the window. The coal-yard there. Full of good coal. Best coal money can buy. Go into town. Chust go into town and ask the peoples. Ask them, I tell you. Do they want the coal? Do they? I tell you, they do. Sure they do. I've got the coal. They've got the money. They want the coal, I want the money. But how? Can I get the coal into their cellars? Can I, I ask you? Can I? I cannot. For why? I no can put the coal in a paper-bag and tell them, There, take it. I've got to send it to them, on a wagon. Have I got the wagon? I have. I have the mules to pull it. Nice little mules, slick little beasts! Oh, they are beauties! Oh, they are pretty! They are birdies! Well, then you say. Well then, why not? Because! Chust sit down. Sit down, sir, and let me explain. No driver, no help! Here I am with a mill. Capacity five hundred barrels. Do I grind the five hundred barrels. Do I? Perhaps you think, I do? I don't. For why? Help, I tell you. I no can get help. The farmers bring their corn. They want it ground. Take it home, my friends, I tell them, take it home. I no can do it. I no can. They've got the corn; I've got the mill. No good. No good these days. I tell you, in Chermany . . . But what's the use? Peoples owe me money. Peoples buy flour. Here they come. Charge it, they say. Charge it, Mr. Miller. We'll pay on the first. No, I have to say no. For why? Do I trust them? Do I? I do. Why? Have I not known them all along? Don't they always pay when they've got the money? Don't they? They do. Well, you say, well then, why not? I'm coming to that; chust wait a moment; don't be impatient, sir, don't. Charge it, they say. No, I say. I no can. For why? I've got the flour. They've got the money. Maybe not now. Well, then, next month. So far, so good. But a bookkeeper! Have I a bookkeeper? Have I? Well, sir, I have not. And there you are!"

"Mr. Miller," I said when I contrived to get a word in, "that is just what I want to talk about."

"That? What?" he asked, completely at a loss. "What? What, I ask you."

"Help," I said succinctly.

"Help?" he repeated and gasped.

"Yes," I replied. "You took me for a salesman. Well, Mr. Miller, I am. But I sell help."

"Whose?" he asked.

"My own," I replied. "To put it briefly, I want to go to work for you."

He sat down as if a strong fist had hit him. "A chob, you mean? You vant a chob?"

"Exactly."

"Vell," he said; and again, "Vell?" as if taken unawares.

"Look here, Mr. Miller," I said. "You've got the work. I want the work. You've got the coal. I'll deliver it for you. You've got an engine. I'll start her up for you. You've got the books. I'll keep them for you."

"Vat?" he shouted, for he was getting excited. "Can you drive mules?"

"Sure," I smiled.

"Vell," he said; moving restlessly about on his stool. "Vat do you think about that? You can drive mules? You can?"

"That's what I said."

"Lissen," he went on, "lissen. They're ugly . . . "

"You said they were pretty," I objected.

He laughed uproariously. "So they are! So they are! But they kick!"

"No mule has ever kicked me," I replied truthfully.

"You must be Dutch," he exclaimed. "A Dutchman and a mule always get along together."

"Perhaps," I agreed. "In all my dealings with mules I have never given them a chance to kick me." Which was perfectly true. I had never been near one.

Again he laughed. "Say," he said, "Mr. . . . "

"Branden's my name," I said, "make it Phil, for short."

"Vell," he shouted, "you said something, Phil. That's vat you vant to do. That's it. Don't give them a chance. You give them a chance, they kick. You don't, they don't. And there you are."

True enough, there I was. It seemed too good to be reality. "And in the morning," I hastened to say in order to hammer the iron while it was hot, "before I go out with the mules, I'll start your engine. You show me how. At night I'll keep your books."

Again he laughed. "Three in one," he said "three in one. But you no can do it all."

"Sure," I asserted. "I'm a devil for work. I just eat it up. If I can get a place around the mill to sleep in, I won't even bother about a room."

"Vait," he shrieked. And he jumped up and ran to the window. "Look," he said. "See?"

"The house?" I asked; for in the far corner of the well-kept yard stood a miniature house.

"Yes," he nodded. "Sure, the cottach! I built it. For the hired man. It's yours."

"Fine," I said. "I could bach it there."

"Sure!" He was full of enthusiasm. "Sure. Bach it. That's it. No cost much."

He paused, suddenly pensive, stroking and rubbing his bewhiskered chin. And, a note of suspicion creeping into his voice. "Vat do you vant?"

"Want?"

"Yes. Vages. How much?"

"Oh," I replied. "That's up to you. Enough to live on. Whatever you say, till I have delivered your coal. After that, if I give satisfaction, we'll see."

"Vell," he went on dryly, "four dollars a veek. How about it?"

"All right," I said, "I'm willing to work for four dollars a week."

"Start right avay?"

"The sooner the better."

"All right," he said in an absent-minded way. "Maybe I hire you; maybe not."

"Not?" I echoed.

"Yes," he said. "I like you. I like you fine. You chust suit me. But I've a partner."

"A partner?"

"Yes," he said. "My vife. A fine voman. A very fine

voman. Ven ve married, she had the mill, I vas a miller, and there you are."

"Well," I said, disappointed at not getting immediate action, "if you mean to say that you have to consult her . . ."

"Consult her? Sure, I've got to consult her."

"Certainly," I agreed, "if she is your partner. But the sooner you do so, the better it will suit me."

"Right avay," he said, "right avay."

He went to the door, opened it, and peered out.

"Villie," he shouted to a little boy across the road. "Villie, come here!"

The boy came running across the driveway.

"Villie, you run up-street, to my house. Tell my vife, Mrs. Miller. I'd like to see her, you tell her. Can she come?"

The boy ran off.

"Well," I said, "if you have the time, you could show me the mules meanwhile. If Mrs. Miller agrees, I'll start right in."

"Yes," he replied, still absent-mindedly, "sure. Come along."

He led the way through the door behind the counter, into the mill, where he took a flour-dusted cap from a nail, and down four or five steps into the yard. When we came to the stable, he pushed the door aside.

"There," he said. "There they are." He pointed to a team of as ugly and mean-looking beasts as you care to imagine.

The floor of the stable was choked with manure.

"Need a brushing," I said, looking at the mules.

"Yes," he agreed. "Sure. I no can do everything. I got the mules. I got the vagon. I no got the driver. Nice beasts. Chentle as lambs." He approached the near mule. "Ho boy," he said and patted him on the rump. "Chentle, you see." But the mule gave a vicious kick without hitting him, for he was clearly afraid and did not go near.

I laughed. "You can't hurt the air, boy," I said to the mule.

Mr. Miller laughed loud and long. "No," he exclaimed, "he can't hurt the air."

"It's all in keeping out of the way of his feet," I said and quickly stepped between the two brutes, although my heart was pounding like an engine. "Hold on," I said to the same mule and hit his nose with my fist; for he turned around, teeth bare, ready to bite. "Pretty set of teeth you've got!"

"Dat's the vay," praised Mr. Miller, his enthusiasm reviving since I was less afraid than he. "Dat's the vay to handle them. I can see. You know them. They won't bite *you!*"

At this moment the boy joined us in the stable.

"Vell, Villie," asked the miller, "vat did she say?"

"She's coming," answered the boy.

Mr. Miller was in a great hurry to get back to his office. There was no mistaking his nervousness. I was expectant and just a little afraid.

"Where did you come from?" asked Mr. Miller when we re-entered the office.

"Down the river," I said. "I heard from a man at the other end of the town that you were in need of help."

Mr. Miller did not reply but gave himself over to impatient waiting.

We did not have to wait long.

Mrs. Miller appeared in the door; the moment I saw her, I might have returned to my friend, the river.

She was a tall, bony woman, slender, skinny, who in walking held her hands stiffly in a tiny worn-out muff, a smooth, flat stole of the same, cat's-eye yellow fur on her shoulders. She held herself erect and seemed to try hard to avoid giving one the impression as if she had legs; she glided along. Her mouth was closed in a straight line. A pair of horn-rimmed spectacles rested on the bridge of her nose. Her small hat bore an upright aigrette of short plumes which looked as if they had been pulled through a rat-trap.

I rose and greeted her with a pleasant, "How do you do, madam."

But she ignored the greeting. For a moment she stood by the door and swept her eye over me from head to toe. Swept, I say, for it felt as if somebody were sweeping me down with a single, rough stroke of a coarse broom. And I stood bared of every pretence at respectability.

Then she slid past, with an air of injured dignity which brought a rueful smile to my face.

Mr. Miller had hurriedly preceded her into the private office, the door of which remained ajar.

The beginning of the conversation escaped me; but soon the woman's voice cut out like an icy knife.

"No," she said with great precision. "Not under any circumstances. It is the worst element, the scum of the country, which comes down the river."

A few muttered words.

Then again, "No. Not under any circumstances. I should consider myself criminally negligent. Reflect for a moment. Think. Suppose a house was broken into! Worse maybe! A murder! Who would be to blame?"

A few muttered words again.

Mr. Miller appeared. He was the picture of dejection; he was all apology.

"I'm sorry," he said; "the river; it's the river!"

I was mad clean through. "No," I said, "Mr. Miller, it's you! Do you mean to tell me that, because that skate . . . "

"Sh!" Mr. Miller hissed warningly. "Sh! A fine voman, I tell you; a very fine voman!"

"All right," I said and reached for my cap. "Suit yourself. Don't blame me if your coal remains undelivered. Good-by."

I went back to the river as if I might miss a train.

FIVE

I Become a Hand

I MADE MANY other abortive attempts. Details seem irrelevant.

One morning when I awoke my face felt strangely wet and cold. On carefully lifting myself, penetrated as I was with a feeling of otherworldliness, I found that the outline of my body, as I lay in the bush, was softened by a mound of snow. The snow had come down soft-footedly, over night, like a benediction. I had slept through it all; my fire had gone out.

My body did not feel cold; not in the least. There seemed such a lightness, speaking of weight as well as of colour, in everything, that the illusion, had it lasted, might have persuaded me that I was still dreaming. I sank back to my bed of willow-boughs and lay there, staring thoughtlessly at the world transformed. Gradually, as my circulation adjusted itself to the quickened pace of wake-fulness, my face began to glow, my ears to tingle. Infinite comfort seemed to creep through my limbs; it was good to lie still. My worries seemed dead and forgotten. I thought of nothing with any degree of intensity.

I seemed to review my life as you may look on at a play when your seat is too far from the stage to understand the words: you miss, therefore, all the vital connections: tragedy may be a farce; comedy may touch you with tears. I lay for hours. I was utterly indifferent to everything except the strange feeling of comfort, of well-being. I dozed again.

Hours later, I started up. This time a wild fear possessed me; a feeling of being hunted and tracked. I sat and stared blankly. Everything was dripping. The snow on the ground and the bushes was a mere slush. The sun was getting in his work.

I felt my pulse. My watch had been spoiled when I lost my raft; so I could not count the beats; but even thus I could feel that my blood was racing through my veins at fever-rate. I rose in terror, picked my things up, and started to stumble blindly along the beach. I do not know how far or how long I went. But I know that some time during the day, when the snow had melted and showed only here and there in patches along the hollows of the opposite, southern bank of the river, the sky became overcast; the usual wind sprang up, a bleak, raw, wintry wind that drove huge waves on the river upstream. Simultaneously, I believe, I began to cough: a hard, dry, racking cough that brought sharp pain to my side and the lower part of my chest. I began to grope along the steep but low bank which followed the curves of the beach at some little distance from the water. I had to stop often; when the cough caught me, I had to bend down, to support myself with my hands on stones, roots, fallen logs.

At last I found a sandy nook in this bank and lay down again. I had not eaten all day; but I had wetted my lips repeatedly with water from the river.

The wind howled dismally through the bare stems overhead. One of the last things which I observed was that the river was rising fast. I slept. A fitful sleep it was, filled with ravings and nightmares, and broken by frightful attacks of that dry cough which seemed to shake my body.

Again I awoke with a wild start in the morning – a start which this time sent me up on my feet. I had to clutch at things in order not to fall. Then I saw the river. It had risen prodigiously. It was full of drift. But the drift consisted, not of logs and boards, not of household articles and fruits of the field, but of large slabs of ice which danced wildly in the wind-lashed floods.

I was beyond myself with unreasoning fear.

I could not stand; I could not walk. I peered up the steep bank and caught sight of the edge of a roof; but between the house and myself rose a formidable hedge of honey-locust with thorns like daggers, ten, twelve inches long.

I struggled up to the hedge; and then I broke or stumbled through it, the huge thorns tearing my clothes and lacerating my flesh with their points. I emerged into the yard of a small farm, swept by the tearing, icy gale.

To the right stood a house. I went to the door and knocked.

A man came out, closing the door behind him. He was in a shirt and trousers only, bareheaded and barefooted; and as he stepped out, he shrugged into the shoulder-loops of his suspenders; he had apparently just been getting up. His empty face expressed only horror at my sight.

I swayed, and the words I spoke came in a painful gasp.

"Have you some stable?" I asked. "A hayloft. I came down the river. I'm sick. I've *got* to get out of the wind."

He hastened to lead me around the house. I followed, holding on to house and trees to steady myself and not to fall headlong. We came to the barn. It was of that half-open type that marks the tobacco-barn, boards and open spaces alternating in the walls. He opened the door. The floor was a mire of manure and trampled-up mud.

I shook my head and waved my hand in his face. "Won't do," I gasped, "too wet."

I could see that the man was nearly scared out of his wits. He slammed the door shut and looked about.

"The smoke-house," he said; "it isn't warm, but its dry. We aren't using it."

Again he led the way.

The smoke-house was a tiny building opposite the dwelling. Its walls were slatted only, but there were all sorts of discarded things in it which offered shelter; the floor was dry.

I nodded, and the man left me.

I sank down and rested. Then I began to crawl about on all fours, like a beast in distress, trying to find the most sheltered spot, not by looking for it, but by the sense of feeling only.

After a while – I must have been lying there for an hour or longer – the door opened, and I saw a woman of ample proportions, a small boy hanging on to her skirts and peering around them, half impertinent, half frightened. The woman looked at me.

"You're pretty sick," she said. "I bring you some broth."

"Put it down," I replied. "Put it on the floor there."

And she placed it within reach of my hand. She hesitated a moment; and then she went away.

I shivered in my chill. After a while I propped myself up, reached for the cup, drank what I did not spill, and sank down again. I lost consciousness.

Hours later I felt that I was being handled. The woman was bending over me.

"We are going to take you into the house," she said.

I offered no resistance. I did not care. But while they laboured in supporting me across the yard, a paroxysm of spasmodic coughing seized me; and when they stopped, trying to uphold me, I noticed a boy hitching a very mockery, a veritable skate of a horse to a decrepit buckboard.

I lost consciousness again.

Days, maybe weeks intervened of which I know nothing.

But through those weeks, scattered in, as it were, among the fever-phantasies and nightmares of my illness, there flit visions of a man who was deftly putting his fingers to my chest and applying a stethoscope.

Him I see very distinctly when I close my eyes. A medium-sized, quiet, unobtrusive man in a black suit, awkward-looking, with hard, gnarly fingers, a coarse, angular face marked by a grey moustache, his shoulders sloping, his neck enclosed in a stiff, very white, but home-laundered fold-back collar with a ready-made black bow tie – the kind that fastens with a rubber-loop and a crescent-shaped pasteboard shield.

A homely figure; ridiculous in its stiff clothes which are too large; I cannot help laughing when I think of him and how he looked; but the laughter is undershot with tears; a strange lump rises in my throat. No offence is meant, doctor, if I laugh at you! Believe me, I bow down to the very earth and touch the ground with my brow!

A consultation took place. I was conscious again by that time of what was going on around me; I was very, very weak; so weak that I could not move my hand without help.

There were three men in the room. "My" doctor and two others, slick and competent-looking men who fairly dwarfed my doctor as they applied their instruments to my chest. I wondered.

A weird conversation took place in which formidable and learned words caught my ears; words like "hyper-resonant rather than hyporesonant" – "hematogenic" – "peribronchial", and others. "My" doctor hardly took part in the discussion; with an apologetic smile he listened; and as I watched his face, I could see, now agreement, now disagreement under that smile. His whole mind seemed to become transparent to my eyes. When one of the young men wound up with, "The prognosis is bad, if not hopeless. Don't you agree, doctor?" he shrugged his shoulders; his smile seemed to become ever so slightly ironic.

The young men took their leave with elaborate, formal courtesy which but thinly disguised their contempt for their homely colleague who thanked them humbly for their help.

As soon as they were gone, "my" doctor got busy. It was the first time that I consciously heard him talking. I remember every word.

"Oh, these young doctors," he said. "They have had so much more of a chance than I ever had! They know so much more! They are so much abler! They have so much more confidence in their diagnosis! When I went to college, we did not have half the opportunities! We were sent out very inadequately equipped indeed. But I am going to wager on Nature. I am going to help Nature along the slightest little bit. I am going to give her a chance to get in her work."

And he rolled me over on my side and bared my back.

"Now, my dear young man," he went on. "I am going to hurt you. I am going to push a pretty stout needle in between your ribs. Here it is," and he showed me. "As I said, it is going to hurt; but I cannot help that. The more it hurts, the greater the hope for you. Pain is not pleasant, I know; but it is an attribute of life."

He was working with wonderfully deft fingers on my back, at the lower edge of the ribs. Those gnarled hands of his were not clumsy. The smell of ether struck my nostrils; he was squirting it at the skin of my back. And then, suddenly, I felt him gather a lump of flesh in one sure, unfailing hand, a hand that knew what it was about – and the next moment the other hand pushed the needle through that upgathered flesh, in between the ribs and through my body. And from my lungs there detached itself, against my will, a yell of pain.

I heard the doctor's quiet, reassuring laugh.

"Good," he said, "fine! Why, there must be a great reserve of strength left if you can still yell that way. One day you are going to be a noted athlete yet. The pain is all over now. Of course, it does not feel natural to have that needle in your chest. But it will take only a few more minutes. Only a very few minutes now. I am working the aspirator."

And thus he talked on; and at last he said, "Now one more second. I am going to withdraw the needle, and then you will be all right; on the road back to health and strength if Nature wills it."

I sank into a sleep; and when I awoke, the pain was gone.

From that day dated my recovery. One morning when the doctor called I tried to speak; but he laid his hand on my mouth.

"Not yet, my friend," he said. "Not yet. To-morrow maybe. You are doing fine. Soon, soon we are going to sit up. But not yet. And no talking yet. But the time is coming fast."

I began to take note of my surroundings. I was still in that house on the riverbank. I was lying on a wide, soft bed opposite an open window through which the wintry air came in, pleasantly cold. Snow was on the ground and lay in heavy layers on the branches of an evergreen outside. There were goings and comings into the room, and gradually I realized that I was lying in the kitchen of a two-roomed house. I do not know how the next bit of information reached me; but I found out that this family of four with whom I was staying had moved into the parlour. I was lying in the one bed which they owned. They were sleeping on straw spread on the floor, there, in their dingy parlor. The fat woman was nursing me under the doctor's direction. The whole household had reorganized itself with this one view, to save me from dying. Poverty was written all over the place; but I lacked nothing that might be needed.

A thought began to puzzle me. One day I asked the doctor when he sat on the edge of my bed.

"Doctor," I said in a thin, strange voice, "who's paying for all this?"

"Don't think of that," he said. "Get well first. You are among friends."

When he had gone, I beckoned the fat woman to come.

"Who is paying for all this?" I whispered.

She smiled. "Doctor Goodwin says you are not to worry."

"But I do," I replied.

"Well, don't," she admonished. "We'd be willing to do it for the Lord, but the doctor won't let us."

So I knew.

"Why do you do all this?" I asked the doctor the next time.

He smiled his deprecating smile. "Your case has been interesting," he said. "I am always glad to take on a case from which I can learn."

"I am a tramp, doctor," I said on another occasion. "Just a common tramp."

"You're not," he replied. "Don't do an injustice to yourself. You may have been tramping, but you are not a tramp. There's a difference."

"How do you know?"

"I can tell," he said; "and what does it matter?"

Then, as my strength returned, we talked.

"Our policy is at fault," he said. "We lose sight of the immigrant. But I suppose it is the same all over the world."

"It is, and it isn't," I replied.

He looked a question.

"Who would think of going to England, to France, to Sweden – anywhere," I argued, "without carefully laid-out plans and prearranged connections?"

"Yes," he agreed, "there is something in that. We invite the immigrant. We tell him, Come and you will find freedom and economic independence. And when he follows the call, we turn him lose to shift for himself."

"You even forbid him to make arrangements beforehand. And think of the countless thousands who do not even know the language of the country."

"I know," he said. "I've sometimes thought of that. Unless they gather in alien communities, they become a prey to sharp practice."

"And it is the one who comes in good faith who suffers most," I went on. "You match two men for a fight. One you strip of his weapons; the other one you leave fully equipped."

The doctor got up. "Don't rub it in," he said.

But I did. "And because they are foreigners, you turn

them over to the scoffing derision of thoughtless ignorance. No wonder you remain foreign to them. Yet they,
too, have made part of America."

"Yes," he said. "In one sense they have."

"Are you done with tramping?" he asked when I had
told him part of what I have told in this record.

"No," I said, "I have only begun. So far I have drifted.
After this I want to drive."

"I think I understand," he smiled. "But you can't go on
now. You will have to lay off for the winter."

"If I can find work."

"Don't worry. Get well. We have provided for that."

I wondered who "we" might be; but I did not ask.

I was sitting up again. I was relearning to walk. My
recovery was rapid; the doctor's calls became rarer; I
missed them.

One day, he took me out for a ride in his buggy. It was a
mild winter day; gratefully I drew the air into my healing
lungs. I waited for him in his vehicle whenever he entered
a house to make a call. All his calls were made in poor
country-houses – his clientele was not among the well-to-
do nor in the nearby town.

Then, on our way back, he broached the subject which
he had been pondering.

"I don't know," he said, "how you feel about it. We have
a mill in town, a veneer-factory. How are you with tools?"

I laughed. "Give me a hammer and a nail, and you can
rely on my hitting the wrong one. But it doesn't matter."

"The druggist, too," he said, "is looking for a clerk."

"No," I said, "no selling for me. Let it be the mill. I'd
like to try out what it is to be a hand."

"Well," he replied, "I've spoken to the manager. They
are shorthanded all the time. We'll fix you up."

"Will they take the vagrant?"

"You are no vagrant now. You have a roof overhead."

"Doctor," I said inconsequentially, "what is the difference between a jail-bird and a respectable man?"

"The respectable man is forehanded," he replied, looking puzzled. "He has an intenser fear of the future and a greater desire for manifold things."

"True," I said; "you might add, a greater dependency on the judgment of his neighbours. But that was not what I meant."

"Morally speaking?" he asked.

"Ethically," I nodded.

"None, necessarily," he answered. "It all depends."

"Doctor," I laughed, "you are an anarchist. I have suspected for some time that all really good people are anarchists."

He too, laughed. "Of sorts," he agreed. "But the really intelligent man, no matter who he is, longs for one thing above all."

"What is that?" I asked.

"Production."

"I have lived off the land," I objected.

"A child," he said sententiously, "is entitled to his infancy."

I felt very grateful for that word.

"The Abraham Lincolns live all around," I added after a while.

"Who are they?" he asked.

"You are one of them," I said.

He frowned quizzically, but kept silent.

And so we returned to what, for the time being, was my home.

A week or two later he dropped in again. I was walking in the yard, looking down at the frozen river, when he pulled his pony in. I smiled and went to meet him.

"Get your coat," he said. "Jump in. I want to show you something."

We drove to town. At the edge of the village he stopped in front of a tiny house; he tied his horse.

"Come on," he said, "I've got the key."

The tiny house held one room, eighteen by eighteen feet. There was a small stove, a bed with a mattress and a blanket, a plain deal table and one chair.

"I'll charge you two dollars a month for rent," he said. "The stove costs two and a half. You owe for it at the hardware store. The bed was given by one of the bankers who wants to be nameless. Table, chair, and blanket are mine, to be returned when no longer needed. You will want some dishes, maybe, and similar things. I am going on your security at the general store. As for fuel, I advise to get half a ton of coal at the yard. That will set you back another two dollars; but it will be cheaper than gathering drift, for you will need to husband your strength. You better stay right here now. To-morrow we shall go to the mill. My office is across the road. You might call there at nine o'clock."

"But I cannot leave those people without thanking them or saying good-by," I objected.

"Well," he said, "they wanted it so. You will see them later."

Thus, that day, I set up a bachelor's establishment.

Next morning we went down to the mill by the river.

I was bewildered when we entered the huge brick building – bewildered by the roar of machinery and the great number of men handling logs, planks, and all kinds of timber in all stages of finish or lack of finish. But more than anything else one thing struck me: these men who were, so it seemed, mere parts of the intricate machines they fed did not seem to mind it in the least: they had time to joke and to laugh.

Doctor Goodwin led me into a small room on the ground-floor, a room which was partitioned off from the rest of the building, but which nevertheless seemed to shake with the pulse of the work.

He bade me wait while he went away, upstairs.

After a while he returned, accompanied by a tall, fleshy man of truly senatorial proportions. This man moved about in a detached sort of way, as if he did not care where he was or went; but on closer observation I saw that his alert little eyes were shooting about in all directions.

"Well," he said when he entered, "so this is the young man?"

And he looked at me with a humorous flicker in his grey-blue eyes. "We can always use an additional hand," he said with a note of irony and the slightest possible emphasis on the last word. "The doctor tells me you are long on brains and short on muscle?"

"I am afraid," I said, "as far as the muscles are concerned, the doctor is right."

"Well," he went on, "as it happens, we need a fellow with an ounce or so of brains just now. In the glue-room. Things are not going there as they should. We make veneers, you know. But we also sell table tops and such things ready veneered. That is a side-line with us, lately introduced. And somehow it has not been a success. We are always behind our orders, way behind. And we are thinking of dropping the whole department for lack of the right kind of a man. It is not a nice place to work in. It is hot, there. Everything needs to be hot. Glue does not smell like perfume either." And he paused with an ironical, questioning inclination of his head.

"Never mind," I said; "where others can work, I can, I suppose,"

"That's the spirit," he replied, still with his ironical drawl. "There are three hands working there now. But they are mere boys. They don't have much sense of responsibility. Naturally, we have to draw on the town for our help; and the glue-room is not popular. The best men do not care to go down there. But if I put you in, I should expect you to see to it that we catch up with the work. Three men should be able to keep the store room empty. But one of them has to be the boss. Of course, I cannot engage you as foreman of a department. You will have to start in on the wages of a helper. But unless you make yourself the boss, you know, you can be of no use to the mill."

Again he paused questioningly. He spoke very much "de-haut-en-bas". But that, I found later, was his way with everybody, even with his fellow-citizens of high standing in the town.

I smiled ruefully. "Well, sir," I said, "I suppose you know all about myself. I am afraid I shall disappoint you."

"The work does not need to be hard," he went on. "It is a case of using an ounce of brains or so."

"It is not that," I said. "But will the boys obey a man who is new in the country?"

"Well," he drawled, "if it is any comfort to you, I will tell you this. The best worker we have at present – I mean by that, the man who is most anxious to do an honest day's work for a day's wages – is a Russian who has been in this country only four months. He is just beginning to pick up his first words of English. He has no education, either. In fact, he can neither read nor write. He was quite unskilled when we shipped him out from Pittsburg. He is kiln-boss now."

"If *you* will risk it," I said.

He turned and looked out into the machine-floor. He raised a finger to a man who was walking about, there, inspecting the work of the roaring machines. A shout would not have availed out there.

The man came, deferential in his bearing.

"Mansfield," said the manager, "this man here – his name is Branden – will report to-morrow morning for work in the glue-room. See me about him later on. Better show him around."

"All right, sir," replied the foreman.

And with a brief nod the manager turned away; and Doctor Goodwin followed him.

Mansfield, a short man with quick, shifty-looking eyes in an elderly, colourless face, beckoned to me to follow him as he began to thread his way among the machines. When he came to an elevator-shaft, he stopped and pressed a button. The open platform of the elevator began to descend. It was encumbered with two low-wheeled trucks loaded with "cores" of worm-eaten chestnut wood.

We descended. It was cool down there, in that huge store-room of the basement. Cores of various sizes, similar to those on the trucks, were piled all around to the height of the ceiling. The whole centre of this basement was occupied by long strips of veneers of quarter-sawed oak, mahogany and poplar.

"Arrears," said Mansfield, pointing with a sweep of his arm, and he laughed. "Need a boss here to catch up."

We went along one of the main aisles, ducking under swinging belts and whirling shafts. Even down here Mansfield had to speak at the top of his voice in order to make himself understood.

Then we came to the glue-room. Intense heat struck us like a blow when we entered. Wide racks of hot steam-piping were loaded with cores. Veneers were spread on long, shelf-like desks. A huge hydraulic press occupied the centre of the room. Along the far wall glue boiled in steam-jacketed pots. The smell was certainly not like perfume; more like that of burning fishbones.

Three young boys were working here, none of them, more than fifteen or sixteen years old. They scanned me with curious looks.

We left the room through a door at the opposite end.

"Can't get a decent man to take hold here," said Mansfield. "It's the heat and the smell."

"I don't mind," I said, "but I don't know anything about the work."

"You'll learn," he replied.

"When do I start?"

"At six sharp, second whistle."

I was a factory-hand.

SIX

I Widen My Outlook

NEXT MORNING I arrived at the factory at a quarter to six, with the piercing yell of the first whistle, and started in. I cannot follow events in this interlude very closely; it would lead me too far afield. I will briefly state that I found the management considerate in the extreme and that, if I made a success of the task as outlined to me by Mr. Warburton, the superintendent, I owed it chiefly to the circumstance. It was no easy work for me; but I have always considered that it was worth while. Three factors made it so: Mansfield, the foreman; Gawrilucy, the Russian kiln-boss; and my study of the general run of workmen employed.

As for my own career, suffice it to say that within a month I was "boss" in the glue-room – the word "boss" implying that I took orders from nobody except the superintendent himself – that within three months the department under my charge had caught up with orders and that, when I left, the work was running smoothly enough to be left to the boys whom I found in charge. My own earnings had remained modest enough. I had started in on seventy-five cents a day; this was raised to a dollar the second week; and by the end of my first month I was getting seven dollars and fifty cents a week – the highest wage that any one below the management could boast of; and even Mansfield, the foreman of the machine floor, received only twice as much.

I said that Mansfield's eye had impressed me as shifty-looking. He seemed to avoid your eye. But I soon found out that the reason did not lie in any inability on his part of treating the men over whom he held authority in a straight-forward way; he was simply excessively modest.

He, too, had come to this mill as a "raw hand" – and not so very long ago. He had worked for maybe eight or ten years and had been foreman for a matter of three or four. His promotion, which he had literally thrust upon him, was due, not so much to sheer ability, as to his vision. Many of the other men could beat him in speed and accuracy of manipulation; but – and here is a very important point – suppose you had slipped him in among them as a mere hand, without their knowledge, at any one of the machines, say at a sandpaper-belt – though they *could* have matched and excelled him in quantity and quality of their output, not one of them *would* have done so. If it had been a contest, entered into with the full knowledge of all concerned that it *was* a contest, many a one would have outdone him. But without such a stimulus, only he would have put forward his full effort. The reason was simply this: that he saw the mill as a thing alive – as a living organism whose performance was his very personal pride. He had that curious ability of loving a dead machine; he adopted it into his affections as nowadays a man may love his car and never be satisfied unless it shows at all times at its best. He could tell you the history of every one of them; how the inventor had met with difficulties in getting his improvement adopted – and how, gradually, it had swept the country and come into general use. For him there was romance in machinery. When he fed some such moving structure of knives and saws, he felt exactly as Dr. Goodwin had felt when he said at my sickbed, "I am going to help Nature along the slightest little bit."

All this implies that he was a reader. He had started with trade-journals, but had soon gone on to reading books of a technical nature; and Mr. Warburton, the superintendent, had encouraged him in every possible way – till one day he had said to him, "Mansfield, I believe you know as much of veneers as I do. Would you like to come into the office." "No," Mansfield had answered. "I don't care about veneers. I want to stay where I am, with the machines." "All right," Mr. Warburton had continued, "but not as a hand, not with a single machine. I am going to put you in charge of the whole floor."

The Russian kiln-boss presented a different problem to me. Like myself he was a recent immigrant; unlike myself, he had at once made a complete and permanent economic success of his new life. But in one respect I found him to be very much in the same difficulties which I had experienced. He was the first of a long line of inarticulate immigrants with whom I was going to come into contact; and from the first I was drawn to him. Many Americans have the idea that the immigrant, as they are used to see him nowadays, is completely satisfied with material comforts. Nothing, I found, is farther from the truth; and that is precisely why I have felt encouraged in giving this record of my own struggles. Very few of them will speak up, even if they are able to do so.

This man, when he came to the United States, left a family behind in Russia. He had saved enough money by this time to let them follow him; but he hesitated.

"This country," he said to me, "good country to work in. Bad country to live in."

I questioned him on this point; and gradually I found out what was his point of view. Immigrants from Eastern Europe were wanted to do the hard work in America, that kind of work for which the man born in America had become too soft through easy living. They were highly welcome to employers who found it increasingly difficult to secure help for that class of work. But they were not at all welcome to those whom they regarded as their equals in the country.

"Why," he would say, "why me kiln-boss? Heavy work. Why no machine hand? Light work. Others do. Handle small piece. Out here, in kiln, heavy pieces. Big logs, big planks, hard work."

"But do you object to hard work?" I asked.

He laughed. "No. Not me. Like it. Can do it."

"Well, then . . ."

"Oh," he said, and his laugh died out. "We here like Pollacks in Russia. Despised. Americans good – we no good. Just beasts, like cattle."

"Does Mr. Warburton treat you like an ox?" I insisted.

"Him, no," he replied. "Him make money. Need me. But boys, how bout them? Slant-eyes, they say. Low-ears. Bones stick out. Cannot speak English. They laugh."

"What do you care?" I objected. "That's only the riff-raff. They do the same with me. A blistering Englishman, they call me. They can't even distinguish between an Englishman and a Swede, when the Swede happens to speak better English than they do."

"I no care," he said. "I no care for myself. But the children. I care for them. I go back to Russia. All Russians there. I got money, I all right. I buy land. My children good. I stay here, my children no good. I no want my children laughed at. Not their fault, have slant-eyes. Not mine. I can't help. Slant-eyes just as good. I speak English; they no speak Russian. I honest. I good father. I good worker. But no good here. Why? Russian! Liberty, Freedom?" He laughed. "Freedom to joke. Freedom to hurt. Fair play? Foul play!"

The upshot of it was that I started to teach him English. He proved a remarkably able scholar. I marvelled at the speed with which he learned, and above all with which he learned to read and write. In two or three months he read magazines. The paradox in it all was that he still had to go to a professional scribe to get his Russian letters written to his family – at fifty cents a sheet – when he could easily have written them himself in English.

Then I came back to the charge. I knew Russia too well to let him go back – Russia as it then was, no matter how much certain people may praise it now.

"You are making good," I told him, "you are an American. Those boys in the mill that make fun of you might be Americans; but they aren't. They are too ignorant. They don't know any better. Your children? Why, bring them over. Teach them yourself for a while. Then send them to school. Will they ever have a chance in Russia?"

"Not much," he agreed.

"Well," I went on, "here you can give them a chance. You say you came here on their account. It's on their account that you want to stay and to bring them over."

"Maybe," he said. "Maybe in fall."

Meanwhile Mr. Warburton began to notice a change in him; one day he sent him to Cincinnati to appraise and to buy, if up to standard, a supply of timbers from the raft.

Once I had a brief talk with the manager about the Russian.

"It's next to uncanny," said Mr. Warburton, "the way that man can see into a log. He'll take his axe and swing it into a timber, and he can tell what the flake will be when it is quarter-sawed. If I did not need him, I'd send him up to Chicago or Grand Rapids. But, I suppose, he'll find out himself, soon enough, that there are better places for him to work in; places where knowledge and power will bring him better pay."

As for the boys with whom I had to work, one little episode will illustrate their psychology. As the time was approaching when I intended to leave – for, as soon as we had caught up with orders, I lost my interest in the task – I mentioned one day that I should not be with them much longer. One of the three, Dan, I felt sure, would be able to keep the glue-room going, provided that the other two would support him. Of these two only one gave real trouble. His name was Jesse, and his aim in life seemed to be to get as much fun and to do as little work as he possibly could.

"I want to help you," I said to him, "to make your job permanent. Unless you show them that you can do as much work as others do, that job will disappear."

"I guess," he shouted. "I can do as much work as the next one."

"Sure," I said, "and get as much pay, too. The trouble is you aren't doing it."

"Well," he exclaimed, "let's get busy."

And for a day or so he outdid every one.

The desire to do his best could be awakened only by a sporting proposition. Make it a case of rivalry, a contest, and he was as good as any one. In the daily grind of routine he fell down.

Spring came, and one day I sought Mr. Warburton.

"I'm going to leave," I said.

"That so?" he asked, unruffled.

"Yes," I said, "seven and a half dollars a week do not seem so alluring to me that I should give up a wider outlook."

"Anything in sight?" he enquired in his ironical way.

"No," I said. "But I want to move on. I want to see things."

"Well, Branden," Mr. Warburton proceeded, somewhat annoyed, "I've always thought so. The lure of the river's got you. It's always the same with the men that drift down the river. Spring comes, and the wanderlust gets back into their blood."

"Partly; maybe," I agreed, though I was nettled at being thought so shallow. "Yet I am not going to follow the river. I am going to foot it, but only because I haven't the money to pay my fare."

"Where do you intend to go?"

"To Indianapolis," I replied. "Maybe to Chicago. I want a wider field."

"As a veneer-hand?"

"Maybe, for a while."

"Look here, Branden," he said. "I don't want to hold you back. But I believe you are making a mistake. Here, in a small mill, you have made good. Don't think for a moment that I want to deny it. But in a large mill you will be just a hand again. Of course, you may make good there, too; don't forget, however, that you are not very strong. Will you be able to stand the pace?"

"I don't care," I replied. "It is beside the point. It does not enter into my ambitions to make a career out of this thing. I have an idea that there is something bigger and more important which I can do."

"Oh?" said Mr. Warburton vacantly.

"It isn't money," I went on. "As far as money goes, very little will satisfy me."

"Money is power," he drawled ironically.

"Money is slavery," I replied. "At any rate, it is not the kind of power I want. Most of you industrial Americans overrate the value of money or of the material things which it buys. Your higher standard of living, as you proudly call it, does not seem so all-satisfying to me. Life has to yield me more than a competence or even an abundance of things necessary or desirable. But I suppose, it is useless to discuss it."

This, in turn, nettled Mr. Warburton; he closed his shell, as it were. His judgment was formed. He did not say it in so many words; but in his features I read his estimate of the tramp.

Dr. Goodwin, with whom I sat during the following afternoon – it being Sunday – took a different view.

"So you are going? he said. "Well, I don't blame you. But will you find what you want?"

"I don't know," I replied. "I'll find it or perish in the attempt."

"Nothing like perishing in a worthy cause," he said. "There is a great deal of satisfaction in it. Though it sometimes seems selfish to me. Don't forget that for us ordinary mortals it is quite a worthy task merely to make an honest living."

"Not for me," I replied, "nor for you."

He laughed an embarrassed laugh. "Well . . . " And his tone was half deprecation, half admission.

"Doctor," I shot at him suddenly, "how much do I owe you?"

He was still more embarrassed. "I really couldn't tell you offhandedly," he said. "I've never figured it out. I'd have to look it up in my books."

"Suppose I wait a week before I ask you again?"

"All right," he said, visibly relieved.

This time it was I who laughed. "Do you want me to tell you what would happen?"

"How do you mean?" he asked.

"I'll tell you," I said. "Either you would not be able to find it in your books or you would try very hard to avoid me. Perhaps you'd be tempted to make a little trip in order never to see me again."

His face was a study.

I was determined, however, not to let him get away with it. I had saved a tidy little sum out of my wages. So I drew a roll of bills out of my pocket and put it on a little table which stood at my elbow.

"Listen, doctor," I said. "I am not going to offend you by insisting that you accept a fee. I have seen the good people who nursed me. They will get my bed and whatever else I own in the line of such trifles. With you I am going to leave four-fifths of what I have saved, in trust as it were, to be used by you for the relief of suffering in your parish. It is not much. Only forty dollars. But I should feel better if you would take it on these terms."

"I will," he said; "thank you."

That settled the matter.

I had still another interview, this time with Mansfield.

"Do you think," I asked him, "that Dan will be able to carry on the work as glue-room boss?"

"I do," he replied. "He has learned to see the employer's point of view, and he has given in to the better methods."

"Very well. Then you had better count me out a week from next Saturday."

"I'm sorry," he said. "But if you wish to go . . . ."

"I'll go," I replied.

As it happened, that was, against my expectations, the

end of my career as a factory hand. Just a word about what it seemed to teach me.

There are three classes of men engaged in the industries of the nation: born leaders, born servants, and the rest of them who are neither the one nor the other but who work for others because they cannot help themselves.

Nothing needs to be said about the first two classes; if all men belonged to them, there would be no industrial troubles.

Nor do troubles necessarily arise in the third class, either. Not without intention have I given details in this chapter about the foreman of the machine-floor and the Russian Gawrilucy. They fitted in; they were unable to be leaders in a large sense; they were not necessarily servants. On the other hand they did not object to the fundamental condition of being led. Being led, they had made a success of their work in life; they were satisfied. Chance had been kind to them: they lived "in abundance" where chance had dropped them. If the world as it is had been put down before them as a toy-shop, Mansfield would have chosen machines for his toys, the Russian would have chosen logs to toss about, to pick them for their flakes and figures, and to cut them open in order to verify his conjectures. They were not only satisfied with what they were doing; they were happy in doing it.

I think I can say that, without exception, the other workmen in this factory were doing what they did – like myself – by chance. When they had reached the age at which they thought they should be making money – or at which others thought that they should do so – they had gone to the mill which happened to be near. A job was easily secured. Work was work; what did it matter? But it surely does matter what we do with two thirds of our waking hours. So long as work is work, and play play, just so long do we want to get as little of the one and as much of the other as possible; that is human nature, not here, but the world over; not now, but in eternity.

We will, for a moment, disregard that small fraction of the human race which would choose to live in utter sloth. We can disregard them for, I believe, humanity could afford to "carry" them as parasites. The loss entailed by them would be small as compared with the loss entailed through present, faulty distribution. For the rest, we will assume that the great majority of humans want to work, want to exercise, not only their physical powers, but also their mental equipment, whatever it be.

We will, also, assume that every human being has, hidden away, maybe, in his innermost heart, never awakened perhaps, but yet has his leanings, his pet inclinations, his hobbies. Why, then, does he not make his hobby his occupation? Because he cannot do so. Chance guides him. When he starts life on his own account, at fourteen, let me say, some mill is nearby, and he goes to it. Money looms bigger than the "abundance of life". And for one thing, very few children know at fourteen years anything of themselves. They start drifting.

Raise the school-age to eighteen, and you will have made a step forward in the right direction; but you will not have solved the problem.

Alas! Our schools! We worship the fetish of reading and writing. Useful arts they are, of that there is no doubt. But – I speak from manifold experience – show me the grown-up who wishes to master the arts of reading and writing and cannot do so in a short time – in one-hundredth the time which we waste on them in our schools, incidentally making our children into verbalists and spoiling them for reality – and I will show you a mental laggard. We say that there is an age for these things; that beyond that age it becomes nearly impossible to acquire that knowledge. That is simply one of the superstitions of the ages. Reading and writing and similar inessentials have formed the curriculum of our schools since time immemorial. Why? Because in by-gone civilizations the man who received an education was the man of leisure. He was taught to read; he was taught to write, not because these things were prime necessities of his life, for they were that less then than now; but exactly because they were not necessities, because they were luxuries, because they were the distinctive accomplishments of his class; they marked him off from the multitude.

We want, or regard as desirable, only one class of our population: the workers. What, then, is the distinctive accomplishment which we should nurse in our schools? There is only one answer: Work which satisfies.

Why do our children break away from school as soon as they can? Because they are forced to follow what seems to them futile, silly, purposeless routine. The children are right. Convince yourselves by going to their schools yourselves; by acquiring some art which is taught there in the same, deadening way in which it is presented to them: I believe I should soon catch you yawning; I believe I should soon catch you playing truant. We are everlastingly hitching the buggy in front of the horse; and we think that unfortunately it cannot be helped. A more systematic, organized, wilfully cruel waste than that conducted in our world-wide systems of education no genius of perversity could invent.

Meanwhile there waits that one great problem of life, to be solved by chance for the countless millions. And we let it wait!

Why is the boy with fingers adapted to tinkering, with a mind inclined to mechanics – why does he think he is satisfied with his work in a machine-shop? Because chance was good to him, *so he thinks*; it placed him where he belonged. But did it? Maybe the time will come when he is at the end of his possibilities for lack of deeper knowledge. He will be a labourer when he might be an executive – leaving all thought of the money-rewards aside for a moment. Then his life will suddenly lack that "abundance". Equal opportunities for all? Indeed! Do you call it giving that man an opportunity if you point back into the past and say to him, "You should have made better use of your school-days?" Was he the man he is now when he was a child? Could he foresee? As a child he looked into that school-room with horror. That was the school-room's fault, not his; all the more so if the school-room sugar-coated things. The task allotted seemed and was slavery and drudgery; Life beckoned, clad in light and the wind of the wild. Maybe it was only tinsel and shoddy: could he distinguish?

But if, when he was a boy, you had led him into a giant work-shop of all the essential industries of the land and had spoken to him somewhat as follows: "Go to it; satisfy yourself; find out in the next year, or in two or four or five years, what kind of work you would like to do; then do it. Whatever you do will be paid for at current rates; henceforth you are self-supporting; the work we are turning out here is not idle play; we are doing part of the work of the world; we do not ask you to weave little paper-mats or to sew little picture-cards which seem silly to you and which indeed we should drop into the nearest waste-paper basket as soon as you do not happen to look; whatever you make, unless in the process of making it was spoiled beyond the possibility of use, will be used; in fact, our shops differ from those of our great industries in only three points: they are here brought together within a comparatively small compass – we watch that you do not overwork, for there will, I trust, be no need of watching you so you won't underwork – and you can get help at any moment in whatever may seem puzzling to you. Above all, find out where your inclinations are; we are going to let you work in many departments; work in them all and find out what you like best. And whenever you run up against that which you do not understand, for which you need theoretical knowledge, well, my boy, against that case we have provided class-rooms where such things are taught; you can avail yourself of them or not, as you please. But till you are eighteen years old, no matter what you may choose to do, you are going to do it right here, on these farms, in these workshops and offices. But, if we do not ask you to spell out silly words which you do not understand and for which you have not now and may never have any use, we do ask you most earnestly never to persist in a task which seems hateful; we require you to find a task that is pleasant to perform. By doing that you will be doing your duty" – if you had said that to the boy or the girl, would they have responded? It is my unalterable conviction that they would.

That is nothing new, of course. I do not mean to palm it off as original thought. I hold no monopoly in common sense. But, couple such a system of education – which would breed craftsmen instead of labourers – with a half-ways sensible system of labour-exchanges – as any group of intelligent men could work out in an hour or so – and you will have done away with the major part of the causes of present unrest; but you will also have done away with what brought the French Revolution about and which is by no means dead: with privilege in all its forms.

No amount of literary cramming will make a good, loyal, intelligent citizen out of a reluctant child. But a craftsman who loves his work and takes pride in his work, who would rather do his work than joy-ride over the country – such a craftsman cannot be a disloyal, trouble-some, unintelligent citizen, even though he can neither read – nor write. But, of course, he would have mastered both these arts without wasting eight years of his life on them, endangering his health to boot.

SEVEN

I Am Kidnapped

ONE DAY in May I left the little mill-town on the Ohio River and struck out north. Thoughts like those which I have outlined at the end of the preceding chapter occupied my mind.

I had seen something of menial service, something of commercial life. A glimpse at industrial activities had followed. One of these three aspects of the work of a nation was warped, it is true, by the unfortunate chance which had led me on to the crooked paths rather than to the straight and narrow ones. But I could close my eyes to that part of my experiences. Two had proved distasteful to me in their very nature. One, the last, had left me feeling clean, untainted, but still dissatisfied. I attributed my dissatisfaction to the circumstances which had led me to one of the smaller enterprises. More and more I became imbued with that old conception of mine that I was cross-sectioning the life of a nation. I must not stop before this task, for as a task I viewed it, was completed. It seemed to be something imposed, a mission, something I could not escape in any case and which I might well further. There was no ulterior motive in it. The thought of writing, of some day telling others about my life, was very far from me indeed. I was merely trying to work out my own salvation; and to do it in my own way. Just now the labourer was in my mind; I wanted to see more of him; I wanted to study him in the mass. Indianapolis was my immediate goal; beyond it loomed Chicago with its multitude of immigrants.

I had set out from New York in order to search for that America which bore Abraham Lincoln. I thought I had found it. I thought that I saw the Lincolns all over the country, in little villages, little hamlets, little farmsteads and smithies – wherever men sacrificed their own selfish ends for the general good – and, above all, of course, in little doctors' offices.

There was, from the outset, no fear of the unknown in this second tramp of a hundred and fifty miles or so. I had only a little money in my pocket, it is true; I went in overalls; but I went, determined and confident that I could make my way without suffering. Nor was that confidence disappointed. I travelled like the travelling journeymen of old.

I will give three examples of how it worked out.

The first evening I came to a farm which stretched along between a creek and the road. House, barns, and stables were strung out to the left of the road, behind a stone-wall. The farm sloped down over bottom-lands to a quick-flowing stream.

It was at the horse-stable where I stopped. A man who had just come in from the field was taking the harness off his horses. I bade him good evening and stepped in. Without leaving his work he returned my greeting and looked me over.

"I'm on the tramp," I said, "I've been working down at the mill on the river and am trying to get to Indianapolis. I'm a veneer-man. I wondered whether I could get a bite at your place and a corner in the hay-loft to sleep in?"

"I don't know," he replied, still looking me over with a look of appraisal.

"I'm willing to pay whatever is right," I added.

"Take that horse, will you?" he exclaimed; for one of the horses was trying to get away from him.

I grabbed the halter-line.

"We'll see," he went on. "I've got to take the horses down to the creek for water first. I'll ask the missus."

"All right," I said. "I'll help you; how many are there?"

"Five," he replied; "yes, if you'll take two, we can make it in one trip."

"Sure," I agreed, dropped my bundle, and reached for the halter-shank of a second horse.

We wended our way down to the creek, through a field in which the corn stood a few inches high.

"Nice corn," I praised.

"Pretty fair," he replied.

And when we were waiting for the horses to drink, he enquired, "Nice little mill they've got down to the river. Are they making money?"

"Hand over fist," I said.

"Why'd you quit?"

"Oh," I said, not caring to discuss my real reasons, "mill is too small. They don't pay enough."

"How much?"

"Six, seven dollars a week, according."

He laughed. "A farm-hand gets that, all found."

"That so?"

I felt sure of the night's accommodation by that time.

When we returned to the stable, we fed the horses and went to the house. The man entered alone.

"All right," he said when he reappeared. "The missus is getting supper. We haven't a bed to spare . . . "

"Never mind," I interrupted. "I'll sleep in the loft. I'm trying to spend as little as I can."

And we sat down, till the "missus" called.

Next morning I was up at the break of day and started brushing the horses and throwing the manure out. I was thus engaged when the farmer entered.

"Well," he said. "Working, are you?"

"Might as well help while I'm here."

"Come in and have breakfast," he said.

When I took my leave and asked what I owed him, he answered, "Oh, I reckon you've paid by your work."

"Well," I said, "thanks."

And I was on my way.

Another night I reached a very small farm just at nightfall. It was a dairy-farm, worked by a young newly-married couple. They were in the cow-barn, milking, when I found them.

Again I started in by giving them some data about myself. They looked at each other. I could see they were glad of a stranger's call. Their lives did not offer much entertainment. To have me there, for the night, was a break in the monotony of their daily grind. They were beginners; their work was hard; and since they had no help, they had to share it.

Still, all their talk at supper was about hiring a man, only to end in a sigh with the words, "Well, we can't. Not just yet. A year from now, maybe."

The woman was expecting a baby as I could see. I carried water and stove-wood in while the young man watered and fed the cows.

Next morning he took a cream-can to town, and, his road coinciding with mine, I had a ride. They refused to accept any pay though they had given me a bed in the house.

A third night which I remember was spent on a large farm conducted by a city-bred man who was trying to use the most modern methods.

Again I came across the owner in the barn. He was standing on top of a load of fodder-corn, and a number of men were feeding the horses of which there were sixteen or twenty, all of them splendid animals with high-arched necks, Percherons and Belgians. I waited for him when one of the hired men had pointed him out to me as the "boss".

"Well," he asked when he fell into step with me, "what can I do for you, sir?"

I told him.

"Sure," he said, "we'll put you up."

A slight shower had fallen during the afternoon, and the air was fresh – of that spring-freshness which seems like a caress.

He stopped between house and barn and looked out over a field sloping away to the setting sun; the corn stood knee-high.

"I've known that corn to grow six inches in a single night," he said. Then he turned to me. "Going to the city, you said?"

"Yes," I replied. "I'm a veneer-man."

He laughed. "I got out," he said.

"From veneering?"

"No, from the city."

I looked at him. He was still a young man, thirty-five maybe – a pleasant, vigourous type.

"Hard on the women, though," he went on when he proceeded towards the house. "Farm life, I mean. My mother and two sisters are with me. I am unmarried."

"Well," I said, "of course, you can't have city conveniences on the farm . . . "

"You can, too," he interrupted. "One day I am going to build the right kind of a house, if I make a go of this."

"You have not been on the place very long?" I enquired.

"A little over a year," he said. "I'm all for it, too. But I doubt whether the women like it."

We reached the house.

"Mother," he called when he entered, "I bring a guest."

A white-haired lady stepped into the room. At a glance I saw why she suffered: she had lived with social niceties for the breath of her life. But she was brave, "game", for she adored her son. I somehow divined as much; and I treated her with formal courtesy.

Before we sat down for supper, I had become a friend of the family, a confidant of their troubles.

We sat till late into the night, the mother depicting, not without a sense of humour, though it was of the ironic kind, the trials of her life among the "rustics".

"But my son says that is honesty," she smiled, "and it is, of course. But it seems to me mere honesty is nothing much to boast of."

We laughed.

"When a man is worried about the mortgage on his farm," I said, "I suppose he has not much to say for the white table-cloth."

"He should," she answered; and again her son laughed.

"Mother doesn't believe in mixing homelife with business-worries," he said. "When a man takes his overalls off, he should be a gentleman even though he may be a roughneck in the barn."

"Above all he *should* take his overalls off once in a while," she added.

I had a room to myself, with washstand and bureau. It would have been an insult had I offered to pay when I said good-by after breakfast.

I gained an insight into the lives of men in the country, a straighter, juster view of things, superficial though it was. During the preceding fall I had looked on the farms which I passed with suspicion and hostility; I doubt whether the mere tramp would have been welcome. Now I kept up the fiction that I "belonged" somewhere. I thus began to feel that a new vista was opening up. What were cities and towns? Mere specks on the map. Here was the ground-mass of the nation – the soil from which cities sprang, like strange, weird, sometimes poisonous flowers in the woods. For the first time I saw the true relation: the city, the town working for the country: the farmer, though not yet realized as such, the real master of the world who would one day come into his own. I understood that, before I could say that I had a fair view of America as it is, I should have to mingle with the men who tilled the soil. And no longer did this seem a formidable task, as it had seemed when first, in the east, I had had a vision of the continent which stretched beyond the rim of the coast-lands. I looked forward to it with pleasure and anticipation.

But I did not swerve from my immediate objective. The labourer was the man whom I wanted to study; unconsciously I understood by that the labouring immigrant: others who, like myself, had come into this country to make a living, but who had the strong arm to make a success of it. I wanted to seem them in the mass, to weigh their chances for a real life. I myself seemed very unimportant, very irrelevant, for I realized by this time that mine was of necessity an exceptional case.

I also pondered a good deal on the curious plan which seemed to underlie my wanderings, though I could not see as yet that it was the natural and necessary outcome of conditions. Here I was, in the middle west, walking the highroads to my destiny. I had started life on this continent as a waiter, feeding the city-masses; had looked in upon straight and crooked business; had taken a glimpse at one of the essential industries, helping to make the accessories of civilized life; and at last I was seeing myself, in the future, among the fundamentals of life – where the food was being grown for the seething world.

What had I done, so I asked myself again, to bring these steps about? Nothing! I had drifted. It was as if a higher power had led me blind-folded. Is it not time, I said to myself, that, instead of resisting, I help it along, that I assist it in bringing about what seems to be my destiny? Oh, how proud I felt when I surmised that one day I was to be master supreme of myself and my fate!

There is humour and irony in the fact that I should just have reached this summit of self-approval, this reconciliation with, and acceptance of, that which I fondly imagined to be my destiny when fate took a hand and played a little trick on me, so as to take the starch out of my most wonderful conceit. For Fate did take a hand and literally railroaded me into the next phase of my life.

This is how it happened.

I was now very close to my immediate destination. That day or the next, I thought, I should have reached the city. But the weather had taken a nasty turn. In the morning a heavy and cold rain had started, soaking the roads till they were mere mires of clayey mud. A drizzle persisted all afternoon.

I came to a farm. The owner whom I saw at once when I turned in at the gate was closing the slide door of a big red barn. I waded across to him and, with a greeting, stated my desire.

He interrupted me gruffly – the weather was enough to spoil any man's humour. "I don't keep a boarding-house," he said, "why don't you go to town?"

I referred him to the state of the roads, but enquired about the direction.

"Follow the track," he said and pointed north.

I went.

I found that I had to go about a mile before I reached the track. I was tired and wet. This last piece of the road was a veritable quagmire, that kind of tough clay-mud which smacks its lips at you when you withdraw your foot. I was hungry, too – though I still carried some bread, the left-overs of my lunch. But since the town was said to be near, I did not stop to eat.

It was a relief when I reached the track; but I tramped along, walking the ties, for another three or four miles before I finally saw lights ahead. At the same time there loomed a water-tank to the right. On a spur of the opposite track stood an open box-car; its doors showed it to be invitingly empty. I still had ten dollars or so; but I was anxious to hold on to that much cash. I crossed over to the car and looked in. It was getting dark by that time; but I could see a litter of hay on the floor.

Here was an opportunity to save money. I had enough bread to allay the worst of my hunger; and I was dreadfully tired. The town seemed to be another half mile ahead.

My mind was quickly made up, and I jumped into the car. I raked the hay together with my foot, making a pile of it in a dark corner. I reached into it with my hands: it was clean and dry.

So I crouched down at the door and ate my supper. I carried a tin-flask with water; and I drank.

Then I lay down on the hay and covered up with my damp raincoat. In a very few minutes I was sound asleep.

A rumbling noise and a strange, half tossing, half shaking motion waked me up. For several minutes I remained where I was, lying still and staring into the darkness. Gradually an uncertainty as to where I was took hold of me. Then a panic seized me.

I remembered where I had gone to sleep. I shot up into a sitting posture and realized that I had a bad headache. I jumped up. There was no doubt any longer; the car was moving, rolling along in a steady swing. This was no mere shunting; the car was coupled to a train; and I was going God and the train-crew only knew where.

I saw grey light which filtered from the cracks of the doors into the dark interior of the car; and the next moment I was groping along one of them, clawing for something to catch hold of in order to pull it open. But I was wasting my effort and merely breaking my nails.

Just then the car lurched over, and I fell against the door, so that it swung outward. In desperation I reached into the crack, trying to catch its edge with my fingers. But the car lurched back, and my hand was caught. With a yell of pain I jerked it free, leaving a piece of my skin in the crack.

I was beside myself with rage and fear; and in my foolish panic I began to hammer the door with my fists, and to yell and to shout at the top of my voice, till I was hoarse.

Then I sat down, in front of the door; and tears of fury coursed over my cheeks. I raved in insensate anger against God and fate and the world. I felt cheated and trapped, like an animal, like a wild beast. And as a trapped beast will – to the very last, to the limit of its strength – rather than give in, fight against the trap which has caught it, so I fought on again, without thinking, without reasoning. I stood and hammered away at that door till the knuckles of my fists were bleeding; till I had spent the last of my strength. True symbol of much of the immigrant's life!

Then I sat down again and held my head as if I were trying to shut out the deafening noise of that car, the roar of the sledge-hammer blows which followed each other in quick succession as rail after rail flew along underneath.

Sunlight replaced the grey dawn in the cracks of the doors, and the atmosphere heated up. The air became stiflingly hot.

I broke down; I relaxed. I threw myself back on that pile of hay. And now I seemed to become conscious of a mocking note in that succession of pounding blows of the wheels on the rails; and impotent rage took hold of me again.

It must have been afternoon before quieter counsel prevailed. I could not see the humour of the situation, of course. I did not laugh at the futility of my planning. But I began to say, "What is the use?" And finally, I believe, I said, "What is the difference, after all?" Still, that goes without saying, I had only one thought: how to get out of this.

But I began to reflect. Trains do not go on for ever. They get to a destination. It might well be, however, that this was one going to California or to the Atlantic coast. It might run on for days. We were going at fifteen or twenty miles an hour, I judged. But they also have to stop for coal and water. And not all the cars were going right through to the same place either: some were "kicked off" now and then; others were picked up. It was at the stops that I must try to call attention to myself. I resented having been so foolish as to waste effort and emotion while we were rolling along.

And suddenly I realized that we were slowing down. That put new life into me. My throat was dry; but as yet I did not think of the fact that perhaps I might have a few drops of water left in my flask. I got up and stood ready at the door. With a screeching of all the brakes and the clangour of clashing car against car we came to a stop. I started to hammer and to shout again; not hysterically this time; methodically, husbanding my strength. But even so it was exhausting work. Then I stopped and listened. Not a sound anywhere. Nobody could possibly suspect my presence: why, then, should anybody happen to come near me? I stood and listened for a long while.

Then I heard a shout and running steps outside. I broke into a frenzy of noise, kicking, hammering, shouting – nothing happened; for just then a sudden jerk and a roar of clashes nearly shot me off my feet; the train went on.

I staggered back to my bed of hay and sat down. I was exhausted with hunger and thirst. I took my flask out, shook it, and inverted it over my mouth, reclining to catch a few precious drops which leaked out. I began to see the possibility of starving in this car. I felt strange waves of panic running over my consciousness. But I fought fear down: it led to insanity. Not that, I thought, not that!

I tried to occupy my mind: I looked at the light in the door-cracks – it conveyed the message to me that the sun was setting – there was a reddish glow to it as of fiery masses of cloud in the sky. And another message: the sunlight struck the front crack of the door: we were going west. It was not much information, but it was something; something to think about: I began to canvass the map of America which I carried about in my head. I indulged in conjectures as to our probable destination, then I started to doze; and at last I slept.

When I awoke, I believe it was the feeling of soreness that made me do so. I do not remember details beyond the fact that for a long while, probably for hours together, I lay perfectly still, in a kind of stupour.

Somehow the feeling of soreness departed when I was awake; whenever I dozed, it returned. My hands were sore, my back ached, my bones seemed to be jarred loose throughout my body. It was as if my physical self awoke to the consciousness of these things whenever my mental self went to sleep. I tried to keep awake.

Without stirring I noted, in a half unconscious way, that a thread of light came through the near crack of the door to the right. Daylight dawned. I wondered what stretches of the country might lie outside; what stretches we might have run through overnight, while I had been sleeping. Truly, I was going "out west" at last with a vengeance!

After a while I tried to rouse myself. I wanted to transfer my bed of hay to the space between the doors. It took me hours to accomplish that. My throat was dry, my tongue swollen. That was my last effort. When I lay down again, I gave in, yielded to fate. I did not care any longer even to arouse the attention of the train-crew by futile efforts. Had I tried, I should probably have found that I lacked the strength to shout or hammer. It was the lack of water more, I believe, than the lack of food which made me so utterly weak.

Another day went by as it had come.

Of the night which followed I know not.

But at last I see a young man with demented eyes and feverish head stagger out of that car – into the arms of a horrified train-man – gasp for water, and faint away by the side of the track in the greying dawn.

I was in a little town west of Springfield, Missouri.

BOOK FOUR

The Level

"None can be an impartial or wise observer of human life but from the vantage ground of what we should call voluntary poverty."
— Henry David Thoreau

I Learn to Beat My Way

E VERYBODY, I suppose, has played with a half-grown
pup. He tries to get at your fingers and to lie down
under your hand. You push him away, into some corner of
the room; as soon as he is on his feet again, he starts back
for your hand. His pertinacity is wonderful. He will wag
his tail, deprecatingly; he will perhaps feel aggrieved; he
will even emit a growl or a bark; but he will start back for
your hand.

I cannot help seeing myself like that. I had been on my
way to Indianapolis. Why? It was the nearest centre of an
industry of which I thought I had taken hold. The hand of
fate had picked me up and thrown me into some far
corner of the land. Hardly was I on my feet again, when I
started back for my original goal.

I followed the track over which I had come. I struck a
bee-line, walking the ties. This tramp back east was little
of my own choosing. My wish and will had nothing to do
with it. For more than a month I kept at it obstinately.
Since I followed the track, I met few farms but many
towns – little outright hospitality, but many opportunities
for occasional work – "odd jobs". I had ten dollars or so in
my pocket, and I held on to that. I adapted myself again.

Sometimes, when I came into these towns, I told the
story of how I had been cast away in this corner of the
world; sometimes I did not; but always I walked boldly in
whenever I was hungry or when night fell. I picked a few

houses and made a back-door canvass for work till I found
it.

The chief result of my experience was the realization –
come to with something akin to amazement – that it really
mattered very little where a person was. So long as I was
content to go on with the kind of life I was leading, I could
make some kind of a living anywhere. I do not think that
such would have been possible in Europe.

Also, a lucky chance thrust a new trade upon me. One
of the first women to whom I spoke in this way asked me
whether I knew anything about pruning trees. She pointed
to the cherished plantation in her front-yard with which a
recent wind-storm had played havoc. It had never before
struck me that I did know something about this art. I had
grown up in a tree-nursery; I had never done any of the
work myself; but I had looked on so often, and I had so
often heard the directions given to "new hands" by a
trained superintendent or foreman that I knew the underlying principles thoroughly; I felt sure I could adapt my
hands to the mechanics of the trade. I undertook the work
for this good lady; and when I finished, I felt it to be a
success. She asked for my charge; and since I had worked
at it for a day, getting my meals – and good meals they
were – I asked for a dollar.

She exclaimed in surprise. "I should think it would be
worth more than that! That is skilled labour! I should not
have minded paying five dollars for what you have done."

She gave me two and half; and I felt rich.

Henceforth when I went into a town, I no longer asked
for "work"; I went from house to house with this question,
"Any trees to prune, madam?" And when I was asked for
my terms, I replied, "Twenty-five cents an hour." If materials were needed – wax, wire, cement – I charged for
them, of course, making it a point to discuss the problem
in hand with the owner of the trees, so as to underline the
fact that my work was that of an expert.

By this time it dawned upon me that I could also graft,
bud, and transplant; and if, in this tramp, I had run across

a tree-nursery, I might have been sidetracked again; my whole life might have been deflected into a different channel.

Financially speaking, I got ahead of the game and laid money by; geographically, of course, my progress was much retarded. And I believe I can say, not without taking a certain childlike pride in the fact, that for once a "peripatetic tree-pruner" was not a "tree-butcher". I even bought the best tools which the market afforded, though I limited my outfit to saw and knives; yes, I went to the extent of discontinuing the work as a regular trade when I judged the season too far advanced, though I still offered to remove dead limbs which were a menace to the welfare of trees and advised about early spring pruning.

At last I began to think of boarding a train. For the first time I questioned the wisdom of returning to the middle west. If I had thought things over more carefully when I first landed west of Springfield, and if at that time I had been in my later mood, I believe I should have gone west instead of east. But the baffled feeling of being railroaded out had prevented me from reasoning coolly. By the comparison of my behaviour with that of the pup I have already indicated that this tramp back east was undertaken by instinct; and instinct is as often wrong as it is right, for it is blind. Now I was nearing St. Louis. "Beer, Tobacco, and Boots" – three things of which I knew nothing except as a consumer.

To the north there was the Missouri River. It was summer. Crops were ripening; the great northwestern wheatfields beckoned. But how to get there was a problem. Might I not, so I thought, look in upon those farms, upon the granary of the western world? Did I really know anything of America, even granted that I had to restrict my view of it to the view from below, to the perspective of the frog, unless I knew the life of the farm where farming is an industry, done on the large scale, not with the primitive methods of mere husbandry with which I was already more or less familiar?

Several days I spent in intense uncertainty, hesitating at every cross-roads where a trail led north. The economic problem had ceased to worry me. No longer was I going to go hungry; no longer was I going to lie in the bush, under no other cover but that of the whirling snow – unless I chose to do so.

I did not realize it at the time; but I had been a tramp; I was becoming a hobo.

The tramp is the outcast, the victim of his nature which is at variance with constituted society; he goes hungry and thirsty and without shelter by sheer necessity and in distress; he is unhappy and to be pitied; his rambles are always at random and lack purpose and plan.

The hobo is, at least in his own estimation – and what else counts? – the lord of the world; deliberately he follows his inclination; if constituted society is at variance with him, so much the worse for constituted society for it is the slave of convention and greed! The hobo never goes hungry and thirsty but lives on the fat of the land; he goes without shelter merely from choice, when the weather is golden and propitious; he is happy in his mode of life, strange as it may seem, and he pities you, gentle reader; work is to be found for the asking wherever he goes – for he goes where it is to be found; he often rejects it because it is not to his liking, or because the pay or some other conditions are not up to standard; he travels, and his rambles are continent-wide, though following definite, well-laid-out channels; if he wishes to spend the winter, the inclement seasons, in softer climes and in idleness, he does so. He is often a coarser and de-sublimated Henry David Thoreau. There is poetry in the hobo's life; and strange to say, though his instincts are not those of the settled citizen, he still has or at any rate had a definite function in the nation's economy.

Of course, there are between the two types all stages of graduation, as we shall see; occasionally one finds a tramp among hobos, and a hobo among tramps, and individual hobos are often victims of very cruel conditions.

But before I go on with my story, I must once more speak of myself. For, quite independently from my haps and mishaps, I went at about this time through a series of deductions which finally determined my life for the rest of my days.

By no trick in the chemistry of my nature, nor by any inclination or choice of my own was I a tramp or a hobo. No matter how much I had sometimes loved my rambles; no matter with how much longing I sometimes looked back with my mind's eyes on this or that scene – in the mountains, along the river, or in the plains – still there was in my heart, deep down, a craving for peace with society, a desire to take root somewhere and to fit myself into this scheme of life in the western hemisphere as a cog which furthered its design in some definite way. Although I saw suffering and injustice on every hand, I began to sense the great undercurrent of an evolution towards fairness, towards that which is morally right and true. Individual men and women might resist this current, might heartlessly, thoughtlessly step down on those who were less fortunate than they; they might be heartless and thoughtless as that freight-car had been heartless and thoughtless in throwing me into that corner of Missouri – yet I began to see more and more clearly that the very essence of the nation's life was a recognition of that which is fair and just, and a firm resolve to help it along to a final victory. With these, the less obvious but, in the long-run, all-powerful tendencies I wished to side, I wished to ally myself if I permanently became an American. Money and glory in the eyes of the world seemed by this time very small things indeed. I no longer cared for them. But here was a task, and a task, so I thought, for which I was fitted. It was, after this, a question of how to go at it; and that became a problem which remained unsolved for a little while yet.

And then, one night, I had a revelation. In Europe I had dallied with the thought – as a possible way out of my economic difficulties – of fitting myself for what should always be an avocation but which at that time would have been no more than a profession for me; and though the thought had never led to anything beyond a dallying with possibilities, I knew suddenly that this was my avocation and that it was to be my destiny. The thought took possession of me; it seemed to solve all my problems. I knew now that, whenever I chose to leave the life that I was leading, I could do so. I saw the gate which led out of the wilderness into the garden of civilization where I, too, might be useful in exterminating weeds and maybe even in planting the trees which would bear fruit. It is significant that I did not choose to do so at once and that I postponed it from choice. Henceforth I could plunge down into the very depths of humanity, knowing the while that I was merely rounding off what I now called my education in the "true humanities".

Thus, one day, I left the track of the railroad and struck north. In the course of a day or so I reached the Osage River and followed it, down to its confluence with the Missouri.

Now there began a strange trip along the river. I have said that, without knowing it, I had become a hobo. It is one of the distinguishing features of the hobo's travels that he neither goes alone nor necessarily afoot. I did not know that either at the time; but I was an apt learner, and I learned from a man who, by chance, was in my own position in as much as he happened to be, for the moment, alone.

I met him one evening, somewhere along the river, between St. Louis and Kansas City. When I came upon him, he was sitting on the river-bank and feeding a little fire over which he was cooking his supper.

He was not tall – a strangely sallow-skinned man, his face framed in a brown-black beard of soft, curly hair. What struck me more than anything else was the resemblance he bore to Titian's paintings of the Lord of Christianity. His was the mild eye, his that exceeding delicacy of skin and features, that near-transparency of the flesh, his the traditional beard.

By his side, where he sat, lay a neatly-rolled bundle done up in waterproof canvas.

Altogether he reminded me of certain people whom I had seen in Russia; all of them belonged to the "Intelligentzia" of that country; and from what I knew of them – which was not much – most of them were fanatics, politically or religiously. Instinctively, I put him down as of Slavonic origin. There was something refined and gentle about him which attracted me. I could not help thinking of Tolstoy's Sergei Ivanovitch. I do not remember whether Tolstoy's description of this figure would have fitted him; but the picture I saw when I stepped up to his fire would have fitted the character.

"Mind if I sit down?" I asked.

He invited me by a motion of his hand, without a word.

It was a beautiful early-summer night. To the right, the river meandered over its wide flood-plain of pebbly rock – to the left stretched the willow-clothed bank. The sun had just sunk down below the horizon; it was an hour for silence, not for talk; and his wordless gesture had something noble in it.

I had been thinking of camping out myself. I had brought a can of baked beans from the store in the last town which I had passed. I opened it and prepared to have my supper.

Meanwhile the stranger's eye appraised me, silently.

I stood up and looked out. There is about the lower valley of the Missouri a suggestion of width, of large spaces, of an infinite beyond which has always thrilled me. It did so that night.

I walked down to the edge of the water to fill my flask. But when I came back, the stranger raised his finger and shook it.

"No good," he said; and, pointing to the northwest, he added, "The city." He raised a little kettle. "Have some tea," he invited. "I have plenty."

"Thanks," I said, nearly in a whisper, for I was hushed by the wide silence of the landscape.

By the time we had eaten our supper there seemed to be a perfect understanding of mutual helpfulness between us. Neither of us had spoken. But I had offered him some of my beans, and he had retaliated by sharing the meat which he had cooked, the boiled hock of a pig, seasoned to a nicety.

At last he unrolled his bundle, and so did I. He had a blanket and a pair of overalls in his. He was wearing a black suit which was rather neat for that of a tramp, for as such I had put him down in my ignorance. The duck in which his bundle was rolled was large enough for a man to lie on or to cover up with. This canvas he offered me when he saw that I had nothing in the line of bedding.

"You need a blanket," he said. "It's cold overnight along the river."

His English was perfect. I could not help wondering about his status. Neatness, delicacy, and refinement were features which I did not expect to find in people "on the tramp". Much against my nature I had been trying to suppress my leanings in that direction so as to fit myself better into the part I was playing. I accepted his offer of the canvas and rolled up. The quiet breathing of my companion soon showed that he was asleep.

Next morning, when I awoke, I found him up already. He had a fire going and was boiling water for tea. He smiled at me with a strangely brilliant smile which uncovered white and well-kept teeth.

"I have been away for water," he said.

I sat up. "Are you tramping it?" I asked.

His face was a study; it looked nearly pained. "Going north," he answered. "Harvest. You, too?"

"Yes," I said, "if I can get there. Where did you come from?"

"Florida," he replied and busied himself with the boiling water.

"Florida!" I thought with a gasp. "How did he manage to get there?"

He read the thought in my face; for he laughed and enquired, "Ever been up before?"

"Up?" I repeated.

"In the Dakotas."

I shook my head. "First time," I replied. And after a while I added, "How do you go? Walk it?"

He smiled again. "No," he said. "Beat it. By train."

This left me pretty much where I was, in darkness. But I did not say anything for a while. I had learned that most things come to him that waits.

We had our breakfast consisting of tea, with sugar and condensed milk, and of fresh bread. I was thinking hard, trying to find a way to make him yield me his secret. But there was no need, for, when he rolled up his bundle, he broke the silence.

"Want to come with me?" he asked. "We can be partners."

I did not then grasp the full significance of this word, nor the honour conferred upon me; but I accepted readily enough.

"If you don't mind," I said.

"Not at all," he answered.

So we both got our bundles ready, he swinging his, hanging from the handle of a stout walking-cane, over his shoulder; I breaking the stem of a willow for the same purpose. Thus we struck out to the west, away from the river, till we reached the track. There we walked the ties for a mile or two. It was on this stretch that he gave me his name.

"Call me Ivan," he said.

"My name is Phil," I reciprocated. And at last I asked, "You are Russian, are you not?"

He nodded. "Born in Russia; but I have my papers," meaning apparently that he was naturalized.

Mostly we walked in silence; there did not seem to be any need for words.

We came to a point where we saw a town ahead. To the right of the track stood the usual water-tank and a coal-bunker, a few hundred yards ahead. Ivan stopped and carefully studied the lay-out, shading his eyes with his hand. I could not guess at his purpose, but I did not like to ask questions. I felt that I was in the hands of a competent guide and did not worry.

At last my companion, having satisfied himself as to the object of his investigations, pointed to the left, down the embankment of the track, and said "We'll wait here. I think we'll make Kansas City to-day."

We cut slantways down the side of the road-bed, to a cluster of brush behind which we sat down for a patient wait. Ivan apparently had a good store of everything; for after an hour or so he got out a little parcel and opened a can of sardines on which we lunched.

"Better have a bit now," he said; "we can't tell when we'll eat again."

Not long after that a train announced itself by a distant rumbling. At once Ivan was on the alert. He put his bundle into ship-shape and kept on the look-out. But above all he listened. The track stretched away in a curve to the south-east.

"Freight-train," he said before we saw it.

I was to find out that he could distinguish the sounds which trains make at great distances.

Then he nodded across the track where, a hundred yards to the northwest, the water-tank loomed.

"They'll stop for water and coal," he said. "We'll board a car."

The train appeared around the curve in the distance. Its rumbling grew louder. The side of the roadbed began to quiver as if in anticipation; and at last I watched the rails on the track, as slowly they began to heave and to sink when the engine approached. Ivan kept carefully out of sight, under the cover of the willows; and whatever he did, I did, too. No words were exchanged; there was tension in the very air. And slowly, with slackening speed, the heavy cars rolled by overhead. They were mostly box-cars, with their doors closed and sealed; but in their rear followed flat-cars piled high with timbers. Those Ivan watched.

The train came to with a sudden roar of clashes and screaming buffers. The flat-cars were only a few steps to our right. But Ivan did not move as yet; and I watched him closely in order to do as he did. I should have hated to make a mistake. He gave no explanations, but the thing explained itself when I saw the legs of one or two members of the train-crew running up from the caboose on the other side of the train.

They had hardly passed opposite our hiding-place when Ivan nudged me. We ran. Ivan had already picked the car he wanted; and with extraordinary agility he boarded it by jumping on the coupler and climbing on to the timbers, flattening himself, so as not to be visible above the box-cars in front. I followed his example, but made the mistake of choosing the far side of the timber pile.

Then I heard Ivan's voice. "Come to this side," he said. "The station is on your side, ahead. Climb down again, the way you came, and come over here."

I did as directed.

"Lie down," he said when I joined him, "till we are past the station. Afterward we can sit up and be comfortable."

I flattened myself between the timbers.

He spoke again. "It does not matter much if they do find us. But it will cost us a dollar. So long as nobody sees us, it's free."

I do not think I shall ever forget the exhilaration of that train-ride. To the right we had glimpses of the river; to the left we looked out upon farms and wooded hills. It was dusty, it is true; the engine seemed to throw out cinders by the shovelful; but it was the first voluntary train-ride which I had since I had left New York; and like the first involuntary one it was free.

Shortly after the noon-hour, houses began to stand in clusters; then straggling clusters arranged themselves, unwillingly, so it seemed, into streets. We were going into the city. What with the sharp draft, the cutting cinders, and the rough jolting, I felt dazed by that time; but I kept up a brave show.

"We'll drop off as soon as she slows down," my companion said. "We'll take a street-car into the city. You better buy yourself a blanket here, and a piece of oil-cloth to wrap it in. That's cheaper than duck."

"You are the doctor," I thought, rather exulting in this new lore of the road. What I said was, "Do we stay in the city overnight?"

"No," he answered, "I want to get out as soon as we can. We are behind the harvest as it is."

So the next time the train slowed down we climbed off to the coupling-gear between the cars; and there we waited till my companion thought the moment propitious to drop to the ground and to dive out to the side.

Then we quietly started to walk to the west, crossing the maze of tracks, and emerged in a dingy street beyond the round-houses. Ivan seemed to be perfectly familiar with the surroundings. We turned a few corners and came to a street with the double tracks of a street-car line. We waited and boarded a car.

In spite of my former cosmopolitan life I was awed by the city traffic and the city manners of the people. I felt like a prodigal son.

At the large and new Central Station we got off our car. My companion led the way to the waiting-room where he immediately began to study a time-table. When he joined me again, after a few minutes, he said, "We'll go out to-night. We may go as far as Omaha. I'll see."

"But," I objected, "I don't know whether I shall have enough money to pay my fare."

He smiled. "Don't need any money," he said. "Just wait. I want to wash."

It was about three in the afternoon.

After a thorough cleaning-up we left the station and went to a big department-store where I, on Ivan's advice, invested two dollars in a blanket and a few cents in a piece of oil-cloth.

"They charge you cut-throat prices for everything farther north," he said. "You will need it anyway. You don't want to horn in with the roughnecks."

This was the only piece of slang which I ever heard him use; it was expressive of the contempt which he meant to put into his words. Otherwise, syncopated as his language was, stripped of unnecessary words, it kept even in the most trivial every-day things to an astonishing level of clear English. "Horn in with the roughnecks" I found to mean sharing the bunks in the atrocious accommodations provided by the farmers of the northwest for their floating labour-supply.

A perverse desire to use the conveniences of the city prompted me to suggest going to a restaurant for our supper. But Ivan flouted the idea with a motion of his hand.

"No," he said, "no good. Need something solid. We'll have a hard night."

And, of course, I gave in to his better judgment.

We bought a supply of good things and returned to the waiting-hall of the station to consume part of them.

Ivan was quiet. He was resting up. His whole attitude showed that this was a serious business with him; that success or failure in any point might mean at least partial success or failure of the season's work. I did as he did. But for me it was no more than a lark – a new experience, to be sure; yet one that was not very serious.

About nine o'clock in the evening Ivan became restless.

"Train leaves nine thirty," he said. "We'd better get ready."

In a dark corner of the waiting-hall he slung his bundle over his back, fastening it with a stout cord and pushing it under his left armpit. He also tied the bottom of his trouser-legs and the wrists of his sleeves with pieces of string. Lastly he pulled his cap securely down on his head. I imitated him in everything; and when we were ready, we left the station, lighting a cigarette as we did so.

For a while we walked briskly along, turning corners

and following glaringly lighted streets. Then we came into darker quarters along the river front; and Ivan's movements became more furtive. We passed under the arch of one of the bridges. It was very dark here, the bridge being lighted only by the red and green signal lights of the railroad. When we came out on the other side of the structure, Ivan stopped. I was now a prey to intense excitement. My heart pounded, and I had a lump in my throat. Instinctively I felt that there was adventure ahead, and that it would be a test of nerve and staying-power. Even Ivan, the mild and delicate one, seemed tense.

He started to climb up along one of the spans of the bridge, working with hands as well as feet. I followed. Several times we had to pull ourselves up by our hands alone, performing athletic feats of no mean merit, with the river darkly gurgling underneath.

At last we stood on the bridge; and at once Ivan eclipsed himself in the hollow of a huge H-shaped girder.

Then he spoke. "We'll ride the rods," he said, "on the flyer. If we are in luck, we shall go right through to Council Bluffs. We shall get there about five in the morning. The train runs slow here on the bridge. You watch me. Climb in beside me. When I get in, you walk alongside the car till I'm on the rods. I shall make room for you. I"ll shout when I'm ready."

"All right," I said.

We waited another five minutes. Then there was some motion of shifting lights on the bridge in front.

"She's coming," said Ivan. "Keep out of the glare of the headlight. Don't get out of the shadows before I do. Got your gloves on?"

That moment the cruel pencil of the headlight touched the girders where we stood. The whole bridge with its sleepers and its thin bands of glittering steel seemed to leap out of the dark. Its floor began to vibrate and to swing rhythmically as the engine, belching steam and smoke in brief, angry snorts, struck rail after rail. It was as if some giant monster were approaching, deliberately, carefully groping its way along a suspected path. The moving shadows of the girders were inky-black.

And suddenly the cloak of darkness fell over us again where we stood; the screeching and towering monster had passed us. The engineer was leaning sideways out of his cab, his eyes rigidly fixed ahead. There was an hysterical, uncanny temptation to shout at him; but I swallowed it down.

Slowly but irresistibly, baggage and mail-cars hove by. The first Pullman appeared. Ivan looked back and stepped out into the narrow aisle between the girders of the bridge-span and the shoulder-high edge of the moving cars.

"Third car," he said and began to walk slowly ahead, with me in his wake.

Suddenly all the brakes began to grind.

"Luck," said Ivan and halted. "She's going to stop."

The third car came by. Then the buffers squeaked, a rumbling noise ran through the monster; the cars seemed to rear as their connections telescoped together.

"Now, quick," said Ivan and dived behind the wheels.

"Come," he said again.

And half against my will I found myself diving in. I was just following him when the train moved with a jerk.

"Watch your feet," shouted Ivan. "Swing up."

The next moment I lay across the rods?* There were four of them. Like Ivan I was on my belly, holding on to the rods with my hands.

"Hook your feet under," shouted Ivan when we were getting under way, "we'll soon be off the bridge; then she'll turn loose."

Once more he shouted. "When she's going, hold your face down on your arms."

The rails were beginning to pound. The rods were by no means rigid. It felt oddly as if they were living things,

* This description was written many years ago, shortly, after a similar experience. To-day I search in vain for the rods; apparently there have been changes in construction.

trying to throw off their riders by bucking. I looked over at Ivan whom I could just see as a blacker bulk against the dark background.

Then it felt as if a restraining hand were withdrawn, or as if we were starting to go downhill.

Faster and faster came the blows of the rail-endings, like hammer-blows on the steel of the wheels. The air began to roar past us; and, as we were picking up speed, first a fine, cutting dust, then sand, and finally gravel was pelted up against my body, caught in the roaring whirl of the wildly rushing air.

I laughed, somewhat hysterically, and buried my face in my arms.

At last we were thundering along. The whole universe seemed to be one deafening bedlam of noise let loose. We swayed and swung as we were holding on for dear life, our hands getting sore from the pelting gravel, our eyes closed tight, our faces pressed down on our sleeves. The track seemed to be a succession of hills and valleys; the rods, a mere vibrating mass of whipping cords; our arms, springs now stretched to the snapping-point, now compressed beyond the power of re-expanding when the roadbed rose and pressed the steel-truck upward. I felt dazed and frightened beyond anything I have ever gone through; and I should surely have got out and relinquished the attempt had it been possible to do so. But as I thought of it, I saw myself lying on the sleepers, a mangled mass of bloody flesh and crushed bones. I did not believe that I could hold on for an hour. Long before that, I thought, my fingers would be numb; they would let go; and if they did, that would inevitably be the end. Again, I thought of Ivan; if he could do it, I should be able to. And I clutched the rods with the effort of desperation.

Yet it seemed madness incarnate. I thought of the delightful tramp it might have been – in the green river-valley with its flood-plain, its sandbanks, and its shady trees. And again I thought how slow it would have been – what a snail's-pace as compared with this tearing speed.

But then, that was life – this was Purgatory at the very least, even if there was an escape, which as yet I could not know. And still, in dumb determination I held on, for hours and hours, so it seemed to me.

Then, after half an eternity of titanic effort and ceaseless sameness, broken only by the scream of the whistle which seemed oddly dull and ineffectual in this roaring noise, the train slowed down. Imperceptibly at first; then with an ever-increasing screeching of brakes close to my ear. The pelting against sore finger-knuckles and body became less violent; the knocking of the rods against knees and thighs less breathlessly frequent and inexorable; the rush of the air roaring past my face less like an irresistible blast.

We were rounding a huge curve; lights flashed by, seen through tightly closed lids; my arms and muscles relaxed.

Slower and slower we went; and at last I heard Ivan's shout. I opened my eyes – the lids seemed stiff with embedded sand – and looked across at him. He seemed ghastly pale in the flashes of light. His face was coated with dirt; his clothes, in their creases, stuffed with thick welts of sand and fine gravel.

"St. Joseph," he shouted. "Only stop. We've got to get off. They look the wheels over. Let's drop at the water-tank."

"All right," I shouted back.

When we got out, I could hardly trust my legs. I swayed as the voyageur sways who for the first time has weathered a storm at sea.

Ivan laughed. "Want to quit?" he asked.

"No," I said; I felt ashamed to own up.

We crossed several tracks to the left, away from the train, avoiding the lights. On the track next to the one on which our train had been running, several loose cars stood strung out in a casual-looking, disconnected line. As soon as we came up, abreast with them, we crossed back into their shadow and started to run.

The station with its glittering lights was just ahead. Our

train was moving up, now. I bent down and looked along under the cars at the crowded platform. St. Joseph, I thought – we had not made more than fifty miles yet. I figured it must be about two hundred and fifty to Omaha.

"You hold on too tight," said Ivan. "When the car throws you to the right, she'll throw you back to the left. Let yourself go more. I'm not tired."

He jumped on to the coupling-gear of one of the idle cars and motioned me to do the same. We were opposite the station. If it had not been for the intervening glare of the sheaf of light from the engine of our train, we should have been in plain view of the waiting people. As it was, we saw them, but they did not see us. Then the engine passed us, and we were screened by the train. It stopped, and people began to run along on the far side, hurrying down to the day-coaches at the end of the train.

Again I felt nervous; we sat and waited. A labourer with oil-can and hammer ran along on our side, reaching in here and there with the spout of the oil-can and tapping the wheels with his hammer. Still we waited.

Then Ivan nudged me, jumped to the ground, and ran. I followed; and when we had climbed in again, I noticed that our relative position was reversed this time.

"All aboard!"

We saw the legs of the brake-man who stood quite close by. There was a general shuffling; the bell rang out; and with a jerk we started to glide along. I could plainly look out on the station-platform where still a few people lingered as we slipped by. A high building intervened. There was no light except from little, one-eyed lanterns hung to posts here and there. And at last, as we were getting under way again, streets flashed by in their nightly aspect; we closed and buried our eyes again.

Once more Inferno started; and this time it lasted for a matter of five or six hours. I heeded my companion's advice and strained my muscles less than I had done before; but, when at last, in the cool dawn of a summer day, we dropped off our rods, at the weirdly benighted-looking grey station of Council Bluffs, I was hardly able to hold myself on my feet.

I staggered along like one drunk; and I was more than glad when Ivan threw his bundle down on the riverbank, so we could rest.

But we did not stay long. Ivan left me as soon as he thought the bakeshops were open. He wanted fresh bread for breakfast.

In half an hour or so he came back; we picked our things up and started on a short tramp in the river valley.

As soon as we were out of sight of any buildings – on the opposite shore, Omaha was still in plain view – we stopped again and made camp. We could not help laughing at each other; we were so black and dirty. But we had a bath in the river; and then we had breakfast.

I praised Ivan because he had thought of fresh bread; he laughed pleasantly, showing his snow-white teeth which were brightly set off by his soft, dark beard.

"I feel as if I could sleep for twenty-four hours," I said.

"Do," he answered; and we laughed. "We shall wait till to-morrow morning anyway," said Ivan. "I don't suppose you want another night-ride again."

"Not just yet," I replied. "Later on. Since I've lived through this one, I won't mind any longer."

"Quick trip," said Ivan.

"Quick," I agreed, "but rough."

I did not know what our final destination might be; nor did Ivan. For the time being, I understood, he was trying to get to a certain town in South Dakota where there was going to be a meeting of some kind.

Next day we made Sioux City on a freight train; then we left the Missouri River, going straight north. We began to pass miles of waving wheatfields. Barley was ripe; whirring binders were cutting the crop. I suggested stopping and hunting for work. But Ivan shook his head.

"Small farms," he said, "poor grub. Too many lay-offs going from place to place. They pay more, too, up north; their season is shorter. Sometimes they will pay as much for haying as these fellows pay for stooking. We shall see at the camp."

He often alluded to "the camp" now, and one day I asked him about it.

"Oh," he said, "the hobos from all over the country come together there. We can find out what the wages are and where the crops are best. No use losing time in beating about."

I had, so far, only the vaguest idea of how things worked out in this great garnering of America's wheat-crop.

North of Sioux City our progress became slower. We had left the district of south-eastern Nebraska and Missouri where the net of railroads overlying the country was narrow-meshed and where traffic was heavy, fed as it was by great industries. Trains were not always forthcoming when we needed them; often we had to wait for many hours. But we went to the stations now when waiting and did not hide any longer; and when they came, we were not the only passengers who were travelling unbeknown though not unsuspected by their crews. Once or twice one of these "blind" passengers was caught; then, as a rule, a search was made by the train-crew over all the cars, and every one of the "bums" who was found was laid under contribution. Once, when the conductor was "grouchy" or conscientiously honest, every one of us was chased off, a few who were not quick enough to take the hint being badly rough-handled before they at last escaped; we were a motley crowd as we stood there along the embankment, roundly cursing the crew for inhuman fools and destitute of common decency!

I cannot say but that, once I was hardened to this way of travelling, I enjoyed it hugely; especially the righteous indignation of the ever-increasing crowd when something was done which did not seem "fair" to them.

I remember one case with more than common distinctness.

All the passenger-trains along this line were day-trains. Ivan and I gave up waiting for them. It was not advisable to travel the rods in daylight; you cannot hide.

Ivan and I were sitting – in a crowd of fifty or sixty others – on the platform of a small way-station, waiting for a freight-train to turn up.

A passenger-train was due and appeared, not more than an hour or two behind schedule-time – so much was usual on those lines.

When the train pulled out, we saw a dozen rod-riders in broad daylight before us; and like one man the whole assembly stood up and cheered them for their audacity.

The conductor had swung up on the step of the last car. When he heard our cheering and saw us wave our hands at the luckless fellows, he bent over to see what was wrong.

"Well, I'll be jiggered!" he exclaimed and jumped into the car to pull the signal line.

A few minutes later the train came to a stop; the rod-riders had to decamp in a hurry.

The train went merrily along without them; but they were more than mad; and though they were in a hopeless minority, they offered to fight the whole crowd of us, getting no satisfaction, however, beyond being laughed at.

I proposed in all seriousness to take up a collection for them and to pay their fare on the next accommodation; but they took that as an aggravation, thinking I was poking fun at them.

When at last, coming from nowhere, so it seemed to me, the news spread that a freight-train was approaching, the crowd which had been thronging the platform broke up. A pair here, a group of three there would walk along the track ahead. Ivan and I, too, picked up our bundles and started out. There was a grain-elevator not far from the little station-building. Ivan rounded its corner; we stood there, waiting.

Several times another group thought our post a likely place; but when they saw that it was occupied, they would turn and walk on. One member of such a group, on catching sight of us, remarked contemptuously, "There seem to be bums around everywhere!"

Ivan and I looked at each other and burst out laughing.

It is characteristic of this unstable flood of floating labour that there is a great feeling of solidarity when they are together in a crowd. Then they are the hobos, as opposed to the great, contemptible mass of the respectable citizens; I should not wonder if I heard that nowadays they had formed a "hobos' union". But when we met them singly or in smaller groups, that feeling of solidarity was non-existent. Every individual feels himself better than his neighbour; his neighbour is a "bum"; he himself is the Lord of Creation. There are exceptions, of course, but they are few. Rarely has one of them, as Ivan did, simply and as a matter of course accepted me on a dead level. Those who did stand out in my memory as my friends.

More and more numerous did these crowds become. Oftener and oftener we saw more or less elaborate camping-outfits along the track, at the outskirts of towns. Sometimes there would be camps for two or three, sometimes for a dozen, sometimes for a hundred men or more. There were men from all the corners of the world; Swedes, a decent lot, but clannish and none too articulate in English; Russians in number galore, sometimes not very clean; Germans who knew the language but mangled it; Austrians, Croatians, Armenians; but very few Latins. Slavs and Teutons – in the wider sense which includes all the minor populations of northern Europe – formed the mass of the foreign element; but Americans and Anglo-Saxons were about as numerous as all the other groups together.

Gradually there formed in my mind the impression of a vast exodus, or rather a vast confluence of numberless multitudes engaged in a pilgrimage to some Mecca.

TWO

I Start Work in the Harvest

A T LAST there were unmistakable signs that we were approaching some great centre of hobodom, some world-capital of floating labour. For though the itinerant "bums" were ever increasing on the trains, the camping sites by the line were decreasing in number and finally disappeared.

One evening, when we rode on an empty flat car into a small town of the northern part of South-Dakota, I caught sight of a camp that was of truly gigantic proportions; we began passing alongside of it at least five minutes before we reached the town, and it extended right up to the town limits. On the west-side it touched the track; on the east-side it stretched away as far as the eye would reach. Everywhere fires were burning; everywhere men were engaged in the task of cooking their suppers.

When we dropped off our car and walked back through the camp, Ivan apparently looked for some one whom he knew.

I was struck by the variety of devices adopted to provide shelter. There were tents; there were open flies; there were poles driven into the ground with wattled walls stretched between them; there were regular cabins built of a few pieces of lumber and covered with building paper; there were ropes fastened to the limb of a tree, running down to a peg in the ground, with coats of the most diverse descriptions hung over them, stretched sideways by cords, so that in the evening breeze they gave the odd impression of great flapping birds, as the sleeves or skirts were raised by the wind.

Right through the centre of the camp ran a pretty little creek with clear, slow-flowing water. And everywhere there was activity and evidence of the most varied household-industry. Here you came upon a group engaged in washing their clothes: huge iron kettles – God only knew where they came from – hanging over fires to boil them in; there a group was demonstrating some new culinary feat; here a man was sitting on the ground and plying the needle on the buttons or patches for coat or trousers; there one was squatting on a low box, his chin well lathered, while another stropped a razor preparatory to shaving him. Games were going on in various places, card games and quoits being those most in favour.

The assembly was truly polyglot; I heard most of the languages of eastern, central, and western Europe, though English seemed to predominate. But in spite of the fact that in the flood pouring north I had found a goodly number of groups of Swedes, the fact struck me that I found none of them here. Again the entire absence of the Latin languages was a conspicuous feature.

Ivan and I joined a group composed of one Russian, one German, and two Americans. Greetings between him and these four were cordial; there was much shaking of hands, slapping of shoulders, laughter and shouting. To my astonishment Ivan showed that he spoke German as fluently as Russian or English. I was introduced; soon we were squatting on the ground, by the fire, and partaking of a good and substantial supper. I do not remember the talk that was going on, but it was lively enough.

After supper we smoked; for the first time it struck me that, though Ivan was a most persistent smoker, he never had any tobacco himself. The conversation turned upon crops and the chances for work. It appeared that the four whom we had joined had been at work for over a month. They had slowly come up through the wheat-districts of

Kansas and Nebraska. But in the southern part of South Dakota crops had been poor; the chances for work had been slight. I gathered that cutting was in full swing all over the state as indeed I had inferred from what I had seen. But the farmers were holding back in engaging help; they preferred to work on a cooperative plan.

North Dakota with its big "bonanza-farms" was the general goal. They had had the needful rainfall there, and wheat stood well. It seemed that the result of the camp-discussions had been something like a general consensus, amounting to, though not actually taking the form of, a resolution not to start work at stooking for less than two and a half dollars a day.

Ivan did not say much but seemed to ponder what he had heard.

I was more than surprised by the independence these people displayed. They were not suffering from their mode of life. Nor were they, even now, in any hurry about securing work. They were going to hold out for high wages.

Our group had a wall tent, with all the paraphernalia of a complete outfit for a prolonged stay in the open. Ivan and I were offered a corner in this tent, but Ivan declined; and when the others betrayed the wish to retire he nudged me with his elbow and rose.

I followed him.

"Where do all these people go?" I enquired, actually awed by the numbers I beheld and those I inferred from the innumerable fires that punctured the night.

Ivan laughed. "Not many here yet," he said; "still early in the season. They're just haying in North-Dakota; haven't started cutting yet. These fellows won't work at haying, they wait for cutting and threshing – there's not much work in South-Dakota."

He picked a place for the night; and while we were unrolling our bundles, he told me that he had left his friends because he wanted to talk things over.

"I go north-west," he said, "if you come. Rather stay in one place, on a big farm, for haying, cutting, and threshing. More money in it in the long-run. No lay-offs hunting for a new place. Grub is better, too. When the rush comes, better wages. I've tried it often enough. What do you say?"

"Anything," I replied. "You know best. How much do you think we can get just now?"

"A dollar and a half a day," Ivan answered; "a quarter a day more from week to week. Four dollars in threshing time. We'll try to beat it up to Walloh, then buy a ticket and strike west. Big farm there. Work for three months or longer. We'll average two and a half a day."

"Good," I said.

We remained in camp the next day. More than anything else the general prosperity struck me. There was no want of anything; the merchants of the little town were waxing rich by the purchases of this vast crowd.

I saw others this day, besides the group of four which we rejoined occasionally. Above all there was one man who looked more like a Bohemian of the Quartier Latin in Paris than like a labourer – both in features and clothes. I heard him speak to several people; invariably his accent was that of authority; his vocabulary, that of an educated man. On his hand I saw a solitaire ring worth the year's income of a well-paid clerk.

"He doesn't work," Ivan explained; "He's rich. Son of a millionaire. He likes this life and travels about with the crowd. He spends his winters in California."

"What were you doing in Florida?" I asked irrelevantly.

Ivan shrugged his shoulders. "Picking fruit," he said, "for some time anyway. Resting, mostly."

There were still a good many things about Ivan which seemed mysterious to me; he was not given to talking beyond that which it was necessary to discuss.

On the evening of this second day we pulled out in an empty box-car, having for once voluntarily paid our contribution to an accommodating train-crew so they would leave the doors open for our convenience. I had told Ivan about my being railroaded in spring; and though he laughed and thought it a good thing that I had never reached my destination, it made him chary of open box-cars. But this night we had straw aplenty in our car and made up a comfortable bed; and while we were sleeping, we travelled at much greater ease and with about the same speed as the average passenger in the day-coach of a way-train. The first greying of the dawn found us at a tiny hamlet in the upper Red River valley where our car had been kicked off, forty-five miles from Walloh, our first objective.

It being a beautiful day and we well rested, we tramped it for a while. Here the waving grain on the fields was still green, and Ivan seemed satisfied. By and by we boarded another freight-train which in the afternoon took us to Walloh.

On the outskirts of the town we had seen the usual hobo-camp, and as soon as we could drop off our car, we did so and footed it back. Ivan bade me wait for him and went down. He exchanged a few words, in Russian, with one of the men who was lying on his back, enjoying his idleness. Then he rejoined me.

"They're haying out west," he said, "on the big farm. It's only fifteen or sixteen miles. We might tramp it?"

"Suits me," I replied.

We set out at once, swinging along at a good gait in the freshening afternoon, walking now the track, now the road which skirted it and offered a smooth though dusty gumbo level.

We did not speak; I believe, for that very reason this vigorous evening march stands out in my memories. A soft and yet cool breeze was blowing; the prairie with its illimitable horizon stretched endlessly ahead; the grain on the fields was waving; the farmhouses stood so still and foot-bound that I readily entered into that hobo-spirit of joy at being "on the go"; my chest expanded; the exertion of marching was grateful.

Odd combinations of words, idle plays of my brain, kept floating through my mind and sometimes wove themselves into disconnected lines of verse. Some of them recur to me even now, at this belated hour, as I try to re-visualize myself, walking along those roads into the setting sun. Others merely peep up through the darkening oblivion which has settled like a cloak over the details of my life.

I also remember that to myself I seemed at the time very old, very experienced, very clear-sighted with regard to the ways of the world. I thought I saw through the futility of much, and that I perceived the high worth of much which was not highly valued by others. The phrase of a German philosopher about the "recasting – revaluation – of values" was much in my mind. I seemed to be looking back upon millennia of thought and accumulated wisdom. I vaguely felt as if it were given to me to solve the problems of a world. It is characteristic of my essential youth at the time that I still believed a solution of the problems of the world to be possible of attainment through such a process as a recasting of values – in other words, through theories and the erection of ideals. It is also characteristic of the eternal egotism of youth that I should have felt myself to be chosen as the one to effect this revaluation of the values of life. Ideals are the play-things of immature minds.

Another peculiar conception arose; that of an assembly of the days, all telling of the errors into which they have fallen and of the truths they have found; and after many speeches and beautiful thoughts have been uttered, the Dean of the Days arises, the oldest Day, and solves the riddle in perfect simplicity.

When we rolled up for the night, in the shelter of a cluster of wild plum trees, by the side of the road, the elation persisted. I felt as if I were standing on the very heights of Life and looking down on the world below. I felt – as well I might – that I had solved at least one great problem for myself: He who asketh little enjoyeth much. With that thought patience came and hurry departed. I was no longer the "modern man" who has not Life.

Early the following morning Ivan and I set out again; as was usual with us, we swung along without words. Never in my life have I met with a companion who could so well keep silent. And he was a hobo!

We came to a place where a road ran up from the south and crossed the track. Just north of the line of steel stood a group of gigantic barns, by the side of which two or three small white houses looked singularly dwarfed. The road from the south was lined with poplars, tall, stately trees – cotton-woods they must have been, from the picture in my memory. It seemed to spring out of a large compound of buildings half hidden in the cluster of its trees.

A low, open buggy, drawn by a team of swift-footed, rangy-looking horses, came rolling along the smooth, shady driveway.

"That's Nelson, the superintendent," said Ivan and stopped at the crossing.

"We are there, then?" I asked.

He nodded and we waited for the buggy.

As it approached, I saw its occupant, a rather small, good-natured and efficient-looking man who sat in the seat, relaxed and nonchalant, negligently and yet firmly holding the horses in with one hand.

At sight of Ivan he stopped and smiled. "Back again? I did not see you last year."

"No," said Ivan. "I went farther west. I have a partner this year. Have you any work yet?"

"Yes," said Nelson, "I can use you two. I can use more, in fact. I am going to town to see whether I can get any men at our price. We're paying one fifty so far. They're holding out for the higher wages, as usual. But the smaller farmers don't hire help yet. They will have to wait."

"Haying?" asked Ivan.

"Yes."

"Which camps are open?"

"Three and eight," was Nelson's answer. "And head-quarters, of course. But there we don't need any more help just now."

"We'll go to eight," said Ivan.

"All right," Mr. Nelson assented. "Want to wait for a ride?"

Ivan looked at me. "We'll walk."

"Leave your names at the office. Tell them I sent you."

With that he clicked his tongue to the horses.

We turned south, into the nave of the poplar trees.

"Camp eight!" I thought and I asked, "How large is this farm?"

"Don't know," Ivan replied; "twenty, thirty thousand acres."

I felt dazed. "Owned by some company?"

"No," said Ivan. "Man's name is Mackenzie."

I pondered that. A farm, many square miles in extent, owned by a single man! Nothing was further from my thoughts than envy; had somebody offered me the place as a present, I should not have accepted it. But it struck me as incongruous. I was awed and felt as if I had run up against some barrier in a valley along which I had been travelling – a barrier of forbidding aspect, insurmountable. This feeling did not leave me either when later on I learned the explanation of the fact. The present owner's father had invested the savings of a lifetime in this land which he had bought at ten cents an acre – before there was a railroad, when nobody yet thought of making it the granary of the world. Now it was worth fifty dollars an acre – hardly allowing for buildings and other improvements at figures which represented real values. Was that what was called "enterprise"?

The road to the great compound of buildings was not much more than a mile long. We passed a handsome white frame-house, surrounded by trees, to our left.

"Superintendent's house," Ivan commented.

Then we emerged into a yard of truly gigantic dimensions. Huge barns stretched out to the west, with horse-lots enclosed by high board-fences. Other buildings stood in front of them, one a blacksmith's shop as I inferred from the clanging noise that proceeded from it.

To the east a number of scattered buildings made a straggling group; these, with the exception of one huge red structure, were all painted white. One of them, occupying the centre of this east half of the yard, reminded me of the "cook-house" on that Ohio "company-farm" of nine months ago.

In this part of the compound a cement sidewalk ran along the northern edge of the yard; and as we proceeded across the open expanse, another view opened up on a cluster of buildings in the northeast corner. There was an unmistakably residential air about them. They were sur-rounded by a small park; well-kept lawns encircled them; and at the entrance of the central house in this group a carriage was waiting, with a team of magnificent, coal-black hackneys hitched to it. Just as we were nearing the building which Ivan was bound for, a young man of ath-letic build, clad in white flannels, walked briskly along the sidewalk, westward. Ivan saw my look, as I glanced back at him and the house.

"That's the boss," he said. "And that's the White House. He lives there with his mother."

This pleasant-faced boy was the owner of all these square-miles! And he lived with his mother! That seemed to imply that he was unmarried. The fact that his mother kept house for him made the whole thing somehow seem still more preposterous; it made the young man seem still younger; it made it a certainty that this farm was not earned. I felt as if some uncomfortable facts, some dis-quieting realities were obtruded upon me, at variance with my last night's mood.

Ivan and I registered, much as we should have done at an inn. A tall young Jew of dandified appearance looked indifferently and yet disdainfully down on these two more bums who henceforth would figure upon his books and time-sheets. I paid scant attention to him; in a few minutes we were on the road again, going south.

Far to the east we had a glimpse of another huge com-pound of buildings; and as soon as we swung out between the fields, we caught sight, way ahead of us, to the south, of the camp for which we were bound.

"All this still the farm?" I asked at last, looking out over endless fields of barley, oats, and wheat.

Ivan laughed. "Yes," he said and waved his arms through space; "as far as you can see; and also north of the track. There is another camp, way north, twenty or twenty-five miles from headquarters."

We came to a place where east of our road a summer-fallow, half a mile wide, seemed to stretch away to the southern horizon. Three steam-tractors travelled along the far edge, each drawing three disk-harrows spaced behind and beside each other. They travelled along at about our speed and kept abreast during the whole walk of four or five miles which we made to reach our camp.

"Big farm," said Ivan and smiled his enigmatical smile.

I nodded in silence; I could not shake off that feeling that something was fundamentally wrong with this world, even though I did not desire one single thing from among its wealth.

The camp which we reached at last made a less well cared-for impression than the one which we had passed through before. The buildings had, in their arrangement, something casual, as if they had been erected without a previous plan, or as if they had been dropped out of some giant's toy-box.

Close to the road, in the centre, stood the cook-house. To the east a towering, barn-like structure, painted red, had something sinister about it. It was the bunk-house, as I found. To the west, at an acute angle to the road, stretched the horsebarns with their accompaniment of high board-fences enclosing the paddocks.

It was there we went. By Ivan's watch it was nearly noon. We would wait for the foreman, he said; we squatted down against the wall of a barn. The only signs of activity were at the cook-house. Otherwise the compound looked deserted.

After a while a two-wheeled cart, drawn by a neglected-looking bay nag came rattling in from the south.

A dirty, stunted little runt of a fellow got out of it in front of the barn and unhitched the horse while he greeted Ivan. We had risen and were walking towards him.

"Hello, Ol'-timer," he sang out in a shrill, mocking, cynical voice. "Got a pardner this time, have you?"

"Yes," said Ivan; and for the first time his smile was embarrassed. I had the impression as if he felt the need of apologizing to me for the fact that this was the foreman of the camp at which we were going to work.

"Going out this afternoon?"

"Don't mind if we do," Ivan answered.

"Who's going to be the teamster?"

"We work together."

"All right, pal," the foreman acquiesced. "Suit yourself. Two miles south, one west, along the track; that's where I want you to work. Come on; I'll show you your team."

And he walked off, leading his horse into the barn.

We followed, taking our bundles along.

The foreman, in passing, pointed to a stall where two big Clydes were standing. "There," he said and walked on.

Ivan reached for my bundle, stepped in between the horses, and climbed up on the manger. He hid our belongings overhead, in a corner of the beams.

"We'll sleep in the hay-loft" he whispered; "that's against the rules; but the bunk-house is alive with vermin."

I had learned to trust Ivan's leadership and nodded.

He started at once to harness the horses. I watched him and did as he did, thus taking my first lesson in harnessing up a draft-horse.

The men were beginning to come in with their teams, and a bell rang at the cook-house. I noticed with satisfaction that on the whole they seemed a decent lot. They were Swedes, for the most part, speaking a broken

English. Most of them greeted Ivan as an old acquaintance, some calling him "Old-timer," some by a name which made me look up at him. Again I saw that embarrassed smile on his face.

He laughed and said, "No use getting mad; they've always called me that. Why, I don't know."

The name was Jesus.

We went to the cook-house for dinner. The food was good, consisting of soup, meat, vegetables, and pudding. Plenty of pies were scattered over the tables which were covered with white oil-cloth; there were large stacks of fresh bread, both white and brown, dishes of butter, pitchers with milk, and pots full of coffee and tea. As once before in similar surroundings I marvelled again at the capacity for eating which these workers of the soil displayed.

Nobody seemed to take notice of myself, though a few more greeted Ivan in a half friendly, half ironical way. There was a rough-and-ready, but healthy toleration about it all.

I found that the majority of these Swedes were not hobos, but young homesteaders from the north, from Canada or the northern edge of Dakota where crops were later – men who were only just establishing themselves, who needed the ready cash to pay for farms or stock or equipment and who went out to this one place only, where they were working for monthly wages till threshing was over. They lost the advantage of higher pay when the price of labour rose; but they gained inasmuch as they were sure of their pay, rain or shine. When the harvest was finished, they left to attend to their own small holdings; and they returned again when winter had set in and when only the vast numbers of horses and other farm-animals had to be fed and looked after. The crew numbered no more than fifty men at present. Ivan and I were the advance-guard, here, of that vast army which had to march in to take care of the crest of the wave of work.

That afternoon I had reason to congratulate myself on the partnership I had formed with Ivan. This quiet and unassuming man with his intelligent, delicate face was endowed with a body able to stand up under any strain. I did his driving and stood on the load which we gathered; Ivan pitched the hay. When he picked up with his fork what he intended to lift, I could only marvel at his strength and skill. Slowly, without hurry, but also without waste of time, he would force the fork with its tremendous load up, with a steady exertion, till he held the handle high overhead; and he would throw the load off with the slightest of jerks so that it fell just where he wanted it. His body seemed to shorten and to broaden when he did that; and never did I see a wrong move or a lost motion, never hurry, never delay. Meanwhile he would call out directions to me, instructing me in the art of building the load, and cautioning me against the mistakes which I made. He was patient, as if he had known that the work was new to me.

Whenever we pulled up to the stack, our load was wider and higher than any other; and it was certainly none of my doing.

In the evening, when we returned to the camp, Ivan looked a different man. He was streaming with sweat; on his bare arms powerful muscles played. He did not remind me of Sergei Ivanovitch in Tolstoy's Anna Karenina now, but of Levin himself – the man who stands squarely upon the soil and who, from the soil, from his soil, reaches out with tentative mind into the great mysteries. This man was to me, on this evening, while we were rattling along the road, the personification of all that is fine and noble in bodily labour; of the joy of muscle and sinew that want to play in mere exertion. I envied him his strength.

From him was reflected into myself, into my own weary limbs and aching joints, an exhilaration, a quiet satisfaction with weariness honestly come by, with pain resulting from having used and called into action hidden reserves of bodily powers of whose very existence I had been in ignorance.

Ivan glowed and smiled; to me it seemed that in his smile there were the infinite sympathy and tenderness which are the attributes of the strong in contact with those who are weak but whom they love.

From this afternoon dated a deeper friendship between us, a friendship still less in need of words than it had been before. I saw a deeper, truer, less obvious significance in the name by which most of the Swedish farmhands called him and which was meant as a mockery suggested by his physical resemblance to the type.

Never, during the month that followed, did Ivan and I discuss the slightest thing of any importance beyond the work in hand. Not once did we touch on anything wider, on our intellectual or emotional lives; and that was very much as it should be. Little was said, much done.

It did not take Ivan long to find out that I was hardly equal to the strain of the work; and since we were working in partnership, he invariably and unhesitatingly and without a word assumed the harder part. So long as the haying proceeded, he harnessed the horses in the morning; he unharnessed them at night; I drove the team; he pitched the hay. And I did nothing for him except that I supplied him with tobacco which he apparently craved but never bought.

Gradually, as the cutting began in the fields of barley, the bunk-house filled, for wages rose. At first only a few stragglers came in; but when the daily pay had reached the two-and-a-half-dollar mark, hobos appeared by the dozen; soon our camp had its full complement of a hundred men. Even then more were hired every day and sent down; if there was no work for them with the field-crews, they were kept busy, drawing pay for every day which was fit for the work in the field, while they were splitting wood, drawing water, and doing similar chores; to be sent out behind the binders when others left unexpectedly.

For there was a constant coming and going; you could never be sure that you would see a face that had turned up to-day again on the morrow. I did not, as yet, take much interest in these men; the reasons which sent them back on the road, away to the next place, seemed utterly trivial. "This eternal beef!" one would say. "This eternal pork!" or, "These eternal stewed prunes!" said the next ones; they asked for their "time", and went. It was mostly the food which served as pretext. By and by I saw more of them, and I shall give a glimpse at their lives as I proceed.

So long as Ivan and I were employed in haying, we saw very little of the foreman. True, he drove by in his cart when we were loading the rack; he stopped at the stack when we pitched the load off; but he never spoke to us. When cutting began, however, he always seemed to be on our heels.

I found that stooking sheaves was much harder work than haying. The twelve or fifteen binders which did the cutting for our crew were given, as a matter of course, to the Swedes who were in the steady employ of the farm. When I saw that, I was strongly inclined to leave, simply as a matter of fairness to the management. I felt that I was no longer doing a day's work for a day's wages. But, again without words, Ivan opposed such a plan. He worked harder and harder, fairly revelling in exertion; more and more frequently he would say, "Take it easy! Take it easy!" I hated, in leaving the work, to leave him.

Once, of a hot afternoon, we two being alone on one side of the field, I was suddenly taken sick.

Ivan looked at my face, pointed to a place on the ground, in the shade of a stook, and said, "Lie down."

There was no choice; I obeyed. While I lay there, I watched him with ever-increasing wonder, for he worked as if he were engaged in a contest of speed and endurance, fairly leaping from place to place and throwing the heavy sheaves which he picked up, never less than two, and sometimes three at a time, with infallible precision, lifting them shoulder-high and flinging them down so that they stood as if planted. He went on for an hour or longer. Then he called me; and when I reached him, he pointed across the field, where the barley was still standing on a shoulder of the ground. A black spot was moving along, just above the waving grain.

"Foreman coming," Ivan said. "Work till he's gone."

"Oh," I said, "I don't care. I shall have to report sick anyway."

"No," he exclaimed. "I've done enough, and more, for any two of them. You take your wages."

"All right," I said and made a pretence at working till the foreman had passed us.

"Lie down," said Ivan as soon as the man was out of sight; and again he started to work as he had done before.

Next morning I felt still weak, though somewhat better. Nelson, the superintendent, was down at our camp when we were ready to go to the field. But the foreman was not around. Since we all knew what had to be done, he had not been missed till Mr. Nelson enquired after him. There was a commotion, then; and several men went in search around the buildings. They found him at last in an empty stall of one of the stables, in a state of brutish intoxication. Our start was delayed. Mr. Nelson summarily dismissed the man and called one of the big Swedes aside. But after a short discussion the Swede rejoined the waiting men. He had declined to act as foreman. Mr. Nelson gave the necessary orders, and teams and crews went out to the field.

Not much later a new man made his appearance in the foreman's cart. As luck would have it, he came at once to where Ivan and I were working, I no doubt not doing a full man's share of the work. He stopped his horse and started his task of looking on. He was watching me. Had he spoken to me in a decent way, I should have explained. But he did not choose to do so; he merely looked on and scowled. He was a fat, florid man with an ugly-looking face. Ivan, too, was slackening in his usual speed. He did not want to outwork me under the eye of the "boss".

Suddenly, after having stopped there for twenty minutes or so, this boss drove up close to us, jumped out of his seat and started to swear and to shout, flinging out obscene words and profane language in such an amazing manner that both Ivan and I straightened up, each of us a sheaf in his hands, looked at each other, and burst out laughing.

This drove the man frantic, and he lifted his hand against me.

But Ivan was faster than he. Before he realized what was happening, Ivan had thrown him off his feet by merely pushing the sheaf he was holding into his face. The man tumbled over, and Ivan, still laughing, held him down.

It was characteristic of Ivan that he looked up at me before he jumped back and said, "We are through."

The newly appointed foreman must have had an inkling of the iron strength in those arms which had tumbled him over; for he simply got up, took a slip of paper from his pocket, scribbled a word or so with a pencil, and handed it to Ivan, saying, "All right."

He had given us our "time"; and we returned to camp to roll our bundles.

Before we left, a dozen or more of the hobos were coming back from the field. There had been no further provocation, we heard. But an example like ours sets the crowds of the hobos going. It works like revolt in a long oppressed country. Somewhere a clash occurs, and soon the whole people is up in arms. Before evening forty of them left this camp alone; yet nobody had had any personal cause for complaint. There is nothing that binds the hobo when he wants to go; he is always willing to leave the best of places.

Ivan and I went to headquarters to draw our pay. At the office there was a stampede. A number of the men who had quitted at our camp had called out their "pals" from other camps; the young Jew found himself swamped with the work of figuring wages and writing cheques. The men were crowding the office; some of them were in an ugly mood. They refused to take cheques and demanded cash. Before long the bookkeeper used the telephone and summoned help.

Soon after, the young man whom a few weeks ago I had seen on the cement sidewalk of the yard came in. He was not more than twenty-five years old; but he had an air of quiet assurance which strikingly lacked the Jew's particular shade of disdain. His mere appearance brought a hush.

He calmly seat down at a desk and turned about. "Who's next?" he asked.

The men held back. The one of them approached and he started the others going.

Suddenly Mr. Mackenzie turned again, "Listen here, you men. What's wrong? What are you quitting for?"

"Oh, I don't know," said one.

Others looked at each other.

Mr. Mackenzie picked out the one who bore himself most boldly. "Here, you, what are you quitting for?"

"I guess I have the right to quit if I want to," replied the man defiantly.

"Sure," said Mr. Mackenzie amiably; "sure. But what do you want to quit for?"

The man looked about, he saw me; with a nod of his head he said, "Ask him."

Mr. Mackenzie looked a question at me.

I could not help but admire his composure. "Well," I said, "I can't speak for these men. As for myself, I am sick. I was not doing my share of the work this morning. The foreman at number eight took the wrong tack, swore, and offered blows. My friend here bowled him over. We could hardly stay after that."

Mr. Mackenzie nodded. "Willing to work at another camp?"

I saw an opportunity here. "Certainly," I said; "but I am not very strong. I think it only fair to tell you that I cannot do what some of the men can do."

"That's all right," he replied; "some work is easier, some harder. We need a store-boss just now. How about your partner? Oh, it's Ivan, is it? Hello!" He nodded to him. "What do you say, Ivan? Willing to stay?"

Ivan nodded; he, too, was smiling.

"How about you?" Mr. Mackenzie asked the next one; in ten minutes more he had hired half the number back.

The rest had made up their minds to leave, and leave they did.

When a man refused to accept a cheque and demanded cash, Mr. Mackenzie told him to wait. "You don't expect me to carry as much loose cash about me as you men are getting these days," he said quite pleasantly. "I'll send to town after a while and have it brought out."

Before long the man stepped up again and declared himself willing to take a cheque.

"That's sense," said Mr. Mackenzie. "You are going to town anyway. They'll cash my cheque at any store."

Mr. Nelson, too, came in after a while. He had had word of the stampede.

He and Mr. Mackenzie held a brief, whispered consultation, in the course of which Mr. Mackenzie pointed me out.

When they had finished, Mr. Nelson came over.

"We need a store-boss," he said. "It's mostly driving. There is more honesty needed than strength. Want to try?"

I did; emphatically; but meanwhile it had occurred to me that to accept meant leaving Ivan. I hesitated; but Ivan nudged me with his elbow and nodded without looking at me.

So I said, "If you think that I can do the work, I'll be glad to try. As for honesty, I can promise you that."

"You'll have to start right away," he went on, "we need some things from town."

"All right," I said.

Ivan drew his pay and told Mr. Nelson that he would not start before morning. He wanted to go to town; since I was going, he had a ride.

THREE

I Become Acquainted With the Hobo

MY NEW JOB as "store-boss" and later as "driving-boss" threw me into closer contact, first with the men, then with the management of the farm. It separated my close relation to Ivan; it made me independent of him. We still remained friends, still saw a good deal of each other for two more months; but no longer did I do what he did – no longer was he the determining factor in my life. That is the reason why he disappears from this story. I cannot but think that he had foreseen this and wanted it so. A few more words about him will be sufficient to resolve the reader's curiosity as to the motive behind his life.

The very evening after I had assumed my new duties I came upon him, sitting on the ground behind the southern-most building of the vast compound which I came, for the time being to regard as my "home". It was after supper, just before dark, and I had been looking for him. He had gone to town with me and cashed his cheque which was for some fifty dollars or so. When I found him behind the "old granary" – which, since Mr. Mackenzie had erected three large grain-elevators of his own, was used as a store-house for such supplies as binder-twine, canvas, and so on – Ivan was sewing at his coat.

He smiled at me with his usual brilliant smile and explained what he was doing by showing me a secret pocket in the lining of his coat which he was sewing up. That was the place where he kept his money!

"Say, Ivan," I said. "I have long been wondering. Just why do you lead this life?"

"Well," he asked, astonished that I should ask him such a question, "why do you?"

"Chance," I replied. "I met you and went along. I liked you, I had no money, and it did not matter what I was doing, so long as I saw something of this country. But I see you have money; more than I have ever seen since I came to this country."

"Maybe," he replied. "I have close to four thousand dollars. It's taken me ten years to save it. I like this work, and don't like any other work. That is why I do it."

"Well," I went on, "what do you intend to do with all that wealth?"

"Buy a farm," he said. "One more year, then I'll be ready. Those Swedes buy the land and work out in order to pay for it. I don't like that. I want a wife and little children around."

He laughed, shamefacedly.

"There's another thing I have been wondering about," I went on. "Just how old are you?"

"Thirty-five," he said.

After that, as was usual with us, we sat in silence.

Ivan was no hobo after all; he had a purpose in life beyond the immediate present. The hobo has not; the hobo never saves; the very essence of his being is spending.

As I found out, the round of my duties was as follows: I had to watch the trains for arriving shipments; I had to haul the provisions out to the store – which was located in the rear of the same building which held the office; I had to visit every camp – we had seven of them open, now – to take out groceries, vegetables, meat; I had to keep an exact inventory of the things on hand and to keep tab on outgoing and incoming items; I had to bring the men hired by Mr. Nelson into the central camp and to distribute them among the other camps; I had to round up the beef-cattle for the butcher – there was, on an average, one steer killed a day; I had to look after the cleaning of the two store-houses; I had to bring the mail from town; and I had to sell such necessaries as overalls, socks, underwear, and such luxuries as tobacco and candy to the men.

In order to enable me to look after all these various duties two teams were at my disposal, one a team of heavy draft-horses, the other a light driving team for a democrat. For rounding up the cattle I had a well-trained saddle-horse besides.

My wages were the same as those of the harvest-crews, except that on rainy days and Sundays, when all the other men lost their time, I was paid at the flat rate of two dollars a day. I had bettered myself, quite apart from the fact that with rare exceptions – as, for instance, when heavy barrels of lubricating oil had to be unloaded – my work was brain-work rather than physical labour. The drives, though sometimes long and tiresome, were on the whole to my liking. I had been rather a horseman in Europe, and I took readily to handling my bronchos. I had no "boss" except Mr. Nelson, who was invariably kind and courteous; I came into close contact with many of the men, of whom there were now eight or nine hundred employed.

Again all nationalities except the Latin ones were represented; all mingled freely except the Swedes. Swedes are clannish; they kept to themselves, slept – by connivance of the superintendent, himself of Swedish descent, in the haylofts of the barns, played their own, innocent games – horse-shoe quoits – and worked with the steadiness peculiar to their race.

All the other hands employed at headquarters lodged at the bunk-house, a huge, barnlike structure in the extreme south-east corner of the yard. The upper floor of this building was the dormitory. The beds or bunks were roughly put up of lumber; they had no mattresses but were filled with straw; the straw was never renewed, and consequently it swarmed with vermin. That was the one unpardonable feature in the accommodation provided. Two heavy blankets of wool shot with cotton were assigned to every bunk. When I first saw this upper floor where a hundred men were crowded together, I thought of the stifling lack of fresh air which must prevail there overnight. But, strange to say, only one or two of the hundreds of men with whom I came into touch ever objected to this accommodation. The ground-floor of the bunk-house was a large hall provided with long tables and wooden benches. Here the men assembled on rainy days.

As for myself, it was not only my right but my duty to sleep in the store-house whenever I was at headquarters for the night. There was a bunk; but I never used it; I preferred to bed myself down on the floor. Occasionally it happened that provisions or men had to be taken to that northernmost outpost of the farm which was twenty-six miles from headquarters and which was now opened at last. When I went there, I had to stop over at an intermediate camp, not on my own account, but on account of the horses, especially when I was driving a wagon with the heavy team. My meals I took at whatever camp I could make in time; I did not mind if I had to skip one now and then.

Ivan slept – by my connivance – in the second store-house which I have already mentioned.

A specimen or two of my encounters with such of the men as obtruded themselves on my attention will be necessary.

One day when I had gone to town in the morning, I picked up two men whom Mr. Nelson had hired. There was the usual hobo-camp at the outskirts of the village, occupied by those who were still holding out for higher wages or who had left some other farm and were going idle till their money was spent. It was here that the two men boarded my wagon.

One was a German of slight proportions, a mere boy; the other a middle-aged American of burly build. Both were taciturn; both seemed to be at outs with their fate. As it happened, they were to be the ones who roused my interest in the great mass of hobos.

There was no immediate vacancy for them in the crews at headquarters; Mr. Nelson put them to splitting wood.

In the evening the German kept lingering in the neighbourhood of the store-house; when he saw me closing the slide-doors on the east side, where the loading platform was, he spoke to me.

"Can I sleep in there?" he asked.

"I'm sorry," I replied, "it's against my orders."

"The bookkeeper gone?"

"Yes," I said, "he has his rooms in the cook-house. Want to see him?"

"I want to quit," he said.

I looked at him. "You came only this morning. What's wrong?"

"I'm not going to sleep in that bunk-house," he said vehemently.

I could understand that and felt instant pity. Most of the men who were seized with the sudden desire to leave used the "grub" for their pretext. The food was good; I had no sympathy with them, though I came to view even these men differently. This boy objected to the one objectionable thing.

Suddenly he sat down on the platform and buried his face in his hands. I was shocked and frightened.

"Don't do that," I said. "I'll see what I can do for you. I can't put you up here, against definite orders. But there is the driving-stable with a good hayloft above. I have no orders regarding it; I'll show you how to get up there if you will wait till I have locked up."

He did not stir.

I bent down and laid my hand on his shoulder; he was shaken by sobs; in an impulse of pity I sat down beside him. "Is there anything I could help you in?" I asked.

He shook his head.

"Are you new in this country?"

Again he shook his head.

"I did not think so," I said, "from your English."

"I can't stay," he cried out. " I can't stay!"

"Why not? Is the work too hard?"

"No," he said. His whole body began to shake with sobs. "My poor mother!" he cried out.

For a moment I was unable to speak. "Is she here in this country?"

"No," he answered, "she's in Germany. When my father died, she had to go out to work, washing and scrubbing! I was to go to America to make money. She's waiting, has been waiting for years, to hear from me. And what have I done?"

"Well," I said softly, "look here. You are making three and a half dollars a day; you have no expenses. There is work on this farm for another two months. Why not stay and then send her a hundred dollars? A hundred dollars is quite a sum over there."

He was still sobbing. "No use," he said. "I can't stay anywhere. I've tried it for years. I can't."

"But why?" I persisted. "Where do you want to go?"

"Nowhere," he answered. "I don't know. I get work, and I leave it. I can't stay. It's stronger than I. I'll go to-morrow." He seemed to pull himself together. "Never mind," he said. "Don't ask me. I won't bother the bookkeeper to-night. Show me the hayloft. I'll stay till morning."

I felt helpless; the thing was beyond my understanding; but I saw suffering; the seat of the pain seemed to be beyond my reach. My impotence was complete and baffling.

Next morning the other of these two men whom I had taken out brought himself to my notice. He, too, lingered about that group of buildings which comprised cookhouse and store. Since I had the impression that he was looking for something, I went and spoke to him.

"What do you do with your garbage here?" he asked gruffly.

"Our garbage?"

"Yes," he replied, "what's thrown away, the offal from the dishes and the kitchen."

"That's thrown out into a barrel and drawn away to be fed to the pigs."

"To the pigs!" he snorted contemptuously and hitched his trousers up. "You'll have to keep it if you want to keep me."

"What do you mean?" I asked. "What do you want it for?"

"To eat," he said with another snort.

I stood aghast. "Did you not get in in time for breakfast?"

"Oh, breakfast!" he fairly shouted. "I don't want none of your beastly feed. I want the garbage."

"You don't mean to say that you prefer it?" I asked, half disgusted, half horrified.

"You don't mean to say," he mocked my voice. "Yes, sir. I do mean to say. I've gone without dinner, and I've gone without supper. If I've got to go without breakfast, too, I'll quit."

"Well, what on earth made you that way?" I asked.

"What on earth, eh?" he mocked again. "Tastes better, that's what. More flavour to it. I can't digest the feed you serve."

With that he walked off. He left that day.

Both these incidents may seem funny to some, disgusting to others; but I had gone through too many things myself in the vicissitudes of my life to let it go at that. Nor did they remain isolated happenings, now that my "job" brought me into constant contact with the men and that as one who stood apart from the crews. They spoke to me as being one of the lesser members of the administration. More than once, when I was taking newly-hired men out to some distant camp – especially to that northernmost outpost of the farm which was some thirty miles from the nearest town – did one or two of them refuse to go on when they discovered that they were being taken far away from the beaten trail. They simply dropped off the wagon and started back, walking.

"Where're we going?" was invariably their first question when they were alone with me on the road. When I told them, they swore or grumbled at the distance; still most of them went on, hoping, that when the spirit moved them to leave, they would find some conveyance to snatch a ride on, if only for part of the way.

As the season advanced, two measures were taken to prevent them from lightly throwing up the work; for when the harvest on the smaller farms was finished, the supply of this floating labour gave out: the wave of hobodom struck farther north, towards the Canadian border where crops were noticeably later, even within an easy day's drive from headquarters; the camp, for instance, on that outpost of Mr. Mackenzie's holdings had not been opened at all till Ivan and I had transferred to headquarters. It was I who drove the cook and the first provisions over, followed by a long string of fifteen binders and as many wagons, with a hundred draft-horses or so behind.

One of the measures to prevent, or at least to impede the drifting away of the men, at a time when they were most urgently needed for threshing, consisted in strict orders issued to the foremen to put only the most reliable hands on the wagons and grain-tanks as teamsters; these in turn, as indeed myself, received strict orders never to give anybody a ride unless authorized by a foreman or the superintendent to do so. Accordingly those among the Swedes who were homesteaders were picked out for hauling the grain when threshing started. To them the threat of instant dismissal in case of disobedience held terrors.

As for myself, one day Mr. Nelson became emphatic about this order, reiterating that it was meant literally; for I had been seen returning from one of the northern camps with a passenger. This had been an independent farmer who, on a rainy day, was walking to town. I explained this to Mr. Nelson, adding that surely I was to use my judgment in such a case; it could not be the intention to antagonize the permanently settled population.

Mr. Nelson smiled. "Just take the order quite literally. If a foreman is around or I, ask. But don't take anybody without being authorized to do so. As for the small farmer, we do not intend to curry favour with him."

Mr. Nelson actually used the word "we". To me this seemed utter autocracy, besides being a narrow-minded policy, as "we" were shortly to find out when the herd of cattle kept on the farm stampeded and broke through the fence; it could not be located for several weeks because every "small" farmer in the neighbourhood did his best to cover the tracks; to find them involved the management in no end of trouble and expense.

As it happened, I had an opportunity to express my opinion in a practical way. A day or two after, when I was driving along a muddy road, I saw young Mr. Mackenzie's car lying on the grassy slope of a cross-road, not far from where it joined the trail which I was following myself. As luck would have it, I was driving the light broncho-team hitched to the democrat, and they were capable of considerable speed.

As soon as Mr. Mackenzie saw me coming, he started on a run for the crossing, leaving his car.

I touched my horses with the whip, and they responded. When I shot past the crossing, Mr. Mackenzie began to shout and to wave his arms. As soon as I had put a hundred yards or so between him and myself, I pulled my horses up short.

Then I turned and called back. "Strict orders from Mr. Nelson. Nobody to get a ride without permission from him or a foreman!" And I drove on, leaving him to tramp home over four or five miles of muddy road.

In the evening he came over to the store, accompanied by Mr. Nelson.

"Nelson," he said, "better tell this man to give me a ride when I ask for it. Make it a standing order, will you?"

I grinned; we all three burst out laughing.

The other measure was of a more serious character.

Everybody who was newly hired was now required to sign an agreement whereby he promised that he would not leave before it was Mr. Mackenzie's pleasure to dismiss him.

I understand that, the men being hired by the day, at day wages, and no definite term being set to end the agreement, nor any definite remuneration being agreed upon – the phrase used was at "current wages" – this agreement was void in law. I know it worked hardship on many and raised a good deal of bad blood. The men, as most men do, signed blindly, some being unable to read, others not caring to go to the trouble. The few who refused to sign were left free to walk back to town – a distance of five miles – or otherwise to take themselves off the premises in any way they pleased.

The way this measure worked out was instructive. As many men left their work as before; for there is always, in the hobo, the desire to move on. When they came to the office, they were refused their cheques; the foremen had already refused them their time-slips. Some took it meekly and went back to work. Some insisted on leaving and were told to come back for their wages when the work was completed; if the impulse to leave was strong enough and the sum owing to them not too large, they simply threw up their wages, for I am sure that nobody returned for them. Some, lastly, got into a temper, demanded to see Mr. Mackenzie, and threatened when he came – as he invariably did – with legal proceedings.

"Go to law, if you want to," Mr. Mackenzie told them. "I doubt whether you can find a lawyer to take your case. If you succeed, all the worse for you. I'll fight you up to the supreme court; whatever you may have coming will disappear in fees and costs, and more besides. If you'll take my advice, you will go back to work and wait till I have finished. There will be something coming to you, then."

Being stationed in the store-house, when I was not out driving, I saw a good deal of this; for I also had a small desk in the office itself.

Some incidents gave me a good deal to think about, for I had taken a great liking to the young owner. I saw his side, of course. It was in the interest of the country, and even of mankind at large, that crops like his should be safely garnered. Lack of labour might prevent this from being accomplished. The men were unreasonable, there was no doubt about that. But I had learned, by that time, that at least nine-tenths of all our behaviour is unreasonable. And I could not help pitying them; I felt sympathy even with their impotent rage, for I knew how the feeling of impotence hurts. What I saw and heard made my heart sore for the underlying conditions that have created hobodom. There is, in most cases, first the inability to secure steady work at any one place; partial or seasonal employment is to blame for that; thus arises, in the individual, an inability to stay with the work; the men have to move sooner or later; they want to choose their own time; and this desire becomes at last a mania for which they can no longer be held responsible. Where hobodom has not been created in this manner, it is a case of congenital disposition. At any rate, as things were, it was one of the conditions of human life; to ignore it and not to make allowance for it, seemed cruelly callous to me.

Slowly my liking for Mr. Mackenzie faded; I found myself slipping into an attitude of animosity.

Then a case came up which relieved me, at least partly, of this gnawing discontent with the order of things. I saw that Mr. Mackenzie tempered a cruel policy with discriminating humanity.

A man had left his camp, asked for his cheque, and was refused. He demanded to see Mr. Mackenzie, saying he had to catch a morning train to the east. Unfortunately Mr. Mackenzie was out in the fields, in his car, and could not be reached. The man, a quiet, unassuming fellow, walked restlessly up and down while waiting.

As soon as Mr. Mackenzie returned, he came over. Two or three others were waiting for him by this time.

"Well, what is it" he asked.

"I am a married man," the first of those waiting said in substance. "I have a family, and I received a letter last night telling me that my wife and two children are down with typhoid. I've got to get home. I have missed to-day's train; but I can walk it to Walloh and catch a night-train. I must have my wages."

"How much have you coming?"

The bookkeeper answered for the man.

"Well," said Mr. Mackenzie, "I can't pay you your wages. I have made a rule; I have to live up to it. But I shall fix you up somehow. Where do you live?"

"Near Fergus Falls, Minnesota," the man replied.

"Mr. Mackenzie studied a time-table. "You can make the night-train from Barnesville," he said at last; "that is thirty miles from here. Have your dinner first; after that I shall take you over in my car. As for money, I shall loan you a hundred dollars in cash. You leave your address with the bookkeeper, and we shall send you the balance by mail when the season is over. Will that fix you up?"

"Yes," said the man, "thanks."

The other two found the young owner inexorable.

I could not excuse the cruel condition; but I could at least view Mr. Mackenzie less harshly than I had done before. Much of our suffering is inflicted by thoughtlessness. Lack of humanity is lack of thought, insight, imagination.

It was at this time that the old feeling of wonder took hold of me again; I marvelled at the plan of my life.

Had I gone through those things which I had endured and suffered myself – on that tramp from New York to Indiana – in preparation for what I was witnessing now? Doubtlessly my own, direct suffering, little as it amounted to, had prepared me for the vicarious suffering of the present. Doubtlessly I should – as others did – have shrugged my shoulders at the agony of the German boy; I

should have turned in disgust from the "garbage-eater".
Doubtlessly I should have looked with the Jewish bookkeeper's distant and hostile disdain upon this flood of
questionable humanity, had not my own experience taught
me a deeper sympathy. I had at that time no thought for
myself; I had nothing to worry about for the future; I felt
that my great idea, my revelation of only a few weeks ago,
secured me, insured me against all threats of an economic
nature which the invaded continent might hold. As far as I
personally was concerned, I could step out of this condition of hobodom whenever I chose to. But what difference
did that make? It did not change one single fact in the
cruel conditions which surrounded me.

And then, somehow, I received a hint of what was going
on at the bunk-house at night and on rainy days.

I knew, of course, that the big hall on the ground-floor
was the scene of the recreations of the hobos. For me
there lay a certain glamour over that hall – that kind of
fascination, I suppose, which in former years, in the
Quartier Latin of Paris, had lured me on occasional ad-
venturous trips into the "dives" of the criminal underworld.

All these men were harmless enough, taken singly.
They were men like you and myself, men with personal
worries and sorrows, likings and idiosyncrasies; above all
weak and suffering men who appealed to my human sympathies. So far I had steered clear of them in the mass. I
knew that Mr. Nelson, the superintendent, a quiet, coolly
courageous man, did not like to interfere with them, there.
Sometimes it was whispered that drinking was going on
in the hall; and though it was strictly against the rules to
bring liquor in any form into the camp, so that, if it was
done, in violation of the rules, it became Nelson's duty to
do something about it, I could see a look of annoyance
cross his face when he was informed of the fact. He would
have preferred not to know about it, to let them get drunk
and sleep it off the next day. It was a dangerous task to
investigate and to seize the whisky. Once, when the report

came that the men were far gone in drink and that an ugly mood was prevailing, he held a brief conference with Mr. Mackenzie, and the two went together. Unflinching courage I found to be the most redeeming feature of the young millionaire-owner.

There was no need for me to go near the place. No duty of mine led me there. But I felt that my knowledge of this particular brand of humanity was incomplete till I had seen it in its orgies.

At last, one evening, after a sudden thunderstorm which had brought the work in the fields to a stop in the early afternoon, I went.

It was after supper; the hour was late; I could not quit work at the usual time. This was especially true on rainy days because then we always had a rush on both office and store; everybody drew a cheque on account; everybody bought what he thought he needed. So night had set in when I reached the hall of the bunk-house.

To this very day I see the scene when I close my eyes.

Innumerable more or less smoky lanterns stood on a long table placed in the centre of the huge barn-hall. The rest of its spaces were in darkness; for the table was surrounded by a dense crowd of excited onlookers whose dim but gigantic shadows checkered and moved over the slanting beams, the walls, and the ceiling of the structure. The atmosphere reeked with the smells of coal-oil, soot, and whisky-exhalations.

When I penetrated the surrounding wall of humanity, edging in at the upper end, near the top of the table, so as to get a look at the game, I was struck by the feeling of tension which prevailed.

To me a game had always been a game – a give-and-take, in which a loss had to be borne with the same equanimity – at least in appearance – as that with which you rake in a gain. But these twenty-odd men who were seated on the wooden-benches around the table played for what to them were fortunes. Their stakes were the earnings of weeks and months of unremitting labour; to some a gain might mean comparative ease and leisure during the coming winter; a loss, slavery in a sweat-shop of the middle west. Winnings were taken with a grim sort of satisfaction; losses, with an obscene curse; sometimes with a vicious word against the winner.

The game was poker, of course; with the bets running high – "the sky was the limit". That is the most deplorable form of the game because it allows the skilful "bluffer" to "squeeze out" an unfortunate antagonist whose holdings have run below his own. It was on that score that the brawls arose; for, as soon as you passed, unable to follow up the expert "pyramiding" of the bets, you lost the right to demand a "show-down".

I saw at once that the game was dominated by a young engineer from St. Paul, sent out by the Tractor Company to supervise the working of the new engines used for steam-plowing and threshing. Engineers and separator men could command as much as ten dollars a day during the high-pressure of the work. But this young fellow was engaged for three months at a flat rate of six dollars a day, all found, rain or shine. His earnings during the season may not have exceeded those of any other engineer – there were eight on the farm; but his bragging certainly did. The fact that he went on drawing his money when rainy weather threw everybody else out of employment, except the low-paid Swedes who never appeared here anyway, put him in his own estimation on a sort of pedestal where he glorified himself.

Once, when he came to the store for a new suit of overalls, he spoke in the most patronizing way to me: and though I coolly discouraged his confidential talk, he rambled on for a quarter of an hour or so, sitting on an up-tilted box and keeping me from attending to my work.

"Money piles up pretty fast," he said, "when it keeps coming in at the rate of six dollars a day whether you work or not. Besides, I have a whole crowd here working for me. They can't keep their money; it burns in their pockets. They come and beg for a game. They know or if they don't, they should know that, when I sit down in a game, I take the money and nobody else. Oh boy, when I get back to the Twin Cities, won't I have a sweet old time with the girls? I'll say I will."

This man who had nothing to recommend him except his never-failing nerve, sat in the centre on one side of the table. On either hand he had a lantern, in front of him a half-empty bottle. At his right lay a long folding-knife which locked in the handle; at his left a pile of bills, cheques, and IOU's. His voice dominated the bedlam of shouts and laughter.

There were others who had made large winnings; they, too, were noisy.

But most of the gamblers sat tense and silent, except for an occasional muttered curse or a whispered accusation. What I could not understand was that they did not unite to down the bully in their midst. But the prevailing spirit seemed rather to narrow the circle by "squeezing" more and more of the less able or less fortunate players out, and then, when only two or three players were left, to spar for position and opportunity and finally to stake everything on one bold throw.

To me the game became a symbol of much that is horrible in modern life.

Here was a handful of the drifting population of God's earth; here were men who owned nothing in the world beyond what they carried about and what might be waiting for them as a balance on the books of the farm. They threw down what they had and mortgaged their future into the bargain by giving IOU's and orders on wages not yet earned. They were virtually selling themselves into slavery. For what? For the thrilling and gripping excitement of a moment; and then maybe in the vain hope of recouping themselves by hanging on; and in a game in which nothing counted in the long-run except nerve.

I watched the engineer. He took his cards up as they fell, hiding the first in the hollow palm of his hand and laying those which followed on top of the first, slowly and deliberately; he never looked at his cards again, never spread his hand out; he hardly ever discarded to draw a new supplement. It hardly mattered to him what his hand might hold. He waited for the first bet; he hardly ever "passed", never accepted a bet as offered. Swiftly he pyramided, in his shrill, tense, ironic voice which stung his opponent like an insult and which seemed to have the power of depriving his victims of their cooler reason. He sat like a hawk, apparently nonchalant, in reality with every muscle taut; his whole attitude one of studied contempt.

I was to have an illustration of the fact that even chance counted for little or nothing in the game as it was played.

Where I stood, a commotion arose among the onlookers. A broad-shouldered giant of a man sat right in front of me. When my eye followed the excited looks of my neighbours in the group, I saw that he held "four of a kind".

I stood tightly wedged in at my post; but somehow I managed to edge up a little closer behind him.

He had a small pile of bills at his right, amounting to maybe twenty dollars or a little more.

Betting started somewhere around the table.

The giant seemed to bide his time.

The engineer's voice was pyramiding the bets, quickly, sharply, skilfully.

More and more betters dropped out of the game; at last there was a momentary pause. I saw that the pot held the stakes left over from a draw.

The deep bass of the giant in front sang out, "Wait a minute, you pup."

And then he made a fatal mistake. The betting stood at fifteen dollars; he should have accepted the bet as it stood. but, instead of merely "staying in," he raised it to twenty dollars.

That gave the engineer the chance for which he was waiting. With a swift side-look of his eye he appraised the giant's pile. I doubt whether many saw that look; but I knew that very moment that the giant was not going to win even though chance had dealt him a "hand among hands". The engineer calmly raised the bet back on him, to an amount way beyond the giant's holdings.

The game stood between the two.

I think, the giant realized at once that he had made an irretrievable mistake. But his fist came down on the table with a tremendous thump which sent the lanterns jumping up into the air.

"I'll call you," he roared, "you son-of-a-gun!"

The engineer sat coolly unmoved. "Put up," he said, throwing his money into the already large "pot".

The giant looked about, as if reading the faces. None of those he saw held the slightest encouragement.

"Loan me thirty buck," he called to no one in particular.

Not a man made a move.

There was a cruel perseverity in this indifference. If I had had the money in my pocket, I should have slipped it to him. He was sure of his game. His "hand" could hardly be beaten. But, of course, it was not the possible or certain chance of recovery which would have prompted me. Iniquity was being perpetrated, even though in a game; I heard the unspoken call for redress.

A pleading look crept into the giant's face. He bent over and showed his neighbour what he held.

The only answer that man made was to close his hand over his pile of bills.

The giant muttered. He turned back to the engineer; but his voice sounded hopeless when he said, "I have sixty dollars coming to me at the office. I'll give you my IOU."

"I won't accept it; I am not a fool," replied the engineer with a steely sneer.

The giant clenched his fist as if ready to spring; his eyes bulged; he bent forward.

The engineer, piercing him with his steady look, reached with a blind hand for the handle of his knife.

There was a moment's tension which came close to sending a sob into my throat.

Then the giant relaxed, threw, with a coarse word, his cards on the table, got to his feet, and shouted, "Count me out. You can't beat the devil."

The engineer smiled his smile of bravado and for a second spread his cards into a fan, for the onlookers to see his hand.

Then he raked in the pot.

I squeezed myself out of the crowd. When, on my way to the door, I passed those who stood behind the engineer, I touched one of the men on the shoulder.

"What did he have?" I asked in a whisper.

"Nothing," was the reply.

Next morning, when I went out into the fresh, rain-washed air, one of the men who, the night before, had seen me in the hall said in passing, "Three of them are still at it, over there."

FOUR

I Meet Mother and Son

THE FIRST building in that long row of stables and barns which ran along the southern edge of the western half of the yard was the "driving-barn". It consisted of two parts: the front-shed which held an astonishing array of buggies, old-fashioned carriages, dog-carts, and so on, a harness-room, and the quarters of the "driving-boss"; in the rear, the stable where four or five driving-teams and four or five saddle-horses had their stalls. Over the whole building stretched a hayloft.

The quarters of the driving-boss were connected by telephone with the White House, the office, and the superintendent's residence.

The driving-boss, as he was called – the word "boss" meaning in this connection that he took no orders from any of the foremen – was a middle-aged little Scotchman of real horsemanship. His temper, however, was that of the man suffering from chronic stomach-trouble – an American disease due, I believe, to the so-called high standard of living. During my month as store-boss I had been thrown with him a good deal, for the broncho-team was quartered in his stable.

One evening, when I was closing up for the day, Mr. Mackenzie appeared in the store-house.

"How are you with horses, Branden?" he asked.

"Oh," I replied, "about as good as the next one, I suppose."

"Well," he went on, "I need a substitute for the driving-boss. He is going on a spree. Do you think you could handle the hackneys?"

"On a spree?" I said, without answering the question. "I thought you don't allow anybody to leave till you have finished threshing?"

"Oh," he replied, "it's different with Standish. He's a permanent employee and has his privileges. When he wants to get drunk, there's no holding him anyway. I'd rather have him away, then. He picks his own time. It is inconvenient – just now; but he gives satisfaction and we want him back. How about the hackneys?"

"Well," I said, "as far as the hackneys go, I'm not afraid. How about the wages?"

"Same as here. Two dollars for rainy days and Sundays; on workdays what the field-crews get."

"All right," I said.

"That's settled, then," said Mr. Mackenzie. "We've got a man to take your place here. Better move over tomorrow morning."

Thus, for the second time, I changed my status on this farm.

Again I will briefly summarize my new duties.

First among them was, of course, the care for the horses. This comprised feeding and brushing, watching the state of their health, looking after their shoeing, and taking them out for exercise when they were not being used. Further, I had to get the teams ready when they were needed; for the owner, for the superintendent, and now and then for the bookkeeper, too. And lastly, when Mr. Mackenzie or his mother wished to be driven, I had to act as coachman.

Mrs. Mackenzie, whom I had never seen so far, was a white-haired lady of bourgeois habits and conspicuously expensive tastes. Her late husband had, in his earlier life, been a section boss; that explained it. She was given to visiting and church-work, so that, whenever the weather was propitious, I was kept busy in her service during the afternoon.

Hers was the black team of hackneys of which she was at the same time excessively proud and inordinately afraid. They were high-strung beasts, but so easily handled and so responsive that to me it was a never-exhausted pleasure to drive them. They were so infinitely superior to the dowdy old lady who sat behind my back that I sometimes smiled and winked at occasional passers-by in town who would invariably stop to admire their arching necks and the thin bones of their fleet, dancing feet.

Once, when we were crossing the crowded freight-yard in town where cars were being shunted and locomotives unexpectedly blew off their steam, the funny bundle of silks and ribbons in the carriage flew into a panic and screamed at me, "Do you see that engine, coachman? Take the whip!"

She did not know that to use the whip on horses like that would have been at once dangerous and foolish.

I nodded; but I merely watched for the moment when the passage ahead was clear and then clicked my tongue: the prancing horses straightened out and shot away.

The old lady never called me anything but "coachman" – that seemed to her a symbol of the gulf which gaped between us. She was, to herself, the "grande dame"; I was a nameless menial. She is dead, now; so this will never hurt her.

On another occasion she telephoned an unexpected order for her team, adding, "Hurry up, coachman. I want to be in town in twenty-five minutes."

The town was five miles away; twenty-five minutes was rather short notice. I came very near recommending the use of the car; but I knew that nothing would have induced her to enter such a vulgar conveyance. I also knew the horses and what I could ask them to do when it came to an emergency. I had the carriage in front of the White House in less than six minutes.

She stood on the steps; and when I held the door of the carriage for her, she threw her order at me, "To the rectory. And remember, coachman, I promised to be there at half past two. Don't make me late."

"Very well, madam," I replied and touched my cap; for I was wearing a uniform when I took her out; her son was just as well pleased with me in overalls.

We had nineteen minutes to make five miles; but we made them. The horses, not used to such speeding, were speckled with the foam thrown from their mouths.

"Wait here," said Mrs. Mackenzie when I opened the door for her, touching my cap.

But I judged it expedient to walk the horses up and down the street so as to prevent a chill.

When, twenty minutes or so after that, Mrs. Mackenzie appeared on the steps, with the rector, she had to wait a quarter of a minute before she could re-enter the carriage. I saw at once that she was displeased.

An hour or so later, when we were back at the farm, her son came into the driving-barn and asked me, "What's that my mother is complaining about?"

I stated the facts and showed him the horses which were still nervous and which I had blanketed.

"Well," he said, "you did right, of course. Never mind mother."

With that he walked out.

It was quite a different matter to drive Mr. Mackenzie himself. I have already mentioned that he never stood on form. He liked to tinker about; so he used his car mostly. Cars gave ample scope, at the time, for the exercise of mechanical leanings; I have heard they do so still.

But when the season advanced, he liked to go out shooting birds in the evening; and whenever he did, he asked me to drive him. If we missed the supper-hour, he would take me to the kitchen of the White House where a pretty maid would serve both of us with a snack.

We used to take a broncho-team for these drives, and they were sometimes not easy to handle. One of the horses we had, occasionally, to chase for five or ten minutes around the stable before we could slip a bridle over his head. And when we had hitched them to the democrat we were using, we had to jump in as fast as we could, for there was no holding them. The young owner invariably helped me in these preparations, and we had a good deal of fun.

Then, when we rolled along the smooth roads between his fields, Mr. Mackenzie dearly loved to talk.

Since we were going out to shoot birds, I told him of the game reserves in Europe. I told him especially of a certain evening which I had once spent in a deer-park; I contrasted that careful policy of conservation with America's wastefulness.

"Oh yes," he said, "but all that's only for royalty."

"Not as far as their presence goes," I replied. "Of course, as for shooting them . . ."

"Well," he asked, "what else should you want to keep game for?"

"That's your American view," I assailed him. "You people still have the utilitarian idea; the fight for the backyard is still in your blood; you haven't had time to put your frontyard in order . . ."

The young owner laughed. "I like your way," he said. "You are hard on America, are you not?"

"On some phases of its life," I argued. "Do you know why?"

"I am curious," he said.

"Because you are wasting the biggest opportunity any civilized nation ever had; because there is even in you a spark of that spirit which found the word Government of the people, by the people, for the people."

"The people!" Mr. Mackenzie scoffed. "Who are they? I am the people."

I gasped. "Do you know," I said, "that you are not the first one to use words to that effect?"

"No, I don't."

"You should read," I went on. "Read history, above all. There's something to be learned."

Mr. Mackenzie laughed it off. "You are a funny fellow," he said.

But he came back to the topic. A few days later, when we were rolling along the roads again, we passed the field on which the crews were threshing. We approached behind a screen of poplars and came unawares upon some of them who were loading the sheaves. At sight of the young owner they changed their gait.

Mackenzie laughed again. "There is your people for you," he said. "Did you see how they speeded up when they saw us?"

"Of course," I replied, "what else can you expect? They have nothing at stake."

"They are taking my money," he objected.

"You have taken their land," I countered, waving my arms across the landscape.

"It's honestly come by," he said.

"It's come by through chance," I challenged.

He laughed.

"I have often wondered," I went on, "how much of what is called enterprise is really chance."

"You're a radical," he said.

"Of course," I agreed. "How can anybody with imagination, sympathy, and brains be anything but a radical? You are a duke, a lord, or an incipient king."

"No kings in this country," he said.

"Well," I replied, "do you think that kings in Europe had a different origin? It has always been that way. Who grabs most becomes the founder of a great family. What did you do to become the owner of this principality? You went to the trouble of being born, to quote a Frenchman."

"I am a good farmer," he defended himself.

"You're not," I accused. "Have you ever spent a night in a bed of your bunk-house?"

"Well," he exclaimed, "you are the limit! I am not fond enough of lice."

"So you have not even the excuse of ignorance! Do you think the hobos are?"

"They must be, or they would get rid of them."

"Have you ever seen them squatting along the slough, of a Sunday, boiling their clothes?" I asked.

"Yes," he pondered, "I have. Why don't they go and clean out the bunks?"

"I wish you would try to pitch sheaves for twelve hours, one day, and afterwards clean house."

"There may be something in that," he agreed. "But there are the rainy days."

"I should not like myself to sleep in wet straw," I answered.

Next day I was thrilled to hear that a man had been appointed to look after the cleaning of the bunk-house. All the bunks were treated with coal-oil and gasoline; the straw was renewed.

"You're learning," I praised the next time. "I wish you had given orders to have the blankets burnt."

"Say," said the young man, "don't you think you are asking a good deal?"

"Just what does your harvest amount to?" I countered.

Mr. Mackenzie looked at me, quizzically. "I know what you are driving at. I'll tell you. Suppose I did all that. What good would it do?"

"It would set an example," I replied. "You see, I am a better American than you are. Do you know what I believe to be the fundamental difference between this country and Europe?"

"I wonder."

"The whole civilization of Europe is based on the theory of the original sin. Right is done only when might enforces it. Even the life of the individual is regulated. But here there is a profound suspicion that in his heart the human animal wants to do right and is good. Take the case of mere honesty. The railway-system, the customs, the police-organization of Europe – they are all built up on the presumption that everybody, unless watched, is a crook. Here the presumption is that the average American is honest."

"I wish I had more of that average," said Mr. Mackenzie.

This time it was I who laughed. "Hold on," I said. "Now you are the radical."

"I don't see that," he replied.

"According to your fundamental tenet all men are born free and equal."

"A beautiful phrase!"

"Do I hear an American say that?"

"You don't want me to assume that the hobo who has to be watched at his work from morning till night is my equal?"

"Are you so sure that, if he had been born in your place, he would not make as good a millionaire as you are? Or that you would make a more industrious hobo than he is? – I am a hobo myself."

"You don't seem to be one," he said. "You are too outspoken."

"Do you know what I have made up my mind to do?"

"Well?" he asked.

"When I leave this life, I am going to talk Red to every man like you," I replied. "But I am going to be the most conservative of the conservatives when I talk to the men. I cannot help believing that at heart you mean right, even where you are doing wrong."

There was quite a break, after this, in our conversations, occasioned by the fact that visitors arrived at the White House. For a week or longer there was only one of these evening-excursions; and that time Mr. Mackenzie was accompanied by a guest.

When the guests were gone, Mr. Mackenzie resumed the drives. The first time we sat in silence for quite a while. Then it was he who took our old topic up again.

"I've been wondering," he said, "what you would have done if you had had the misfortune of being born in my place."

"Don't be so ironical about it," I said.

"Well," he countered, "your talks have made me feel quite blue."

"Good," I exclaimed. "Though they were not meant to work that way. If it is any comfort to you, I will first of all say that probably I should have lived a life of ease as you have done. You rich people don't have half a chance. Your education is neglected."

"Our education?"

"Yes," I replied. "A man like Judge Gary is to be pitied only. It would do him, and incidentally a few thousand workmen, a world of good if he were turned out on a tramp in a foreign country for a year or two, penniless, in order to learn. I contend that, as things stand to-day, the most fundamental part of your education is forgotten. You are not taught to see the other fellow's point of view. But, of course, if you were, you might lose sight of your own, though that would be distinctly the lesser evil. Equality of opportunity! Nothing but a phrase. You poor rich people simply do not stand a chance!"

"It strikes me," laughed Mr. Mackenzie, "that this time it is you who are ironical."

"Very well," I said, "I'll be serious. What you really meant to ask is this: What would I do if a property like this fell into my hands at the present time, I being what I am and having gone through what I have seen of the world? I will tell you; but it will seem Utopian. First of all I should spend some hundred thousand odd dollars in providing proper dormitories for the men – a white-tiled bunk-house with proper bathing and washing facilities and decent beds: that would settle the vermin. Then gymnasium, reading-room, and play-room equipped for the proper kind of games: that would settle the goings-on in that bunk-house hall of yours. Next I should provide proper work for them the year around. You would soon anchor that part of your floating labour supply which can take root. And lastly I should divest myself of my property."

"What do you mean by that?"

"I mean, I should feel that it is sinful for me to let even an appearance persist as if I were really the owner of all this and as if the men were working for me. It is surely better for the country if the same amount of grain, or even a smaller amount, is produced by a greater number of independent farmers, each holding a fraction only of what you hold. I am not an economist, but I can see that real democracy can be arrived at only in one of two ways, by collective ownership or by a limitation of wealth. I do not presume to decide on their relative merits; I do not expect to see either way realized in my lifetime."

"How old are you?" asked Mr. Mackenzie with seeming irrelevance.

"I am young, thank God," I replied with fervour; "and so are you. Youth means courage and adaptability; old age means ossification. I hope I shall never be old, even though I live to be a hundred or more."

"I sometimes wonder," he sighed, "whether you are right or merely crazy."

And at that we left it.

Harvest was finished; the regular driving-boss returned. I drew my pay – it amounted to two hundred dollars or so – and got ready to move.

I said a personal good-by to Mr. Mackenzie, and he offered me the position as bookkeeper on his farm.

I declined. "I want to see a little more of this life," I said; "My place is with the men; you are the past, they are the future. I have my plans, and I see very clearly what I want; it is not within your gift."

FIVE

My Problem Defines Itself and I Solve It

THIS IS the last chapter of my wanderings.

Light gleamed ahead. My life-work was clearly outlined in my mind. I had discovered the soil in which I
could grow. This book has nothing to do with that life-
work itself; it does not deal with the growth in that soil. Its
topic is the search and its end. I might stop here; I had
found.

Unfortunately, and typically for the immigrant, a conspiracy of circumstances seemed to arise, bent upon, and
well capable of, shaking the strongest faith of him whose
wider outlook was none too firmly established as yet.

I was reconciled to America. I was convinced that the
American ideal was right; that it meant a tremendous
advance over anything which before the war could rea-
sonably be called the ideal of Europe. A reconciliation of
contradictory tendencies, a bridging of the gulf between
the classes was aimed at, in Europe, at best by concessions from above, from condescension; in America the
fundamental rights of those whom we may call the victims of civilization were clearly seen and, in principle,
acknowledged – so I felt – by a majority of the people.
Consequently the gulf existing between the classes was
more apparent than real; the gulf was there, indeed; but it
was there as a consequence of an occasional vitiation of
the system, not of the system itself. I might put it this way.
In Europe the city was the crown of the edifice of the

state; the city culminated in the court – a republican country like France being no exception, for the bureaucracy
took the place, there, of the aristocracy in other countries.
In America the city was the mere agent of the country –
necessary, but dependent upon the country in every way –
politically, intellectually, economically. Let America be-
ware of the time when such a relation might be reversed:
it would become a mere bridgehead of Europe, as in their
social life some of its cities are even now.* The real reason
underlying this difference I believed to be the fact that
Europe, as far as the essentials of life were concerned, was
a consumer; whereas America was a producer. The masses
were fed, in Europe, from the cities; the masses were fed,
in America, from the country. Blessed is the nation that
remains rural in this respect, for it will inherit the world.
Freedom and happiness flee, unless "superest ager."

That was my idea; and it contained the germ of an
error. In my survey of the American attitude I was apt to
take ideals for facts, aspirations for achievements. From
the vantage-ground of retrospection, I can only be glad
that an anticlimax intervened before I set about building
my life.

When I came from Europe, I came as an individual;
when I settled down in America, at the end of my wanderings, I was a social man. My view of life, if now, at the end,
I may use this word once more, had been, in Europe,
historical, it had become, in America, ethical. We come
indeed from Hell and climb to Heaven; the Golden Age
stands at the never-attainable end of history, not at Man's
origins. Every step forward is bound to be a compromise;
right and wrong are inseparably mixed; the best we can
hope for is to make right prevail more and more; to reduce
wrong to a smaller and smaller fraction of the whole till it
reaches the vanishing point. Europe regards the past;
America regards the future. America is an ideal and as

---

* I must repeat that this book was, in all its essential parts, written
decades ago.

such has to be striven for; it has to be realized in partial victories.*

When I walked back to Walloh, I had two hundred dollars deposited to my name in the bank of the town, and some little sum in my pocket besides. I carried my bundle as I had done three months ago, when I had walked the same road in the opposite direction. Financially I was very nearly where I had been when I had walked the same road in the opposite direction. Financially I was very nearly where I had been when I had first landed at Montreal. But then my only idea had been to make money; now my one idea was to live and to help others to live.

Three months ago I had been a hobo; now I adopted the disguise of one. I have since gone out like that again, a good many times; I have always enjoyed such holidays.

I reached Walloh late in the afternoon and boarded an evening train going north. After a ride of seventy or eighty miles I dropped off at some junction and struck west again. For two or three days I tramped it, alone. The crops stood in stooks; I should find work at threshing.

Then I came to a town. As it chanced, I hit upon a livery-stable, somewhere along the track. The front of the building was occupied by a real-estate broker's office.

I entered the stable and found the hostler, a morose elderly man crippled with rheumatism.

"Any work around here?" I enquired.

"Sure," he grumbled. "Might pull the harness off that horse there." He stopped at a stall, looking with helpless eyes at a long-legged driver.

"I'll do that for you," I replied, for he was bent double with suffering. When I had finished, I turned and said "But, you know, that was not exactly the way I meant it."

Since I had helped him, he softened. "I guess not," he said with a sigh and went to the front of the building.

---

* I have since come to the conclusion that the ideal as I saw and still see it has been abandoned by the U.S.A. That is one reason why I became and remained a Canadian.

I followed him.

"No," he answered my question at last. "Not yet. They are through cutting, and haven't started threshing. But in a few days, I suppose. You see the boss."

"The livery man?" I asked.

"Barn belongs to two lawyers," he said. "Real estate and farm loans, too. They've got a big farm south of here, fifteen miles out. Three thousand acres or so."

"Where can I find either one?"

"Stick around," he replied. "One of them will drop in before dark."

In the dusk of the evening a small, stout man appeared in the office in front of the stable. I followed him in.

"Have you any use for a harvest-hand?" I enquired.

He looked me over. "I can use some teamsters," he said. "Can you handle horses?"

"I can," I replied. "For threshing?"

"Yes; but we won't start before next week. Meanwhile I need a man to look after a bunch of horses here in town if you are satisfied with the wages I offer."

"How much would that be?"

"Well," he said, "I'll pay you a dollar and a half a day. You will have to board yourself. Not here. In the stable at my house. You can sleep in the hayloft, if you want to. Meanwhile you can haul hay for my drivers. When I take you out to the farm, you get your board, of course, and the current wages."

"All right," I said. And thus it was settled.

I began work next day, hauling hay from a nearby half-section of land owned by my employer. There was a man living on the place, a Finn who spoke only the most broken of English. Since he was getting ready to move, I presumed him to be a renting tenant; I was interested in his experience. My curiosity as to the economic life of the immigrant settler led to enquiries; and they disclosed a startling condition.

This man had come to America five or six years ago; he

had brought a family which had since increased by three or four members. This family he had at first left behind in the city, while he himself was drifting about. He had come to this town and started to work for my present employer who, seeing his great strength and his love of work, had treated him well, had gained his confidence, and finally had made him an offer which had seemed good to the Finn. It had even seemed kind.

The offer was this. The lawyer would sell the Finn a half-section of land at twenty dollars an acre, to be paid for in half-crop payments. He would build a shack and a stable for him at so-and-so much, and equip him besides with all the machinery and the horses he needed at stated prices. The machinery was second-hand; I do not remember the sums involved; but I do remember that the price as stipulated was what it had cost when new. Of horses there had been five – good horses, the Finn admitted; but colts, not broken or trained for the work. The price of these was one thousand dollars. For the whole of this equipment the Finn had been induced to give five notes, lien-notes, with that iniquitous clause, " ... Or if the party of the first part should consider this note insecure, he shall have full power to declare this and all other notes made by me in his favour due and payable forthwith, and he may take possession of the property and hold it until this note and all other notes made by me are paid, or sell the said property at public or private sale; the proceeds thereof to be applied in reducing the amount unpaid thereon; and the holder thereof, notwithstanding such taking possession or sale, shall thereafter have the right to proceed against me and recover, and I agree to pay, the balance then found to be due thereon."

This, I am aware, is perfectly within the law; it may even work without hardship where "the party of the second part" is fully aware of what he signs, though I doubt it. This Finn was an intelligent man; he could read and write his own language. But, as far as English goes, he

was to all intents and purposes illiterate; through none of
his fault. He had been turned loose on American soil,
equipped for the struggle of life with nothing but an inherent trustfulness; he was paying for his lesson with bank-
ruptcy. My own, comparatively trifling and mild experiences, annoying as they had been, here widened out for
the first time into the experience of a whole class of immigrants, and that the most desirable one. In every nation
there are sharks, of course; it is only just to say that in
later years I found the worst of the sharks among successful immigrants. In every nation there are brutes and fools;
we cannot charge their doings to the collective score. But
children need looking after; and the immigrant is, as far
as the ways of this country are concerned, no better than a
child. Here was a bona-fide settler, a prospective citizen
of the most promising kind, turned into a sower of discontent. Do you blame him?

Let me explain how the compact between the lawyer
and the Finn worked out.

The lawyer played the part of the lumber-dealer, the
contractor, the implement-dealer, the horse-dealer, the
real estate agent, the collector, the bailiff. At his disposal
were willing friends and helpers; there was, above all, the
whole, inexorable, and irresistible machinery of the law
which he knew well how to handle. With all these assis-
tants, he stood arrayed against a single man who was
helpless because he did not even know the language of the
country.

The lawyer made a profit on the lumber, on the building, on the implements, on the horses, and on the land; but
he was not satisfied with that.

If he had rented the land, he would have had to furnish
all that he had furnished the Finn, free of charge; his only
gain would have been the customary half-share of the
crop. It is true, he would have remained the owner of the
land and the equipment; but he also would have had to pay
the taxes on the property. As it was, the Finn paid the

taxes and the interest on his debt for two years, in addition to two payments on the capital involved.

Then one of the horses fell; the machinery – which had not been new in the first place – began to go wrong at a critical time. When the third of the notes fell due and he found himself unable to pay, the bailiff seized machinery and live-stock. These were offered at private sale and readily found a buyer who proved to be the second lawyer of the little town, the seller's partner; he paid a laughable price for the whole of the outfit and shortly sold it back to the first owner at a profit, but still at considerably less than the Finn had paid. His profit was his part of the loot.

The Finn still owed a considerable balance; his equity in the farm and whatever he had acquired in the first two years of his life as an independent farmer – two cows, some pigs, a flock of chickens, the furniture in his shack, and so on – came under the hammer. The net result was that the Finn had worked three years for nothing – not as a renter would work – with an eye only to his advantage – but as the owner works, from sun to sun and longer, straining his powers to the very limit.

I might add right here that the same farm was sold again, equipment and all, under exactly the same conditions – with the price of the land raised to twenty-five dollars an acre – before I even left town, that is, within three or four weeks.

My first impulse was, of course, to leave then and there; but on second thought I decided otherwise. To leave would have been a weakness. If at any future time I wanted to be of help, I had to study just such cases. I saw even at the time that, unless such problems are faced and the easy remedies applied, nothing could come from the indiscriminate admission of immigrants, but unmitigated evil. I might add that most of the fashionable talk about Americanization strikes me as mere cant. I know of no more effective means towards that end than the open, frank, unsugared square deal.

With my new employer no relation was possible as had sprung up between Mr. Mackenzie and myself. The farm was a matter of fifteen miles from the town. Its lay-out resembled in a general way that of the outlying camps on the Mackenzie place, though, of course, things were on a smaller scale. There were only twenty-five men in the crew; but in the absence of the owners of the land – which was primarily held for speculation and disposed of in parts as buyers were found – there was again that imper-sonal air about the work which had characterized the organization on Mr. Mackenzie's farm.

I found the crew in a turmoil. When I appeared, I was questioned about wages offered in town. I was little inter-ested in the amounts I was making and could give no information on this point.

The foreman asserted that the men were getting what anybody else got in this neighbourhood. But they de-manded certainty. They were in a strange isolation on the farm. They were kept busy throughout, rain or shine; and the only way to get to town would have been to ask the foreman to let them off from their work for a day and to give them a ride to boot. They were all of that type of men who, like the Swedes, hang on to the work as long as they can, most of them being Finns. I was most forcibly struck by the way in which nationalities ran in streaks in this northern harvest-migration of floating labour. At Mr. Mackenzie's place the Swedes had predominated; here it was the Finns.

I had been on the place for two weeks or so, driving a four-horse team with a load of wheat to town in the morn-ing and coming back late at night. Then, one evening, the men held a secret meeting in the horse-barn, and I was asked to come.

When I entered, I found them talking in a lively and excited way, in Finnish, which I did not understand. What struck me, however, right at the start, was the air of mis-trust, of suspicion with regard to the management of the farm. Apparently the owners enjoyed a "hard name". On the Mackenzie place nobody had ever questioned the perfect fairness in money-matters between men and owner. The wages had been about twenty-five cents above those which other farmers of the neighbourhood were paying; whenever an advance took place, the foreman had made it known at the breakfast table. Here it turned out that nobody knew exactly what he was being credited with. All of them had been engaged at "current wages"; the foreman, when asked, was evasive; he never stated a definite sum without adding "I think"; the last sum which he had mentioned that way had been three and a half dollars a day; but even that was no more than "he thought" they were getting. The season was drawing towards its end; none of these men had any particular reason to work on this farm rather than on any other. There was no consideration of loyalty involved. They were after the greatest number of dollars in the shortest possible time.

As it happened, it was my turn next morning to take the first load to town; my tank had been filled just before quitting time at night. Under these circumstances I would start before break of day and reach town in time for feeding the horses; that would leave me an hour or so for my own meal and for whatever else I might wish to undertake.

The men asked me to go to the station at train-time, when farmers would be in, looking for help, and to enquire about the wages paid elsewhere. I promised to do so, and we dispersed.

At the station next day three or four farmers addressed me, offering work; an enquiry as to the wages disclosed the fact that nobody offered less than four dollars, while one of them offered four and a quarter a day.

It was about five o'clock in the afternoon when I got home. As soon as I appeared on the road, within sight of the crews, the whistle of the engine blew for me to come out to the field and to reload for the next morning. I turned on to the stubble and, when I passed through the corner where the men were loading sheaves, they crowded around me and asked for the news.

Everybody, as if by a concerted plan, dropped his work and jumped into the box of my grain-tank. It was thus, with a load of seething humanity, that I reached the separator.

The men at once called the foreman aside and surrounded him, clamouring, threatening. I heard the foreman protesting, arguing, promising; and after a short time, while I was waiting for the grain to begin pouring into my tank, the men dispersed, going back to their work.

The foreman came over to where I was waiting.

"Get out of that tank," he shouted to me, his voice nearly drowned by the vibratory pounding of engine and separator which were running empty.

"I'll give you your time," he went on; "I'm going to town, you come along."

I jumped to the ground. "What's wrong?" I asked.

"No damned foreign agitators wanted around," he shouted angrily.

I shrugged my shoulders and walked off to camp.

When we reached the office in front of the livery stable, the foreman and my employer held a whispered conference. Then the lawyer went to a desk and made out a cheque.

I sat down and waited till he tossed the pink slip across the small table at which I was sitting. I looked at it and did some rapid mental arithmetic.

"Just what do you call current wages?" I asked.

"What I pay the rest of my men," he replied. "How much that is is none of your business. You don't think that I pay current wages to a man who quits before the work is finished, do you?"

"Oh," I said with a shrug of my shoulders and a smile, "that explains this cheque."

I crushed it into my pocket and rose.

That was the end of my work as a harvest hand.

Now those were the years of tree-planting in these parts. Every house in town was surrounded by a yard with young plantations a few years old. It had struck me that many of them needed attending to. The tree used was box-elder, a bad choice in a windy country, since it is apt to break in the crotch. I still had my tree-saw and pruning knife; and somehow I did not wish to leave the town just then. I went out offering my services as a tree-pruner, charging forty cents an hour, and finding an ample clientele.

One day, a man who reminded me of the senatorial Mr. Warburton, the manager of the veneer-mill in the little Indiana town, had been watching me for some time at work and at last addressed me.

"You seem to know your business," he said. "I have a large plantation at the north end of the town. Do you care to look it over and see what you can do with it?"

"Certainly," I agreed. "I'll go with you now."

We came to an agreement on the basis of my usual charge; I estimated that the work would take me five or six days.

I did not know the man; but an enquiry brought out the fact that he was the partner of my previous employer; a curious coincidence, I thought.

I went to work with even more than my usual vigour and alacrity; I was anxious to show that I, at least, was willing to give a square deal even though I had not received it at his partner's hands. Frequently, while I was at work, the man would come and look on, asking questions, making suggestions. By dint of special efforts I managed to finish the work in four days.

On the morning of the fifth day I wrote a bill for sixteen dollars and went to the law-office to present it. A stenographer took the bill and asked me to return in the afternoon. When I did so, she handed me four dollars and stated that her employer had said that was all my work was worth.

I refused to take the money and asked to see him; but he was not in.

I went to his house, and he was not there; nor could I find him anywhere else. A sullen anger took possession of me; at him and his partner. They were the lawyers in town; they were prominent and respected citizens; but they were crooks, and I longed to tell them so.

To this very day I hope they will read this record; if they do, they may rest assured that I hoard their names in my memory.

In the evening I was sitting at the station, on the platform, talking with the section-boss with whom I had fallen in and to whom I told my experience with the noble pair, when a tall, skinny man touched me on the shoulder and gave me a sign to follow him. He led the way to the side of the station-building.

"I'm the chief?" he said by way of introduction.

"The chief?" I asked blankly.

"Yes," he said, uncovering a badge on the edge of his vest. "The chief of police. You better leave town; there are complaints against you."

"Complaints?" I asked. "Of what nature?"

"Never mind," he said and turned to go. "You know. You can't go about here and threaten respectable citizens. Take my advice and clear out." With that he walked off.

Then I returned to the section-boss and told him of the new development.

He, too, laughed; but to my amazement he advised me to take the hint and go. "Can't beat politics in this country," he said.

"But what can they do except expose their own crooked dealings?"

"Railroad you on a trumped-up charge," he replied.

I mused for a while. When my first anger had cooled, I decided that the advice was good. What did it matter? I wanted to get out in any case. After I had made the big change, then it would be time to go after men like these. I had meanwhile seen enough of America to put the incident down for what it was: an incident. It no longer clouded my whole horizon for me, as my experiences with Messrs. Hannan and Howard, Tinker and Wilbur had done. I had simply run up against a pair that were sailing close to the wind; I had hit upon another crooked game;

crooked games were no longer the world. The immigrant always sees only a partial view; but I had seen enough partial views to make their average more or less true to reality. I even thought myself lucky to have run up against this case; the very fact that I could take it as I did seemed to prove that I was ready for the work which I had chosen. If you run down a river in a boat and your boat brings up against a snag, you do not get out to dam the river and to dislodge the snag; you simply turn your boat and push it off into the current; the snag is not the river, after all.

As it happened, the section-boss could offer me the means to leave town. He was shorthanded in his gang; that very morning a man, after receiving his wages, had quitted work, leaving at his tool-shed a hand-car which was needed further back along the line. The signal-posts along the track were to be repainted before snow-up; there was a week's work to be done, at a dollar and seventy-five a day. If I cared to take the "job", I could have it; he would get into communication with the district-superintendent over the wire.

Thus it came that my rambles ended by a week in the open. I shot along the line of steel at a speed which depended only on my endurance and strength. There was fun in the work. Sometimes I wished that one of my old friends in the capitals of Europe could see me thus. Whenever I met a signal-post, I got off my hand-car, armed with paint-pot and brush. At night I made some station and stayed in town. To all whom I met I was no longer a tramp or a hobo; I was a duly labelled painter of signs for one of the great lines on the American continent; as such I "belonged".

For the first time in a year I thought of young Ray; one day I wrote to him to find out where he might be. I gave the city of Winnipeg as my address; for by now I felt that I wanted to become "repatriated" in Canada where I had made my first fight for economic independence.

At last the day came when I reported at the office at Grand Forks, handed over my car, and received my pay.

I have mentioned a little notebook which I had started to use soon after I had first set out from New York. A few years ago that little booklet was still at hand. It held my accounts, among other things; and I remember that, when I had received the wages earned on Mr. Mackenzie's farm and left on deposit in the bank, the net result of my season's work as a harvest-hand showed a saving of $249.35, on the day when I bought my ticket for Winnipeg.

When I arrived there, I had a number of interviews. I wanted to go to foreign settlements and help recent immigrants to build their partial views of America into total views; I wanted to assist them in realizing their promised land. The upshot was that I applied for and obtained a position as teacher.

I have been a teacher ever since; and not only a teacher, but the doctor, lawyer, and business-agent of all the immigrants in my various districts.

And twenty-seven years after the end of my rambles I published the first of my few books.

Author's Note to the Fourth Edition (1939)

Since this book, written in 1893-1894, appeared in print in 1927, I have often been asked whether the story which it presents is fact or fiction. My answer, a prevaricating answer, was that every event in the story was lived through; but that only a very few events that had taken place in the years with which the book deals found their place in it; and among them there was not one of the terrible things.

I should like to seize this opportunity to add a word or so.

Every work of so-called imaginative literature, good or bad, is necessarily at once both fact and fiction; and not only in the sense that fiction is mingled with fact. In every single part fact and fiction are inextricably interwoven.

Imaginative literature is not primarily concerned with facts; it is concerned with truth. It sees fact only within the web of life, coloured and made vital by what preceded it, coloured and made significant by what followed. In its highest flights, imaginative literature, which is one and indivisible, places within a single fact the history of the universe from its inception as well as the history of its future to the moment of its final extinction.

The reason for this is that, in imaginative literature, no fact enters as mere fact; a fact as such can be perceived; but, to form subject-matter for art, it must contain its own interpretation; and a fact interpreted, and therefore made capable of being understood, becomes fiction.*

The book which followed is essentially retrospective; which means that it is teleological; what was the present when it was written had already become its *telos*. Events that had followed were already casting their shadows backward. By writing the book, in that long-ago past, I was freeing myself of the mental and emotional burden implied in the fact that I had once lived it and had left it behind. But the present pervaded the past in every fibre.

One more point. Why, so I have been asked, did I choose a pseudonym for my hero? Well, while a pseudonym ostensibly dissociates the author from his creation, it gives him at the same time an opportunity to be even more personal than, in the conditions of our present-day civilization, it would be either safe or comfortable to be were he speaking in the first person, unmasked.

---

* See Hueffer, *Joseph Conrad: A Personal Remembrance*, for Conrad's perfectly sincere reminiscences of his seafaring life. In their oral presentations, they varied as their significances unfolded themselves in the telling.

Afterword

BY W.H. NEW

A Search for America pretends to tell a straightforward documentary, one about real life, perhaps even the author's own. But except indirectly, it does nothing of the kind.

Grove's most accomplished novel, *A Search for America* tries continually to make fictions seem real, at the same time calling attention to its own pretences, as though waiting for someone to ask why masks are necessary. Even the linear form is illusory. The story only pretends to begin at the beginning and end at the end. In fact it starts over every time Phil Branden sets out to begin his life anew, and it does not end at all. Nothing is finally resolved. The narrative simply stops, just as another story is about to begin – or be written – and any suggestion that Branden's next move will be his last is merely another carefully crafted illusion.

The numerous beginnings and the unresolved ending stress the power of fiction to make almost any narrative seem "real." They emphasize the artifice of stories and the effects of contrivance. Hence Branden's "autobiography" is told in such a way as to invite readers to accept heroic romance as though it were documentary truth – in its second edition (1928), the novel is subtitled, significantly, "The *Odyssey* of an *Immigrant*," a phrase that reads social history as narrative adventure – but it exposes this equation as false. The result is a deliberate double

461

vision, and at some point readers are bound to ask whether the duplicity demonstrates the *narrator's* compulsion to construct fictions and pass them off as real – or the *author's*.

Branden is more of an enigma than he professes. He manipulates the world around him, despite which he seldom seems aware of his own limitations or the transparency of his ambitions. Possibly he is a fraud; possibly he is a victim of fraud. But Grove, who *lived* a double life, seems to want his readers to see from the outset how often and how effectively people wear masks. Disguise lies everywhere in this book; it shapes themes and characterizes the recurrent technique. Disguise also, contradictorily, helps reveal truths about desire, ambition, and behaviour. Hence the subject of this novel may well be the author rather than the character, but not exactly as might be expected.

The author's disguise begins with the dedication to the "illustrious triad" of Meredith, Swinburne, and Hardy – which sounds on the surface like a simple compliment to three famous writers; indirectly, however, it shapes a reader's expectations about the narrative that follows. The way it suggests a familiarity with the "great" serves to elevate Grove himself to their company, a strategy that has echoes in the subsequent story. Compounding the effects of illusion, Grove later hinted that his novel was his own memoir – not by openly saying so, but by relying on the effects of partial truths and implications. In his preface to the fourth edition (1939), he claimed that he wrote the novel in 1893–94, though he actually wrote it in the years immediately preceding its publication in 1927. This somewhat stretched truth provided a plausible context for what followed. For when, responding to the question of whether the novel was fact or fiction, he constructed an elaborate passive evasion ("every event was lived through") instead of a direct reply, he left readers to infer that Grove and Branden were one. Readers who accepted this suggestion unequivocally equated the first-person narrator with the author and read the closing sentence ("I published the first of my few books") as Grove's own initiation into writing. Prepared by this impression to accept the *narrative* events as *documentary* reality, these readers did not notice the numerous textual revelations of pretence, the hints that reality was unlikely to be this simple. Neither Grove nor Branden was quite what he seemed; the connection between author and character, consequently, lay less in documentary detail than in the psychology of behaviour.

Stories of confidence tricksters abound in *A Search for America*: Frank's graft in the Toronto restaurant, Tinker's fraudulent bookselling scheme, the various lawyers' and landowners' and cardsharks' manipulative skills with glitter and money and language provide a range of examples. Such stories, entertaining as anecdotes, seem designed to reveal the devious nature of the "real" world; they also, however, help construct a public image for Branden. Throughout, the narrator makes trickery seem the attribute of others; *other* people are the rogues who shape the designs in which "honest Phil Branden" gets accidentally enmeshed. Paradoxically, the more Phil looks like the victim, the more he looks like the innocent hero, the one who gives up European condescension and learns to appreciate natural American goodness. But a lot hinges on expectations of innocence and definitions of "natural." Appearances can mislead, and while the narrator constructs an image of himself as an ingenuous but honest man, his narrative reveals a bleaker version of his "Odyssean" heroic behaviour. Branden's is a tale of conversion designed to win sympathy. But why does he want sympathy? One answer is that he wants to validate a presumption-laden claim upon power and position.

For Branden is no innocent. To listen to him closely is to realize how often he uses discriminatory stereotypes – castigating Jews, self-righteously dismissing smalltowners, patronizing women. He repeatedly caricatures women (particularly those who occupy positions of authority, including all mothers, who seem to represent a threat to his independence). When he condescends to Mackenzie, the young landowner, calling him a "boy" because he still lives with his mother, the implication is that Mackenzie is not a "real man" and that Branden, the solitary, ostensibly self-sufficient wanderer-hero, is. The dismissal consequently reads as an intricate technique in self-justification. And the faults Branden sees in others – disdain, distrust, insecurity – are the failings in himself that he never quite acknowledges but never quite hides. Dismissive of other people's game-playing, he is delighted to participate in the "sophisticated" game of identifying vintages, for example; articulate in his condemnation of capitalist profiteering, he never gives up his own preoccupation with money. Such revelations of character cumulatively call into question the high values for which he says he stands; his version of "equality" and "morality" prove to be not without self-interest. The revelations also call into question the very narrative he tells. The more his sequential stories unfold, the more they begin to read like another version of the confidence game, one constructed not in currency but in words.

The novel frequently calls attention to the power of appearances; given an effective context, they can reshape the world. When Branden begins his narrative by claiming a privileged Swedish upbringing, Grove demonstrates how such appearances work. Although the character soon avers that his family was in truth penniless, this admission never erases the effect the initial claim created. Illusion is all. It is one of the classic techniques of the con artist: to make an initial premise so convincingly that the victim (in this case the reader), armed with preconceptions, will treat all subsquent confessions and inconsistencies as natural signs of modesty rather than as glimpses of complex truths.

In the novel, everything follows from the initial illusion, and one of the fascinations of the book is to decide whether Grove accepts the first premise or questions it.

Branden's claim that he has a privileged European background conventionally associates him with such notions as wealth, education, ethics, "breeding," civilization, and social hierarchy. The more he moves into the rural American heartland, the more he seems to question the validity of this association. But "seems" is the important word here. In the greater scheme of his narrative, hierarchy and wealth are precisely the values that finally give him position and authority. He becomes a teacher, an attorney, a doctor, a business-agent: in other words, in all that gives him position, he remains fundamentally concerned with the discriminations inherent in the social system. While he renders his story of success as a progress toward *natural order*, this outcome is his narrative illusion, the version of self he would like accepted. Underpinning it is a development of a different kind, a princely progress toward *rulership*. Ultimately it is not an American dream of equality that Branden locates, whatever he might say about unlearning his past; it is a romantic *European* dream – of a rural America waiting "naturally" for benevolent European regulation. Branden tries to write this dream into existence. But it is a false dream, one predicated on inequality, for in it, he, as the "civilized" European, designs for himself a superior role.

The way the novel is put together reiterates this design and emphasizes its persuasive power. Branden constructs his story in three consecutive ways: as a quest, as a series of revelations, and as a descent into a maelstrom – thus combining the familiar motifs associated with Classical, Christian, and Byronic heroes. The familiarity of the motifs makes them seem natural, unchallengeable, and Branden makes almost subliminal use of them. Not for nothing does he cite Jesus and Lincoln and carry with him into the "wilderness" of the American Interior the *Odyssey* and the New Testament. By associating himself with men whom the culture reveres, he blurs his own identity; the associations work for him, however, manufacturing the public image he desires, that of a brave, moral, innocent wanderer besieged by the ruthless forces of others' selfishness.

This image, too, must be seen in context, for Branden's character is neither unitary nor uniform. All along he has assumed whatever identity others have discerned (or desired) in him: "Baron," "infant," hobo, intellect, farmhand, friend, boss, saviour. He is all of these – or none – and duality marks every role he adopts. Even at his most apparently "natural," living the life of the country tramp, he is self-consciously re-enacting the role of the "explorer," the exploiter. Though he writes, too, of "submerging," "drowning," and facing the "maelstrom," as though water were a threat, he also matter-of-factly declares that he is "by nature nearly amphibious." Such utterances ask to be heard carefully. "Philip" (meaning "lover") claims he is one with the "river"; his surname ("brand") says he is one with fire, too. To what end? If he is a reformer, why does he collaborate so readily with the systems in place? If he is an agent of received conventions, why does he overtly reject authority?

Political expedience does not seem to be an adequate answer. Branden does tell Mackenzie that landowners are incipient kings in the New World, and that anyone with imagination and brains must be a radical; at the same time he chooses to be "conservative" when he speaks with ordinary working men. Habitually speaking with two tongues, moreover, reiterates the duality on which pretence and trickery depend; but in this novel that is not all it does. It also epitomizes Branden's condition as immigrant-outsider and begins to reveal the insecurities that underlie his behaviour. Because the world he observes seems to operate by illusion, Branden creates his own masks to function in it; they give him power – or at least appear to him to do so. Yet though he dons masks in order to assert control over the world, he can never give up his need to confess his fear that such control will be recognized as unreal. The tension between these two impulses carries him along for most of the story he tells, but there comes a stage in his "progress" when mask and man get debilitatingly confused. Reality has been nagging at Branden all through his story. At this point, the fiction takes him over completely.

When Branden declares that his love for America designs the country as neither his friend nor his mother but his bride, all three branches of this declaration reveal his insecurities. Mothers, throughout his story, are mere figures to be dispensed with, indications of immaturity and naiveté; friends are extensions of the self, but self constructed in such absolute terms that imperfect reality is bound repeatedly to prove disappointing (as do all the male "friends" in the novel: Frank, Hannan, Williams, Ivan). A bride, however, is a sign to Branden of his own potent authority – something he apparently requires in order to confirm his status to himself. Despite this need, he dissociates himself from it. Locating his "bride" in place rather than in person – presumably to avoid the possible dangers of reality or disillusionment – he lives with a paradox of his own construction. If he conceives of his status as permanent and fixed, he invites disaster, and so he moves, in order to avoid exposure. If he can avoid exposure, he can conceive of his identity with the land as permanent and fixed. Fiction and reality hold each other tautly apart. But once he begins to identify with his own mask – especially his version of himself as the wise writer, teacher, and lawgiver: Lincoln, Christ – then he is no longer even alert to the psychological paralysis that his narrative reveals. Although he claims to come to a conclusion by moving to Canada, the claim can readily be interpreted as self-deception or deliberate misdirection, given the stories he has already told. Probing this ambivalence, the novel moves to its uncertain close.

The book's section titles – "Descent," "Relapse," "Depths," and "Level" – allude to the standard stages of progress in quest romances, during which the young quester characteristically survives his trials, overcomes his enemies, marries his bride, and comes into his kingdom.

As a paradigm for an egalitarian reformer, this pattern seems ironic, or unusually circumspect; as a paradigm for a self-deceived or self-deceiving radical, however, it offers an implicit commentary on the psychological ramifications of image-making. Personal authority and political convention can both be masks. And for an ordinary imperfect man to construct an identity for himself as hero is a dangerous exercise in folly. The novel's closing irony – that the narrator himself does not seem to realize quite what he has written or revealed – means that he ends up not a hero after all, but the pathetic victim of his own performance.

Exactly what this failure of self-recognition has to do with Grove remains unclear. The life that Branden tells as a "search for America" was probably never intended as Grove's autobiographical lie, however much readers turned it into one. The interest in the book rests more in its concern with the psychology of language – the unconscious revelation of personality – than in any documentary details surrounding character. And the novel does not so much reveal the deliberate fabrications of a confidence trickster as it demonstrates the unconscious adaptation of the art of counterfeiting to the invention of a fantasy self.

Branden may pretend his story ends in an ideal community ruled by rural benevolence. That is what Grove (intruding through his final footnote into his own story) says "Canada" meant to him, and perhaps glimpsing an ideal was all the novel ever meant to do. But the words of the novel ask to be read for what they hide as well as for what they say, and in any event the illusions, by this point in the book, have cumulatively called the teller as well as the tale into question. Even though readers might continue to sympathize with a character – or an author – who depends so desperately on fictions, they are unlikely to accept readily, or entirely, his compromised versions of truth.

BY FREDERICK PHILIP GROVE

AUTOBIOGRAPHY
In Search of Myself (1946)

ESSAYS
It Needs to Be Said (1929)

FICTION
Settlers of the Marsh (1925)
A Search for America (1927)
Our Daily Bread (1928)
The Yoke of Life (1930)
Fruits of the Earth (1933)
Two Generations (1939)
The Master of the Mill (1944)
Consider Her Ways (1947)
Tales from the Margin (1971)

SKETCHES
Over Prairie Trails (1922)
The Turn of the Year (1923)

LETTERS
The Letters of Frederick Philip Grove
[ed. Desmond Pacey] (1976)